MW00934540

SIEGE OF EDEN:
THE RISE OF THE ILLUMINATI

SIEGE OF EDEN: THE RISE OF THE ILLUMINATI

by

C.D. BAKER

ISBN: 9781701608733

AUTHOR'S NOTE

THIS BOOK IS A WORK OF HISTORICAL FICTION based on real people and events. The warring spirits of history did ignite the lives of the main characters. The quotes preceding each chapter are real. Many of the scenes you will encounter are grounded in fact, and the conspiracy that sprouted in this time still grows. I have provided summary documentation for interested readers in the notes. For these reasons, the book may be better considered a 'docu-novel.'

But we do have a novel, after all, and so I have taken plausible liberties with the story. For story is how we experience reality, and the realities of this story are far too important to disappear under raw fact.

DEDICATION

To my father, who would have wanted me to write this book and in this way.

"In the beginning, men enjoyed two of Nature's blessings: Liberty and Equality. But property came into existence and so Liberty was ruined and Equality disappeared. Eden was lost. Now subjects of sin and slavery, men were reduced to servitude beneath Kings. Hence rose nations, and at the formation of nations, the world ceased to be a great family."

ADAM WEISHAUPT

CHAPTER ONE

SEPTEMBER, 1771

GERMAN IMPERIAL CITY OF FRANKFURT-AM-MAIN

"YOU SAY THAT A TROUBLED HEART IS NOT enough?" Professor Adam Weishaupt kept his face fixed on the squalor passing slowly by the window of his two-horse cab. "I agree, sir, but what can we *do*?" The twenty-three-year-old waited for a response from the stranger seated across from him. Hearing nothing, he said, "Nature intended gods in paradise but tyrants have chained their souls."

Weishaupt drew warm, rain-scented air through his long nose and turned toward the large man who had introduced himself simply as 'Lucius.' The stranger's face remained hidden within an ample black hood. The professor cleared his throat. "Before she died, my mother shared with me a beatific vision of a world that *could* be. The sights out there must have weighed heavily on her—"

"As they did on your father, and as they now do on you," said Lucius.

"Sir?"

"I know you by reputation, *Herr Doktor.* You are the much-admired professor of law at the University of Ingolstadt. Your father was a good man who died too soon. Your godfather is brilliant." Lucius' accented German suggested a foreign birth. Greek? Egyptian?

Weishaupt shifted in his seat. *Much-admired? And who is this man?* He answered carefully. "Injustice has always weighed on my family. It should weigh on every man."

"Few understand the errors of the world more than you."

Weishaupt sniffed and then reached into a pocket to withdraw a silver coin which he flipped at a startled woman shuffling close to the coach. She dropped to her knees and clawed the shiny coin from the dusty street, hissing at a rival. "You see, Lucius? Property turns humans into animals. We must change everything."

"Yet, you seem to enjoy the wealth of your godfather."

Eh? Weishaupt flushed at the sudden turn. "I protest, sir. Must I shout to the whole world that I did not seek my privilege?" He took a breath. Settling, he said, "Oppression is the dark side of ownership. Despite my present advantages, I imagine a world in which all is held in common." He fidgeted with his silver-headed walking stick. "If only everyone simply had *enough.*" He glanced outside. "They have nothing. And they are so unhappy——"

"You have much, but are you happy?"

Weishaupt stiffened. "You overstep, sir."

"Your pardon, Herr Professor. Perhaps I have overstepped, but I have studied your life from afar. . .as have others."

Studied my life? Weishaupt adjusted his sleeves, thinking. "This is not about me." He pointed at a head-drooped beggar. "These wretches are not only oppressed, they are also shamed."

"As you have been."

Weishaupt grit his teeth. "Again——"

Lucius changed course. "You are well-versed in *Agathon.*[1] A happy society free from religion and other servitudes. The end of nations. Enlightened leaders guided by the secrets of the ages——"

"I have worn its pages well."

"It is no wonder. Many know how you suffered at the hands of the Jesuits.[2] Your godfather did not intend that, of course, and your poor mother was too sick—"

Unnerved, Weishaupt raised his hand. "I am flattered by your interest, but I now insist that you reveal your face."

"Perhaps another time."

Another time? The professor struggled to collect himself. "Then I prefer you to look out there." He tilted his head toward the window. "They are whom we should be discussing. Superstition, ignorance and fear rule them all."

Nodding, Lucius said, "Yes. The unholy trinity."

The coach eased to make way for another. Weishaupt withdrew a kerchief and wiped perspiration from his broad brow. A dirty hand suddenly reached into the window. He recoiled, slapping the hand away.

"Ah, when the gods get too close—"

"Enough!"

Lucius leaned forward. "The world needs a plan to turn your vision into practical effect."

The way Lucius' eyes had just blazed through their dark recess sent a sudden shiver through Weishaupt's bones. "Who are you?"

Not answering, Lucius went on. "I know your godfather's library well, thus, I know what you have been reading since you were a boy." He paused. "He has 4200 volumes that share a unifying truth. Have you noticed what it is?"

Unsettled, Weishaupt's mind ran to Hermes, Spinoza, Wolff and others.[3] "Nature as the source of reason and happiness," he muttered.

"Yes. But there is another layer. Taken as a whole, the library reveals something *else*."

"What is that?"

Lucius ran his fingertips along the smooth leather lining the coach's window. "I leave that for you to discover." He paused. "Nevertheless, you are nearly ready for us."

The comment jolted Weishaupt. What did that mean? "Nearly ready? And for whom?"

"You are a topic of conversation among men who dabble in, shall we say, 'unusual' things." Lucius remained deep within his hood. "Can you imagine yourself leading a movement to change the world?"

Taken aback, Weishaupt guarded his words. "I…I would need help." What was happening here?

"Of course. You will need philosophers, teachers, booksellers and bored princes. Even magicians and revolutionary priests. And financiers." Lucius abruptly laid a huge hand on Weishaupt's forearm. "You will center them in a secret purpose that is disclosed gradually." The coach bounced across a gap in the cobblestones. Lucius released his grip and leaned back.

In the long silence that followed, the professor's mouth began to dry. *Something is afoot. Wait. Is this a Jesuit trap?* A wave of unease passed through him. "Enough," he mumbled. Weishaupt leaned out of the window. "Driver!" The carriage shuddered to a stop. He grabbed the brass handle. *"Auf Wiedersehen,* Lucius. Perhaps we meet again someday." With a grunt, Weishaupt pushed opened the door and dismounted.

Lucius called after him. "Do they permit Jews outside the ghetto today?"

Weishaupt bristled. "There. Something you do not know about me after all. I am not a Jew."

"This is Frankfurt, the police do not know you here…and you look like a Jew."

"Look like a Jew? Bah. Do you see? This is why the world must change." Weishaupt slammed the door.

Standing in a puddle of fresh urine, Dr. Adam Weishaupt stared at his buckled shoes and cursed the departing coach. He lifted his feet and covered his nose with a gloved hand. A passing drunk then spat on his white stockings. A hard shoulder knocked him to one side.

The small, delicate academic forced his hand off his nose only to retch. "Christ almighty," he grumbled. Weishaupt had only known the wider world through the distorting windows of fine libraries. But he now stood on a very real street shielded only by his fine education and his exquisite suit. The sounds of jeering women and honking geese filled his ears. *Get a hold of yourself.*

The young professor summoned a reserve of courage and clutched his walking stick, firmly. He tried to take another breath. *These poor wretches are your mission…*Thus resolved, he moved deeper into the neighborhood called Sachsenhausen—a part of Frankfurt lying opposite the river from the wealthy city center. Nearly everyone was dressed in rough, homespun wool. They were sooty and reeking. Weishaupt reached for his nose again, wishing the clouds might finally open and wash them all.

Carts groaned close; Hogs squealed from the slaughter field not far away. Several men began fighting nearby. The brawl began to spread and a surge of anxiety raised the hair on Weishaupt's skin. He pressed his way ahead, politely at first, but within moments he began to shove milling folk out of his way, rudely. "Move! Move!" It was then when an imp yanked the hat off his head. His wig fell away, revealing a closely shorn scalp. Snatching his wig up, he burst from the mob and chased the ragamuffin for his hat.

Items reclaimed, Weishaupt spotted a wider street beyond a gap in the crowd. He sprinted for it. Arrived, he looked about, panting. This street was less threatening. Not far away he could see the masts of resting boats and the broad sky above the river. Open space. Trembling, he wiped his face, rubbed his head, and then confirmed that his purse had not been ripped away. He wiggled his wig in place and then plopped on his tricorn hat. His breathing began to ease. *Beer*, he thought. *Beer and a pretzel.*

Hurrying to the docks, he bought a tankard of beer and a hard pretzel before collapsing on a bench. Birds swarmed. Hay carts groaned past. Fishing boats and barges destined for Mainz and beyond rocked dockside in a light breeze. The sun broke through. Adam swallowed a long draught. Settling, he wiped foam off his mouth and took a deep breath. The air smelled of river mud and fish and manure.

Relaxed, Weishaupt bit through his pretzel. *I had no reason to be afraid.* He chuckled to himself and watched simple folk do whatever it was they did in a day. His sense of paternal care slowly returned. He handed what was left of his pretzel to a lame lad limping by. *And as for that Lucius fellow, perhaps my reputation*

HAS caught the imagination of others. Educated, caring men. Men looking for leadership. He smiled. *I should not see Jesuits everywhere...*

Weishaupt then stood and stared across the river at the orderly rooflines peeking above the city walls rising from the far bank. His mind's eye pictured ladies in plumed bonnets and ample gowns. He knew well the world from which they came and the advantages they enjoyed. The professor smiled, smugly, believing that their privileged world—their 'over there' world—would soon be reduced. "No one can become rich without others becoming poor," he pronounced rather loudly to a lonely pigeon. "So, we must even the scales." His mind raced through the books in his godfather's library, resting on the Third Earl of Shaftesbury,[4] one of the writers from which he derived his notion of the noble savage. "No. Humanity is beautiful when free, and it shall be free again."

About a hundred yards to his left he noticed a policeman and two priests pressing through the moiling crowd. "Do you see, Mistress Pigeon? Oppressors from the state and from religion lurk everywhere." Then from his right, a young girl in a coarse shift emerged singing a country melody. The sight of her captured his attention. "Ah, but she—" The girl passed close by Weishaupt bearing a heavy yoke of two tin milk cans. She cast a curious eye at the professor. Smitten, Weishaupt stood and followed. She moved toward a ramp leading to the water. He watched her set her milk cans down and add river water to dilute them.

Clever girl. Weishaupt moved closer.

Finished, the girl curled her neck beneath the yoke and strained upward. Blowing air from puffed cheeks, she struggled back up the ramp with her swinging cans until she returned to the flat of the dock and set them down.

Gott in Himmel, Weishaupt thought. Before him stood the female archetype of the new world he envisioned. Fresh and free and ripe. Bursting with primitive vitality. "*Fräulein?*" Weishaupt could barely form the word.

The pink-cheeked girl wiped her brow with the back of her arm. "Ja?"

Beer-brazen, he said, "You are beautiful. You are more than beautiful, you are...you are magic. You are magically beautiful." *Magically beautiful? Scheisse. Why did I say—*

She cocked her head with a smile. "Ja?"

Weishaupt's breath quickened. This was a goddess...*his* goddess. He wanted to devour her. Abandoning all reserve, he said, "If you threw off your clothing and bathed in the river, you would be forever remembered as the Goddess of the Rhine."

The girl twirled her braided hair with a playful finger. "So, should I?"

Perspiring, Weishaupt moved close. "What is your name?"

"I am Friederika." Her blue eyes fixed on the professor's crooked hat and wig. She giggled.

He tried to straighten his hat. "I am Adam."

"Like in the Bible?"

"Yes, like in the Bible." Heat rose on Weishaupt's skin. He guessed Friederika to be about five years younger than himself. She was slightly plump and spirited. "And you could surely be Eve."

"Well, I am sorry, Adam, I have no apple for you." She lowered her face, seductively.

Weishaupt thought he might burst. *She is everything! I shall take her here and now.* He swung his small eyes about and they landed on a shed door that was partly open. He withdrew a pouch of coins from within his jacket. "Shall we walk?"

The girl stared at the ample pouch in his palm. "What about my milk?"

"How much for all of it: cans, yoke, milk?"

"Twenty *Thalers.*"

Without so much as a grimace, Weishaupt produced twenty silver coins and eagerly dropped them into her open hands. "Someday none of us shall need money."

She quickly hid them away in an apron pocket. "And what is a walk worth?"

Very clever girl. Weishaupt licked his lips and sunk his fingers into his pouch for more. Hurriedly handing her nearly all the coins he had, he said, "There. Now, I should like to see what is in that shed."

Pocketing her fortune, the girl followed his finger to the door and tittered.

Limbs light, the young professor took Friederika's hand, firmly. He approached the shed and pushed the door farther ajar to peek into a sailmaker's shop. A broad pile of coarse canvas lay to one side, coils of rope on the other. Believing the building to be vacant, he led Friederika inside. Slanted light filtered through the wide gaps in the siding. The place smelled of wet canvas and hemp, river mold and stale oils. It would do.

"My dear Eve, let me look at you." Visions of play in fields of plenty filled his mind. He could not stop smiling.

The buxom girl did not blush.

"Oh, my dear. You and I—" Weishaupt began to circle her, slowly. "Ripe daughter of Nature; Maiden of Liberty." He stopped and cupped her face in both his palms, lightly. He could bring her such happiness. "You are the one I have been shown in my dreams." He removed his hat, coat, vest and shirt. He could already taste her. Bare chested, he said. "Do I still look like a rich man?"

Friederika's eyes fell to his fashionable breeches, silk hose and buckled shoes. She nodded.

"Then..." Weishaupt removed every article of clothing until he stood naked in front of her. "And now?"

The girl tittered. "Now you look like a Jew."

Weishaupt blushed. Born a Jew, he had been circumcised. "Think of me as just a man. Not a rich man or a poor man, not a Jew or a Christian...just a man." He moved closer to her and took a light hold of her homespun shift. "And beneath this?"

Taking the cue, Friederika removed her apron and pulled her shift over her head. Without hesitating, she then removed her under-linen to stand naked in the dim-lit shed.

None of his books on libertine ecstasy had prepared Weishaupt for this. Unable to speak, he reached for her hand. He kissed it and drew her against him. He moved his lips close to hers.

Friederika submitted.

The young man pressed his lips against hers, slowly, as if savoring a supple fig. Life pulsed through him. The warmth of her arms enveloped him. He loved the strength in them. He kissed her neck, her ear and her lips again. Her breath was warm on his skin and smelled of honeyed milk.

Weishaupt then led her toward a stack of folded canvas where he laid her down. He ran his fingers along her arm and one leg. Her skin was soft and unspoiled. He prepared to claim her...until he felt something was amiss. A discomforting sense of presence startled him and so he raised his face.

An icy chill took his breath.

A single eye was staring back at him from between a space in the wall boards.

He could not move.

The shed door burst open. Friederika screamed. Two priests charged forward with a policeman in tow. "You, Jew," shouted one. "What are you doing?"

Hard hands threw Weishaupt to the ground. Helpless, he cried out as a priest dragged his beautiful Eve away. He struggled until the policeman pressed his body hard atop the shed's floor. "I am not a Jew!" pleaded Weishaupt. He watched the man's baton lay back. "I was baptized—"

The policeman's arm fell. Adam Weishaupt's world turned black.

The notes that follow our chapters are intended to provide the interested reader with historical context regarding persons, ideas and circumstances relative to the story.

CHAPTER ONE NOTES

1 *The History of Agathon* was an extraordinarily popular German novel by Christopher Wieland (1733-1813). The protagonist enjoys peace by shedding the rule of religion and the state, attaining an enlightened way of life that made him a god beyond the chaos of a struggling world. Adam Weishaupt considered the book to be a key influence in his life and vision.

2 The Society of Jesus, or 'Jesuits' within the Roman Catholic Church answers directly to the Pope. Their many schools throughout the world have been accused of numerous political and ecclesiastical conspiracies.

3 Adopted around age five, Adam Weishaupt had unlimited access to his godfather's (Baron von Ikstaat) extensive and controversial library. The sampling of authors below represents typical influences that shaped his ultimate worldview comprised of a hybrid tension between materialism and theosophy.
Hermes Trismegistus, (5000 BC?), mysterious author of the *Hermetica*, was considered the father of holistic spirituality and progenitor to Greek philosophy, Christian Gnosticism, Eastern religious traditions, etc. Some claim he was an incarnation of the Egyptian god of learning named, Thoth; others say he was a representative amalgamation of ancient wisdom teachers. His principles of a unified cosmos made him a primary source of metaphysical* insight for those working toward a realignment of the world's spiritual/philosophical center.
*Metaphysics is the philosophical study of the meaning, structure and natural principles of the whole of reality, including the spiritual realm.

Baruch Spinoza (1632-1677), a Dutch philosopher who argued for the essential unity of the cosmos, leading to his conclusion that God and Nature are expressed as the same reality. The attainment of knowledge was the path to salvation rather than adherence to divine revelation.

Christian Wolff (1679-1754) was a German philosopher whose work impressed Adam Weishaupt through mathematical views of metaphysics. A primary influence on the German Enlightenment, he believed that human reason could direct men toward moral perfection.

4 The notion of a 'Noble Savage' was important to Weishaupt's coming movement in that it assumed humanity—when free to exist in its natural state—was essentially good and would therefore assure mutual happiness for all.

Anthony Ashley-Cooper, 3rd Earl of Shaftesbury (1671-1713) was an English philosopher and politician who urged trust in the people. He sought the development of political and economic institutions based on the essential goodness of free men.

"For our struggle is not against flesh and blood, but against the powers
of this dark world and the spiritual forces of evil in the heavenly realms."

FROM THE BIBLE, *BOOK OF EPHESIANS*

CHAPTER TWO

28ᵀᴴ JUNE, 1772
OYNE, SCOTLAND

GRANDMOTHER 'GRUNNIE' HORN ONCE TOLD LITTLE ALEXANDER THAT love was the
securing presence in all things, the very essence of a joyful God to whom we
belong. She assured him that on this account he should fear nothing.

But just twelve hours before, the boy had watched Grunnie's coffin disappear beneath stony Scottish soil. He would no longer see her smiling or hear her
song. Perhaps that is why the priest had said, 'Love is now laid to rest.' Those
words may have been offered as a kindness, but they stung the lad and he could
not put them out of his mind.

What did it mean for love to die?

Most especially, what did it mean for *him* that it had?

And so, on this—the wee hours of his tenth birthday—Alexander Horn
raced as far as his skinny legs could take him from his family's estate near the
village of Oyne. Panting heavily, the wiry, brown-eyed Scot raced northwest
along the Huntly Road—a well-worn dirt highway scratched neatly into the
hilly landscape of Aberdeenshire. To his left the solid silhouette of Bennachie
Ridge blocked the stars. He strained to hurry past it and see the fullness of the

night's sky. It was something Grunnie loved. Maybe he could see her there, in the stars.

Pressing forward, he resisted the urge to stop and weep. "Go, y'dolt," he muttered. He tossed his head to steal a look behind. Did anyone yet know that he had left? Was his father in chase? Seeing no one, he slackened his pace a little. The only sound was his even panting and that of his leather soles padding the hard roadway. Oh, how he wished he could fly away from the fear. His grandmother had been his everything. She was his safe place, she was his happy welcome, the song in his heart. Grunnie Horn really was the face of love.

But they had buried love. The only face remaining was that of his father and there was nothing lovely about that.

The boy ran under starlight until he finally arrived at a small rise just before the village of Insch. He stopped by a stone fence and bent over to lean his hands on his knees and sob. It felt good to weep, even defiant. Last evening his drunken father had dragged him from his bed in Westhall and beat him for crying over Grunnie. 'Ye sound like a blubbering lassie!' he had screamed. Thanks be to God that Alexander Horn the Elder—the raging Catholic of Oyne—was now three miles behind and snoring.

Young Alexander sat down in the dark weeds by the side of the old road. There the boy wept until he finally laid back to draw a deep breath of dewy air. A hint of brine belied easterlies, and that might mean rain. No matter. Grunnie liked the rain. She said it was Heaven watering God's garden.

The boy relaxed, smiling to think of that. Grunnie always had a way to find the good. Even when his recurring dream frightened him—the one in which some unseen voice hissed, 'A-L-E-X-A-N-D-E-R' in the night—it was she who comforted him by suggesting the hissing of his name was no hissing at all, but a kindly whisper from his angel.

Surely, Grunnie Horn had blessed the boy with many ways to see the world and to see *in* the world. Among her blessings was handing him the secret key to his late grandfather's library. That and giving him the notes that Granda Horn had written for him about the most difficult of the books. Books and learning quickly became the boy's other comforts.

Alexander smiled again, thinking of how he confounded his tutor with un-accounted for knowledge of the ancient philosophers. He liked watching him scratch his bald head.

Settled, he stood and stared ahead. Then, with a grunt he began to run again, hurrying to find the ruin of Dunnideer Castle before the sun melted the mist. The lad listened to the steady rhythm of his own feet, thinking. It was true that Grunnie had never sat with him at Dunnideer, so this was not exactly about her. Although whenever he had described it to her she smiled and stroked his hair, and always said that it sounded like the perfect place to find the enduring peace of the Presence.

But there was another who had spent time wandering the stones and the ruins and the river with him. Alexander now begged the Holy Mother for her to be there as she so often was whenever he needed a friend. Of course, if his father knew that he was running to see *her* he would beat him all the more. He was cruel enough to say that she did not even exist. "She's a figment or a witch!" Old Horn once shouted.

"Or maybe an angel?" his sickly mother once dared to whisper.

Or maybe just a little girl?

Alexander guessed that he had less than an hour before the sun would rise. He pattered his way through the silent village of Insch and then along the low banks of the mist-shrouded River Shevock. He found the shallow ford marked by rock pillars. Arriving, he paused for just a moment to watch silver-tipped water glide cream-like over unseen rocks. He bent over to scoop its cold water into his mouth, then pulled off his shoes and wool stockings.

Picking his way over slippery rocks to the far bank, he sat in a thick patch of blooming globeflowers to wrestle his stockings back over his wet feet. He lashed his shoes. He then ran toward a stone fence which he easily hopped, and dashed forward until he came to Dunnideer's ancient stone circles standing in a foggy grove of leafy birch. There he paused. Fiona had met him at the stones most often. He looked about. "Fiona?"

A sheep answered from the darkness.

"Fiona?" He waited. Silence. No, his little green-eyed friend was not wait-ing for him there, not by the magic stones. Not on this morning.

Undaunted, Alexander hurried from beneath the birch boughs and emerged onto a grassy clearing at the base of Dunnideer mountain. He worked his way upslope and soon came through curling mist to see the summit where stood the silhouetted ruin of a rectangular wall of vitrified stones. The only remains of an ancient castle and keep, the wall appeared more like a squared archway…a dolman with two supporting walls and a mantle.

In his reading, Alexander had learned that dolmans—like the eight-angled pyramids of Egypt—could increase the earth's natural energy said to flow in massive ley lines like great streams of unseen force. If that were true—and why should he doubt it—then he would be wise to sit within the opening and feel the strength of God's earth. Especially in such a terrible time as this. Most especially with Fiona.

With his goal in view, Alexander Horn strained upward. His legs began to burn as he climbed up the conical mount upon which Dunnideer was perched like the throne of its ancient Pictish overlord. His feet dug through clumps of green heather, slipping on bare patches of flinty stones. He breathed, hard. He cast a nervous look eastward into a now starless horizon fearing the sun might crest before he stumbled into his place. "Hurry."

Up he ran, panting.

He clambered over all that was left of St. John's Chapel, startling a tiny herd of sheep. "Fiona?" he cried as he pressed upward.

Gasping, he finally arrived at the dolman. He collapsed, sucking for breath, and laid his face against the lichen-patched stones. "Fiona?" he wheezed.

He hurried to sit in the center of the square opening. He licked his lips and wiggled his way into a notch worn by a thousand winters. The boy caught his breath, hoping to feel some influx of power. He gripped the stone walls on either side and summoned his friend once more.

It was then that a vision of the furious flames that once fused the stones startled him. He could feel the heat blasting against his face. He closed his eyes until the heat passed. A waft of fresh air lifted his long hair lightly and cooled his skin. Alexander Horn then opened his eyes and she was there, smiling in the first blush of dawn.

"Fiona!" Alexander's face lit. "You've come!" He leapt from his seat and hurried to be close.

Fiona stood there as a spindly, strawberry-haired girl, perhaps a year younger than Alexander. The girl smiled, kindly. She was petite and pure, and moved like a tender willow. Yet, for all her fragility it seemed as though the whole of nature's power was hers to summon. "I heard about Grunnie Horn," she said. "I am sorry." She reached her hand and touched Alexander's.

Tears swelled the boy's eyes.

"Let them fall." Fiona squeezed his hand.

Alexander began to sob again, and the two children held one another other as the sun crested the rumpled landscape far below. The boy then wiped his face and trotted to a clump of bell-heather. He snatched some purple petals into his hand and presented them. "My queen, Queen Fiona of Dunnideer."

The girl giggled.

The two then sat in the crux of the dolman and watched the sun move the mist. "The priest said that Grunnie was the face of love," said Alexander. "And that 'love is now laid to rest.'"

Fiona said nothing.

"That makes me afraid. With no Grunnie at Westhall, it shall just be ma and myself to face *him*. And ma's always sick."

Fiona nodded. "Your poor ma hides in corners, but she has hopes for ye." She then pointed to the sprawling panorama of shadowed hills and squares of green. "Do you remember how Grunnie said we all must learn to look beyond our world for the center of things."

"Aye," said Alexander. "She said, 'look beyond to see what's already here.' I never quite knew what she meant by that one."

"She was clever." Fiona smelled her flowers. "You should remember that about yerself. And when you do, you shall become all of who ye are."

The boy blinked.

She then climbed off the dolman and picked up a stick. She drew a circle and dug a hole in the middle. "Love is at the center of everything."

Hopping down, Alexander wrinkled his nose. "Father Moore says that *God* is at the center."

"But what is God?"

He scratched his head. "Grunnie said that he is love."

Fiona smiled. "Aye. And he knows yer name, Alexander Horn." She touched his arm, smiling.

It was then the boy heard a raging voice crying from the bottom of the hill. "Alexander! Alexander Horn!" He chilled and whirled around to see his father charging uphill, shouting and shaking his walking stick. "Run, Fiona! Fly away."

Wheezing, Alexander Horn the Elder arrived at the ruin to throw himself atop one of the rough rocks. He wiped his brow and threw his well-worn bonnet to one side. "By God, y'little shite." He struggled to catch his breath, then drew a long draught of water from a leather canteen. "Stand here, in front o'me."

Alexander obeyed, white-faced and trembling.

"You defied me!" Horn seized Alexander's shoulders. His weathered face was taut; his eyes, fired. "Y'made me chase after ye all this way!" He squeezed his thumbs into the boy's joints.

Alexander stifled a cry and slid his eyes to one side. *She's gone. Good. But I am alone with HIM.* He shuddered.

Horn eased his grip and stared at the boy for a long, silent moment. "Bah. By the saints, yer lucky it's your birthday." He pointed to a menacing bank of black clouds gathering in the distance. "It's coming." An eagle screeched from far above. Ignoring it, he scowled at Alexander. "Christ almighty, you are forever tormenting me. You and yer brother. So y'know, he's now to be called, 'Brother John.'"

Alexander nodded. His elder brother was a faraway monk in a Scots' monastery sitting in the middle of the German Empire.

"He always thought himself to be a saint and me a devil." Horn spat. "By Christ, at his age I was chasing girls in Aberdeen." He took another breath, then more water. "I'm glad to be rid of him."

Old Horn fixed hard eyes on Alexander. "Look at ye. Bony. Thin. Yer lanky like yer mother, big brown eyes like your granda." He spat. "You got that hint of red in yer hair from me, you know." He took hold of Alexander's ears. "But these stick out like yer grunnie's." He gave one a hard twist and shoved the boy away.

Keeping his feet, Alexander winced, calculating it to be a foretaste of what was coming. He dug for courage.

Horn scratched his jaw. "Yer not the thistle in my arse that Robby is, but you're not like any of the other bairns in Oyne, either. And you're surely not like me." He paused for a long moment. "Yer grunnie said God made ye different than all of us. She said I should honor your fine mind. It was her dying wish."

The boy held his breath.

Old Horn grabbed Alexander's arm, firmly. "Ten years old now. Time to be a man and not a little fool searching for sylphs and fairies in this place."

What was coming?

His father then grumbled something incoherent, masking the melancholy suddenly thickening his voice. He released his hold. "Yer Grunnie was too soft, but I grant she was wise. Lairds and yeomen alike sought her counsel." Horn kicked a stone, lost in some memory. "She had a favorite proverb: 'The fear of the Lord is the beginning of wisdom.'" He then grabbed Alexander by the jaw and leaned close to the boy's face. His breath smelled like last night's whiskey. "She said if we forget that truth, all is lost. There, I just gave ye something worth keepin'."

Head bent backward, Alexander nodded. *What is this?*

Old Horn grunted. "Remember it, and you just might change the world." He shoved Alexander's face away, lightly. "Bah. But what is wisdom, anyway?" He wiped a large hand over his face. "Ask me something about breeding horses and we can talk, but philosophy and high things? Not interested. Which is why I quit the university. Did I ever tell you I went?"

Surprised, the boy remained quiet.

Horn coughed mucus up from his throat and spat. "I'd rather *shovel* shite than bury my nose in it." He sat and peeled some white lichen off the rocks with his thumbnail. He then looked squarely at his son. "But you like books, and you don't care one whit about breeding horses."

Alexander often wished he did. If he could occupy his father with talk of horses or rents or the tricks of managing the family estate, the man might not be forever reaching for something in him that was not there. The boy tried to swallow. "Em...horses are beautiful—"

"Enough." Old Horn shook his head. "You and I are as different as the Pope and a Calvinist."

He supposed that was something of a relief.

Horn took a drink of water, then tossed Alexander his canteen. "So, impress me. Tell me what you think 'wisdom' is."

Confused by the unexpected turn, Alexander stared at the canteen. "Em. Methinks wisdom is…seeing the world from God's heart."

Horn blinked.

Dare I? Alexander cautiously picked up a stick and dragged it through the dirt in the shape of a circle. In the middle he dug a dot. "God is at the center of the universe, like an eye, watching."

His father stared at the drawing for a long while. "'Tis what a Freemason[1] would recite. Nay, something's not right with that." Horn struggled. He picked at his nose and snorted. He stood and poked at the sketch with his staff. "You say God is at the center?"

"Aye." The boy shifted his feet.

The man shook his head. "God is not the center of anything."

What? Alexander bit his lip.

"Nay. Otherwise he'd be trapped inside what he made. The center might be a portal to him, but it cannot *be* him." He rubbed the circle away with his foot.

Alexander gawked.

"I am not a complete fool, y'know." Horn fixed his eyes on his son. "You are like yer granda, what with all his books you read. Aye. You dig around his library against my rules. Yer grunnie's secret key is no secret to me."

Alexander knew that was cause for another beating.

Horn scratched his jaw and looked at a slated bank of clouds gathering in the east. "Tell me what's so important to you on those shelves."

The poor boy could barely think.

"Who are you reading?"

Alexander strained to gather himself. Answering would be an admission he sneaked into the place; not answering would defy his father's question. He yielded. "Em, some from Hermes the Egyptian. Sometimes Dr. Dee[2]…but they were both hard. And then there was—"

His father folded his arms. "Dee was Queen Elizabeth's sorcerer. He summoned spirits and shared wives with an earless medium. Have a care what he says. Go on."

Earless medium? Alexander licked his lips. "Francis Bacon?[3]"

Horn raised his hand. "Bacon was a fool who meant well. Lots of men mean well." He tapped his foot, thinking. "I learnt something from the horse track: Know *who* a man is by what he *does*. That's better than Bacon."

Alexander liked that. Should he say more? "Em, most of the philosophers want to find Eden."

"Eden? Shite." Horn snorted. "I tell ye this: if men could make their way back to Eden they'd be gobbled up by pride of purpose. And then we would lose Eden all over again anyway." He spat. "Do not be blinded by the high intentions of clever men."

The boy blinked.

Standing, Horn lifted his face to follow a winging gull. "Evil is always crouching, ready to pounce on little shites like ye. But enough of that." He weighed his walking staff in his hands and stared at his son. "I'll grant that you have an extraordinary mind and yer grunnie's good heart. But neither can shield ye very well in all the darkness that is out there. 'Tis why ye need me." A stiff easterly tossed his hair. He drew a deep breath through his nose. "We'll be wet on the hurry home."

Alexander remained silent. His father seemed deeply troubled.

"I remember something *my* grunnie told me once whilst she was mashing neeps. She said that forces ride the winds, forces that move the affairs of men."

Wait. Was his father afraid of something?

"Such talk gives me shivers." Old Horn ground his jaw. "I have a dark feeling lately." His face tightened. "The world is what it is, which is why I am not easy on ye. You shall thank me someday."

Alexander glanced at his father's hands, noticing how the man was tightening his grip on the staff. He braced himself.

A sharp gust ruffled his father's linen shirt. "You've been sneaking about granda's library against my rules. Ye ran out of Westhall without my permission, and you came here again to find yer witch, also against my rules. I do not care that it is your birthday."

The boy was ready.

Then, like lightning snapping a sapling, his father struck him with the oak staff.

Alexander squealed in pain as he crashed to the ground. Blood burst from his left ear and scalp.

Horn loomed over his son, straddle-legged and squeezing his walking staff with both hands. "Yer days of disobeying me are over," he shouted. "Stand up. 'Tis all for yer own good."

Whimpering, Alexander climbed to his feet, slowly. He cowered and closed his eyes, imagining himself to be flying away with Fiona.

"Eden?" Horn cursed. "This should remind you that Eden is long gone." He jammed his staff into the boy's belly, bending the gasping lad in two.

Crying out, Alexander sucked desperately for breath. He was faint. The little fellow staggered backwards and fell to one side. He tried to fight the tears. Then, from beyond he spotted the proud form of a red stag. He fixed his teary eyes on the stag's and slowly stood upright.

The animal snorted, switching his eyes to Old Horn who whirled about. "I wish I had my musket," the man grumbled.

Alexander set his small jaw. "I am very happy you do not."

Cursing, his father grabbed the boy by the shoulder. "Which is why I will be doing with you what I must do."

CHAPTER TWO NOTES

1 Freemasonry (also referred to simply as 'Masonry' or the 'Craft') was (is) a secret society committed to the betterment of humankind by building character. It developed from the legacy of medieval stone masons who traveled from city to city to ply their trade. In so doing, they evolved a fraternity involving secret practices that protected them. Some developed alternative religious practices and imagery.

In 1648, an English astrologer, occult mystic and alchemist named Elias Ashmole (1617-1692) became the first non-craftsman to be accepted into a guild of masons. His membership began the important transfer of the philosophical/mystical secrets beyond the world of craftsmen and into secret gatherings of educated men, thus creating Freemasonry as we know it.

As we will see in the story, the Craft is organized into 'lodges' which are local cells supervised by their corresponding 'Grand Lodges.' Since Freemasonry's philosophical purposes have strong esoteric (hidden or secret)/spiritual assumptions, their meeting places are called Temples.

For any men considering non-traditional ideas, the secrecy of Freemasonry provided a secure place of discussion and planning. The first formal Freemason lodge (of non-craftsman) was established in England in 1717. Others quickly followed such as: Spain in 1728, France in 1728 (debated), the American colonies (as per Benjamin Franklin) in 1731, Russia in 1732, Germany in 1733, and the Netherlands in 1734, etc. Eventually, a complex collection of lodges expanded throughout the world organized by a dizzying array of rites and degrees of advancement.

Adam Weishaupt would soon recognize the value of infiltrating the Freemason's lodges to use their secrecy as a cover and their liberal atmosphere as a place to recruit members to his vision of building his new world order.

2 **Dr. John Dee** (1527-1609) was an English alchemist, astrologer, chemist, spiritualist and trusted advisor of Queen Elizabeth I. At the height of his influence he shared his vision of a coming British Empire with the monarchy,

thus inspiring English colonialism. He carried a stone which he claimed help him discern good vs. demonic spirits. His occult interests influenced Elias Ashmole, the first modern Freemason, as well as others who directed a variety of secret societies in the later centuries.

3 **Sir Francis Bacon** (1561-1626) was one of the primary Enlightenment agents of a Utopian future for the New World. His secret philosophical society in England was called the 'Knights of the Helmet' and birthed what was known as the 'Invisible College'—a secret gathering of wisdom seekers, astrologers and alchemists. This, in turn, contributed to the creation of the Royal Society which became the British home to Enlightenment elites within science and philosophy, most of whom vigorously but secretly endorsed natural reason and not religion as the source of human salvation. His esoteric vision of an enlightened new world provided a foundation for the masonic influence on North America, and metaphysical ground for later Illuminist arrivals.

"There has existed for thousands of years enlightened humans. To them it has been revealed that civilization has a secret destiny."

MANLY HALL [1]

CHAPTER THREE

December, 1773
Ingolstadt, Duchy of Bavaria

PROFESSOR DR. ADAM WEISHAUPT BROODED FITFULLY OVER A frothy tankard of dark beer. Outside, a cold rain muffled the carriage wheels rolling over wet cobblestones. He murmured as church bells rang their deadened tones for Sunday's mass. *"Schwachköpfe.* More than fools. Dangerous fools." The twenty-five-year-old moved to his small, square hearth and dropped a chunk of coal into his ashy grate. He drew a soot-scented breath through his nose and turned to his bride. "Stand still and let me look at you." He surveyed *Frau* Afra Weishaupt like a buyer at a horse auction.

Weishaupt drank more beer. "Buy some new clothes. You know how I adore beauty. Why can you not dress like Sophia?" He had always preferred his brother's wife.

She nodded.

"Sit."

Afra sat.

"You know, my mother was a lover of beauty, too. She saw it in all people, as do I."

"You see no beauty in priests."

25

"You correct me?"

Afra lowered her face.

"Good. Now what was I saying?"

"The foolishness of church bells."

Weishaupt sniffed. "Indeed. The idiots in pews sicken me. And their priests enrage me. Whatever good my mother might have seen in them has been corrupted. Every unhappy thing in the lives of men is their fault. Their system has infected every layer of civilization with inequality and subjugation."

Afra looked up. "They have made your life difficult."

He grunted. "Difficult? They ruined my father—I still say they murdered him—and they've made my godfather's life miserable. They degraded my mother, they humiliated me as a child and nearly killed me in Frankfurt—" Memories of Friederika were never far.

"Converting to Lutheranism has not helped your cause."

The man huffed. "Those *Arschgeigen* are no better. I would rather announce myself as a Manichean.[2] At least Manes understood that we are saved by *thinking*—"

"You will put them all in their place, husband. Then they shall see who you are."

Weishaupt threw himself into a chair remembering one particular September day when two Jesuits mocked him as child. He closed his eyes. "The baron had me baptized, but the priests still called me a 'little Christ-killer.' That was just the beginning." He opened his eyes and stared at Afra. "In the end, the Lutherans are no better. They hate Jews and everybody else. They drowned the Anabaptists, and exchanged slaughter with the Catholics for thirty years...for what? So they might close men's minds in a different way."

The professor stood and folded his arms. "Enough of their hypocrisy and fairy tales. Let me be satisfied reading Pythagoras or Hermes, or rest in the wisdom of Isis, or let me get lost in the peace of the Eleusinian Mysteries—"[3]

"My father says you will change the world."

He looked at the ceiling. "I want you to listen to this recitation of an Eleusinian:

'I came close to the chamber of death.
At midnight I saw the sun shining in all his glory.
I approached the gods and I stood beside them.'"

Weishaupt turned to his wife, his brown eyes suddenly alight with passion. "Can you hear it? A man moves from darkness to light and *stands among the gods!*" The professor paced about the room, animated. "This is my quest! Nature urges mankind to be free. I want us all to be happy. To take our places with the gods. Is this too much to ask?"

Afra smiled. "No!"

The professor stroked her hair "The good news is that the stage is being set. We will grind away the foundations of thrones and altars. Ja, thank Almighty Nature for Voltaire, Mirabeau,⁴ and their friends in France. And may fortune forever shine upon Frederick in Berlin!"⁵ He threw himself back into his chair.

Afra knelt by his side. "And yet, you are different than them." She kissed his cheek. "Better. Wiser. If anyone is destined to lead us to happiness, it is you, husband."

Weishaupt nodded, then closed his eyes. *Oh, how that might feel. To lead. To be understood, recognized. To be complete——* His attention was abruptly taken from out-of-doors. "Do you hear that?" He moved quickly to the front window and divided the heavy drapes with one hand. Outside, an ornate red coach had arrived at the curb in a great commotion. An impressive team of six black horses pawed at the puddles. Three uniformed postilions scrambled about under the severe eye of a motionless rider sitting atop a single white horse tightly reined at the rear. "What is this?" The professor narrowed his eyes. A finely dressed traveler beneath a large Spanish hat emerged from the coach. Dressed in black, he passed through his armed guards. "What the devil?"

Professor Weishaupt pressed his nose closer to the window and studied every motion of the curious arrival. He chilled. A dark agent for the damned Jesuits? The Jesuits had been recently suppressed by the Pope and all hell was breaking loose. There were even rumors of Jesuits assassinating free thinkers like himself. Was he one of them?

Unless an avenger of one of my lovers...

Weishaupt's face flushed. He snatched a blue coat off the arm of a chair, pushed his white-sleeved arms through it and checked for the small pistol hidden in a deep pocket. He then faced a gold-framed mirror. The professor smoothed the form-fitted breeches clinging to his stocky legs and squeezed the powdered curls suspended over each ear. He picked a cake crumb off his small chin, then clenched his fists, faced the foyer and pursed his lips. He squared his narrow shoulders and took a deep breath, thinking. *Or maybe just a man of means come to call? That is most likely. But perhaps I should answer the door myself*— "Wife, tell the servant to make ready beer and sausages. Go."

The brass knocker fell heavily on the oak door. Weishaupt drew another breath. He strode forward and threw open the door.

A huge stranger removed his hat with a flair.

Weishaupt faltered. The square-jawed man was as magnificent a specimen as he had ever seen. With a swarthy complexion, black-hair, and amber eyes, the handsome visitor offered a smile that might melt the Danube in February.

"*Herr Doktor* Adam Weishaupt." The man stepped forward.

Adam shuffled backward as the man filled his foyer. "Ja?" His belly churned. His nose filled with the aroma of a peculiarly sweet tobacco.

The stranger shut the door and then took Adam's hand, swallowing it as if it were a child's. "My great pleasure." Grinning, he swept past Weishaupt and entered the side parlor as if he were intimately familiar with the space. He tossed his large hat into a corner and threw his wool cape to one side.

The professor hurried from behind and pointed the stranger to a red chair.

"No. I should rather like to sit there, by the fire." He took his seat in a green chair alongside the small fireplace and stretched his long legs forward.

Weishaupt closed the parlor door. Facing the oak panels with his back to his guest, he gathered himself. He then glanced out his front window. The stranger's escorts were guarding the entrance with shouldered muskets. *Who is this man?* He struggled to place the man's accent. *Greek? Egyptian?* Something about him seemed familiar. He turned. "Sir, who are you and why are you here?"

"I am of no consequence."

The man's sudden turn of tone puzzled Weishaupt. "How can I help you?"

The stranger laughed, loudly "Oh, Herr Doktor. If only I had the time—"

Weishaupt pressed his back to the door and summoned his courage. "Sir, I must protest."

"I am here to help you."

"You must first explain your presence."

"Must I?"

Weishaupt shifted on his feet. "You must."

The stranger shrugged.

A bead of perspiration slid along the professor's temple. "Tell me your business or leave." He watched the stranger reaching into a leather bag. *What's this?* He moved his own hand very slowly into his deep pocket.

The visitor retrieved a rolled object wrapped in brown paper. "You have no reason to fear me." He set the item on a side table near his chair. "No need for your pistol. Correct me, but it is a little Willmore from London with a nick in the walnut."

Weishaupt gawked.

The stranger folded his large hands over his flat waist. "I would like more coal. It is quite damp in this room."

Confused, Weishaupt obeyed, cautiously. "You refuse to introduce yourself?"

The visitor stared at Weishaupt for a very long time. "You have been chosen. Now sit by me."

Weishaupt hesitated until the man's penetrating gaze moved him to submit. He pulled a high-backed Windsor chair close and sat.

"Your mother knew it before you were born. She sang songs to you, even in your cradle—beautiful songs of *you* as the hope of the world." The stranger leaned forward. "And you loved her for it, even then." He sat back, smiling. "You pretend modesty, but you know that others have told you the same. Your godfather[6] told you this when he adopted you at age five. At fifteen your professors chose you for advanced study. Just months ago, a colleague said the Universe had chosen you against the Jesuits for your present university position." He paused and crossed his leg. "Now I tell you. We all know you know. We just need you to believe."

Heat flushed Weishaupt's cheeks. We? *Who is this man to toy with me?*

"I am not here to toy with you, professor." He stared through Weishaupt with other-worldly eyes. "But before you launch your calling, are you going to offer me anything to eat or drink?"

Weishaupt's mind whirled. He licked his lips, thinking, then tilted his head toward the window. "First tell me why you have armed guards at my door."

"We have enemies."

"We?"

"You and I."

"The Jesuits?"

"Of course. But there are others."

Weishaupt was near his end. "Tell me."

"Fear, ignorance and superstition." The stranger smiled.

Adam Weishaupt grunted. It was then that a sudden realization came over him. *Lucius?* His jaw dropped. "You are Lucius. You rode with me in Frankfurt." Was that who he was?

The stranger said nothing.

Weishaupt's mind spun. He studied his guest. "But wait. I never did see his face. No...you... no..." He thought for a long moment. "Ah! No. You must be Kolmer, the merchant from Jutland. [7] Everyone is talking about you!" Standing, Weishaupt clapped his hands together. "They say you are a giant in both stature and insight. Ladies swoon for you, men hang on every word—"

"Am I? Do they?"

Fussing about the room, Weishaupt called for his wife. *Finally, he has come. The great adept who inspires and vanishes...* "Ja, ja, I have been writing to you—"

Afra entered hastily with her servant carrying beer, plates of sausages and an aromatic cherry strudel.

Weishaupt began the excited introduction. "This is Herr Kolmer, a man of letters from afar. Herr Kolmer, this is my wife—

"Of course. Frau Afra Weishaupt née Sausenhofer von Eichstaat." The man stood and bowed with a flair. "This is the fine woman whom your godfather disapproved. On this matter, the baron is quite wrong." He took Afra's hand and kissed it. Motioning toward the woman's belly, he said, "And you are carrying a girl."

Afra stared at her husband.

"Sir?" said Weishaupt.

The stranger shrugged. "Consider it my gift to such a splendid hostess." He then received a pewter tankard and a china plate from the servant.

Weishaupt's mind was reeling and he thought his wife might swoon on the spot. "Herr Kolmer brings, shall we say, insight. Now, leave us."

The men watched the women disappear before the professor continued. "So, how may I serve you?"

The man did not acknowledge his name but took a long draught of beer.

Pondering it all, the professor returned to his chair. Kolmer certainly did not appear to be from Jutland. What Dane looked like this? But—

Sitting, Kolmer said, "The world needs to be saved, Herr Professor. I and the others have been patient for a very long time. We 'hurl the javelin but hide the hand,' as it were. Nevertheless, we reveal ourselves to the chosen in due time. Therefore, I am here."

Emboldened, Weishaupt asked, "Who are these 'others'?"

Kolmer popped a generous slice of sausage into his mouth. "As I said, in due time." He chewed for a long moment and then swallowed. "I begin with this: You must learn to first deliver men *from*. Then you can lead them *to*."

Weishaupt strained.

"You will understand." Kolmer leaned forward. "Now, tell me, professor, what is the foremost voice you hear in your life?"

Weishaupt was confused.

"When you are alone in a very quiet place, whose voice do you hear?"

"My own?"

"Really?"

Weishaupt struggled.

"Men yield to the most demanding voice speaking into their souls. So again, whose voice rules you?"

Weishaupt stood. He walked to the window and squeezed his fists. "The Jesuits." He turned. "I hear them scolding and mocking and demanding and denying, shaming..." Tears welled.

Kolmer raised his hand. "I am impressed."

Weishaupt wiped his eyes, hastily, and sat. He stared at his feet.

"The wise can name the intruder, and in the naming they steal his power. Thus, you are wise…and now free."

The professor looked up. "And so, you are here to deliver me *from*—"

"The chains of shame." Smiling, Kolmer lifted another sausage to his mouth. "I see why you have impressed influential men. You are considered one of the finest minds of our time. You are not like others. We know what you have read in the baron's library—all those books banished by the Jesuits. We know what you despise and what you love." He leaned far forward. "Tell me, sir. Do you play chess?"

Weishaupt nodded.

"Are you ready to win the greatest chess game of all time?"

Adam Weishaupt sat very still.

"Herr Professor?"

Weishaupt licked his lips. "I am ready."

The visitor stood and walked to the professor's desk where he sank the point of a sharp quill in ink. He drew a perfect circle on a piece of paper. He placed a dot in the very center. "Symbols do more than words." Weishaupt studied the sketch.

"Symbols transfer the power of invisible forces into the psyche of men. Good ones evoke layers of meaning. The Freemasons understand this, well. [8] Now look at this."

Receiving the drawing, Weishaupt focused. "The circle is nature's unity. Reason is her center, like the sun radiating light into the universe."

The visitor closed his eyes and recited, "'There is only one name under heaven whereby mankind can be saved.'"

Weishaupt was suddenly disappointed. "You quote St. Paul?"

Kolmer returned to his seat, laughing. "No. I quote the Roman army. Paul stole it like he did everything else.[9] It is time for you to take it back." He looked carefully at Weishaupt. "We must replace the authorities that rule men. Kingdoms must fall, and we must surely 'crush the Wretch' of religion…as our friend Voltaire so elegantly puts it."

Weishaupt listened, eagerly.

"Ah, but all men need to worship something. Our simple task is to free men to worship something *else*. Do you understand?"

"First *from* and then *to*. Yes, I understand."

Kolmer then bent over and picked up the item wrapped in brown paper. Handing it to the professor, he said, "A small token to mark the passing of the torch from chosen to chosen."

Curious, Weishaupt opened it. "Ah, Diderot's *Encyclopédie*,[10] first edition folio! Thank you. This is turning the world upside down."[11] The professor set his short forefinger on the title page and traced the image of a winged creature with a flame dancing atop its head. "Lucifer, the Light Bearer—"

"The true Illuminator."

"And there…the Masonic square, compass and triangle, all hidden in plain view."[12] Weishaupt set the folio down. "So, how do I proceed?"

Kolmer smiled, then studied the strudel. "In time. But now, I am tired of admiring this pastry. I want us to devour it, every flake and cherry."

CHAPTER THREE NOTES

1 **Manly Hall** (1901-1990) author, lecturer, mystic and sympathetic scholar of esoteric (hidden except for the enlightened few) movements including Freemasonry.

2 **Manes** (i.e. Manicheanism) was a third century A.D. Persian theologian known as the 'Apostle of Light' or the 'Supreme Illuminator' who attempted to reduce all known religions to their common essence that was devoid of a personal God.

3 **Pythagoras** was a 6th century B.C. Greek mathematician and philosopher who was heir to the ancient Egyptian wisdom traditions. He conceived the universe to be a unified whole with a mathematical, impersonal 'First Cause' at its center. His ultimate goal was to reclaim the essential natural wisdom found in the center of all things and thus teach the ascent to human completion. Masonic and eventual Illuminist degrees model similar premises and aspirations.
The worship of the goddess, Isis—often associated with universal wisdom—was part of a complicated evolution of Egyptian religion that centered on the allegorical story of the unifying sun god, Osiris.
The Eleusinian Mysteries of ancient Greece invited initiates into increasing states of alignment with the spiritual forces of the cosmos. These and most other ancient religions loosely shared a common understanding of the universe as a whole governed by an impersonal force.
The Illuminati was eventually grounded on the shared metaphysics of these ancient 'mystery' traditions, thus generally assuming a general religious monism—the unity of all things within an unknowable Source—as illuminated by natural reason. Human divinity (completeness) is thus attained by ascending through enlightened degrees toward spiritual perfection.

4 **François-Marie Arouet, alias 'Voltaire'** (1694-1778) was a French philosopher and prolific writer interested in a variety of Enlightenment concerns regarding civil freedoms. Credited with over 2,000 influential books, he was especially known for his strong criticism of Christianity generally, and the Roman Catholic Church in particular.

Honoré Gabriel Riqueti, Count of Mirabeau (1749-1791) was something of Weishaupt's parallel force in France. He was a philosophical nobleman who, under the pen name Arcesilaus, wrote about the gradual undermining of Christianity and the overthrow of the existing political order. Benjamin Franklin used him as a ghost writer for some of his own more extreme works that needed to be kept anonymous. The count ultimately served as a critical player in the launch of the French revolution.

5 After taking control of the French Academy (a prestigious literary club that controlled much of French thinking in the mid to late 18th century) Voltaire and his accomplices created an insider group called 'The Economists.' Meeting in the Parisian Hotel de Holbach, their secret mission was to promote revolutionary political and social reform. Christianity was considered the supreme obstacle to human happiness.

King Frederick II (the Great) of Prussia was an enthusiastic philosopher who invited open discussion for improving society. He claimed that orthodox Christianity 'grew nothing but poisonous weeds.' He eventually preferred the pseudo-Christian mysticism of the Rosicrucians against the more materialistic views of the Illuminati.

6 **Baron Johann Adam von Ikstaat** (1702-1776) was a professor and director of the University of Ingolstadt. Considered a champion of the Enlightenment, the baron compiled an impressive library of books, many of which were deemed controversial, if not heretical. His presence at the university was doubtlessly a point of friction for the Jesuits until they were disempowered. He must have had a sincere interest in Adam Weishaupt, having adopted him at the death of Weishaupt's father. His famous library became an informative refuge for young Adam.

7 The shadowy **Merchant of Jutland** (Denmark) was identified simply as 'Kolmer,' and was a traveler who roamed central Europe in the 18th century sharing the 'secret Mysteries' of the ancient philosophers. He was believed to have been either originally Egyptian or to have studied the hermetic mysteries there. He influenced men of high station to replace the world-view of Christianity with the assumptions of alchemy, astrology, and cosmogonies native to ancient Egypt, Persia and ancient Greece. (Their shared conclusion is, simply put, that the completion/perfection of humankind can be achieved by human effort.)
Some claim that the 'merchant's' primary aim was to insert a revolutionary purpose into the masonic lodges. Others interpret his mission more spiritually as insinuating occultism into the Western religious tradition. After spending time with chosen elites—like Adam Weishaupt—he was known to vanish.

8 The transformational effect of images has been a theme in esoteric teaching through the ages from ancient Egypt, Plato and forward to Carl Jung. Symbols communicate the essence of realities. For some, images simply express ideas and feelings; for others they are objects of worship because of their association with ethereal forms and presences. Secret societies like the Freemasons recognized the power of images and used them to influence the philosophical direction of nations. Weishaupt quickly recognized their potency in mysteriously affecting consciousness and would embrace them as tools.

9 From Acts 4:12. The New Testament has many examples of slogans or declarations taken from the Romans and used to make the superior claims of Jesus Christ.

10 The largely forgotten French periodical known as the *Encyclopédie* was published in France by philosopher Denis Diderot (1713-1784), and mathematician Jean le Rond d'Alembert (1717-1783). Its first folios were released in 1751 as journals claiming free thought in a wide variety of intellectual categories. Offering natural reason and humanist ideology, the journals were friends to Deist (believers in an impersonal Creator) and Atheist alike, and therefore suppressed by the Roman Catholic Church in France. The influence

of the periodical was significant, and in association with allied thinkers such as Voltaire and Mirabeau, it contributed a great deal toward the unsettling of established norms and the inspiration of revolution in both France and America.

11 Thomas Jefferson wanted the *Encyclopédie* distributed throughout the American colonies. He and Madison were avid readers, inclining Franklin, Monroe and the Marquis de Lafayette to become regular subscribers.

12 Three of Freemasonry's important symbols derived from antiquity are the square—representing the materiality of the earth; the compass—representing the spirituality of the heavens; the triangle as either equilateral which represents the unnamed Creator, or as a right angle representing the forces of Nature.

*"True wisdom has been preserved by an advanced school, illuminated
inwardly by the Savior, and continued from the beginning to the present
time as the Invisible Celestial Church."*

A.E. WAITE [1]

CHAPTER FOUR

1ST MAY, 1776

GERMAN IMPERIAL CITY OF REGENSBURG

ON A SUNNY WEDNESDAY, THE ALMOST FOURTEEN-YEAR-OLD ALEXANDER Horn made
his way slowly through the streets of Regensburg with a letter in his hand.
The letter returned his mind to the shocking day descending Dunnideer some
three-and-a-half years ago when his father announced that he'd be sent away.
Alexander paused for a moment to remember being tossed aboard a crowded
ship bound for Rotterdam. He recalled being alone and afraid as he then tra-
versed the fragmented princedoms of the so-called German Empire. [2] He finally
pictured that dreadful day when he stood in front of the Scots Monastery in
Regensburg to enter school as an oblate *puer oblatus* just like his brother, Robby,
had done some years before.

It all had proven to be a blessing, however. The auburn-haired youth had
grown like summer thistle into a lean lad with broadening shoulders and strong
features. An excellent student, he had become an attractive conversationalist
through an emerging charm that he could already muster as either a grace or as
a shield. Most thought him to be happy.

Alexander sighed and began to hurry on until he arrived at the threshold of a bakery where he inhaled the delicious aromas of warm bread and confections. He leaned against the door frame to re-read the contents of the letter his mother had written. His father had been swindled by a Calvinist in a rigged horse race, leaving Alexander Horn the Elder waging a private war against the Protestants of Oyne.

Just reading of his father's rage sent a shiver through the boy. He folded the letter in half and then in half again. Chased from the bakery, he moved through the busy streets of tidy Regensburg assuring himself that he was out of his father's reach and that his mother would be fine.

Choosing to think of Oyne no more, Alexander turned his attention his new home. He liked Regensburg. It was an ancient city set on the banks of the Danube River about eighty miles north of Munich. Independent from surrounding Bavaria, the city was ruled directly by Emperor Joseph II of the Germanic Holy Roman Empire—a scattered collection of competing European principalities. Since the emperor's parliament met here, diplomats from much of the world conducted financial and political intercourse in nearby cafes and taverns. The colorful presence of internationals enriched the small city with the kind of cosmopolitan intrigue that kept Alexander's fertile mind fascinated.

The young man finally arrived at his destination—the cemetery just beyond the walls that enclosed the monastery's complex. Here he was to meet with his superior. He was late.

Brother Benedict Arbuthnot[3] walked toward his student with a patient smile. The soon-to-be abbot was a handsome man of middling years with a fresh complexion and friendly manner. "So, my dear friend, where hast thou seen God today?" He folded his arms within the folds of his black habit.

Alexander bowed his head. "I do not know, *Nonni*."

"It is a question thou art instructed to ask thyself every day."

The young man said nothing.

The senior monk pointed upwards. "I shall answer it for thee: The sun is warm with God's love. It rises faithfully to cast the light of truth over us all."

He waited, then leaned forward. "I see that I have not impressed you. What troubles you?"

Alexander hesitated.

"Speak."

The young man obeyed. He told his senior about his father's story, to which the monk quoted some Bible verse and dug in his purse.

"See this?" asked Benedict as he retrieved a copper coin. "An Austrian *Pfenning* worth no more than four farthings. 'Tis a small thing...just like thy problem." He leaned forward.

"Thy father shall learn,
      the cheat shall burn."

Alexander stared. "This is your counsel?"

"Disappointed?"

"Aye."

Shrugging, Brother Benedict pulled some Dutch gouda from his bag. "It will have to do. I've bigger things to speak about." He lowered cracking knees to the grass. "Sit."

The young man sat.

"You smell like pastry. Strudel? I hope you bought some to share."

Alexander shook his head. "I prefer to wonder at beauty than to gobble it down."

The monk grunted and tossed the penny to his student. "Next time. Now to my point. Yesterday I told thee that I've a sense that something's afoot. I notice that the printers are seeking certain kinds of books. Mostly blasphemies. Last night I had a dream. A hand reached from a grave at noon and tried to grasp the sun." He took a bite of cheese. "It was not a very pleasant dream."

Alexander perked up.

"Aye. Unable to seize the sun, the hand snatched butterflies and birds from the air and squeezed them to death."

Alexander raised his brows.

The monk leaned forward. "Then I heard the King of Prussia laughing at King Louis of France."

"What does it mean?"

"I am not finished: The fist then divided itself into two, then four, then eight. Soon the whole of the horizon was covered with fists grasping at songbirds and butterflies." He shuddered. "It was all quite terrible."

Alexander was spell-bound. "And then?"

"I woke up. That was it. Quite enough, actually." Benedict blew air from his cheeks. "I've shared this with the abbot but he is obsessed with his retirement." The monk ate more cheese. "But I tell you because I want you to keep an ear to the ground. Something is afoot—"

"Or something is 'afist.'" Alexander laughed.

"Not funny. Hear me. Diplomats are telling me that some kind of change is coming through the *literati*. They are spreading words and images within the safety of the Freemason temples, especially in France but also here. And I am told that some clever American printer is their bridge to the American colonies. The secrecy of it all casts a dark shadow.

"This is to say nothing of the universities. The Jesuit vacuum down in Ingolstadt opened the doors for that self-important sophist, Dr. Weishaupt. I have been warned about him."

"By whom?" Alexander feigned interest.

"No matter, I am told he teaches odd notions. But whether here or in France, men are whispering that property is evil and unrestrained natural urges are good. They want equality for all with no regard for accomplishment, virtue or breeding.

"Pamphlets cover tavern tables in Paris despite threats from King Louis. Some devil is even spreading these heresies amongst the pig-heads of Switzerland. Apparently, King Frederick encourages this kind of 'free thinking' in Prussia; Catherine does the same among her elites in Russia. A Swede swore to me that their royal house is likewise active and the Poles are following suit."

"Maybe they just want to make the world better. Do we not preach equality and brotherhood?"

Benedict frowned. "Do not be naïve. The elites have no intention of being equal with commoners. And they hate the holy Church. One of their philosophers wrote that the 'fear of the Lord is the beginning of folly.'[4] Can you imagine?" The monk gobbled down more cheese. "They have a false foundation. This all reminds me of Francis Bacon. That fool said there was no divine purpose in the world. What shite! Others don't even believe men have souls."[5]

Alexander tried to insert a word but the monk waved him off.

"It seems their objective is to govern the world with some new order of reason. Of course, the powerful among them would claim some *reasoned* right to rule the rest." He took a breath. "This is to say nothing of their symbols." Benedict leaned forward to whisper. "Numerology and sorcery abound. The rebel flag in America has *thirteen* stripes and was inspired by a mysterious man who vanished after meeting with a *seven*-member masonic committee.[6] These numbers have occult purposes—black magic."

"With respect, I think you go too far," said Alexander. "There are thirteen colonies in America, you know."

Benedict snorted. "Does that not say something!" He studied his student. "You only see the obvious." He drew a deep spring-scented breath as he dug into his bag. "The American rebels have taken arms against our own King George in favor of this bit of rubbish." He tossed a copy of Thomas Paine's *Common Sense* [7] in front of Alexander. "One of the choir monks found it under your bed on his way to evening offices."

Alexander picked up the pamphlet. "Aye. It was interesting…and why was a monk snooping under my bed?"

"'Interesting?' That's all you have to say?" Benedict stared beyond a heavily budded oak and into a blue sky. "This Pennsylvania farmer, Paine, may just turn the world upside down, and you say it is 'interesting.'"

"I am not discounting it——"

Benedict placed a finger against his head.

"There is no power greater among men
than thoughts wielded by the pen."

He then pointed at the pamphlet. "I want to know thy thoughts."

Alexander sighed. He would rather be watching princesses pass the bakery. "Well, Mr. Paine argues that all men are on an equal footing. This is not unlike the Rule of our monastery."

"And?"

Alexander leaned back against his hands and let the sun warm his face. "And he believes nature granted mankind a right to govern itself."

"Do you agree?"

Alexander shrugged. "He speaks of nature as if it is an authority of its own and with reason of its own."

The monk picked a white flower from the grass. "What does this flower tell you of God?"

"That he loves beauty and loves us enough to share it," said Alexander.

Brother Benedict approved. "But..."

Alexander sat forward. "But the flower *is* not God. Neither nature nor reason *is* God, but Mr. Paine fails to make the distinction. So, like others, he errs, though I am not certain he means to do so. I suspect that he believes God made nature, and so—"

"You are too generous." Benedict studied the youth. "I think they willfully deceive."

"I did notice that he speaks of 'mankind' as a whole," said Alexander. "I wonder what he thinks of individual persons."

Surprised, Benedict looked at the boy for a long moment. "You are gifted. Some say you are chosen for some kind of greatness." He leaned forward. "You belong at a university, you know. The world would become much bigger for you, and you would become bigger for the world—"

"My world does not need to be bigger; it needs to be better." Had he said that with too much force?

Benedict narrowed his dark eyes. "I notice the books you read. They suggest to me that you have a dream of self-perfection."

Alexander stiffened. "Jesus says, 'Be perfect, even as I am perfect.'"

The monk leaned close. "He did not mean this. In my experience, those who seek perfection are actually seeking something else."

Alexander flushed. He turned away.

Benedict laid a hand gently on the boy's shoulder. "Have a care:

Pride hath two tricks to make thee stumble,

One is haughty, the other humble."

CHAPTER FOUR NOTES

1 **Arthur Edward Waite** (1857 — 1942) was a scholar of Western mysticism. This quote is paraphrased from his introduction to Karl von Eckartshausen's *Cloud Upon the Sanctuary* in which he concurred with Eckartshausen (a character soon to arrive) that spiritual forces of good were aligned to oppose those forces operating behind most of the ancient mysteries.

2 The 'German Empire' is a reference to the Holy Roman Empire (of the Germans) founded in the year 800 by Charlemagne. The Empire was a collection of multiple principalities, duchies and small kingdoms that became something of a Germanic commonwealth overseen by an emperor. It was dissolved in 1806 by Napoleon.

3 **Abbot Benedict aka Charles Arbuthnot** (1737-1820) was a respected Scottish monk and abbot of the Scots Monastery at Regensburg from 1776-1820. Besides spiritual formation, he was famous throughout Europe for his work in mathematics and chemistry. He served as Alexander Horn's mentor and guide for many years.

4 Demilaville in *Christianity Unveiled*, an influential piece circulated among French intellectuals.

5 From a French work, *Good Sense*, author unknown.

6 In December, 1775, a committee that was formed to design an American flag met in Cambridge, Massachusetts with Benjamin Franklin as chairman and George Washington in attendance. A stranger known only as 'The Professor' arrived to offer comments, the first being that six members would not do as seven was a more suitable number. He went on to offer the flag's design that resulted in the flag known as 'The Grand Union' flag. It incorporated

the British Union Jack in the field and the familiar thirteen stripes. He
then predicted that the field of the flag would soon change. After supper he
disappeared.
On January 2, 1776, Washington raised the flag with his own hands; the
opposing British army approved, saluting the flag with thirteen cheers and a
thirteen-gun salute. By June of the following year, the field was replaced with
the familiar blue with a circle of white stars.

7 **Thomas Paine** (1737-1809) published *Common Sense* in January, 1776. A
farmer and philosopher, his pamphlets inspired American revolutionaries with
a fresh vision of how government and natural law should be reconciled. Paine's
later writings supported the French Revolution, advocated Deism (see later
note) and ridiculed Christianity, claiming that 'the only church I know is my
mind.'

"A time shall come when men shall acknowledge no other law than the great book of Nature; This revolution shall be the work of secret societies."

ADAM WEISHAUPT

CHAPTER FIVE

THE SAME DAY, 1ST MAY, 1776
INGOLSTADT

THE WORLD WAS ABOUT TO CHANGE ON A Wednesday. Professor Adam Weishaupt wiped perspiration from his brow and stared through his third-floor window. Almost two decades of clandestine reading and wary whispers had led him to this day. He drew a deep breath through his nose, listening to his pregnant wife fuss with one of their two daughters.

Gazing across Ingolstadt's fanciful collection of guard towers, baroque cathedrals and stair-stepped gables, Weishaupt understood that this small city could veil secrets, well. Here many of Europe's finest minds gathered for research and discourse without the public display of Frankfurt or Berlin. With the Jesuits displaced from power in its university, the vacuum was increasingly filling with liberal men, even revolutionary men.

Enchanting or not, however, the city was also home to those not friendly to the kind of change the professor was plotting. And so, a gnawing, undefined unease crept through his bones. Was it the echoes of the remaining Jesuits? Fear of failing Kolmer? Fear of failing his deepest longings?

Maybe it was simply fear of Duke Theodore—the prince of Bavaria who ruled over Ingolstadt.[1] Indeed, men could be hanged for the kind of sedition he had in mind.

He shook his head. If only his enemies could understand his vision! No more wars, no more poverty or pestilence. Misery replaced by hope. A rational world free to be happy. Was this all so terrible?

Weishaupt's thoughts drifted to Friederika, the magic maiden whom he had never forgotten. He closed his eyes and imagined her walking with him through the city's grassy garden belt known as the glacis. The glacis provided a green screen for songbirds, butterflies and the occasional lover. Eden? To be with Friederika in that place on this day of days—

His wife's light touch startled him. "What?"

"Everything is ready?"

"Ready? Ja. The chamber is ready." He turned back to his window. "A modest beginning, but a beginning nonetheless. Like the Freemasons, I shall build the Order by way of degrees that men climb like steps." He closed his eyes. "Picture an ancient ziggurat, a stepped pyramid—"

"Like the Tower of Babel," Afra offered.

Weishaupt grunted. "The brothers will be guided by twelve counsellors; I will remain as the thirteenth, like Jesus. Thirteen is an important number." He turned and reached for a bead of his wife's necklace. "Did you know that twelve equal spheres can hide a thirteenth in the center? Fascinating, eh?"

Afra walked behind him and laid her head against his back, wrapping her arms around his waist. "And like Jesus, you will change the world. You always wanted to be like a god—"

"Did I?" He closed his eyes, smiling. "And why not? What is God other than Reason by another name?" He turned and pinched her chin, lightly. "And I am a *reasonable* man. I think even more reasonable than that teacher from Nazareth everybody worships." He kissed her, lightly on the lips.

Afra smiled.

Weishaupt abruptly changed his tone. "But hear me: From this day on, you must never ask me anything about this business. Our enemies are ruthless. So, if you hear a word, you must forget it. If you see a letter, you must turn away.

Otherwise, you put the great work in danger, to say nothing of all of us." He cast an eye toward his daughters. "Even they would suffer."

He took hold of Afra's thin shoulders. "You can never know *how* we do it, but you will understand that after today, nothing will ever be the same."

The professor hurried from his home near the city center and moved westward toward the glacis and the city gate. Rushing by the stately homes lining Theresienstrasse, he continued to strive against a vexing inner darkness that clung to him. Just a week before while preparing for this day, he had endured a night of terror. The wind was up that night and a cold rain had battered his window. Anxious from the groans of the empty office building he was in, he had turned to brandy.

He never knew if he had fallen drunk to the floor, or if he had been carried away in some sort of mystery. Weishaupt only remembered being overwhelmed by vivid images reminiscent of the *Divine Pymander of Hermes*[2] he had once studied and recently reread.

But now as he walked in daylight toward the garden park, the same images were finding the corners of his sight. Weishaupt blinked, then slowed his gait. An odd numbness came over him and he steadied himself by a lamppost. Beginning to tremble, he lowered himself on to a bench.

There he closed heavy eyes. He laid his head back and his mind immediately filled with the drama of *Pymander*. He saw the great dragon now hovering close overhead like a winged serpent dripping fire and water on all sides. It claimed to be the mind of the universe. Then, with a terrible shriek it summoned a pillar of flames which it called the eternal *Logos*—the Divine source of reason. The dragon then jolted Weishaupt by shrieking, "This is my Son in whom I am well pleased!"

Transfixed, Weishaupt floated in the silvery darkness of the Milky Way. Stars ejected from all sides like living beings released from some seedbed of souls. A frightful creature appeared, announcing itself as the 'Master Builder.' Suspended between light and darkness, the builder commanded the chaos to find order. Huge geometric shapes began to coalesce…

Paralyzed, Weishaupt could only gape until the dragon returned, trumpeting: "Reason hath redeemed thee!"

The professor opened his eyes, blinking in the light of the May evening. He ignored the crowd of staring passers-by who had gathered. Perspiring profusely, he reclaimed his thoughts. *What just happened? Did the Jesuits curse me?* A stranger's hand helped him to his feet.

Weishaupt drew several deep breaths, still frightened. He then walked weakly to another bench and sat again where he calmed himself by watching a squirrel dash about. An idea arose. *But...could it be?* Only a man chosen for something extraordinary would be drawn into such an encounter.

The professor exhaled, then filled his chest. "By Christ, I understand," he muttered. "I have just been initiated into the mysteries." He laughed. "By whom, you ask? Does it matter?"

Oh, surely his time had come! He must hurry on now. Past the crowded park and the stone wall, the exhausted professor rushed to the Kreutzor—an ancient city gate leading to the green girdle of the glacis. Breathing heavily, he greeted familiar students strolling toward the spring gardens, bursting with green. The day had been spectacularly warm, prompting Afra to say earlier that the sun must be pleased with her husband's plans. Weishaupt recalled her words as he drew a breath of grass-scented air through his nostrils, filling his lungs. Yes! A good day, indeed.

The professor stretched upward on his tip-toes. "Where the devil are they?" He primped his wig and bent over to wipe dirt off a shoe. *What if they don't come?* Straining at every arriving face, he tugged at the lace cuffs of his silk shirt and adjusted his yellow waistcoat one more time.

"Herr *Doktor?*"

Weishaupt whipped his head around to see two of his recruits striding toward him. "Ja, ja!" He welcomed the young men. Both were advanced students of his whom he had worked hard to prepare for this very day. One was nineteen-year-old Franz Anton von Massenhausen. He was a tall young man from Berlin with light hair and narrow-set blue eyes. The other was Adolf Bauhof, a brawny,

Munich-born eighteen-year-old with a perpetual snarl well-suited for law. Both were passionate to be leaders in a changing world.

"Where are the others?" said Weishaupt. He rocked on his feet, happily.

Bauhof turned and pointed. "There."

The final two hurried toward the gate. One was Andreas Sutor, a stout clergyman from the environs of Salzburg. He was twenty-nine—one year older than Weishaupt. The last to arrive was Maximilian Balthasar Ludwig Edler von Merz, a twenty-one-year-old aristocrat from Frankfurt preparing to serve as a diplomatic secretary in Regensburg. [3]

What a day this will be! "Gentlemen, I want you to look at one another. These are about to be your brothers in the Great Plan to bless humanity." The men shook hands and the professor let them get acquainted.

Weishaupt drew them together. "I have prepared each of you for this day, but this is the day we actually begin." He adjusted his coat, casting a smile at the sun setting slowly. "Thus, you must first understand that *everything* we do has a purpose. Look there." He pointed upward toward seven spires jabbing the sky. "Notice that we are gathered within the seven towers of the Kreutzor. The number seven represents perfection. And so, here under this sacred number, we begin to perfect the world."

The men stared upward.

"Follow me." With a burst of energy, the professor led his recruits into the glacis, arriving beneath the securing canopy of a huge, freshly budded tree. Angled shafts of light cast shadows. "Welcome to Eden and our very own Tree of Knowledge. This is the *Siebenstämmige Buche*—the Seven Tribes Beech. Here we have the perfection of the continents represented by Nature, the universal Source."

The men gathered close together.

"Now see, there," said Weishaupt, pointing westward. "The sun. The sun is the visible sign and symbol of the center of all things." Weishaupt held up a finger. "The sun is illumination. The sun is reason, the radiance of wisdom. Therefore, I now reveal the first secret: We honor the Zoroastrians' sun king, Yaz.[4] From this day forward, our secret calendar shall be his and not that of the unenlightened world." He surveyed each curious face. "Therefore, today is the first day of Adarpahascht, 1146."

As the announcement fell from his lips, Weishaupt blushed. He recovered by challenging the others. "Who has an objection? Who cannot comprehend why we do this?"

The men stared at their feet.

The professor closed his eyes and breathed, deeply. "You will be privy to many secrets that would be judged foolish by the ignorant. As with the Freemasons, every symbol, every liturgy, every recitation, every teaching has many layers of meaning." Weishaupt placed his hands behind his back and began to pace. "These are our fundamentals:

"First, the Source of all things is revealed in Nature. Look around you. What do you see? Life! Harmony!" He pointed to a cluster of early lilies. "Beauty! Thus, 'nature' is the word we use to reference the Whole, the World Soul, the Logos...pick one as you please, they are all the same.

"Second: The gift of Nature is happiness.

"Third: Happiness is discovered in liberty and equality.

"Fourth: Nature's wisdom is found in reason." He then commanded his initiates to take one another's hand and stand in a circle with him in the center. "And fifth: To secure happiness, enlightened men must unite against the wicked trinity of fear, ignorance and superstition."

The four nodded.

The professor then ordered the men to stand shoulder to shoulder. "Illumined leaders will ultimately liberate mankind to happiness through a cosmopolitan regime—a world commonwealth—directed by wise adepts. Future generations will be educated according to Nature's Reason..."

Ever the professor, Adam Weishaupt lectured on for a quarter hour, mindful to reveal only what might inspire the initiates and not frighten them away. Finally, spent of his declarations, he put his hand on each man's shoulder. "Are you ready?"

Each answered, "Yes."

"Then follow me."

The five walked from beneath the Seven Tribes Beech in silence and in near military precision, passing through the seven towers of the Kreutzor and turning south as the city's lamplighters began their work. They arrived at the gardens leading to the relatively new gem of Ingolstadt—the baroque-styled School of Medicine⁵ designed by the Swiss wonder, de Gabrieli.

Weishaupt led his initiates along a garden walkway and to the front portico. The portico was constructed with thirteen pillared arches and thus Weishaupt chose this particular building for tonight's sacred ritual. He paused to describe how it was that the arches represented Jesus and his Twelve, and that he would be initiating his first Novitiates in an upper room.

The professor used his key to open the decorative front door. Once inside the foyer, he ordered Sutor to light lanterns, then led his four past the dissection theatres and up a long, heavily built stairway. Standing before a wide oak door in a narrow third floor corridor, Weishaupt dug into his pocket for another key which he inserted with force. He turned the key and stepped to one side. He ordered all lamps extinguished but one, and directed his initiates into a stuffy, windowless room.

The men took a position in the middle of shadows, mumbling to themselves. Overhead were bare rafters and the scalloped undersides of damp tile. The room smelled of musty timber and wet clay.

"Silence!" The professor moved carefully to the far side where his shaded lantern revealed a red draped table dressed like an altar. He chased a spider and lit four candles from his lantern. Atop the altar were a sword, four lengths of chain, a small stack of paper, a lockbox and the statue of an owl. "Undress."

The four hesitated.

"I want you naked."

The men obeyed and Weishaupt followed. Five naked men now stood before the altar. The professor ordered each man to grab a chain and lay it over their shoulders. They were to take a candle and walk to the far side of the room where stood a desk with ink and paper.

The room closed in on the professor. His own ritual threatened him. He steeled himself. *First FROM and then TO*, he thought. *From darkness to light*. He drew a deep breath, remembering some night terrors of his youth. "Write your most damning personal secret and affix your signature."

After a considerable time of shifting and awkward movement, the four returned to Weishaupt who collected the confessions, quickly. To the men's dismay, he proceeded to read them each aloud and with flourish.

The men hung their heads.

Finished, Weishaupt said, "These are only to be revealed outside the Order should you betray your brethren." He studied each face. "But I tell you this, nothing you have confessed will matter in the world we are about to make." He eyed two of them. "Homosexuality will be an act of liberty." He turned to another. "Adultery? No such thing if the world is one family." He looked at another. "And theft from a widow? There can be no theft when all things are held in common. The fear of these imaginary sins are the chains we shall lose. Now drop yours."

Four chains crashed atop the wooden floor.

Weishaupt proceeded to lock the men's confessionals in a strongbox. "These serve only to protect you from the temptation of revealing our secrets." He then pointed three of the men to the corridor door. "Wait outside until you are called."

Massenhausen—the nineteen-year-old Berliner—was told to remain. He was commanded before the altar with his candle.

Weishaupt donned a black, hooded robe.

"Honor the owl. She represents Minerva, goddess of Wisdom."

Massenhausen bowed his head and mumbled something. It would have to do. Weishaupt wanted this to be over with as much as his initiate did.

"Now kneel."

The young man submitted, visibly anxious.

"Do you intend to serve the Order of Perfectibilists?"

"I do so intend."

"Why?"

"I see the degradation of mankind."

Weishaupt liked that. "Leave this room and reflect on your intention."

Massenhausen obeyed.

The next initiate entered for the same, and the next and then the last. Each was dismissed in turn and then Weishaupt summoned the Berliner once again.

"Have you considered your answer and do you still affirm your desire to serve the Order?"

"I do."

"Do you seek the protection of the Brethren?"

"I do."

Weishaupt took a breath. "Your request is just. In the name of our most Serene Order, I promise to protect and to defend you. I assert that you will find nothing among us to be hurtful to Religion, Morals or the State..." He then took the sword and placed the point against Massenhausen's bare breast. "But should you ever betray us, be assured that shame and remorse shall follow you, and the rage of the Brethren shall prey upon your entrails."

Massenhausen swallowed.

"Do you still insist on submitting yourself to this cause?"

"I do."

Weishaupt lowered his sword and walked to the extreme rear of the room. There he lifted his candle to reveal a black coffin lined with black satin. The professor chilled. He remembered his mother lying inside one of these, pale and waxen. He shuddered. "Get in."

The youth hesitated.

To make matters worse for poor Massenhausen, Weishaupt revealed a hammer and nails. "There is no life unless there is death. One must pass from darkness to light in order to illumine others." He pointed into the black hole of the empty coffin. "Lie here and die, or leave."

"You will nail me inside?" The young man began to tremble.

"Die to live again, or live and die blind." Weishaupt's tone was harsh. Wrath rose within him.

Massenhausen alternated his eyes between the rigid face Weishaupt and the specter of the coffin. The poor Berliner began to leak urine. "I...I..."

The professor leaned into the lad. His voice had a sudden, menacing hiss. "He that forfeits his life shall save it."

Massenhausen obeyed. He climbed inside the coffin with a submissive whimper.

Weishaupt immediately slammed the lid shut with a terrible, triumphant shout. "You are dead to all that was." He held a nail between his two fingers.

The hammer was ready. Something deep within tempted him to fasten the lid and leave the lad behind to suffer. He set the point of the nail in place.

He heard Massenhausen begin to sob.

No! What? Weishaupt took hold of himself. Breathing quickly, he hammered the coffin edges without nails, then waited for a brief moment before throwing open the lid. "Now live to all that is and all that shall be."

The young man scrambled free.

The professor wiped his brow. What had just happened? He then directed the terrified Berliner to the altar and handed a paper to him. "Read this oath."

Massenhausen put one hand over his heart. With the other he read the oath aloud in the flickering shadows of candlelight:

> "In the presence of almighty God and this most excellent Order, I confess my endless weaknesses and swear to resist the enemies of human nature and society with all that I am and all that I have. I pledge to serve humanity, to improve my mind and apply all my strength to the common good.... I pledge an eternal silence, an inviolable obedience to my superiors and the statutes of the Order.
> I fully renounce my own judgment if ever in conflict with the goals of the Order and accept the greater wisdom of this cause. So, help me God."

Weishaupt handed the young man a quill. "Now, sign as a pledge of your soul."

Franz Anton von Massenhausen signed. Weishaupt deposited the oath in his lockbox, then surprised his first Novitiate with an announcement. "You are dead as Franz Anton von Massenhausen. You are heretofore to be known within the Order as 'Ajax.'" He then handed him a small book containing the new calendar, a secret geography that renamed the cities of the world, and an initial cipher for secret correspondence. [6]

Ajax von Massenhausen then blurted, "Let the world be changed."

The young man's confidence relieved Weishaupt. The oppressing darkness lifted a bit, and he commanded Ajax to stand behind the altar and bear witness to the rest of the others' initiations. When all were done, the professor spread his arms. "Brothers. I am no longer Adam Weishaupt to you, but *Spartacus*, though you must never mention me again. I am to remain behind the curtain. You have much to learn and the world is waiting. But——" Weishaupt rang a small bell and the door to the chamber opened. A half-dozen giggling females and two young males entered. "Until then, Ajax, *Agathon, Erasmus* and *Tiberius*: I invite you to enjoy the sumptuous fruits of liberty."

CHAPTER FIVE NOTES

1 **Duke Karl-Theodor of Bavaria** (1724-1799) A generally unpopular ruler of the German state of Bavaria, the duke was more interested in philosophy and the arts than governance. His legacy includes the artistic improvement of Munich and his ultimate defense of tradition against the rise of revolutionary ideas. A liberal thinker, he was eventually persuaded to champion the cause of conservatives against the radical beliefs underpinning the Illuminati and Freemasonry.

2 The *Divine Pymander of Hermes* is an early Hermetic writing loosely dated from the second century A.D. It includes the story of origins as revealed to Hermes in the primordial past. In it, the texts reflect the claim of many ancient mystery religions that enlightened spiritual life is best personified by a Great Dragon. The dragon is identified as the ultimate Mind (as per the Egyptian god, Thoth) of the universe, and thus is the father of Reason. This text identifies the Son of 'Thought' as the Eternal Logos—a Greek word meaning rationality, dialogue and/or word. The Great Dragon and his Son go on to create the world.
The philosophical assumptions and imagery of this text can be followed through the history of later theosophical traditions that have influenced culture and politics, including those referenced in the context of this story and beyond.
In contrast, Christian traditions identify the Great Dragon as the personification of a counterfeit light, sometimes known as Lucifer and/or Satan. The *Gospel of John* identifies the Eternal Logos (Word) to be Jesus Christ, the true 'Light of the World.'

3 The names of Weishaupt's first recruits are historical as were the great majority of those who are to be mentioned in this story. I refer the reader to Terry Melanson's exhaustive work as included in the bibliography provided.

Of the ultimate 3,000 estimated members of the original organization, some 2,000 names are known.

4 **Persian King Yazdegerd III** was the last Shah of Iran before the Islamic conquest of the region. His regnal date was 632 A.D. and so Weishaupt simply subtracted 630 from the western year to calculate his secret calendar. Yazdegerd and his Zoroastrianism focused on the exaltation of Wisdom as god.

5 As an aside, the astute reader may remember that Ingolstadt's School of Medicine was the setting of Mary Shelley's 1818 novel, *Frankenstein*. Given the themes of the famous book, and given her husband's devotion to the occult, one wonders whether this site was chosen by Mary for its association with the founding of the Order of the Illuminati.

6 This abbreviated description of the initiation into the membership of the Illuminati comes from first hand witnesses as conveyed to Abbé Augustin Barruel (1741-1820). Notably, the oath is intentionally deceptive in any reference to 'God.' Later degrees were introduced gradually and these were used to incrementally reveal the actual intentions of Weishaupt's Order.
Barruel was a French Jesuit and writer who revealed the relationship of secret societies to social revolution. He famously wrote, *Memoirs Illustrating the History of Jacobinism* which included an informed exposé on the Illuminati.

"See to it that no one takes you captive by deceptive philosophy which depends on human tradition according to the elemental spirits of the world and not Christ."

FROM THE BIBLE'S *BOOK OF COLOSSIANS*

CHAPTER SIX

29ᵀᴴ SEPTEMBER, 1779
REGENSBURG

SINCE HE'D BEEN IN REGENSBURG, ALEXANDER HAD SUCCESSFULLY completed his studies amongst the Benedictines, made friends of many, and had grown into a lanky, handsome seventeen-year-old. But on this day, Alexander Horn was to be no more.

After pre-dawn vespers, the top of Alexander's head was shaved to form the tonsure—a ring of hair that symbolized Jesus' crown of thorns. Dressed in a plain shift, the lean lad was led into the torch-lit sanctuary of the abbey church where a group of black-hooded brothers waited, silently. Abbot Benedict commanded him to lay prostrate before the altar, itself ablaze in a constellation of candles. From this position, Alexander Horn would be laid to rest and 'Brother Maurus' would rise.

Alexander obeyed. Arms at his side and his face against the cold terra cotta tile, doubts quickly filled him. Was this really what he wanted? And if so, why? His older brother, Robby, had taken his vows in this same place to escape the world. But what about him?

Alexander's mind raced as several monks proceeded to cover him with a large funeral pall—something of a rectangular black drape with a crimson cross. Buried beneath it, his world now turned black. The drape smelled musty. Feet shuffled nearby and then he heard some chanting. He squeezed his fists.

For the next two hours, Alexander remained in his utter darkness as Abbot Benedict prayed, recited Scriptures and read from liturgical texts. Dust made his nose itch. Even his young joints began to ache from the damp cold of the tile. More than that, his mind continued to churn. *What if I just jumped up and ran away? But run away from what?*

The space beyond his then fell silent. His breath quickened, and he thought he heard the terrible hiss again. 'A-L-E-X-A-N-D-E-R.' *No!* It was as if he were a child alone in his room in faraway Oyne. He ground his teeth and tried to imagine an angel, but that only worked when Grunnie had been near. "Alexander is no more!" he hissed back. "I am Brother Maurus…" Hearing his words caught his full attention. Wait! Was that true? But what of 'Alexander Horn?' A wave of fear crawled through him.

From nowhere, a distant memory found him. He was a small boy. His head lay on Grunnie's soft lap as the two sat on the lawn at Westhall. They were staring at the stars through the cold air one Hogmanay night. She tucked a heavy blanket under his chin as he marveled at the canopy above. "Grunnie!" little Alexander said. "Look how many!"

And he remembered his grandmother answering, "Aye, laddie, and we are so wee beneath it all. Yet so safe."

The simple memory filled Alexander's heart in this moment. "So safe," he muttered. He then thought about how the dear old woman pointed to the Milky Way as the 'Hem of the Almighty.' His spirit quieted beneath his pall. A moment later, a vision of Fiona came to him. She was still little. Her green eyes were bright and she smiled.

An angel after all? he wondered. *Perhaps that would be better, for then she is forever close.* Alexander took a deep breath. Deep peace settled over him and held him. Lost in his remembrances, Alexander released his spirit. He imagined he was floating in the grand shalom of the starry Presence where Love abounded. He smiled in his wonderfully dark place.

A fitful yearning then rose up within the about-to-be monk. *To reach out and take hold of just one star of that hem. To belong to God…* He opened his eyes in his darkness…*To feel his love. To be welcome, to be shielded by his might.*

The sounds of monks chanting the solemn *Litany of the Saints* returned him to his cold floor. Their words declared Alexander's death to the world. Death? The young man did not understand that. Did Jesus not come because he *loved* the world? *Why must I die TO the world he loves? Should I not at least die FOR the world? And how does one do that?*

If only Alexander knew how it was that the very asking of such questions set him apart. The monks never mulled over more than the mundane required. The abbot had a curious mind, to be sure, but even he failed to press beyond the limits. No, Alexander had always been different. His Grunnie thought he was chosen. The lad never knew it, but she had once told Horn the Elder that his son would oppose evil in ways that no one could imagine.

The chanting ended and hands lifted the heavy pall off him. *Now what?* Supposedly rising to new life in the yellow light of the nave, Alexander—or more correctly, Brother Maurus—climbed to his feet, slowly. He was then invited to the altar where he raised his face to the crucifix of his Lord. Turning a deaf ear to more recitations, he spoke to Jesus. *You and I both know this should be about—*

"Brother Maurus!"

"Eh?" The startled young man stared blankly at the abbot. "Sorry."

"Read this." Abbot Benedict handed him his chart on which he pledged his obedience to the Order of St. Benedict. "And then sign it." He handed him a dripping quill.

Alexander took the chart in one hand and began to read it aloud. "*In nomine Filii…*" He paused and gawked at the men in black robes. Was this really to be him? Was there no other path to the hem of the Almighty?

The now Brother Maurus inhaled a deep breath. *None that I can think of just yet.* He finished his awkward reading, exhaled with a long sigh and he signed. This would all have to do, at least for now.

Smiling, Abbot Benedict countersigned the young monk's chart. Alexander—Brother Maurus—then sang the obligatory *Suscipe me Domine* three times, beginning with arms outstretched, and finishing on his knees with his arms crossed over his breast. Thus, his rebirth into new life was proclaimed in Heaven and on earth.

Resigned to the whole business, Alexander almost laughed at the abbot's joy in helping him put his new scapular over his simple tunic. The scapular was an ankle-length, sleeveless black robe bound at the waist by a simple cord. He then donned his cowl. He stood patiently as his superior laid the medal of St. Benedict over his neck and granted him the kiss of peace.

Alexander took the circular medal in one hand. On one side was an etched figure of the old saint; on the other was a cross within a circle. The effect of the symbols surprised him with a securing sense of belonging. He smiled and held the medal to his heart.

With another prayer, the abbot and two priests proceeded to administer the Mass. The new Brother Maurus soon found himself eating the flesh and drinking the blood of Christ Jesus. When it was over, the young monk received the sincere welcome of his brethren and the kind benediction of his God.

Though none yet knew it, in all of this the history of the world was once again changed on a Wednesday.

Later that same day, Alexander was walking the streets of Regensburg winking at girls and self-consciously rubbing the top of his shaved head. His brother disapproved of course. "You took a vow, Brother Maurus," Robby Horn said.

"But look how beautiful she is." One of the many German daughters belonging to the princely house known as 'Thurn and Taxis' passed by in an ornate coach, smiling. "Besides, the quest of my spirit is pure—"

"Even if thy flesh is not? They are joined, brother—"

Alexander put a hand on his brother's shoulder. "I am not a monk because I am afraid of women…like someone I know. I can be pure of heart and still friendly."

Robby grumbled. "I cannot imagine why thou art a monk at all. And why did you choose 'Maurus' for a name? It is ridiculous. Our mother shall not be pleased."

"Saint Maurus was the first oblate of our order. You should know that."

Robby kicked a small stone. "You think thou art the first among lessers... some kind of special being ascending to shame us all."

Alexander shrugged. "Don't be stupid."

"You never get sick, you never get hurt. You excel at whatever you choose. Important men already seek thy counsel and you are not even eighteen! And the ladies—"

A carriage suddenly careened toward the two monks, a wheel cracking loose from its axle. With a cry, Alexander shoved his brother to one side as he stumbled to another. The carriage's startled horse lurched upward. Alexander dashed forward and lunged for one of the reins as two passengers spilled atop the brick street. The driver launched forward, head over heels.

Shouting, Alexander grabbed hold of the rein and strained against the bit of the frightened mare, finally bringing her to a nervous stop. He moved closer, keeping the single rein taught. "Easy, lass, easy..." The horse snorted. Her iron-shod hooves struck restlessly atop the bricks. "Steady, steady." The wide-eyed mare shuddered. "Such a pretty girl..." He took her bridle carefully and fixed his grip near her heaving nostril. Relieved, he laid a free hand on her cheek. "That's my beauty."

A small crowd gathered. Some attended the carriage, others applauded. He released a long breath.

"You there, brave monk!" A tall man with bloodied knees limped quickly toward Alexander. Behind, another disheveled gentleman was on the ground holding tightly to a small girl. "Brother, I cannot thank you enough." The approaching man was five or six years older than Alexander and had the bearing of a diplomat. His slightly accented English suggested he was an American. Arriving, he extended a severely scraped hand. "You saved us."

Alexander offered his free hand to accept the man's own. It was then the mare panicked once again. Without warning, she reared and tangled the young monk's other hand in her head-gear. Before anyone could react, she bolted, dragging poor Alexander. Howling, he hung helplessly alongside the dashing horse. His feet bounced atop the street; his arm twisted. Screams from all sides filled the air. The carriage dashed to pieces, leaving the horse thundering down the street with Brother Maurus.

Helpless, the youth could do nothing as the stocky warm-blood loped and bucked through dodging pedestrians. Battered and numb, he flung about at the mare's heaving shoulder like a limp rag doll. Many were in chase until a wall of men finally filled the street and brought the frightened animal to a full stop.

Alexander remained suspended from the bridle nearly unconscious. Hands loosened his, and in moments he was carried to a wagon for delivery to the small hospital near the city center.

That night Alexander Horn groaned in a clean bed surrounded by a candle-lit circle of familiar men and one he did not recognize. He was in pain and he was afraid.

"Brother Maurus?" Abbot Benedict leaned close. His dark eyes were soft and comforting.

Alexander nodded, and when he did he wanted to cry out for the pain stabbing his ribs, shoulder, arm and legs.

"You have some bones to be set. That shall surely hurt.

But the pain ye feel
Will help thee heal."

Alexander was in no mood for the abbot's doublets. Would he die? Was he ready to die? He felt suddenly trapped. The room was too dark. Too small. The cold chill of terror rose the hair on his skin.

Another brother laid a hand on his shoulder, lightly. "The household is in prayer for thee, Brother Maurus."

The young monk stared, unable to answer. Prayers? Such a promise did not fill him with the comfort he thought it should. He struggled for a calming breath. Pain cut it short. Another voice approached. It was from the man with the bloodied knees. Alexander watched the man striding toward him. Sympathy filled the stranger's face and he reached his hand forward long before he arrived at the lad's bedside.

"Brother, thanks be to God for your courage," the man said with such earnest that a lump filled Alexander's throat.

The stranger knelt to one side and rested his hand on Alexander's shoulder, gently. "My niece was still inside the carriage when you first brought the horse to a stop. She was rescued before the mare bolted the second time."

Alexander smiled. That was good news indeed.

"She sends her thanks to you, Brother. And this." He retrieved a little yellow wildflower from a pocket and held it up to the suffering monk.

Alexander stared at it for a long moment. A tear welled. Perhaps that was where he saw God that day.

"Except for your bravery, she would have been killed." The stranger's face distorted with emotion.

Alexander wheezed something indiscernible.

The man wiped his eyes, then introduced himself. "I am Albert van Loon, agent for the American government in Regensburg."

Alexander tried to open his hand. He winced.

"I see you are in pain, my friend, and so I leave you to your brethren. I promise to return."

For the fortnight to follow, Alexander Horn endured a great deal. Nearby were the rasps and retching of diseased patients and injured men. His own bones had been set and splinted but they ached. The gashes on his legs had been stitched and bandaged but they were raw. His shattered ribs made him dread each breath. Fever found him and sapped his remaining strength. Fever had also prompted confusion and filled his mind with terrible visions. And worse of all, the hissing voice had returned.

He awoke one night to see a priest administering his last rites. "Get away," Alexander gasped.

In time the fever did lift, though the fear did not. Something about death at his door had awakened him to a reality previously pushed away. As Robby had once charged, Alexander had always been spared much that others had suffered. The result of such good fortune did not serve him well, however. Quite the contrary, his 'good fortune' had proven to be an illusion of invulnerability that encouraged him to rely on his own strength. But now that truth had slapped his face, the young monk's prayers were desperate.

Yet his prayers were answered with silence.

And in that silence fear filled him all the more.

By the beginning of the third week, he was in fear of fear, and his fear shamed him. Robby was of no help, but other brethren came regularly with confections and prayers of their own, readings and blessings. Abbot Benedict sat faithfully by his side, assuring him that he was safe. He supposed these charities were something.

Early one morning, the abbot took Alexander's hand. "I see how fear consumes thee, little brother," he said. "But God's love casts out fear."

Alexander stared. "Where is God? And where is his love?"

The abbot smiled. "He generally presents himself in the faces of others."

"Like Robby?" The night before, his brother had arrived to insist that Alexander was suffering a long overdue punishment for his pride and his lusts.

Abbot Benedict raised his brows.

"Well, the Almighty strains with every word
to find a saint and not a turd."

Laughing, Alexander clutched his ribs. Perhaps love looked like this after all.

Abbot rested a warm hand on the young monk's shoulder. "Is that American still visiting thee?"

"Aye." Albert van Loon was a great help translating for him to the German hospital staff, and he had distracted the monk with news of the American Revolution.

But there was another, one whom 'Brother Maurus' was not supposed to notice at all. Her name was Julianna, a fifteen-year-old daughter of nobility with strawberry hair who served the nuns in their care of the sick.

One week later, Alexander finally received the good news of his discharge and he asked that Van Loon escort him home. The tall American entered the hospital dormitory in his tailored suit and fine leather shoes. He was a handsome man with a fair complexion and powdered blond hair tied at the base of his neck.

Well-educated and mannerly, he removed his long coat and took his position on a hard stool by Alexander's bed. "Are we about ready?"

"As soon as the nurse brings my crutch."

"I've had interesting conversations with your abbot, Benedict," Albert said. "He tells me you want to perfect yourself. I found that interesting. Dr. Franklin is of like mind. He recently told me——"

"How do you know Franklin?"

"I am assigned to his staff in Paris. I thought I told you already."

Alexander didn't remember.

"Since I am fluent in Dutch, German and French——"

"Your government sent you here. Of course."

Van Loon nodded. "Precisely. You know of Dr. Franklin?"

"The abbot says Franklin is a blasphemous glutton who likely suffers flapdragon."

The American took a breath. "Dr. Franklin ends each day asking, 'What good have I done this day?'"

Alexander shrugged. "The brothers ask something deeper: 'Where have I seen God today?' I already see a big difference." He chased a fly. "Besides, how does Franklin's notion of 'good' square with his membership in the Hellfire Club?" [1]

The American stood. "Not your concern. But you ought to have a care about rumors."

Rumors? Perhaps Alexander had been rash, though talk of the club's debauchery and occult worship were widespread. [2] Benjamin Franklin's name was nearly always in the mix. "Well, if it is all rumor I apologize. Though you might want to do some checking. The founder of that club worshipped the Goddess of Nature, and his members might just as well be priests to Isis."

Albert eased. "Apology accepted." He folded his hands behind his back. "I was going to tell you about Dr. Franklin's formula for moral perfection, but now——"

That sort of thing made Alexander curious. "No, go on."

Van Loon returned to his seat and crossed his long legs. He paused. "Very well. It consists of thirteen virtues and a table on which he records his daily successes and failures."

"And?"

"He says that he improves but admits he might be happier settling for something just short of perfection." The American grinned.

Van Loon's smile was infectious; Alexander laughed out loud.

From behind, a woman's voice turned both heads. "It is time to go home, Brother Maurus." Julianna Roth von Himmelsberg arrived smiling. She handed Alexander a set of wooden crutches.

Instantly forgetting Van Loon, Alexander stared at Julianna. A flood of boyhood memories enchanted his heart to overflowing. *Fiona? Oh, if only you could be my Fiona come to me like this.* In these past weeks he often hoped for pain just so Julianna might soothe him with a cool cloth and a kind word. "I shall miss you." He swung his legs over the side of his bed.

Julianna took hold of his arm. At her touch life pulsed through him. He stood, carefully, thinking of his days in Dunnideer. "Thank you for your good care of me."

Julianna steadied him. "Care is my duty." She smiled, playfully.

Duty? The word stung the young monk. He glanced at Albert and back again. "Of course." His mind raced. "And...and my *joy* would be to offer you a blessing." He leaned on one crutch and laid his hand atop her head. Her hair was soft. Then, knowing nothing of what he was doing, he went on to pronounce some kind of benediction. "*In nomine Patris, Filii, et Spiritus Sanctus...*"

Julianna shifted in place.

The young monk rambled further to recite some prayer from no book ever written. He would have babbled on forever if it would keep his hand attached to the girl's head. A sharp command from behind startled him.

"Brother Maurus!"

Alexander turned to see Robby running at him. Behind Robby hurried three nuns to Julianna's rescue.

"Enough! Unhand her."

CHAPTER SIX NOTES

1 The Hellfire Club was founded by Francis Dashwood and the Earl of Sandwich around 1755 in London. Sometimes called the 'Monks of Medmenham,' members gathered to celebrate a combination of pagan rites, occultism, and libertine sexuality. Dashwood believed that the wise few could best govern the ignorant majority as long as they were inspired by a true religion. For him and his club, true religion was based upon the male and female principles of nature. The club engaged in orgies and elaborate rituals to celebrate this. The serpent was a favored image and numerology was a strong influence. Membership included many of the British political and social elite, as well as Benjamin Franklin.

2 Broadly defined, Occultism refers to a wide array of beliefs and practices that invoke the supernatural. In the West, however, the term typically applies to secret philosophical/spiritual activities stemming from non-Christian sources. These may include divination, magic, witchcraft, tarot, astrology, alchemy, numerology and spiritism.

.

"Our goal is to restore to man the powers which had been his in Eden before the Fall."

COUNT ALESSANDRO CAGLIOSTRO [1]

CHAPTER SEVEN

8ᵀᴴ FEBRUARY, 1780
INGOLSTADT, BAVARIA

AFRA WEISHAUPT'S CORPSE LAY ATOP HER CANDLE-SHADOWED BED. Her folded hands held a sprig of acacia. Her husband stared into her face, offering no expression—not one of grief, shock or even remorse. By his side stood his oldest two daughters. The youngest two remained downstairs in the care of the governess; another had been buried just months prior.

On the other side of the deathbed stood Franz Zwack,[2] one of Weishaupt's handpicked leaders now known to the brotherhood as *'Cato.'* Cato Zwack was an ambitious twenty-four-year-old attorney from nearby Landshut with a broad forehead, prominent nose and close-set blue eyes. Over the past four years he had risen to the supreme rank of Aeropagite[3] and had quickly become Weishaupt's closest confidant among this ruling Council.

The clock over the crackling hearth chimed eleven times. "The physician pronounced her dead at three o'clock this afternoon." Weishaupt lifted his face to Cato. "That was the exact time my godfather likewise died so mysteriously." The professor had never fully recovered from that shock. It had not escaped his notice that the man who raised him may have been murdered just three months after the founding of the Order.

Weishaupt kissed the top of his daughters' heads and sent them from the room.

Closing the door, he said, "We have enemies, Cato. But this? No one knows my identity other than the Aeropagites." He wiped his nose. "We may be growing too quickly." Weishaupt's clever plan to imbed his Order deep within Freemasonry was proving to be a stroke of genius. Hundreds of members were now active throughout many of the German states.

Cato nodded. A forceful man, he practiced law in Munich and was suspiciously familiar with the worst elements of the city. "Somebody has been talking. Reports have come back to me."

Weishaupt let his eyes fall again to Afra. "Sometimes our friends even become our enemies." He turned to Cato, fully aware of the man's obsessive concern with security. "You are privy to criminal apothecaries, to assassins, abortionists—"

"Yes," said Cato with a steady voice. "All of that and more."

"I am told that you have a collection of recipes for sundry poisons and the like. Even some sort of dust that blinds a man." He paused before adding, "And I am told you have the means to fill a chamber with pestilent vapors."

"As do our enemies," said Cato.

Weishaupt paused. Could it be possible? "I find it curious that my poor Afra died of a very sudden fever that seemed to be contained in this bedchamber."

"We thank the Universe for sparing your children," said Cato. "And for directing you away from here and to Munich last night. That was fortunate, indeed."

Weishaupt sucked a long breath through his nose. The air in the dim-lit death chamber was musty from sprays of dried herbs. "Yes. We must find who did this and deal with him," said Weishaupt. "I suspect a Jesuit was involved." He then pointed to the acacia. "Her physician left that on behalf of the lodge."[4]

"That was kind of him," said Cato.

Nodding, Weishaupt wiped his nose with a kerchief. "She was a good wife, ja? But not very beautiful." His thoughts turned to Afra's excitement on that special Wednesday, now more than three years past—and to the warning he had given her. "These candles make her lips very blue," he said quietly. "And forever still."

Weishaupt then motioned for Cato to follow him into a corner. "Tell me, exactly where are you hiding your recipes?"

Cato lowered his voice as if Afra might hear him. "I had an exploding box built. If a curious meddler attempts to open it, it will be his end and the contents will be destroyed."

Weishaupt raised a brow. "By Christ, you have a cold and practical heart." He thought for a long moment. "Who built it?"

"It is better if you do not know."

"Is it large enough to secure all our papers? I am holding the confessionals of hundreds of initiates in simple lockboxes. I also have the ciphers, our maps and stolen correspondences. I have instructions for every position and thoughts on new degrees. Imagine if the authorities found any of this."

"The box can hold it all, Spartacus. And if I need another, I'll have it built."

"Where is it?"

"Bolted and draped in the cellar of our church for now."

Satisfied, Weishaupt returned to his wife's body. "I wanted her to be happy. I want us all to be happy. Is it too much to ask?" He paused. "She shall have a respectable service and I shall allow it in the Lutheran church. I think it better to wear that mask a little longer…and she would have liked that."

"You are wise, General." Cato stepped close. "You are chosen—"

"I grow weary of that word," muttered Weishaupt. "I would like to be alone." As the attorney disappeared into the dark hallway, the professor closed the door and moved slowly to an upholstered chair in a corner by a table. Removing his coat, he stared across the room at his wife's body. His eyes lingered on the acacia sprig. He wondered about her soul. Did she have one?

Did he? Where would such a thing as that come from?

And what of the day he would lay on some bed like this, eyes under coins and hands folded over a lifeless heart. His mind turned to Charles Bonnet.[5] Bonnet's work had convinced him that Nature guides a perpetual reincarnation of life's energetic essence toward eventual perfection. The notion had been a comfort. But staring at Afra's lifeless body, at that moment he thought Bonnet's calculation to be suddenly useless. She looked utterly vacant. Would this be his end, as well?

Unsettled, Weishaupt adjusted his waistcoat and poured himself a wide-bottomed snifter of Armagnac brandy. "Mysteries," he muttered. He raised his glass to his wife. "Forgive me, Afra." He swallowed a large gulp. "I must leave you behind."

Weishaupt through a log into the hearth and leaned his wigged head against the back of the chair. He stared at the heavily shadowed ceiling, yellowed by firelight. He wondered about himself and his movement—its name now changed to the 'Bavarian Order of the Illuminati.' *Only my Areopagites even know that I am General Spartacus.* Where was the glory in that?

He closed his eyes and let his mind drift elsewhere. He soon pictured the full figure of his Friederika. His thoughts had never been far from that woman over these years. She had made him feel so very much a man. And then there was Sophia, his brother's fetching wife. Oh, how he had longed to bed her. Sighing, he opened his eyes. When he did he nearly fell over. Standing in the very center of the room was the mysterious Merchant of Jutland.

"Kolmer? But how—"

Looming within a large black cape, Kolmer raised a gloved hand. "I am very sorry for poor Afra." He glided toward Weishaupt's corner chair. He tossed his long black hair and laid a heavy hand on the professor's shoulder. "Are you?"

The professor felt as if he were being smashed into his chair. He could not speak.

Kolmer removed his hand. "I have little time so listen carefully." He poured himself a short glass of brandy. "I am concerned that you may not be, shall we say, thinking as clearly as you must."

"I don't understand."

Kolmer darkened. "I am here to…encourage you about a few things." He took a sip. "First, never forget that that things do end—like Afra. You will end." He leaned close to Weishaupt's face. "But the Order must never end." He confused the professor with a sudden grin. "You must infuse it with the ability to reincarnate in fresh forms as circumstances require. Its purpose…*your* purpose…is to cast seeds into the wind like a June dandelion." He tossed a log into the fire, sending a rush of red sparks upward into the chimney.

Weishaupt licked his lips.

"We are generally pleased with you, Adam—Spartacus." Kolmer stepped to another side. "You have insinuated good men. You are soon in control of the masons in Munich."

The professor waited. Wood crackled and popped.

"We are lucky to exploit the Craft, are we not? Those almost-awake men have set the stage for us." Kolmer walked to a window and spread the drapes apart. Below, the dark streets of Ingolstadt were empty. "The Freemasons loosen the grip of men's ignorance. Their ceremonies and symbols distract men from their superstitions." He paused. "Oh, how I enjoy the Order of *Elus Coens*! Did you know that their initiates spend six hours inhaling incense laden with agaric mushroom spores? Ha! Imagine the effect when their blindfolds are removed by brethren behind Egyptian masks and pointing swords at them!" Kolmer laughed, loudly. Turning, he said, "So, we use them for now. In time, we will jettison them all…" He thought for a moment. "Yes. The Craft gets us into all of Europe…and America. What are your thoughts on America? You must not lose sight of her."

Weishaupt wiped his brow. "Franklin is key. He understands what true freedom must look like."

"Agreed. I like him…and Paine and Jefferson. But Washington is a waste. He may dabble in astrology and masonic forms, but he is content in his Deism."[6] Kolmer grunted. "Win or lose their little rebellion, OUR war for America must be for the hearts of its people. They are an obstacle to everything. Their religion has too much effect." He thought for a long moment. "Yet, hope is far from lost. Franklin is developing a creed that has the possibility of reducing all religion to a mere philosophy of good living. A wonderful step. We would simply change the idea of 'good' over time."

Weishaupt nodded. Perspiration gathered along his brow. "As I say, Franklin is key. I wish I would have met with him in France. I think he would have embraced my vision for a happy world."

Kolmer took three long strides toward Afra's body, casting a menacing shadow on the ceiling. Weishaupt suddenly shrank in his chair. The shadow danced like the winged serpent of his night terrors.

Kolmer snatched the acacia from Afra's cold hands. Returning, he held the sprig directly in front of Weishaupt's face. "But all in good time. For now, you must root the Order, deeply, and in realities beyond simple externals. I hope you understand."

Nodding, the professor watched Kolmer disappear as quickly as he had arrived. He exhaled and watched his trembling hands. He tried to swallow. Weishaupt carefully scanned the suddenly hollow room. A waft of sweet tobacco lingered in the air. His nostrils sucked its fragrance into his lungs until he coughed. He wiped his nose and mouth. Standing, he moved warily toward Afra. His eyes followed her form and when they fell upon her hands, a cold chill spread through his chest; the acacia sprig remained neatly held as if it had never been moved.

SEPTEMBER, 1780
INGOLSTADT

"I am very pleased." Adam Weishaupt sat in his favorite tavern near the Danube with his new second-in-command— an erudite aristocrat named Baron Ludwig von Knigge[7] now known as '*Philo*' to the Order. Philo von Knigge was an intelligent young man of twenty-eight, tall and lean, and with a thin nose and soft blue eyes.

Weishaupt reviewed the ciphered document one more time. "You have done well. This is exactly what we need. You have made a mockery of the Jesuits with such literary skill."

Philo took a long, satisfying drink of dark beer. Dabbing froth from his mouth with a napkin, he answered with precision. "My advice remains. Hide your plans for the Church. The Order will be finished if our deeper purposes are discovered." He leaned forward. "The people are not yet done with religion."

Weishaupt grumbled.

"Also, you must not ridicule mysticism," said Philo. "It is simply good logic. The Masons are mystics. To attract them we need to encourage their metaphysics, not mock them."

Weishaupt wrinkled his nose. "You say all this because *you* are a mystic."

"You may think yourself to be only a rationalist; you like to suppose the universe is only material. But you are also a mystic in your own way. You serve the Unknown Superiors in ways you may not fully see."[8]

Weishaupt turned his face. Was it true?

Philo pressed. "Hear me. Anyone is a mystic who understands that forces—and not chance—move men. And only an idiot would deny it."

Weishaupt snorted. "As far as I am concerned, an idea is a 'force.' I want to talk of economics and morality, even science and mathematics. I am sick to death of superstition—"

The baron raised his hand. "With respect, General, philosophy that makes room for the mysteries remains the key. Men feel an instinct for something *else*. They will not accept an overthrow of the present order unless they have something to stand on that rings true to them."

A wave of admiration came over the professor. That and a certain envy of the man four years his younger. Weishaupt stared into Philo's intelligent eyes for a long moment, marveling at the man's insight. He, himself, had experienced the reality of *other* things more than he dared tell. "Then we need some mysteries of our own. Proceed with your reorganization." He took another drink wondering if Philo might not prove to be a rival. He swallowed. "But you may not fully understand the realities I am dealing with. Our duke is a problem. Voltaire loved him for his early signs of liberalism, but the oaf now sees threats everywhere. And watch King Frederick. He says Christianity is poison and yet he is a Rosicrucian[9]—"

"Do not fear the Rosicrucians; the Church's suspicions of them should make them our allies."

Weishaupt grunted. He leaned forward. "The day is coming—"

"I do not mean to challenge you," said Philo. He glanced about the tavern. "As you say, men must be re-educated. But take heart. Time is our friend if we have the patience to walk slowly. Our purposes are shared in France. After we insinuate the German lodges we can eventually claim Scotland and America, especially if the Freemasons win their revolution. All will be well."

That was better. Weishaupt nodded. "Dr. Franklin intrigues me. He is both a rational thinker and a philosopher...though perhaps not quite the mystic you are. He is a master at charm. If anyone can 'hide the hand and hurl the javelin' it is he."

"I met Franklin when he initiated dear Voltaire into the Lodge of Nine Sisters in Paris. I should add that he and his American friends love that place."[10] Philo took a drink. "But poor Voltaire. Just when King Louis finally permits him to return to Paris he has a seizure! Then he dies begging for a priest. A priest! After cursing Christianity for decades—"[11]

"He was delirious," said Weishaupt. "Forgive him." The pair sat quietly for a very long time before Weishaupt reached into a leather satchel and produced a document. "I have what you requested. It is NOT to be shared outside the Council." Weishaupt carefully handed Philo a paper written in cipher. "Do you have your decoder?

Philo quickly dug into a secret pocket in the lining of his coat. "The long-awaited list?"

Weishaupt smiled. "You look excited."

Philo hurried to decipher the contents. Weishaupt had long promised a succinct list of the Order's five primary goals.[12] The first, of course, was to destroy Christianity. Religious devotion and morality were simply in the way. The second one was to overthrow kingdoms in favor of a world commonwealth ruled by enlightened men. Philo smiled. "And every prince imagines he is enlightened."

The third was to replace any latent sense of patriotism with devotion to a world without borders. Philo then laughed at the fourth. "You want to abolish marriage and create one universal family? Ha! I think you just want to bed whomever you want and you make it a point of revolution!" His eyes dropped to the final principle and he read it in a whisper. "Rights of property must be eliminated and all inheritance ended." Philo wiped his brow with a kerchief. "I dare say—"

"As you can see, we must reveal these VERY slowly and only according to the Order's degrees you are about to write," said Weishaupt. "Ah, but can you not see it? I wish my mother could be here. This was the world she dreamt of for us all." He laid a hand on Philo's forearm. "Can you not feel the *hope* in these things?"

"I am speechless," said Philo. "And I am happy to see you chose *five* points."

Weishaupt chuckled. "I thought you might notice."

"Five leads us to the wisdom of Isis; Five relates us to Virgo," said Philo. "Five elements of alchemy[13] contain the mystery of unity." He laughed. "The Americans even put a five-pointed star on their flag—their tribute to Sirius, the brightest star in the sky."[14]

CHAPTER SEVEN NOTES

1 **Alessandro Cagliostro** (1743–1795) was an Italian psychic and theosophist who charmed the courts of Europe with his magic arts and philosophical
commitment to utopian ideals. Though a Grand Master of the Rosicrucians for
a time, his primary effort remained within 'Egyptian Freemasonry' where he
worked to restore the Craft to its deepest occult foundations. His intersection
with the Illuminati was brief, though he shared a common aim for the perfection of mankind through initiation into the ancient mysteries. The accuracy of
his many prophesies unnerved his critics and attracted many to his views.

2 **Lanz Xaver Carl Wolfgang Zwack von Holzhausen**, *Illuminatus Cato*
(1756 – 1843) was a student of Weishaupt's and later a doctor of law employed by the city of Munich. He was one of Weishaupt's closest advisors, a
Freemason, and active in the politics of German states.

3 The Areopagites were members of Weishaupt's ruling council, named after
ancient Athens' elite intellectuals who gathered on a rocky outcropping known
as the Areopagus. In the biblical book of *Acts,* St. Paul famously debated them
over the identity of God whom they considered 'unknown' and thus a distant,
supervising force rather than the relatable person of Jesus Christ.

4 Acacia has been a symbolic plant for millennia. The Bible records it as the
type of wood (Shittim) from which the Hebrew's Ark of the Covenant was
built. Freemasons say that its evergreen sprigs represent the immortality of the
soul and so use it in masonic funerals. Occultists consider it to be a plant with
energy aligned with the sun god and use it in potions related to psychic power
and protection.

5 **Charles Bonnet** (1720-1793) was a Swiss philosopher whose pantheistic
views (God AS nature) inspired Weishaupt to consider spiritual perfection as
inevitable, and thus the destiny of the Order was secured.

6 Deism rose to prominence among Enlightenment thinkers in the 17th and 18th centuries. In essence, it was a philosophical religion that accepted a benevolent Creator but denied his personal involvement in the universe beyond design and general supervision. As such, it was something of a return to the platonic Greek and later gnostic notion of a 'demiurge' which was an impersonal designer that may or may not be the actual Supreme Being--itself left impersonal an undefined. Therefore, Deism was a step away from the personal God-Son-Spirit trinity of Christianity.

Deism was popular among the British and American elites, and in parallel with masonic religious philosophy which identifies the ultimate deity as the 'Great Architect.' Among leading Americans who were Deists were Franklin, Madison, Jefferson and Washington.

Washington carefully masked his private religious beliefs but used the terminology of Deism whenever recognizing religious form. This contributed to suspicions about Washington's Christianity, especially since he never participated in Holy Communion or used the name of Jesus Christ even in private correspondence.

Accepting some sort of spiritual forces to be at work, Deism did not preclude astrology as a guide. Astrology is the belief that the location of the planets and stars have a direct energetic and/or spiritual connection to the earth, thus affecting the affairs of men. Freemasonry invoked a great deal of astrological symbolism in their design of the American capitol. Washington D.C. has more astrological symbolism than any city on earth. In keeping with masonic tradition, George Washington consulted a horoscope to determine the most fortuitous date for setting the cornerstone of the Capitol building.

7 **Baron Adolf Franz Friedrich Ludwig Knigge**, *Illuminatus Philo* (1752-1796) served in the courts of central German states and Frankfurt-am-Main in a variety of capacities. He was greatly admired as a novelist and literary critic. He was particularly fascinated with secret societies, alchemy, and other occult attractions. At one point, he contrived a myth to support the Illuminati, that being its founding by Noah.

8 The notion of 'Unknown Superiors' was an assumption that spiritual entities guide the affairs of men. This claim formed the basis of the masonic Knights of Templar Strict Observance which dominated much of Freemasonry—especially in Germany—from approximately 1751 to 1782. Some believed the notion was invented to enhance an ambience of mystery. Others insist(ed) these entities were/are very real. Examples of mysterious, directing presences like Kolmer abound, including in the writing of later mystics like Allister Crowley, Madame Blavatsky and Manly Hall. Napoleon Hill boasted that he and other influential American political and industrial leaders in early 20th century America were instructed by unseen spiritual presences.

9 The time of their founding uncertain, the Rosicrucians were (are) mystics with Christian sympathies but not associated with the institutions of Christianity. They take their name from the 'Rosy Cross', itself an image of debatable meaning though generally understood as a symbol of spiritual transformation. They were not a secret society, but the complexities of their ancient teachings made them sufficiently inaccessible by the uninitiated as to have the same effect.
Their primary interest was (is) in the advancement of humankind through spiritual enlightenment, itself based in Hermeticism, astrology, alchemy, and the ethical teachings of Jesus. They became enemies of the Illuminati because of their commitment to personal inner transformation rather than collective revolution, though later members adopted a more activist application of their ideals. Their membership in the 18th century included an impressive collection of dignitaries.

10 The Lodge of Nine Sisters was famous for its occultic practices and a membership that included some of Europe's most liberal thinkers such as Bonneville and Mirabeau. The famous American naval captain, John Paul Jones was a guest, as was General Lafayette. Thomas Jefferson, though not a Mason, is known to have frequented this same lodge as well, perhaps only for its political influence. Franklin was its Grand Master for a time. It was considered the bridge between European secret societies and America, especially via Franklin.

11 At 84 Voltaire was permitted by the king of France to enter Paris in spite of the philosopher's lifelong quest to replace Christianity with a philosophy of reason. Excited, Voltaire celebrated the king's hospitality, only to be stricken with several hemorrhages. He quickly suffered both physical and emotional anguish, eventually begging to see a priest and offer his repentance. His philosophical associates interfered, leaving him in an alternating state of either blaming God for not rescuing him or blaming his compatriots for abandoning him to a hopeless end. He died on 30 May, 1778. His heart was saved in a silver case.

On 28 November of that same year, Franklin eulogized Voltaire in a mixed rite of pagan and Christian liturgies, proclaiming him to be a god.

12 The five goals of the Illuminati are well-documented. They should be familiar to most readers since they appear more or less obviously in various movements given birth by Adam Weishaupt, especially in Marx's *Communist Manifesto*, but also in public discourse in our modern times.

13 Alchemy was considered a pseudo-scientific system seeking the material and spiritual essence of perfection in both matter and spirit. Its practitioners believed in a common source of all that is. Reducing anything to the common source then supposedly allows for something else to be rebuilt. Gold was considered the perfection of matter and also symbolized the perfection of spirit. Whereas physical gold could be created by distilling all material imperfection, likewise spiritual perfection (divinity) could be achieved by distilling spiritual imperfections.
Alchemy also proposed that reducing all religions to their common essence might allow for a reconstruction of common religion for all mankind. This and other assumptions collided with Christianity, forcing many European alchemists to hide their work in cipher or keep their studies far from public view.

14 The five-pointed star historically represented Sirius—the star worshiped by the ancient Egyptians for portending the beneficial flooding of the Nile. Marking the new year, they honored it with a hieroglyph called the *seba* which was a five-pointed star enclosing a circled dot.

Representing invisible energies and high spirituality, Sirius figures prominently in masonic traditions, including its astrological significance in important dates such as the signing of the American Declaration of Independence. As with the other important charts for Jupiter and Virgo, Sirius' position figured in the dedication of the Washington Monument, etc.

"We must establish a universal empire over the whole world without destroying civil ties. Under this new empire, all other governments must be able to exercise every power, excepting that of hindering the Order from attaining its ends."

ADAM WEISHAUPT

CHAPTER EIGHT

"AH, MORE BOOKS. YOU MUST BE HAPPY," SAID Abbot Benedict with a smile. From the first day that Alexander Horn—now Brother Maurus—had arrived at the monastery school, the abbot knew that he loved books. The young monk once laughed that he enjoyed the smell of old paper as much as a fresh rose! Therefore, no one was surprised when Alexander was appointed to be the abbot's book agent.

"Van Loon delivered some good inventory." Alexander set a load of books on a table in the monastery's musty library. "Including a new edition of Nickolai's, *Sebaldus Nothanker.*"[1]

The abbot returned his face to the egg he was spinning atop his desk.

"Father Abbot?"

"In a moment, my son." Benedict gave it another twist. As it wobbled a meandering course, the abbot murmured something. He smiled and then looked at Alexander. "I had a meeting with a most interesting philosopher from Bohemia."

Alexander pulled up a stool.

Benedict gave the egg another twist. "He said that life is intended to spin like an egg, not a child's top. Eggs are wobbly ovals; tops are orderly circles. He argued that God permits a bit of chaos—imperfection, maybe even evil—to make room for change. I think he may be correct." Benedict caught it from falling. "Nevertheless, chaos—like evil—does not rule. Do you understand?"

The young monk nodded, respectfully.

The abbot returned his egg to the basket, grinning.

"Forgive this old man the detours of his thought
And know that wisdom is all that is sought."

Alexander waited.

The abbot tapped a finger on his chin. "Brother Maurus, do you happen to know how to discover wisdom for any situation?"

"One measures the counsel of many?"

Benedict wrinkled his nose. "Of course not. One asks the simple question, 'What does love look like in this?'" He leaned forward. "Do you understand?"

"I would have to think about that."

The abbot threw up his arms. "You never just believe me!" He then turned his attention to the bundle of books. "Well *think* about this: Our business is thriving. Regensburg is perfect for us, what with all the foreigners." He reached for *Nothanker,* turning its pages. He then bounced the book in his palm. "We have already re-sold this blasphemy to a Dr. Karl von Eckartshausen, the new censor of the Munich library.[2] He shall be delighted, though I can't imagine why."

"Some complain that we are happy to turn profits on blasphemies," said Alexander.

Benedict waved the comment away. "In the right hands, like Karl's, these can be instructive in spite of their outrage." He leaned close to the young monk. "They prove something's afoot. And that is good, because

What is plain to the eye
Can be made to die."

Alexander spied the abbot's sleeve. A corner of paper peeked from under the man's hem.

Benedict quickly pushed the paper from view and rummaged through a drawer where retrieved an American $40 bill. He handed the paper money to

Alexander who turned it over in his hand. "An English major made a joke of this at the market. Look there, the all-seeing eye of Horus. The American rebels have a sun god on their currency!"

He then handed Alexander an American $50 bill. "And look at this one: an unfinished pyramid. Straight out of Freemasonry magic. These rebels invoke pagan archetypes against our Christian King George—"

"One could argue that they are just pictures, Father Abbot."

Benedict scowled. "Maurus, images have power! These so-called United Colonies invoke a nation *under the sun god*—"

"Or simply the eye of Providence, the Freemasons' 'Great Architect' of the universe."

Benedict drew a deep breath through his nostrils and exhaled. "'There is only one name given under Heaven'…and it is most certainly not 'The Great Architect.'" He picked up a chunk of coal with his tongs. "In time you shall see why I worry." He dropped the coal into the small firebox. "But enough of that. You are troubled about something."

Alexander glanced at the abbot's sleeve again. What was the man hiding in there? "Small things, Father Abbot." But were they?

Benedict waited.

A twinge tightened Alexander's chest. *Small things?* They were not such small things. Benedict smiled kindly.

> "Great or small
>
> I care for them all."

Alexander bit his lip. "Tell me what you are hiding in your sleeve."

Surprised, the blushing abbot fell silent.

"Do you not trust me?"

"Of course I trust you my dear *fratello*." He laid a hand on Alexander's shoulder. "But that does not mean you are entitled to know all that I know." Benedict leaned very close. "Perhaps we are both hiding something."

A week later, Alexander Horn stared through the darkening evening across the sorrowful drab of the monastery's garden. The turf lay in broken clumps, abandoned since the harvest. An early frost had browned the edges of the weeds drooping in the cracks of the stone walls. He wrapped a cloak around himself, then read the letter he'd just received once again. His father had died from an infected wound received in a race track brawl. He had been buried near Grunnie. His frail mother was moving to Aberdeen to live with an uncle.

"Dead. Father is dead." He could barely imagine it. He looked back behind him at the way he had come, surprised to feel tears welling up. Shouldn't he be shouting for joy? He stared at the leaf-littered path ahead and took a step.

Alexander made his way through the narrow gate in the garden wall and to the cemetery where he threw himself atop the cold earth. He crumpled the letter in his fist. He sat there for an hour as dusk fell, considering all the ways he had disappointed the man. Heavy-hearted, he finally dragged his numb body to its feet. He drew a deep, quaking breath and blew it slowly into the damp air. A lone crow cawed from a bare limb. Alexander answered. "Aye. But even he deserved something better than death by fever, alone in the night."

He stared at the letter balled in his palm. It was then he realized a certain relief alongside his grief, and for that he felt sudden shame. He hung his head and leaned against a tree, closing his eyes until a cold wave of fear filled him. Confused, Alexander quickly paced in a circle. He realized that as dangerous as the man had been, Horn the Elder had also been a shield against the world beyond Westhall. Now his shield was gone.

But did that matter? Had there *ever* been anything to fear but him? He stopped and stared at the bare limb of a gnarled tree. "Enough of this," he muttered. "Enough." Alexander turned and walked quickly toward the north entrance to the Romanesque abbey church known as the *Schottenportal.*

Arriving at the 12th century entrance he collected himself to let the magnificence of the wide, carved arch assure him. He breathed deeply to let the presence of the place secure him. Torches to either side cast shadows across the ancient relief. Above the apex was a frieze of Christ and his disciples. He let his eyes follow the line of the arcade to the left. There, Mother Mary was carved as the new Eve. He liked that. Comforted, his eyes moved to find humans caressing one another in love. "Beautiful," he murmured.

Then, perhaps because of his melancholy or perhaps by some other force, his eyes opened to see something they had never before noticed. To his right were vicious beasts and a dragon swallowing a lion. *What?* He scanned other carvings up and down, left and right. In one place was a woman with snakes at her breast; over there, several monks desperately clutching books. He ran his hands over the figures of the brothers. "This is me?" His mouth dried. He stepped back and spotted a hostile crocodile swallowing a hydrus. "Yet the hydrus destroys the monster from the inside," he whispered. He then lifted his eyes, scarcely daring to look beyond it. They fell upon the Siren of Temptation.

At the sight of her, the monk winced. Temptation had been tearing at his heart for months, and her name was 'Julianna.'

Heart pumping, Alexander stepped back. "The war," he said aloud. "The war for mankind. The war for me." He chilled. He had no shield. "Lord, your armies need better men. Better men than me."

Two days later, Alexander hurried to Regensburg's Steinerne Bridge under his heavy cloak. Spotting the man he was to meet, he lowered his hood. An early snow was falling from a pewter sky, each flake melting in the surging Danube. "Good to see you, friend."

Van Loon clasped his hand and the pair walked briskly in the late afternoon air toward a riverside tavern crowded with noisy gentlemen. Van Loon spotted a table by a bright hearth. Shaking snow from his coat, he said, "Now, let me look at you." He sat. "You look troubled as usual."

Alexander threw his cloak to one side and changed course, asking about the American rebellion.

"The British have moved south," answered Van Loon. "And the fighting there is fierce. But with the French now supporting the cause from land and sea, I suspect victory may be within sight."

Alexander observed that the man announced such a bold claim without enthusiasm. "And your family?"

"My father and mother are returned to England. My brother remains in Philadelphia with his daughter—the little girl whom you saved from the carriage."

"England? But—"

Van Loon called for a bottle of gin. He studied the monk. "We shall speak of it later. Now, you must tell me what ails you."

Alexander sighed. "My father is dead. And that is all we need to speak of it."

Albert considered him, then raised his glass. "To Mr. Alexander Horn the Elder of Oyne, may he rest in peace."

The two sat quietly for a long while. Alexander finished a gin and then another. Van Loon wisely ordered food.

"And something is troubling you, as well," said Alexander.

"Me? I am just weary. I suspect my duties in Europe may end soon and so perhaps I am a bit melancholy."

That news was disappointing. "You will return to Philadelphia? Maybe find a wife?"

Van Loon shifted. "I am not certain."

Alexander leaned forward. "There is something you are not telling me."

"I have told you all I can."

More secrets. Alexander bit his lip. *Van Loon and the abbot are both hiding something from me.*

"When the time is right, I shall tell you everything my friend." Albert drained his glass and filled another.

"I am feeling a bit cross about your silence."

"I understand," answered the American. "Friends ought not keep secrets. But others are involved, and there is an oath I have taken. I hope you understand."

Disappointed, Alexander stared into his gin for a quiet moment. Finally, he raised his glass. "To Albert van Loon, a reliable man." Swallowing, he then added, "Seeing you, I am reminded that I need to be a *much* better man."

Van Loon adjusted the fashionable slightly upright collar of his new French suit—a slim, three-piece version of the popular *habit à la française*. "And how do you propose this?"

Alexander knew that a moment was suddenly upon him, a moment he had spent a great deal of time considering. In fact, to think of a crossroads would be too simple. This was more like choosing between ascension and stasis. He worked to compose his thoughts.

The serving maid created a helpful pause. She delivered plates of schnitzel, cheese, bread, and pickled fish. His mind raced to consider whether he should do this. Would such a request create discomfort? He had no idea if it were even possible. He stared at his flatware and food, then peered through the tobacco smoke at the gentlemen all around.

"Brother Maurus?"

Alexander licked his lips. What harm in asking? "I should like to join the Freemasons."

Albert calmly lowered his glass. "Ah." He fell quiet for a long moment. "The Craft needs good men and your abbot says you are guinea-gold."

"But do they accept monks?"

The American paused. "I have seen priests but never a monk. I do not know." He stabbed lightly at his fish. "Why? Why do you want to do this?"

"I want to be a better man."

"Why?"

Alexander grumbled. Why all the 'why's?' "Because...because...I don't really know. I see my shortcomings and think I should do better. Besides, I am very curious about things."

Van Loon nodded, thoughtfully. "Perhaps I should not ask 'why,' but rather *what* it is you hope to get from this."

Alexander was not certain. "I suppose knowledge, wisdom? Perhaps of myself as well as the world."

Van Loon smiled. "Ah, now that is a good answer." He shoved some fish into his mouth and chewed. "I think you are seeking something more. Your betterment is for some other purpose." The American stopped chewing. "I suspect you feel incomplete."

Was that it? Alexander had no answer.

"Well, in any event, would Benedict approve?"

Alexander shrugged. "Would you?"

Van Loon smiled. "Of course. I could sponsor you for initiation into Lodge Theodore in Munich."

"Why that one?"

Van Loon shrugged. "Geography. But are you sure you understand the purpose of the Craft?"

"That being?"

"The improvement of mankind according to the principles of a wise universe." Van Loon tore some bread. "We build men's characters under the eye of a Great Architect—call him whom you will. You might say we strive to complete men. The Great Architect has embedded the universe with principles of natural reason, generally hidden in the ancient mysteries which we reveal through our liturgies and our symbols."

Alexander thought as much. His heart stirred within him.

"There are three primary degrees. First you would be initiated as an Entered Apprentice, then advance to Fellow-Craft, and finally Master Mason." Van Loon continued eating. "I suspect you could be a Master in no time, especially with an aggressive advocate. After that, every mason can choose higher degrees according to the various rites of various lodges."

A pitcher of warm ale was delivered along with two pewter tankards. Listening, Alexander poured.

"The Munich Lodge belongs to those following the system of degrees known as the Knights of Templar Strict Observance."[3] Van Loon thought for a moment. "Its teachings are supposedly guided by the mystical knowledge of some Unknown Superiors."

"Like spirit messengers?"

Van Loon shrugged. "The kind of stuff the Rosicrucians like to talk about."

"And your Rite?"

"American patriots mostly join the Ancient and Accepted Rite of Scottish Freemasonry. It is considered more liberal. By that I mean it is more heavily influenced by the ancient mysteries than by Christianity."

Alexander leaned forward. "Like the Egyptians—"

"Yes," said Albert. "And the Greeks and the Vedics of India." He took a drink. "Did you know that Pharaoh Akhenaton[4] proposed the building of a world government of sorts." Taking a breath, Van Loon searched Alexander's face for the effect of his words. "For centuries, secret societies kept the ancient mysteries safe. Then Francis Bacon started his Society of Unknown Philosophers[5] to advance them into our times. A descendant of his supposedly delivered his secret plan for America to Jamestown.[6] Anyway, Freemasonry is where the ancient movement is most at work today."

Alexander filled his cup. "And the other Rite—"

"Yes. Most loyalists in America follow the York Rite. The York is more in-clined to greater sympathy with Christianity."

"And your preference?"

Van Loon nodded. "I confess a certain discomfort with the occult and mag-ic. The first three degrees are the same in all the lodges, so I may just remain as a Master Mason and not fret about following any particular rite upward." He balanced some schnitzel on his two-pronged fork. "I think Washington may be York, though he certainly is no Christian. He just likes to keep appearances. On the other hand, Dr. Franklin makes room for every sort of notion he stumbles upon." He laughed. "He is the only revolutionary who is adored by all sides."

Alexander reached into his pocket and produced the American $40 bill. "Abbot Benedict is concerned about your drift into paganism. You have the all-seeing eye and Egyptian images on your currency. I suspect this is all masonic—"

"Wait until you see the national seal." Van Loon laughed, uneasily. "But yes. The Masons are embedded in all levels of the rebellion. Why not? Secrecy makes room for new ideas; revolution thrives in dark places." He took another bite of schnitzel. "Now, forget America. What are we to do with you?"

The monk relaxed.

"I can introduce you to the Munich lodge and offer my recommendation. But I fear your tonsure and habit will isolate you. The priests who have joined are so liberal that few think of them as men of the Church. They attend dressed like the rest of us. But a monk? Remember, this lodge is in the Strict Observance and very occultic. Would that frighten you?"

"No. I find it all intriguing." Alexander returned his eyes to the mulling crowd of fine gentlemen now filling Regensburg's tavern house. Few were as dashing as Albert van Loon, but all were dressed smartly in the German way—understated elegance with an air of permanence. He smiled. *Why not just dress like them? I could cover my head with a wig.*

"What about Abbot Benedict?"

"Em, no need to worry him about this. But if he finds out he might just be pleased. I could sell a great number of books in a lodge."

Van Loon roared. "Indeed!" He leaned forward. "You look like you have an idea."

CHAPTER EIGHT NOTES

1 *Sebaldus Nothanker* was a popular novel written by Friedrich Nicholai in 1775-1777. A complex love story, its appeal was primarily in its exposure of the narrow-mindedness and intolerance of orthodox clergymen.

2 **Dr. Karl von Eckartshausen**, *Illuminatus Attilius Regulus* (1752 – 1803) was a highly esteemed philosopher, numerologist, and Christian mystic who published nearly 70 books on a wide variety of topics including literature, science, fine arts and history. After years researching esoteric wisdom, he eventually concluded that Christ was the ultimate location of wisdom and insisted that spiritual forces guided the affairs of humankind. This quote is from his influential book, *Cloud Upon the Sanctuary.*

3 The Knights of Templar Strict Observance was the dominant Lodge of Freemasonry in Germany from approximately 1750 – 1782. The Rite claimed a founding connection to the Knights Templar and demanded loyalty to 'Unknown Superiors' who supposedly ruled from behind the veil. Some thought these superiors to be spiritual guides, other imagined them as simply men in hiding.

4 **Pharaoh Akhenaton** (about 1388 BC – 1353BC, also known as Amenhotep IV) is considered to be the first ruler to dream of a Brotherhood of Mankind. His reign emphasized the benevolent unity of all things as expressed by his new religion known as 'Atenism.' He is considered the founder of the notion of a one world government.

5 Francis Bacon's Society of Unknown Philosophers was a secret organization of men of wealth and vision established in the 17th century. Their goal was to colonize a new world (America) for the purpose of establishing a utopian society from which the rest of the world would be changed. The hope was an eventual world commonwealth guided by wise philosophers. Bacon's work,

The New Atlantis, expresses the essence of the plan which includes a sympathy for Christian ethics if not biblical orthodoxy.

6 According to British historian, Nicholas Hagger (see bibliography), a descendant of Francis Bacon named Henry Blount brought Bacon's secret plan for the future of America to Jamestown and hid it beneath Bruton Church. Thomas Jefferson was the last person to read it and had it reburied in a yet-to-be-discovered vault under the same church. Bruton church no longer stands in its original location. The plan contributed to the masonic vision of the new America.

"Masonry, like all religions, all the Mysteries, Hermeticism and alchemy, conceals its secrets from all except the Elect, and uses false explanations of its symbols to mislead those who deserve to be misled. Truth is not for those who are unworthy to receive it."

MASONIC GRAND MASTER, GENERAL ALBERT PIKE [1]

CHAPTER NINE

APRIL, 1781
MUNICH, BAVARIA

"THIS IS A GOOD NIGHT," SAID ADAM WEISHAUPT. Dressed in a dark blue suit and waist banded by his masonic apron, he adjusted his white gloves. Outside, a soft Spring rain dampened the sounds of arriving coaches.

"Indeed, General Spartacus," answered Philo von Knigge, still the Order's second-in-command. The young aristocrat looked about the Munich masonic hall with an approving air. The Illuminati now controlled this lodge, entirely. His eyes fell to a lanky young man of middling height who was about to be initiated as a Master Mason. "That is Mr. Bergström. He is a candidate for us. Cato Zwack has been studying him ever since he entered the lodge as an apprentice. I suggest we work hard to get him into the Order."

Weishaupt watched carefully as the young man greeted the brethren. He thought the youth to be confident and personable. He liked the dash of his distinctive shoes. The professor smiled. This was just the sort of earnest fellow that could help lead the world to good places.

99

The professor leaned forward and chuckled as Bergström offered the handshake of a Fellow Craft—the second degree of Freemasonry. Bergström fumbled to press the top of his thumb across the second knuckle of his greeter. Weishaupt then scanned the candlelit hall filled with murmuring men in fine attire. Most had dual membership in the Craft and his Order, the Order now being their highest loyalty.

He took some claret from a passing waiter. Staring into the wine, he grumbled. Only his inner council knew that *he* was Spartacus Weishaupt. In fact, initiates were now told that the secret commander of the Order was to be referred to as, 'Basilius.' This would add a layer of disguise as an alias of his alias. But the whole notion of hiding himself was beginning to gnaw at him. After all, how could he ever be properly respected without being known?

Weishaupt let his attention move to the physical space of the temple, marveling at the multi-levels of meaning the aesthetics offered. On one wall was a painting of a pyramid of course, and the all-seeing eye. Over here was the compass and square; there, several triangles, and a skull-and-crossbones. The high ceiling was painted black and displayed the silver stars of the zodiac.

The professor sipped from his crystal glass and then fixed his gaze on the Minerval Owl his Illuminists had delivered to a corner table. Behind it was a mural depicting their circle and centered dot. Clearing his throat, he finally answered Philo. "I am told that Mr. Bergström is everything we are looking for. Not a clergyman, not a dunce. Young. A bookseller and man of letters. Perfect. And his pedigree is odd enough to make him interesting."

Ever cautious, Philo answered, "Ja. A Prussian who can barely speak German, raised by a Scottish mother."

"I have studied his features. Broad shoulders, high forehead, symmetrical face, masculine. He has intelligent eyes. His Scottish connection might prove fortuitous—"

"If his business ever eases in Regensburg."

Weishaupt nodded. "As you know, I prefer to have candidates seek us, but I think Cato should plant some seeds."

"Cato says the man is hungry for perfection. Perhaps too zealous?"

Weishaupt kept his eyes on the bookseller. "I can see that Bergström is sociable and you say he is enterprising. I am intrigued. You and Cato…your suspicions get the better of you sometimes." He sipped some claret. His recruitment scheme had worked nearly flawlessly for the past five years. His only serious failures had been from his first initiates—Sutor and Bauhof—whose boundless debauchery had threatened the public perception of them all. Otherwise, his membership was expanding and in exactly the circles of influence he coveted.

Weishaupt's insinuation of recruits had evolved to follow a careful pattern based on clear preferences. He sought liberal minded young men—particularly Protestants as they could more easily be persuaded from religion, and especially publishers and educators as these changed hearts and minds. Further, he insisted that his recruiters pay careful attention to physical attributes which, he believed, revealed natural qualities.

Mr. Bergström appeared to qualify on all counts.

Changing subjects, Weishaupt summoned Cato to join Philo at his table. "So, the Rosicrucians are beginning to move against us?"

Cato scowled. The Munich attorney gulped his glass of wine. "All on account of that religionist Ignaz Franck![2] One sermon! Now we are accused of betraying Freemasonry to prepare the way for the anti-Christ. And, of course he would have to be the tutor to the Duke's daughter."

Weishaupt leaned close to his officers. "And is he wrong?"

Cato stared for a long moment, then burst into laughter.

Weishaupt continued. "But the Rosicrucians may prove to be rivals of some force. My sources say they are recruiting Prince Frederick. As heir to the Prussian throne, he could be formidable."

Philo grumbled. "I warned you. And why do you think they oppose us?"

Weishaupt darkened. "I know, I know. Our inclination is toward reason and not the magic they adore. But there is more. No one sees them as a threat because their vision stops at personal transformation…like the masons. They want to liberate men; we want to liberate mankind. Thus, they are benign to the rulers."

The professor noticed how Philo glanced sideways at Cato. Both men nodded. Philo spoke. "But I say again, we must appeal to the same thing the Rosicrucians dangle: the notion of spiritual forces. Our embrace of that would attract those seeking personal awakening." He took a restraining breath. "I know you understand this. You have had conversations with Cagliostro."

Weishaupt narrowed his eyes. "Who has not? He hops about the courts of Europe like a flea in a kennel."

"And?"

The professor hesitated.

"I know he is a master among the Rosicrucians," said Philo. "And he is forming an Egyptian Rite in Masonry so that the Craft does not lose touch with its so-called spiritual guides."

"Guides?" Weishaupt feigned ridicule. "Now we have more guides?"

The baron did not flinch. "Guides like Kolmer and the other inexplicable forces we have all witnessed." He set his wine down, hard. "You and Cato pretend superiority to the spirits, but yet you both know that history is moved by invisible hands."

Weishaupt scowled. "Ideas are forces, you know." Why did he have such trouble admitting what he really believed?

Philo pressed. "Five days before news reached any of us, Cagliostro told the world that Empress Maria Theresa had died. Then he prophesied that Marie Antoinette would give birth to a healthy son. Both true."

Weishaupt nodded. "Luck." He lifted his lip. "And do you know what he told me?"

Philo and Cato leaned forward.

Weishaupt snickered. "The man closed his eyes, went stiff, and then babbled a wild vision of King Louis standing before a guillotine. The king's head was then held up by his ear to a cheering crowd." Laughing, the professor poured himself some wine. "Make what you want of Cagliostro." He took a sip. "He will surely prove to be a charlatan."

Philo shook his head. "Nevertheless, he represents an important impulse."

Weishaupt did not want to hear any more about it. The general cleared his throat. "We must not lose sight of our purpose. We can compromise where we can, but we must strip the Craft of these so-called 'Invisible Superiors' because *we need to fill that space ourselves.* All of this spiritual nonsense keeps men from the good world we want for them. Surely you can see this."

Philo would not budge. "Men demand to worship something. They need a vision that makes room for more than mathematics."

Weishaupt took a drink, thinking for a long moment. He conceded. "As I said, we can compromise to a point." He turned to Cato. "And your advice?"

Cato thought for a moment, gazing quietly down his strong nose. Ready, he said, "Philo and I disagree. All of this talk of invisible forces is rubbish. Mystics are fools. But it seems their foolishness is too great an obstacle at this time. So give them something to worship. Maybe themselves."

Weishaupt poured himself more claret. Was Cato right? Were mystics fools? Or was there something greater? Why could not the world just be happy without all this!

Alone, Alexander Horn entered Lodge Theodore on this, the grand occasion of being initiated as a Master Mason. [1] Adjusting his hat, he wished Albert van Loon had not been recalled to America. He had a great number of gnawing questions he would have liked to pose to his friend.

He swallowed. This feat had not been easy. He remembered his first initiation, and his second. But to now advance to the degree of Master meant he had survived a great deal of scrutiny. This lodge had a unique reputation of not-so-restrained hostility toward clerics, no doubt driven by an upstart secret society rumored to be operating at its margins. To counter any such prejudice, months earlier Albert sought an ally for him in Brother Dr. Karl von Eckartshausen. Karl was a customer of Benedict, the censor of the library at Munich, friend of Van Loon and an influential member of Lodge Theodore.

At first, Eckartshausen had been reluctant to help. "They shall never accept you as 'Brother Maurus,'" he said. "No. This is not possible."

But Alexander had persisted, suggesting a bold plan. He very much wanted to find the path to improvement, if not perfection. In a few weeks, the man relented and thus, 'Mr. Bergström, bookseller,' was invented.

This 'Mr. Bergström' required the monk to cover his tonsured head with a wig and exchange his habit for a stylish olive suit consisting of a fitted vest, breeches, silk stockings and low-heeled shoes uniquely accented by four-pronged buckles. A fashionable French coat, white cravat, and a three-cocked beaver hat finished the impressive look.

And so, 'Mr. Bergström' was now standing for a third time within the temple of Lodge Theodore for his final initiation. He searched for Karl von Eckartshausen whom he finally spotted.

"Hello, Mr. Bergström," said Karl. "This is the night!" The kindly man was an almost-thirty-year-old with narrow shoulders and an aquiline nose. He had a gentle bearing and was both loved and respected by all who knew him.

Before Alexander could answer, the Senior Warden of the lodge summoned the temple hall to order. An immediate hush fell over the room and the Worshipful Master moved toward the Oriental Chair positioned along the east wall. The assembly was led in a prayer directed to some vague Source of divine light.

Karl placed a gentle hand around Alexander's elbow and led him away as the formalities of the hall continued. Having been through the first two degrees, Alexander had some sense of what was coming. Each degree had introduced him to deepening meanings of symbols and the influences that might help build him into a better man. Among them was the dot in the center of a circle. In his first initiation he recited that the point was the individual brother, and the circle was the boundary of his proper behavior. In his second, he recited verses revealing the dot as a connection to the life-giving phallus of the Ancient Mysteries. On this night, he would repeat that its deepest meaning was as the sun god, Osiris, encircled by the universe.

He arrived at the door of an ante-room when Karl asked bluntly, "What troubles you?"

Alexander hesitated. In his first initiation he had been told that the important masonic symbols of the square and compass simply represented squaring his duty to the brethren within the circumspect boundaries of good sense. This seemed reasonable enough.

But yesterday he had dug through the Munich library to find an engraving from 1613 of an old Hermetic symbol labeled, 'Azoth.' In it, a square and compass were located within a circle. Above was a dragon. "Osiris, Isis and the dragon," Alexander whispered to Karl. "The compass and square represent false gods. And look over there. We are being supervised by the 'All-seeing Eye of Horus [4]—'"

Karl thought about that. "You do not have to accept the full symbology, just understand it. And think of the eye as the eye of God."

Alexander grimaced. "I fear this all may be built upon a hidden foundation."

Karl nudged him gently into the small room and closed the door. "Now look at me, Brother Maurus. You must decide now. You said you wanted to become a better man, and so I have taken a great risk in this charade—"

"None of this troubles you?"

The man laid his forefinger aside his long nose and breathed, eyes closed. "I have some doubts. As does your friend, Van Loon."

"You have spoken?"

"We correspond from time to time." Karl adjusted his masonic apron now wrapped around his waist. "I would like to think of the lodge as neutral ground that parallels our Christianity. But, if I am honest, this particular lodge does now trouble me. I am told many of the brethren are also members of an order some call the Minervals."

"Van Loon said it was all rumor."

"No. Their members are very secretive, but one told me they want to improve society in very concrete ways. Whereas the Craft builds individual men to help society, these Minervals want to *rebuild* men and revolutionize society—"

"According to what?"

Karl shrugged. "I do not know."

Alexander licked his lips.

"You see, I need an ally in this place to help me sort it out."

Alexander shifted on his feet. "You're asking me to hope for the best but help you watch for the worst?"

"Ja." Karl waited.

Alexander yielded. He removed all his clothing and put on a pair of linen under breeches and a hood for the coming sacred ritual. "I am ready." Karl then blindfolded him and wrapped a rope around his body three times. He knocked thrice upon the door to the murmuring hall.

"What is it you seek?" came a voice.

Alexander took a breath, then recited, "'Brother Bergström has long been in darkness and seeks the light.'"

At the Master's cry of 'more light,' a warden opened the door and took hold of the rope to lead Alexander forward.

The young monk remained in his darkness and stepped lightly on bare feet atop the wooden floor. He could smell candles and the wool of the warden's coat. Stopped abruptly, as the sharp tips of an object were suddenly thrust against his bare chest. They were the points of an open compass.

"Brother Bergström, as a man's heart is contained between the breasts, so are our virtues contained within the points of the compass." The tips were removed.

Alexander exhaled and was then jerked forward to circle the temple clockwise three times. At each geographical point of his symbolic pilgrimage he was struck lightly on the head. At last he was led to the altar where the Worshipful Master commanded him to kneel and rest his hands on a Bible, compass and square.

Alexander obeyed. His belly churned as his fingers felt the objects. *Kneeling before the compass and square?* Troubled, he remained on his knees where he was instructed in the expectations of the Craft. Included was an irrevocable oath of secrecy. He was then to swear to abide all the aforementioned 'without mental reservation,' under penalty of having 'my body severed in two and my bowels removed, so help me God.' The young monk faltered. *Without mental reservation?*

Perspiration ran along the inside of his arms. His knees ached on the hard wood. The silence in the room made him dizzy. Someone cleared their throat. Fear began to crawl through him. Alexander yielded again. He repeated his oath. His mouth felt as if it were filled with wool. He could barely understand his own words.

Finished, he suddenly wanted to fall down and beg God's mercy. The Worshipful Master's voice broke through. "Brother Bergström, what do you most desire?"

Alexander dared not tell the truth. "The Light of Freemasonry," he recited.

"Then let there be light!" The Master tore off Alexander's blindfold.

The monk blinked. On each side stood a line of brothers in their masonic aprons. He was then handed his apron with instructions. Before he could digest any of it, however, hands lifted him from his knees and led him back to the anteroom.

Confused, Alexander listened to the Warden order him to dress. He slowly climbed out of his ceremonial breeches and put on his suit, careful to keep his tonsured head covered by his wig. The Warden threw open the door. In front of the discomforted monk were his brethren, clapping. The Conductor took his arm and led him forward until a voice suddenly boomed. "Stop."

Alexander chilled.

The Worshipful Master hurried forward, shouting. "You are not yet a Master and may never be! Kneel!" The man began to load a pistol.

What is this? Trembling, Alexander kneeled.

The Conductor blindfolded him again as he instructed him to pray for mercy. "And when you are finished, say aloud for us all to hear, 'Amen.'"

Alexander silently begged God's forgiveness for stepping into this.

"Have you finished?"

Alexander choked, "Amen." A sudden hope filled him. *They said they might deny me entry. I can be out of here.*

Nearly all the candles of the hall were quickly extinguished. Behind his blindfold he could see the darkness deepen. Alexander heart raced. Someone slapped a pistol into his hand, no doubt the one just loaded by the Worshipful Master.

"Show us your loyalty!" many shouted. "Shoot yourself, now!"

What? Alexander weighed the pistol. *Would they really load it?*

A score of angry voices accused him of cowardice and faithlessness.

His hand began to shake. Had he been found out? Were they going to execute him by his own hand? *Where is Eckartshausen?*

Someone snatched the flintlock from his hand and placed the barrel against his head.

"Oh God, forgive me." Alexander blurted.

"What was that?"

"Forgive me!"

An unseen hand took a severe hold of his elbow. A rope was again wrapped around him, tightly. Still blindfolded, he heard creaks from above. The tightening ropes squeezed his body and bent him backward. Alexander cried out as he was hoisted above the floor with rhythmic pulls. Having no idea how high he was suspended, he heard the Warden demand that he repeat his oath of secrecy.

Terrified, Alexander did.

He was then dropped to crash atop the wooden floor. The breath left his body and Alexander sucked for air, groaning. A maul struck his head, lightly.

"Lie still!" The same voice then recited the resurrection myth of Hiram Abrif, the builder of Solomon's Temple.

Still blindfolded, Alexander lay helpless. Hands then lifted him atop a blanket in which he was immediately wrapped, tightly. *Oh God, now what?* The corners of his blanket were gathered and he was dragged away to lay in utter silence until a different voice pronounced him dead.

Finally, the Conductor cried, "In whom do you trust?"

Quaking, Alexander replied, "In God?"

"Yes, the Great Architect!" His shroud was opened. A hand grabbed hold of his and he was lifted to his feet. His blindfold was removed. As the brethren applauded, he blinked in the dim light. Now advanced to the degree of Master Mason, he had died to himself and was resurrected to new life.

It was finished. [5]

CHAPTER NINE NOTES

1 **Albert Pike** (1809-1891) was Sovereign Grand Commander of the Ancient and Accepted Scottish Rite of Freemasonry and one of the most influential Freemasons in history. A Confederate general, slave owner, and accused war criminal, his statue still stands in Washington D. C. This quote comes from his opus, *Morals and Dogma*.

2 **Ignatius Franciscus Franck** (1725-1795) was an ex-Jesuit and member of the Rosicrucians (see earlier note) who delivered the first public oration against the Illuminati in 1781.

3 Freemasonry consists of a confusing array of Grand Lodge jurisdictions and various rites. The great majority of lodges share the first three degrees known as Entered Apprentice, Fellow Craft, and Master Mason. These three comprise 'Blue Lodge' Freemasonry which is considered foundational. After that, brothers may follow the path of one or more 'appendant' organizations, each with their own system of degrees. Examples include the Ancient and Accepted Scottish Rite (In modern times this is where the familiar reference to 33-degree masonry is found), the York Rite, Knights Templar, Royal Order of Scotland, Swedish Rite, French Rite, Holy Royal Arch, etc.

4 In ancient Egyptian religion, Horus was the son of the sun god Osiris, and his moon-goddess wife, Isis. Various esoteric teachings later conflated Horus with Jesus, both said to represent a notion of a 'son of god' on earth. The referenced publication claimed that, like other prophets, Jesus was teaching from the truths of Universal Reason as represented by the sun god, and Universal Wisdom as from the moon goddess.
The 'eye of Horus' is considered the All-Seeing Eye of the Illuminati and the Freemasons—and what appears on the American Great Seal and American dollar bill. Some observe that the All-Seeing Eye is actually a synthesis of the

Eye of Horus—which is wise, observant, benevolent—and another Egyptian symbol, the Eye of Ra—which is fierce, combative, powerful.

5 Masonic rites of initiation were/are inspired by the ceremonies of the ancient Mystery religions which emphasized death to the old self and resurrection to new life within the light of the sect. This scene was largely informed by an eighteenth-century initiation into the Esperance Lodge located in London's Soho neighborhood.

"Jesus wished to introduce no new religion, but only to restore natural religion. He wished to unite men in a great universal association...so the secret meaning of his teaching was to lead men to universal liberty and equality. We are the only real Christians."

BARON LUDWIG VON KNIGGE [1]

CHAPTER TEN

THE LODGE NOW ADJOURNED, ADAM WEISHAUPT PICKED HIS way through the hall with Philo von Knigge in tow. "There he is." He paused three men deep from the new Master Mason and watched the young Mr. Bergström engage his well-wishers. Weishaupt leaned into Philo. "He looks a bit shaken, but still the charmer."

When his turn came, he looked up into Alexander's eyes and extended his hand to offer him the lion's paw—the grip of the Master Mason. "Welcome, Brother Bergström." He smiled to himself as Alexander's thumb fumbled to find the space between his second and third knuckle. Feeling pressure on the right spot, he returned pressure in kind. He tilted his head toward Philo. "This is Brother Baron von Knigge. He is all the way from Frankfurt. He tells me you are a young gentleman with an intriguing past."

Alexander forced a smile.

Weishaupt released his grip. "And I understand you are a bookseller?"

"Yes. And you are a professor of the law in Ingolstadt."

The comment surprised Weishaupt. "I am." How did this fellow know that? "You must tell me how you know of me." He studied Alexander carefully. Would the boy maintain his eye contact? Would he hesitate even for an instant? Was he a spy?

"Your reputation lights the halls of gentlemen where ever I travel."

Weishaupt bowed his head, wondering of which reputation Mr. Bergström was speaking. "You humble me, good sir."

Philo offered a faux smile. "And exactly what is the professor's reputation?"

Alexander kept his eyes on Weishaupt. "At the risk of flattery, I am told you are the finest legal mind in Bavaria and beyond. You are said to be a liberal thinker and man of reason."

Weishaupt was pleased but Philo pressed, unable to mask his suspicions. "Who tells you these things?"

Alexander turned his face. "You seem annoyed, Brother von Knigge."

Weishaupt placed a restraining hand on the baron's forearm. "Mister Bergström, we appreciate your encouraging words and bid you a fond *adieu*." With that, he released the young man to others and dragged Philo to one side. "Where is my diplomat? You are too obvious."

"Something about him is wrong."

"Enough. He travels in good company. Why would he *not* know things about me!"

Philo drew a long breath and adjusted his cravat. "As you say, he is a charmer. We need to be sure he does not charm us."

Alexander Horn (Mr. Bergström) continued greeting his brethren with the appearance of enthusiasm. In truth, his face was weary of the false smile he had plastered over it, and the voices within could not be kept mute for much longer. Fortunately, the claret was in full supply and he found some relief in its warm flush.

Somewhere around midnight, Karl von Eckartshausen rescued him. "Come with me, Mister Bergström," said Karl. He led him out of the hall and on to the brick street now slick from an earlier rain.

Alexander breathed deeply of wet air. It felt cleansing.

"You look as if you might sleep for a week."

Alexander nodded.

"Secrets take a toll," whispered Karl. "I noticed you chatting with Weishaupt."

"Yes. What of it?"

Karl thought for a long moment. "I think he may be one of the so-called Minervals taking this lodge over."

Alexander was too tired to care. "My impression is that he is a man desperate for glory."

Karl was surprised. "How on earth—"

"When I told him that his reputation lit the world his chest rose and such a serene look came over him—"

"You told him that?" Karl laughed. "Yes, that little peacock loves to rule. I knew him from my own days in Ingolstadt. And he thinks the ladies swoon for him."

The pair laughed, loudly, until Weishaupt, Philo Knigge and Cato Zwack came through the door.

Weishaupt called out. "Hey ho! What is the joke?"

Quick to adapt, Alexander answered with a sweep of his hand. "Herr Doctor, we were wondering if the maidens of Munich enjoyed talk of phalluses as much as we Freemasons!"

Weishaupt roared but Cato and Philo kept a steady gaze.

"And your conclusion?" asked Weishaupt.

"Brother Eckartshausen, here, suggested that only his phallus is worthy of conversation."

"Then we shall speak no more about any of it!" laughed Weishaupt. He wrapped an arm around Alexander's back. "I understand you have an office in Regensburg."

"Yes." *Who told him that?*

"And do you sell books in Ingolstadt?"

"Ja, of course. And I would be delighted to meet you there." Why did he say that? Alexander's limbs weakened. He had never intended to extend the world of 'Mr. Bergström' beyond the masonic hall. Now he'd have to sell as a monk to some and a businessman to others!

Weishaupt released him. "You have impressed the brethren. But tell me, I meant to ask, why have you joined us?"

Alexander thought Weishaupt's small eyes seemed suddenly serpent-like in the lamp light. "I want to be a better man."

Philo folded his arms. "Than whom?"

"Than the man I presently am, sir."

"And exactly who is that man?" said the baron with a smirk.

What is this? Alexander dared not look to Karl for help. "Why do you ask?"

Philo leaned close, abandoning any pretense of diplomacy. "Because you are a Scot by the name of 'Bergström.' Because your German is terrible. Because something about you is suspicious. Even your postal address is fake."

"How dare you, sir!" Alexander lifted his chin and folded his arms. "As to my postal address, I move from place to place... As to my past, I owe you no explanation—"

"We are now brothers," said Weishaupt. "We keep no secrets."

"No? We have nothing but secrets." Alexander wanted to run. Instead, he watched Weishaupt's face slowly brighten.

"Ha! Well said." The professor touched his walking stick to his hat. "Until Ingolstadt."

JUNE, 1781
INGOLSTADT, BAVARIA

Adam Weishaupt paced through his personal library. Seated nearby was his confidant, Cato. Lonely since his wife's death, Weishaupt typically summoned companionship from various sources according to need. On matters of organizational discipline, enforcement or personal frustration he met with Cato. On matters of ritual, symbolism, recruitment and vision, he met with Philo. When desiring carnal pleasures, he commanded the presence of Ingolstadt's finest erring sisters by way of his new private secretary—a former priest named Johann Jakob Lanz, now known as *Socrates* within the Order.

On this warm day, Weishaupt was irritable and melancholy. He had received news that his brother had died. Never particularly close, the news weighed heavy on his heart nonetheless. "Ja, thank you for your condolences, Cato."

Cato, ever the practical confidant, scratched his stubbled jaw. "You could take his widow as your lover. I think you could use one."

Weishaupt liked that. As with Friederika, Sophia was a woman of his fantasies. "Too soon."

Cato shrugged. "Well, she could no doubt use some comfort. She is not far from Munich, right?"

Weishaupt grunted. "Enough of that." He took a seat. "Philo reports some anxiety among the Council." He dabbed perspiration from his brow.

"Philo overstates things. We have no reason to be anxious about anything. Our brothers have kept all the necessary secrets." Cato helped himself to a green bottle of Mosel Riesling. "We are building upon a solid foundation. Be patient."

Weishaupt stood, nodding. "Good, very good. I will trust you on this." He released a long breath and scanned some new titles recently purchased from Mr. Bergström. "That curious fellow delivered exactly as he promised. Look." He removed a book. "Ferguson's *Institutes of Moral Philosophy*. In here we have a collection of Bacon's elevations of knowledge, Buffon's work on racial characteristics, Hume on population, Montesquieu on politics, and even Marcus Aurelius on true happiness.[2] We need to be sure these are mandatory reading." [3]

"What do you think of our Mister Bergström by now?"

Weishaupt returned the book to its place and turned. "He refers to his friendship with Eckartshausen from time to time. I think that is a clue."

"I serve with Professor Eckartshausen on the censorship council," said Cato. "He is a prospect for us."

Weishaupt nodded. "So, you have no fears of either him or Bergström?"

"I did not say that. Eckartshausen is more of a mystic than either of us would prefer. And this Bergström—there is something about him."

Weishaupt waved Cato to silence. "Just continue our surveillance on them both. Watch for the little things. My only fear for Bergström is his pride. We need men who find strength in our Order, not in themselves. Otherwise they lose sight of how to *serve* their fellow men."

Cato said nothing for a moment, then lowered his heavy brows. "Should I tell the brethren to begin stealing books?"

Weishaupt laughed. "Indeed. But not from Bergström. Have them pick the monasteries as clean as they can without getting caught. They'll find it good sport. In fact, it is time we encourage more rebellion against moral fears. I want them stealing and lying, taking neighbor's wives. 'Holy sins,' Cato. Sins because convention says so; holy because in committing these acts we break down the order of things for the ultimate good." He winked. "The brethren will enjoy it."

Cato made a note. *'Holy sins.'*

"There are many ways to inspire men. Thus, there are many ways to direct the revolution. It is something of an art. Can you see it?" Weishaupt poured himself a glass of sweet wine. He was quite sure the attorney could not see any of it. "You must understand how complicated this all is. Which is why I share what I do only with you and others of the Council."

Weishaupt held the clear, white wine to the light. "Now, tell me, what are we doing about our unremarkable duke?"

"I have followed your orders. One of our forgers has falsified letters that suggest he is contemplating increased taxes and concessions to the Austrians."

Weishaupt was pleased. "That will cause a stir."

"This is the same forger who scandalized the leaders of Strict Observance," said Cato.

Weishaupt nodded. "That trap is now set. We will grab that whole organization for ourselves." He thought for a moment. "On another matter: Philo is of the opinion that our Minerval churches should sponsor reading clubs all over the Continent. This would attract the literati of France into *our* circle. In time, we can recruit them."

"Agreed."

Changing course, Weishaupt stood. "On a final matter, Philo has proposed a deeper organizational model for us. We have decided that the more complex it is, the more men are drawn to it.

"In essence, the Order will soon operate with three tiers. The Nursery for our first four degrees including the Minervals. The second tier will include the next five degrees, all similar to the Freemasons. The third tier would be where our real intentions come slowly forward."

"I remain concerned about our secrecy. Many of our present brethren would fly away if they understood all this."

Weishaupt laughed. "I agree with you. This is why Philo has so carefully designed our curriculum. We must move men slowly. Too much light and they will run." He stood. "Thus, we need to stay hidden within the masonic lodges as long as we can. The public already accepts them. But in time we will control the whole Craft…beginning by taking over all the Strict Observance lodges." He clenched his jaw. "After that, every level of education. Do you not see? If we educate men properly, then Nature will take her own course. Men will embrace our deepest secrets because they will have been properly formed. That is when religion disappears, policies begin to change, soldiers rebel, kings fall. This is when men are set free."

Before Cato could answer, a servant entered the room advising that a guest had arrived. He presented Weishaupt with a calling card.

"See him in."

Mr. Bergström entered the library bearing a large canvas bag. He greeted Weishaupt with the Master's grip and set his bag on the floor, carefully. "Good day, Herr Professor." He pointed to his bag. "I think you shall be pleased."

"I am told that you never disappoint, Mister Bergström." Weishaupt laid a friendly hand on Alexander's shoulder. His spirits lifted. "Now, I cannot wait another moment. Show me what you have."

The bookseller reached into his bag and retrieved a copy of François Fénelon's *Summary of the Lives of the Ancient Philosophers*. "I was able to buy this from a Monsieur de Broulieux, an agent for King Louis in Regensburg."

Weishaupt snatched the copy. "What else?"

Alexander withdrew three books by the French encyclopedist and progressive philosopher, Paul-Henri d'Holbach,[4] including his *Système Social*. "I wish I could attend one of his dinner parties!"

Weishaupt laughed. "Imagine yourself seated alongside your fellow Scots, David Hume or Adam Smith. Or that wonderful American devil, Benjamin Franklin."

Alexander smiled, politely. "'Fellow Scots?' I am a subject of Emperor Joseph, sir."

Weishaupt cast a sideways glance at Cato. "Well then, forgive me young sir. By your Scottish accent I was always of the opinion—"

"My father was a German merchant who married my mother in Aberdeen and then took her to his home in Hanau where he died within months."

Weishaupt was intrigued. "Near the gardens of Wilhemsbad?"

Alexander hesitated. Was it? "Yes, of course."

"Such a humble start, and yet you now work in Regensburg with diplomats from all over the world. Where is your mother now?"

"In Aberdeen."

Turning to Cato, Weishaupt said, "This is a true cosmopolitan man." He flipped through one of d'Holbach's books and then bade his guest to sit. "Do you read the books you sell?"

"As many as I can."

"Good." He took note of the beads of perspiration now gathering atop the young man's lip. "Are you thirsty, brother?"

"Ja." Alexander adjusted his sleeves.

Weishaupt summoned a servant and ordered beer, cheese and dark bread for them all. He leaned forward and studied 'Bergström' for a long, silent moment. "I am very, very pleased that you are a brother in our little lodge. Thank you for telling me a bit about yourself. I think you and I have a bright future together."

Alexander sat back. He ran a finger beneath his silk cravat and cleared his throat. "I am likewise pleased, sir."

"Wonderful." Weishaupt continued to study Alexander, surveying him from his wig to his polished shoes. "Are you married?"

"No."

"Good."

"Why do you say that?"

Weishaupt paused. "Tell me, Brother. What do you seek to accomplish in this life?"

The answer came easily. "I want to be a completed man, one suited to improve the world."

Weishaupt nearly leapt from his chair. "Then you and I share a common *telos*. Thus, you shall find a wife to be a distraction."

Alexander smiled. "So says St. Paul."

The reference annoyed Weishaupt. "Ah, St. Paul." He bit his tongue. This prey was too valuable to frighten. *Is this man not a Protestant?* "So, you are Catholic?"

Alexander hesitated. "Mostly."

"Mostly?" Disappointed, Weishaupt thought quickly. "Yes, yes, I understand this. I was once Catholic, now I am Lutheran." He now knew exactly how to charm Mr. Bergström. "You are a man who likes to think. Bravo."

Alexander smiled. He received a tankard of beer and a small plate of food. "You are perceptive."

Weishaupt cut his sausage, slowly. *We've now a Minerval Church in Regensburg,* he thought. *An Insinuator shall hook him there.* Excitement pulsed through his body. *He could connect us through his contacts in Regensburg...but also in Britain.* "Now, before you and I discuss how to make the world a happy place, I would like to present you with something." He motioned to Cato who retrieved a long, narrow object wrapped in a red cloth. "Here, Brother Bergström. A gift for your exceptional services."

CHAPTER TEN NOTES

1 This quote is paraphrased from Knigge's comments regarding his collaboration on the design of degrees that would appeal to a broad base of initiates. Weishaupt later clarified that true, 'hidden Christianity' was safely veiled within Freemasonry and, properly understood, was really just another expression of Universal Reason. Thus, Reason was as worthy of worship as Christ. This would soon be seen in the French festivals and liturgies of Reason.

2 These books were representative of Weishaupt's emphasis on the inevitability of progressive human development toward a perfected society.
Adam Ferguson (1723-1816) is considered a forerunner of modern sociology. His work points to the improvement of society through proper social relationships.
George-Louis Leclerc, Comte de Buffon (1707-1788) was a French naturalist who wrote extensively about the origins of humankind, believing original man was Caucasian and that humans have descended from this race. He is considered the first evolutionist.
Charles-Louis Montesquieu (1689-1755) was a French political philosopher who greatly influenced the British and American political systems with his emphasis on a separation of powers.
Marcus Aurelius (121 -180) was a Roman emperor who wrote extensively on living a happy life. His *Meditations* coalesce around the theme of abandoning a dependency on exterior circumstances for inner peace. He writes, "The happiness of your life depends on the quality of your thoughts."

3 Weishaupt's revolutionary vision was comprehensive. His primary goal remained the happiness of mankind. To that end, his social policies involved the replacement of all oppressive human institutions with a governing elite properly enlightened by the works of revolutionary minds as found in the collections of his mandatory reading lists.

4 **Paul Heinrich Dietrich, Baron d'Holbach** (1723-1789) was a German philosopher who was raised in Paris. He was popular in international society as an author, philosopher and outspoken atheist. This particular book supported his general view that an inherent social contract exists amongst peoples that creates a natural cooperation for societal happiness. A second contract exists between a people and their government only so long as the government supports the general welfare of its citizens.

"There is but one God, but one truth, and one way which leads to this grand Truth. And the sum of all these perfections is Jesus Christ."

KARL VON ECKARTSHAUSEN

CHAPTER ELEVEN

DECEMBER, 1781
REGENSBURG

ALEXANDER WAS SURPRISED AT THE NEWS. ABOUT EIGHT weeks prior, the British general, Cornwallis, had surrendered to the Americans at a place called Yorktown. Regensburg was buzzing. He was delighted for Albert van Loon, though he had not seen his friend for some time. Yet, this was not what was on his mind.

Hiding in the early shadows of the winter's evening, Alexander adjusted his wig and tricorn, snugged his gloves in place and gripped his new walking stick—the one presented to him as a gift by Adam Weishaupt. A Minerval Owl was etched on its silver handle along with his initial, 'B' for 'Bergström. Uneasy, Alexander chewed on the inside of his cheek. He tucked himself within his wool cloak and stepped bravely into the city's lamplight, hoping he looked wonderfully handsome.

Behind him, the Danube was flat and carried a smooth sheen of starlight. Some drunken gentlemen stumbled nearby. His feet held the icy curb of busy Keplerstrasse. At last, he heard a carriage slow its approach. He drew a breath. Should he be here? The driver reined his single horse and dismounted to help a lady step to the bricks.

Seeing her, Alexander hurried forward. "Julianna, you came!" He tossed the driver a coin and faced the girl. Two years prior, the princess had cared for Alexander at the city's hospital. Since then he had made a point of seeing her from time to time, but thought of her always. He was never sure if it was the meetings or the thoughts that heaped the most guilt on him. After all, he was a monk and the shame of his affections nagged him. But at this moment, he simply wondered what she might think of his new clothes?

Julianna hesitated at first.

"It is me, Brother Maurus…uh, Alexander…uh—"

Amused, Julianna batted her green eyes, seductively. "Well, look at you!" She curtsied. "But what happened to Regensburg's favorite monk?"

Alexander grinned. "My lady, I present Mr. Bergström." He bowed again, then took her gloved hand and kissed it.

Julianna giggled.

Happy, Alexander stared at the young woman with his big brown eyes. She had opted to sneak from her palace dressed more like a merchant's daughter than the jewel of the court, but he would not have cared if she was wearing a canvas sack. Her strawberry hair was hidden within an ample, taffeta bonnet. Over her shoulders rested a long, yellow cloak. He thought she was the most enchanting sight in all of Regensburg.

Julianna clutched her cloak at her heart. "Well, Mr. Bergström, I am at your command."

Alexander wanted to float. He knew that Julianna was not actually Fiona, but what was the harm in pretending the two were some common incarnation? "Then follow me." He took her by the hand, dashing past candle-lit shops and tavern windows dusted with snow.

Reaching the corner of Albanstrasse and Einhorn, Alexander paused and dug into a pocket. He retrieved a key, opened a heavy door and led his princess up two flights of stairs to a small office where a little candle was burning beside a small heater filled with red ash. Saying nothing, he touched the candle to several others until the room was aglow.

"What is this place, Mr. Bergström?" Julianna removed her cloak, gloves, and bonnet. She shook her hair.

Alexander smiled. "I have three lives. This place is for two of them." He set his walking stick against a corner and brushed snow off his cloak. He then held a chair for her before stoking the grate. He pulled his own chair close.

Julianna smiled. "Tell me more."

"I am Brother Maurus, of course. His habit hides under the bed when necessary. Sometimes I am 'Mr. Bergström' whom you behold."

She laughed. "I like it. For bookselling?"

"Mostly."

"And what about the third you?" Julianna reached a hand for his.

At the touch, life filled the youth. He kissed her hand. "The other is Alexander Horn. I fear he is lost between the two right now."

Julianna fell quiet. "And who sits with me tonight? Surely not Brother Maurus. But I hardly know either Mr. Bergström or Alexander Horn."

Alexander faltered.

The young woman fell quiet for a long moment. "If I dare say it—" She hesitated. "I hope the day comes when you are able to step out as who you really are."

Alexander blinked.

"Do you understand?"

"Like an emerging butterfly?" He forced a laugh.

Julianna returned a polite smile. "Yes. Exactly I look forward to that for you."

Alexander quickly stood and walked to a cabinet to retrieve some French brandy and a Christmas treat. "Sugar wafers?" he said.

Julianna raised her brows. "How can you afford these?"

The young man shrugged. "Mr. Bergström can."

"You are playing a dangerous game, young sir," said Julianna. "I presume you have lightened the abbot's book sales with a small profit for yourself?"

Alexander took another firm hold of her hand. "I do what I must." His voice trailed away.

"Ah, and so the costume. Mr. Bergström is not as accountable as Brother Maurus." She tittered and took a cookie.

Was she on to something? The notion of skimming book sales had nibbled on Brother Maurus' conscience for some time. But he did have special expenses...And a 'costume?' He quickly reached for a cookie.

Julianna leaned into Alexander. She spoke in a whisper, letting her warm breath linger on his cheek. "I like when you kiss me. I liked how you touched me in the forest last summer." She sat back. "I have missed you."

Alexander poured them both some brandy. "I have been traveling. The abbot says I am the best bookseller he has ever known——"

"And he still knows nothing of Mr. Bergström?"

"No."

"And he knows nothing of this place?"

Alexander shook his head. "Of course not. It belongs to an American diplomat."

Julianna took her drink. "It seems they have won their war."

Alexander did not care one whit. He drank another glass of brandy. Church bells pealed nearby. They sounded scolding. "Another cookie, Princess Julianna Roth von Himmelsberg?"

Julianna placed the white star in her mouth, slowly. She licked her lips. "I love your baker."

Alexander could not tear his eyes from her. Everything within him was yearning to hold her. He removed his suit coat. The coal hearth was suddenly too warm. He removed his vest. His eyes slid to the corner where Albert's narrow bed stood. He quickly returned his face to Julianna's, lovely-lit by candlelight. Captured, one voice within sang the unsullied wonder of her beauty. Another hissed, urging him to devour her on the spot. The young man fumbled for the brandy bottle. "Would you like more?"

REGENSBURG
MARCH, 1782

Walking through the dead gardens of late winter, Abbot Benedict folded his hands behind his back. "Brother Maurus, something is troubling thee."

Alexander turned his face. A cold wind rustled his monk's cloak.

Benedict sighed. "How many trips have you taken to Ingolstadt in these past months? And how often to Munich?"

"Seven to Ingolstadt. Three to Munich, Father."

"I have seen your book list. What you are trading troubles me. Occult mysteries, radical sciences, ancient alchemy, astrology, social revolution, French atheism…Voltaire! No, I think this goes beyond 'knowing thy enemy,' as you too often answer." He stopped and faced the young monk squarely. "Who *exactly* are you buying from, and to whom *exactly* are you selling?"

Alexander thought the abbot's voice to be uncharacteristically firm. "I buy from diplomats from America, Austria, Russia, France…all over the Continent. A great deal from the Prussians—"

"You read these books?"

"Most of them."

"And?"

Alexander thought for a long moment. "I see a common impulse to create a happy world, safe and free. Things the Holy Church also wants."

The abbot tensed. He closed his eyes. "They are not the same. Your books seek the self-perfection of mankind. No doubt an upset of political order, sweeping changes in economics, an overthrow of faith. From whence comes their power to do so?"

Alexander stiffened. "I do not know. It seems they gather like minds to discuss ideas in secret—"

"In secret. Yes. Like the Templars of the past and the Freemasons. I am well-aware." He drew a long breath through his nose. "A toad is a toad

No matter the road."

"What is that supposed to mean?" Alexander flushed.

"This path of perfection may point where it may,

but its pilgrims are led astray."

Alexander struggled to be respectful.

"I am surprised they deal so freely with a monk. They have no regard for the Holy Church. They have no sense of the sacred, no sense of reverence."

Alexander did not answer. Another gust of March wind lifted the hair from his ears.

Abbot Benedict looked at his young charge. Kindness returned to his face. "My son, these perfectionists assume they can be like god, knowing what is best for us all. Thus, they are humbled by nothing. Remember what you have been taught: humility is the guardian of all other virtues. Thus, a man who is in awe of nothing greater than himself will never respect anything lesser than himself. This makes them dangerous."

"I cannot see how bettering oneself is such an error. I like to imagine a happier world."

The abbot nodded. He laid a gentle hand on Alexander's shoulder. "A noble end, my son." He thought for a long moment. "But if you saddle a unicorn, have a care. For once seated, you may be carried away by a dragon."

Alexander said nothing.

The abbot sighed, then stared carefully into his monk's face. "Dear Brother Maurus, beware the temptations of pride. Even thine own."

The young man chafed, inwardly.

Benedict smiled, kindly. "Accept your struggles as gifts. They remind us that we are human." He eyed Alexander, carefully. "But it helps to name what you struggle against."

The comment caught Alexander's attention. What *was* he struggling with? *Why is it all so confusing?* The young monk's belly churned. He avoided Benedict's eyes. Suddenly, Dr. Weishaupt seemed easier to be with than the abbot. "My struggles are no different than those of others. If you are looking for a confession, I have nothing to say." A wave a nausea filled him.

The abbot exhaled. "I love you, Brother Maurus." He clasped his hands behind his back and began walking. "And therefore, I do not wish to abandon you to your secrets."

Alexander obediently followed in step.

"What are you afraid of?"

The lad wanted nothing more of this conversation. His body closed. "Why do you ask about fear?"

Benedict stopped walking. "Beneath that charming smile, your keen mind and occasional pranks, I sense some kind of terror." He laid a kind hand on the youth's shoulder. "It is only love that can truly cast out fear. And so, I want you to look beyond yourself and see how love holds you, always."

Alexander said nothing.

The abbot fell quiet and the two stood in silence for a long moment. Finally, Benedict spoke. "Of all the brethren, I would say this to you only:

Think less

Trust more.

God's quest

Is sure."

"Think less?"

"Trust more."

Alexander grumbled.

"His quest is to reconcile all things to himself. We do not understand it all, but we can trust it as very good news."

The young man nodded.

Sighing, Benedict said, "On another matter. If thy brother hasn't already told thee, he is to be ordained a priest. Several families of nobility have requested a new confessor and I am considering sending him."

Alexander chilled. Robby hearing the confessions of Julianna?

"What say you to that?"

"Um. His...his German is nearly perfect and he is very pious. If I am honest, however, he lacks grace."

The abbot nodded and he started walking again. "Have you heard from your friend, Albert?"

Alexander shook his head.

"You know about the Americans?"

He hardly cared. "Of course, Father."

"This is not good news for the proper order of things. Their revolution was shouldered by Presbyterians who were led by Diests and Freemasons along a path *away from* our Christian identity. They shall be the first nation of the West to officially abandon Christianity in favor of some neutralizing philosophy. I pray Christ remains in the hearts of her people."

Alexander cleared his mind. "Is a neutral government such a bad thing?"

Benedict thought for a moment. "It is a *risky* thing. For good or naught, the government creates an atmosphere. Replacing our Lord with a vacuum——"

"Leaves room for the Church to serve, freely."

"In a perfect world, perhaps. But I suspect they will chase Christ away in favor of some moral philosophy resting on the wisdom of mere men. That, too, is a religion."

Alexander thought about that. "But they remain affected by William Penn's Holy Experiment in Pennsylvania——"[1]

"Franklin will have the longer lasting effect than Penn. Mark my words." The abbot sat on a bench and bade Alexander to sit by his side. "Franklin is a popular man with nearly everyone, and that is what makes his Christ-less personal creed so dangerous." He closed his eyes. "It goes something like this: 'There is a benevolent, supervising Creator who is worthy of worship. We are to do good to our fellow man, and thus be rewarded or punished after death.'[2] That is the extent of it."

Alexander shrugged. "And?"

"His omissions drain Christianity from sight. His 'unnamed God' is the same as the unnamed Nature gods of all time."

Alexander thought for a moment. "Their new vision of government simply claims natural rights, freedom for the people, of a balance of powers——"

"Rights from their god of Nature. And do not forget their interest in 'the pursuit of happiness.' What exactly do they mean by that? Hear me:

A foundation of sand

Can never stand."

CHAPTER ELEVEN NOTES

1 **William Penn** (1644 — 1718) was an English Quaker who was granted the North American colony of Pennsylvania. His 'Holy Experiment' was intended to manifest divine love in the organization of society. It included religious freedom of worship in contrast to official churches that dominated many other American colonies. On 28 October 1701 Pennsylvania's *Charter of Privileges* stipulated that 'all persons who also profess to believe in Jesus Christ, Savior of the World' were permitted to serve the government regardless of their various Christian denominational difference. Thus, a Christian worldview was presumed to be the overarching religious context, though various sects were permitted. This Christian frame of societal love stands in sympathy with the founders' deistic frame of Natural Reason. Yet, the elimination of Christianity from the institutions of the United States is an important distinction between Penn's experiment and the Founders' vision.

2 Benjamin Franklin's Creed appears in Part Three of his autobiography as put to paper in 1788. He was interested in discovering a single set of religious essentials that could be shared by all men of virtue as the foundation of a benevolent society. A close examination of his creed would reveal what has become the essence of America's present national theosophical consensus.

"The great strength of our Order lies in its concealment; let it never appear in any place in its own name, but always covered by another name. None is fitter than the three lower degrees of Freemasonry. Next to this, the form of a literary society."

ADAM WEISHAUPT

CHAPTER TWELVE

16ᵀᴴ JULY, 1782
WILHEMSBAD, PRINCEDOM OF HESSE-CASSEL

ON THE SAME TUESDAY THAT THE SOON-TO-BE FREEMASON Amadeus Mozart premiered his progressive opera known as *Das Entfuhrung aus dem Serail* in Vienna, Adam Weishaupt raised the curtain on his own drama. He had cleverly incited Duke Ferdinand of Brunswick—Grand Master of the Knights of Templar Strict Observance (the premier masonic organization in central Europe)—to convene a congress of secret societies at a lush spa known as Wilhelmsbad near the German town of Hanau.

Duke Ferdinand was painfully aware of dissention and confusion among the dizzying array of secret societies and masonic rites now competing throughout much of Europe. The French were an exception, having already reorganized 266 masonic lodges within their powerful Grand Orient Lodge under the watchful eye of the conspiratorial Duke of Orleans.[1] But the rest of continental Europe's Freemasonry was in disarray. New rites had risen and with them new ceremonies and symbolism. Fresh doctrines appeared as if out of nowhere. This prompted a great deal of quarrelling. Mystics opposed the materialists;

magicians and scientists were at one another's throats. Occultists and Christians were at severe odds. In all of this, who had time to make men better? Ferdinand's hope was that a grand convention might solve it all.

However, Adam Weishaupt had recognized this chaos as his friend. The time to overthrow Strict Observance had finally come. In so doing, he planned to draw its membership into the orbit of his Order. The professor was hopeful, for Ferdinand had left his underbelly exposed.

"This is our moment, dear Philo," said Weishaupt. He and Philo von Knigge were walking through the shadowed gardens of Wilhelmsbad in the comfort of the summer evening. "We are about to capture a treasure. I give the spear to you. Hurl it straight into the heart of Strict Observance and the day shall be ours!"

Philo was not so sure. "This is an overwhelming task. Delegates are coming from all of Germany, the Netherlands, Russia, Poland, Italy and even France. We need your voice, Spartacus."

Weishaupt took his arm. "I must remain behind the veil a little longer. You are all I need. Get close to as many as you can and as quickly as you can, especially Johann Bode.[2] From what I have heard, he may be essential to our plan."

"I do not understand your interest in him. He is too old and far too ugly. He looks like an unintelligent hog with that pushed up snout——"

Weishaupt laughed. "I've not met him, but I am informed that he is a musician and a publisher second to none. So, hog-faced or not, we can use him. We need to infect art *and* scholarship. More importantly, he is our doorway into this whole business. With him as an ally, we shall sweep the field."

Philo was flustered. "All of this by two of us? This is what you rely on? How am I to snag Bode and also pull the rug out from under the Craft?"

"Ah, Philo. Just knock over the two pillars that Strict Observance depends on: their silly claim that it descends from the Knights Templar, and its lie about Invisible Superiors." Weishaupt toyed with his cuff, thinking. "The entire organization teeters on the edge of a cliff like an overstuffed giant. Even a child could tip it into the abyss. They have gone too far with their fantasies." He wiped perspiration from his neck. The air was humid. "Rational men have grown impatient. Besides, bankers are here to help." Weishaupt smiled. "So, do not lose heart. We have positioned you in many ways for this day. Our, shall we say, 'diplomacy,' has worked."

"You mean forgeries and bribes."

"I mean necessities for a better end." The professor smirked, then laid a hand on Philo's thin shoulder. "You simply need to give one more nudge. I am almost giddy! I wish Mr. Bergström would have come."

"You do not find it odd that he did not accept your invitation? This is supposedly his own home town."

"You sound like Cato. I will invite him to my betrothal party."

Philo grumbled. "As to that, may I remind you—with all deepest respect—that you do not even believe in marriage! You told the Council it is a distraction and a product of false moral convention. Yet you choose to return to chains once again...and to your dead wife's sister!" He shook his head. "May I suggest you do not share any secrets with this one."

"Her family is our door into the entire Continent. Her brother is a prince of substantial means. An intellect, even if she is not. He is a powerful presence." Weishaupt watched a robin jump from a nearby limb. "I can picture him initiated into a high degree of ours in the manner of the French masons. Yes, I see him blindfolded and bound in red scarves. We would command him to plunge his knife into the heart of a traitor. He would do it, and he would be disappointed to learn he had only slain a lamb." Laughing, the professor faced Philo. "He is the kind of man we want to advance."

Philo grunted.

"In any event, I hope you see that my marriage is a strategy. And I hope you see how important it is that you succeed. Your work can deliver us the very heart of Freemasonry."

Three days later, Weishaupt was furious. "What the devil is wrong with you!" He and Philo von Knigge walked through humid evening air along a stream in the Wilhelmsbad gardens. "We are so close and you say that?"

The baron was not about to be scolded like a schoolboy. "You sent me into this to explode the whole business and so I did."

Weishaupt grumbled. He slapped his walking stick against his thigh. "But there are clever ways and stupid ones." He collected himself as he wiped his perspired brow. He drew a deep breath. "You say the reaction was mixed?"

Philo nodded.

"Who was the loudest critic?"

"Comte de Virieu."

"A Martinist. [3] Of course he would complain." Weishaupt took a breath, thinking. "Perhaps this can be salvaged. You say you attacked the Templar traditionalists *and* the Rosicrucians at the same time?"

A voice turned both heads. Johann Bode trotted toward them panting heavily. Weishaupt nearly recoiled. As he had been warned, nothing about the man's appearance recommended him to anything. Heavy-built, moon-faced with a wide nose, a weak chin and a sloping forehead, this man from Hamburg seemed better suited as a butcher than a publisher.

The Hamburger arrived, gasping. Hands on his knees and wig shifted to one side, he sucked for air. Ignoring the professor, he finally stood upright and offered his damp hand to Philo. "I have been looking for you." He wiped his face with a linen kerchief. "The session is in an uproar. We need you, now."

"What happened?" said Weishaupt.

Bode gaped. "Who are you, sir?"

Weishaupt's skin bristled. *You do look like a hog and you have the manners of one.* He opened his mouth when Philo wisely interfered. "This is Brother Weishaupt of Lodge Theodore. He is a friend of mine. A bit curious, but harmless."

Weishaupt clenched. He suddenly wanted to strangle the baron.

Bode's ruddy cheeks were dripping. "I have private business with the baron, Brother Weishaupt."

The professor bit his lip until Philo said, "Speak. I vouch for him."

Bode hesitated. "Fine." He squared himself toward Philo. "After you left, others pounced on the Rosicrucians. Lessing, [4] rallied many delegates against false mysticism and deceptive histories. You, sir, lit the fuse."

Now Weishaupt wanted to shout for joy.

"In turn, others were inspired to stand and to mock all manner of pompous titles and oriental costuming. Some Italian then offered an inspired summons for us to return to the business at hand...the complete reformation of the world."

Weishaupt leaned forward.

Bode grinned. "A vote on three matters is proposed for midnight and we need you to twist arms. First, it shall be decided whether Strict Observance can rightfully claim a Templar birth. Without it, their foundation cracks."

Weishaupt could barely stand still.

"After that, we shall vote on the Unknown Superiors nonsense." Bode wiped his face once more. "It is an embarrassment that keeps us from uniting with the French. Once that silliness is defeated, it all collapses."

Philo then took Bode's arm. "And what of the Jews?"

Weishaupt wondered why he worried about them.

"Lessing kicked that door down as well. He argued that Christianity was simply a newer form of Judaism, but both are eclipsed by Reason. Enlightened Jews should be welcomed to a rejuvenated Craft. We need their money. He credits your insight in all of this."[5]

Like a proud father, the professor studied Philo. *Well done, Philo*, he thought. *With Strict Observance destroyed, we can annihilate the Rosicrucians and scoop up the cream of the Craft.*

The Lodge of Strict Observance was routed at midnight and, in their defeat, Spartacus Weishaupt suddenly became the veiled master of much of Continental Freemasonry. From behind his cloak of absolute secrecy, the professor's machinations had created a vacuum of masonic leadership into which his Order now rushed.

"I can scarcely believe it!" said Philo. He and Weishaupt were now hurrying south toward Ingolstadt in a fine coach. "And to have Duke Ferdinand and Prince Karl—Master of Germany's Grand Lodge—abandon the Craft to join our Order!"

Weishaupt stared at the lush green of the German countryside. He felt light as air. "And so many others. We have taken the archivist—Von Schwartz—and he gets us into Russia. We also get Kolowrat-Liebensteinsky from Transylvania, Count Szapary from Budapest, Chevalier de Savaron from Lyon...just a few on a long list that spreads us across the whole of the Continent!" He closed his eyes and the sun warmed his face. But my greatest prize is Johann Bode. I tell you, hog-faced or not, that publisher won my affections. He will serve us well." He turned. "Philo, I have never been happier than in this moment."

The pair rode on, silently basking in the grand coup. Philo then said, "I should tell you now that many plied me with bottles of English gin, but I kept true."

"Whatever do you mean?"

"Everyone wants to know who the hidden hand is." He smiled. "Everyone is yammering about some phantom named Basilius. You were clever to toss that bait into the wind."

Weishaupt stared at the sharp gables of a distant village tucked into the hills of Hesse. His clever alias for Spartacus did, in fact, have the world chasing a ghost. The fact was both pleasing and not. "I suspect most believe *you* to be Basilius?"

"Me?" Philo looked away. "No. I tell them the unseen hand is best unseen."

Weishaupt grunted. "Ironic. We destroy Strict Observance because of their supposed 'Invisible Superiors' and then insert our own."

Philo hesitated, then murmured, "But we do—"

July, 1782
Regensburg

As Adam Weishaupt was executing his plan to steal German Freemasonry, Alexander plopped himself on a city bench alongside his friend, Karl von Eckartshausen. He was now worried that the abbot would learn of his rise to master mason. "I could be put out of the monastery," he said, catching Karl's eye. "Then what? Do I just become Mr. Bergström? Do I return to Oyne as Alexander Horn, disgraced monk?"

"You worry too much." Karl removed his hat. "He does not *want* to suspect anything so he doesn't watch. You sell too many books for him to open his eyes." He chased a fly with his hand, laughing. "On another matter, are you aware of the congress at the Wilhelmsbad spa in Hanau?"

"Of course. Dr. Weishaupt nearly begged me to meet him there—"

"Because you told him you were *from* Hanau!" Karl puffed his cheeks and exhaled. "Of all places, you chose to be from Hanau. Little brother, your web nearly ensnared you."

Alexander shrugged. "One of my customers was from there and he described Wilhelmsbad as such a lovely garden, what with ponds and swans, a new castle built to look like a ruin. I had it on my mind when I spun my tale to Weishaupt."

Karl shook his head. "I hear that Weishaupt is courting his own sister-in-law."

The news meant nothing to Alexander. "He is a kind man and she is in need of a husband." He tossed a twig into the air. "Tell me, do you think he is one of the Minervals—or Illuminati as some say it should be called?"

"Does it matter?"

Alexander was not sure. "I'm curious about finding something for myself other than the Craft. Ever since they wanted me to shoot myself—"

"The gun was not loaded—"

"I do not like the idea of it. Suicide is a mortal sin and should not be toyed with." Alexander thought for a moment. "I need to be a better man, that is true enough. But I am now doubting Freemasonry. One of the brothers bragged about their spreading of symbolic sun worship throughout Europe by importing obelisks from Egypt."

Karl nodded. "Jeremiah predicted the pillars of sun worship would be demolished someday—"

"My concern is not only on account of their pagan—"

"You impress me, friend," said Karl. "I retreat from these conflicts by hiding within my library and my melancholy, but you *contend* with them."

Alexander watched an ant crawl through the grass by his feet. "I should have attended the congress. I could have spent more time with Dr. Weishaupt. He seems suspicious of the excesses of the masons—"

"Are you sure about him?"

Alexander shrugged. "I have spent enough hours with him listening very carefully. He speaks endlessly of bettering mankind but little about spiritual things. He is truly passionate about happiness. He once spoke of a world without borders, of all men living in equality. He really must be one of these Minervals."

Karl agreed. "And if he is?"

"Then he may be able to introduce me."

CHAPTER TWELVE NOTES

1 **Louis Philippe II, Duke of Orleans** (1747 – 1793) was the Grand Master of most of French Freemasonry. He was a wealthy cousin to King Louis XVI but decidedly revolutionary in his world view. An eventual supporter of the French Revolution (1789), he voted for the beheading of the king only to meet the guillotine himself not long afterward. His liberal philosophical views were common to French Freemasonry generally and, like Adam Weishaupt, were heavily influenced by the philosophy of Rousseau (who emphasized the essential virtue of a primitive world of nature.)
The masonic Grand Orient Lodge was the most potent humanist force in European Freemasonry and included the Paris Lodge of Nine Sisters which was home to Benjamin Franklin and other American notables. Its philosophical views were aligned with the Illuminati and would eventually lead to a divide between itself and the masonic lodges in Great Britain and North America.

2 **Johann Bode**, *Illuminatus Amelius* (1730-1793) was a musician, author, and publisher. He particularly enjoyed performing in musical sessions presided over by the son of Johann Bach. Bode was Grand Master of the Hamburg masonic Lodge of Strict Observance until 1782. After the dissolution of that lodge, he quickly ascended as a prime player in the Order.

3 Martinism was/is a mystical theosophy associating itself with Christianity. It descended from **Louis Claude de Saint-Martin** (1743-1803) and his mentor, the occult magician **Martinez de Pasqually** (1727-1774). It emphasizes the return of man into eternal Wisdom via progressive degrees of enlightenment.

4 **Gotthold Ephraim Lessing** (1729 – 1781) German philosopher and playwright who promoted the perfection of humankind through a universal

brotherhood of love and moral freedom that would transcend all religions. His work provided philosophical grounding for the Order's plan to build a world commonwealth.

5 Until this time, Jews were not permitted into European Freemasonry outside their own Lodge known as 'The Small and Constant Sanhedrin of Europe.'

> *"(After) the overthrow of civil society, its laws and its chiefs, (the Illuminati) shall institute a more liberal opinion of human nature."*
>
> ADAM WEISHAUPT

CHAPTER THIRTEEN

REGENSBURG
AUGUST, 1782

"I AM TO MEET WITH DR. WEISHAUPT NEXT week in Ingolstadt." Alexander walked with Albert van Loon along the Danube, toying with his walking stick. In the two weeks since Van Loon's return, Alexander had hoped to avoid a deep conversation with him. Perhaps it was guilt on account of his using the man's room for secret liaisons with Julianna. That, and some rumors about Van Loon's own secretive past that had begun to gnaw at him.

"Why meet with Weishaupt?"

"He ordered more books for some kind of 'church' he's planning to attend in Ingolstadt. More like an academy for discussion, I think."

"A Minerval Church, to be precise."

Alexander raised a brow. *So it's true.*

Van Loon watched a small bark tack upriver against a stiff breeze. "From what I hear, these so-called 'churches' are springing up in Berlin, Hamburg, Frankfurt, Munich…Vienna, Lyons, Paris…They meet twice a month with at least one meeting held on the full moon. Seems odd for a 'church.'" He shook his head. "As your abbot says, 'something is afoot.' I attended Lodge Theodore last week. The mood is odd. Everyone is deadly serious as if there is some grand venture being planned."

"With Strict Observance dead, something must be filling the void. The Minervals?"

Albert nodded. "Friends tell me they are a subset of some other organization. What do you know?"

"Very little. I have heard the name, 'Illuminati.' Rumors have it that they are philosophical activists. They are more practical minded than the Craft." He answered. "This is good. We need to change the world. Injustice rules. Kings and princes oppress… except in your country."

Van Loon turned away.

Alexander waited, wondering whether the rumors about his friend were true.

The American stopped walking and removed his hat. At last, he cleared his throat. "Alexander, you know what it is like to lead a second life." He drew a breath and faced the young monk squarely. "I have had a second life as well."

Alexander waited.

"I…I was not serving Dr. Franklin in France." Albert began to rub his thumb.

"What?" The rumors were that Albert van Loon was involved with the Russians in some kind of black-market scheme related to arms trading.

Albert drew a very deep breath. "I was not a patriot. I was serving the Crown as a spy in Franklin's entourage."

The words hit Alexander with force. "Spy?" He tried to calculate exactly what that meant. "A British spy *against* the Americans?"

"Yes. I convinced Franklin that I should travel between his offices in Paris and the Diet here in Regensburg where I could keep an eye on Continental politics. In truth, I conveyed information to the Crown about Franklin's seduction of the French."

Alexander gawked. This was nothing that he expected. "A spy? But—"

"I know. It does not seem honorable. And in the end, nothing I did prevented disaster. The French rescued the rebels and all on account of Franklin's charm. I tried to warn the British agents here—"

"But you, a spy?"

Van Loon stiffened. "Are you going to shame me for it?"

The monk blinked. "Shame you? Why would I shame you?"

"Because it is a dirty business."

Dirty?

"Now you know." Albert started walking.

"Wait. No. I do not think less of you for this," said Alexander. He held Van Loon by his forearm.

Pulling away, Albert kept walking and the pair moved quietly along the grassy riverbank where the sounds of snapping canvas and splashing prows occupied them for a quarter hour. Finally, Albert stopped. He turned and explained his loyalty to the Crown and how he had established a new home by some willows in Salisbury, England. He then disclosed his present assignment as a British diplomat here again, in Regensburg.

"You should have no regrets." said Alexander. "You followed duty as you saw duty to be."

Van Loon shrugged. "I followed duty, though I may have left my honor behind. I did not like saying one thing and doing another. I admired Dr. Franklin and despised betraying him. And I actually agreed with the grievances of America. I just opposed their revolution." He paused. "The Pitts¹ asked me to do it as an act of family friendship."

"The Pitts?" said Alexander. "But how——"

"They were close with my maternal grandmother."

Alexander stared at his friend. The Pitt family was of great influence throughout the British Empire. He then exhaled. "You look genuinely troubled. My granda once said men should consider what things trouble them so that they might more clearly see what they love. You are troubled by betrayal and deceit. It is because you love loyalty and honor. Do not be ashamed, Albert. It is plain to see that you are a good man."

Van Loon's eyes filled. "Thank you, Brother Maurus. You do understand."

The pair walked on. Alexander smiled. "And you were right. We both have other lives. Since one life passes quickly, maybe it is a good thing to have extra! I will already be twenty in a month——"

"With the wisdom of a sixty-year-old."

"Wisdom? I don't think so." Alexander slapped his friend's back. "Now, what of America? No treaty is yet signed. Are we sure they defeated us?"

"Yes. King George has no more resources. More than that, I see that America is born of something...something deep. One can feel it from her land. The people are fascinating," said Albert. "Strong, intelligent, centered in their faith, diligent, brave. They have an instinct for justice. They love freedom and they despise privilege; they defend their property but yet are generous.

"Nevertheless, I fear for them." Albert stopped and reached into his purse to retrieve a folded paper. "Too many of their founders follow a different star, so to speak, quite different from the average settler." He found a bench, sat, and flattened the paper on his leg to reveal two drawings. "This is America's new Great Seal.[2] It is a masonic secret in itself."

Alexander stared.

"As to the front side, some say this eagle is actually a mythical phoenix." Albert pointed. "I think not, but who knows? And see the stars? The designers chose *five*-pointed stars for a purpose—occult secrets?"

"Or artistic choices."

"Freemasons designed all of it. With them, nothing is just artistic." Albert tapped on the second drawing. "Here I especially worry. They use the Great Pyramid of Giza—the supreme symbol of the ancient mysteries—oriented eastward. And look, there are seventy-two blocks—"

"Seventy-two is the Cabalist number of the Shemhamforash." [3] Alexander looked up. "Thus, seventy-two represents the forces of nature that perfect mankind."

Evidently impressed, Van Loon said, "Seventy-two is also the number of years in the precession of the Zodiac.[4] The Freemasons are obsessed with the power of the stars. They do nothing without consulting an astrological chart." He then pointed to the top of the pyramid. "Then there's this: their floating Eye of Providence? Some say it is the Eye of Horus."

The monk then studied the Latin mottoes. "*E Pluribus Unum*. Out of many, one—the unified cosmos—the dreamed of world commonwealth." He strained. "Or it could easily simply mean the union of their colonies."

Van Loon nodded. "It could. But this is *masonic* symbolism; it always has layers of meaning."

Alexander read the next motto. "'*Annuit Coeptis*; God has Favored our Task.'" He looked up. "That was a prayer to the god, Jupiter—and the planet named for him is the planet of plenty."[5]

The American then began counting things. "Everywhere is thirteen. Thirteen rows of blocks on the pyramid—"

"Naturally. Thirteen colonies."

Van Loon agreed. "But it interests me that thirteen is also the spiritual number of regeneration. And look. Even the Latin spelling is changed to make sure each motto is thirteen letters." He wiped a hand over his face. "The whole of this seal is a code for those with eyes to see." Albert then blew air from his cheeks. "It is widely believed that a man in black approached Thomas Jefferson in a garden as he was deliberating on this. The unnamed stranger supposedly instructed him on the design. What would be behind that?"[6]

Alexander shrugged. "Sounds like a wild story to discredit the Americans."

Albert became grave. "Perhaps. But far more may be going on than what we can even imagine."

"I do not understand why Bergström could not attend my betrothal announcement. I am right here in Regensburg," said Adam Weishaupt. "I could have introduced him to the visiting Sausenhofers and he could have introduced me to diplomats from all over the world."

Cato Zwack walked alongside the professor on a crowded city street. "We should have had our eyes on Regensburg years ago. The Imperial Diet sitting right under our noses and we failed to see it."

"We? Philo failed to see it. I depend on him for strategy."

The attorney wisely offered no comment. Instead, the twenty-six-year-old vented his increasing frustration over Weishaupt's obsession with the young bookseller. "So why has not one soul ever heard of your Mr. Bergström? I have asked of him in every tavern." He blew his nose into a kerchief. "You do not think this is strange?"

Weishaupt did but would not grant his guard dog the satisfaction of agreeing. "Someone shall know him in there." He pointed to City Hall just a block ahead. "He must pay taxes." He led Cato in a sudden rush, finally turning a corner where they nearly collided with two laughing men. One was a handsome gentleman in a fine blue suit; the other a young monk with a walking stick.

Weishaupt grunted.

The gentleman removed his hat with a sweep, and bowed. "Apologies."

"I know you," blurted Cato. "You are Brother van…van, something. I know you from Lodge Theodore."

"I am Brother Albert van Loon," said the gentleman in adequate German. He reached for Cato's hand and then Weishaupt's, exchanging the Master's grip with both.

Weishaupt then turned to the monk hiding deep within his hood. Something about him… "Brother——"

The monk kept his face down.

"You seem familiar to me." Weishaupt's eyes dropped to the walking stick with which the monk was suddenly fumbling. *Could it be?* He shuffled closer. "Lift your face."

Alexander Horn stared at his sandals. His palm covered the Minerval owl etched on the head of his walking stick. *What do I say? Surely, he sees it's me. This could ruin my membership at the Lodge.*

"Your face, sir?" asked Weishaupt.

Albert van Loon interrupted. "Brother Maurus is not well. We ought to be going." He tipped his hat and took Alexander by the elbow.

"Ah, Brother Maurus." Weishaupt's tone was firm. "I politely asked to see your face, now show me."

Alexander's heart pounded.

Cato suddenly grabbed hold of Alexander's hood and jerked it off his head.

Adam Weishaupt stared into Alexander's wide eyes. "You?"

Mind racing, Alexander turned to Van Loon with a forced flourish. "Sir, our business is concluded. I hope you enjoy your reading. Fare thee well."

Blank-faced, Albert nodded. "Yes?" He strained. "Well, then, I…I bid you and these gentlemen *adieu*." He bowed and quickly faded from sight.

Alexander took a breath and offered Weishaupt an awkward smile. "I needed my client to leave."

Weishaupt and Cato exchanged glances.

"As I always expected, you are the one man in the whole of this city with eyes keen enough to discover me in this...costume." Alexander forced a smile.

Cato grumbled, but Weishaupt said, "Mr. Bergström, I presume?"

"Indeed! And you look surprised." Alexander rubbed his shaved head. "And why not? No fine suit. No wig, no hat. But, ah, as fine a gentleman's walking stick as one might receive from a valued friend."

"Well, I...well, I am not surprised that you are clever." Weishaupt wiped his lip. "Yes, yes. Clever indeed."

"He is a fraud," growled Cato.

Alexander feigned a deep insult. "Fraud, sir? We are brothers in the Craft!"

Cato scowled.

A carriage drew near, one carrying noble family. The driver reined his team and a driver dismounted to open the door. *Now what?* The driver helped a young woman dismount.

It was Julianna.

Alexander paled. He had not seen her for many weeks and now this?

Dressed in a splendid French *chemise à la reine* with a bright red sash, Julianna approached the men with a large chaperone at her side. "*Guten Tag,*" she said.

Adam Weishaupt executed a perfect bow, left leg placed straight forward. "My joy is complete," he said as he introduced himself.

Cato bowed, half-heartedly.

Alexander gawked.

Julianna moved close to Weishaupt. "Dr. Adam Weishaupt? I am told your students admire you like no other."

"And why not?" He took her hand and kissed it, lingering.

"With such a kiss as that I suspect you have spent time in Paris?"

Weishaupt tittered. "Not as much as I would like, *Mademoiselle.* Perhaps a holiday there would be in order."

"My family loves Paris."

"Then, perhaps you and I could someday stroll through the *Jardin des plantes?*" Weishaupt tilted his head and smiled. "Ah, better. What about a midnight bath on the barges at the *Cours-la-Reine?*"

Julianna turned her face toward Alexander. "Greetings, Brother Maurus."

A chill surged through the monk.

"You know him?" muttered Weishaupt.

"Everyone knows him, sir."

Alexander bowed his head, one eye on the professor. "*Fraulein.*" Now what?

Julianna offered her hand, then quickly withdrew it. "Oh, I am sorry, Brother Maurus. I did not mean to disrespect your vow."

"No, sister. I would not expect you would." He felt Weishaupt's eyes on him. "Allow me to move along. I am sure you must have something important to discuss with the professor."

"Important?" Julianna turned to Weishaupt. "No, but I am interested in how a famous professor of Ingolstadt is familiar with Regensburg's favorite monk?" She smiled.

Alexander's mouth went dry. He cast a sideways glance at Weishaupt who seemed utterly confused. Cato, on the other hand, crossed his arms, waiting.

"Ah, that," said Alexander. "Well, it...uh, well things are not always as they seem." He could not gather his thoughts.

"Oh, really?" She blushed, suddenly straining. "Then I shall be content to leave you three as I found you." The princess spun away and hurried to her carriage, leaving Alexander to clean up the mess.

Weishaupt followed after Julianna's fine form and offered a dramatic wave. After all, Cato had recently proposed that the Illuminati begin recruiting females into a special Order, beginning with Cato's own wife. Watching the lovely Julianna disappear into her carriage, it was easy to understand why. Imagining princesses like her sitting at his knee was suddenly appealing.

He stood in place until her carriage rounded a corner. His smile then turned downwards. He marched back to Alexander. "Explain yourself."

"What is there to explain?"

Cato laughed.

Weishaupt flushed. Restraining himself, he stood very close to the monk. "I had very high hopes for you, Brother Maurus…Mr. Bergström. Whichever! I thought that you and I shared a vision of the world, but—" He caught himself. Was he ready to abandon this young man? "I would like to know what this is all about." He gestured at the monk's habit.

Alexander answered without hesitating. "This city is one of intrigue and secrecy, and so monks are trusted. Especially monks from Scotland. Everyone loves a Scot…except the English. So, I pretend to be a monk to overcome the fear of buyers."

Weishaupt was not convinced. "I am confused. Are you 'Mr. Bergström' pretending to be a monk, or 'Brother Maurus' pretending to be a bookseller?"

"Which would you prefer, sir?"

How dare he! Weishaupt reddened. "Whatever do you mean?"

"In Ingolstadt and Munich my bookselling is better as Mr. Bergström. Here in Regensburg I do better as Brother Maurus. What remains constant is my love of books…and my profit."

Weishaupt adjusted his cuffs, thinking. *No true monk would play this game.* "And so, you are no monk at all?"

Alexander hesitated and Weishaupt noticed. He answered, "Can you really imagine me as a monk, sir?" He offered a laugh. "Though I have the abbot believing I am a lingering pilgrim from Edinburgh."

Weishaupt strained. *He is clever. But if he is clever, maybe he is being clever with me.* The professor tapped his own walking stick atop the brick sidewalk. *Then again, I am no fool. I know men. This one is too proud of his game to be lying about it. Of course—*

Weishaupt abruptly wrapped an arm around Alexander. "You are a shrewd fellow! I would like to see more of you. I look forward to drinking gin with Mr. Bergström in Ingolstadt." With that, he bade Alexander an abrupt farewell and watched him hurry away.

Weishaupt then turned to Cato. "It is my wish to know more about this bookseller. If he is this clever we may need him more than I thought. Besides, something is surely going on between him and the princess. Have him followed. I want a full report."

CHAPTER THIRTEEN NOTES

1 **William Pitt the Younger** (1759 – 1806) was a British statesman and son of Lord Pitt the Elder, himself a British Prime Minister with great sympathy for the American colonies. Like his father, the Younger served as Prime Minister with distinction. He would become a nemesis for the Illuminati and its offspring.

2 The Great Seal of the United States was the result of three committees meeting over a six-year period. Members included Thomas Jefferson, Benjamin Franklin, Charles Thompson, William Barton and others, only one of which was not a member of a secret society. Finally approved in 1782, its esoteric reverse side was rarely seen until 1934 when Secretary of Agriculture, Henry Wallace—a mason and world federalist—convinced Franklin Roosevelt to put it on American currency. Since then it appears on the U.S. dollar bill.
One of the seal's mottos is taken from a prayer to the supreme Roman god, Jupiter, who was also known as the 'Light Bringer' (*Lucetius*, or as more commonly known, Lucifer.)
The Great Seal's (and the U.S. dollar bill's) image of an unfinished pyramid represents the Great Pyramid of Giza, considered by the ancients to be the tomb of Hermes. Thus, at one level the image suggests the ongoing project of building a nation, and at another, a nod to the philosophical/religious beliefs of many American founders.
E Pluribus Unum (Out of many, one) offers at least three levels of meaning. First, it clearly refers to the notion of the union of America's disparate colonies. Second, it points to the ultimate political unity of a world commonwealth as expressively promoted by the Illuminati and others. Finally, it correlates with the metaphysical assumptions of Monism (Universal Oneness) as a gathering of the many into one.

3 The Cabalists were/are Jewish mystics widely regarded for their studies in numerology. The Shemhamforash is an ancient term referring to the 72 combinations of the four Hebrew letters that describe the secret name of God.

4 Every 72 years the relative position of the earth to the sun and the planets shifts about one degree. This is called the precession of the vernal (March) equinox. It takes about 26,000 years to return to the original position. This means each of the 12 constellations of the Zodiac advance every 2,100 years, thus causing shifting ages for astrological interpretations of history. We are presently moving out of the Age of Pisces (often associated with Jesus Christ) and into the Age of Aquarius (considered to be the holistic fulfilment of humankind.)

5 The planet, Jupiter, figures prominently in American masonic symbolism. As the planet of beneficence, its proper positions in astrological charts importantly bestow blessings, especially in relationship with Virgo—the constellation claimed by many American Founders to be that of the United States. Thus, as with the star Sirius, Jupiter's location on astrological charts became important for a variety of stone laying ceremonies and building dedications in Washington D. C.

6 The story of Jefferson's encounter with a disappearing man in black was widespread. Were it not consistent with other such 'legends' it might be more easily dismissed.

"Our secret schools of philosophy shall one day retrieve the fall of human nature, and nations shall disappear from the face of the earth. Reason shall be the only code of men."

FROM THE ILLUMINATI DEGREE OF PRIEST

CHAPTER FOURTEEN

REGENSBURG
JANUARY, 1783

"YOU ARE NOT STILL ANGRY WITH ME?" JULIANNA touched the cold tip of Alexander's nose, then rubbed his tonsured head, playfully. Church bells tolled the hour, rumbling low against the stone wall of the Thurn and Taxis palace where the two hid in the shadows of the starry night's sky.

Alexander studied her. Something seemed off. "Of course not. I was already in a pickle when your carriage came by." He masked his own troubled spirit with a false smile. "No harm, though." He took her hands. He sickened. Was this the right time? He summoned every conviction and blurted, "My dear Julianna…" His courage failed as quickly as it had risen. "You…you look beautiful."

She pulled herself close. They kissed.

At the soft touch of her lips, voices filled Alexander's mind. Scolding voices. He wanted to back away. He lingered until he finally retreated a half-step. "I am so happy to see you again. I think of you always."

The young man could barely say the words. It had been three years since Julianna had nursed him to health and his heart had never been the same. Three years of wanting what his holy vows denied. Three years of doubting his virtue

155

in those wonderful hours with her. Three years of doubting his calling. Three years of fearing he would lose her...like he had Fiona all those years past. Yet, also three years of wonder and passionate dreams. The very thought of her made him feel alive, whole. Julianna was a comfort, and that comfort was safety he never wanted to lose.

Alexander drew a deep breath. "However, I...we..." He squeezed her hands and finally closed his eyes. Now was the time. Could he say what duty demanded? Dare he? It was good he was dressed as a monk this night. He opened his mouth. "We...we must no longer see one another in this way."

Julianna murmured something indiscernible. She squeezed his hands and tears rose.

"I live and die a little more with every kiss. I long for you, yet you must understand that I belong to the Church—"

She lowered her face. "Have I always shamed you?"

"Shamed me? No. No. I shame myself. I violate my vows every day and every night because I do not stop thinking about you. I am commanded to pray without ceasing, yet instead I wonder what you are doing, who you are with, what you are wearing. I think of holding you, of your face, your neck—"

"Enough, Alexander." Julianna released his hands and wiped her eyes. She collected herself. "You are a good man and I have been your stumbling block. I have treasured our times together in ways I cannot find words to express." Her voice faltered. "I too, think of you daily." The tears returned. "Perhaps more of late than ever." She clasped her hands over her breast. "But it is good that you say this, for I needed to tell you something and did not have the courage."

Alexander reached for her.

Now Julianna retreated. She stared at him from swollen eyes. "Before I do, I must first say this—" She hesitated, then laid her open hand flat against Alexander's chest. "No matter what I am about to say, you must find a way to set yourself free." The princess gazed deeply into his soul. "You wear three masks to protect this heart of yours." She then wrapped her arms around him and whispered into his ear, slowly, "A-L-E-X-A-N-D-E-R. You are loved. It is safe. Come out and be free."

The young man trembled.

He then wiped his face with a kerchief and stared into her eyes. He could not speak. Awed, he took Julianna's hands. He studied her fragile fingers. *I could abandon all my vows for love like this.* He pressed her warm palm against his cheek. "You are God's gift to me. He shows me his face in yours. Yours is the face of love."

"Oh, dear Alexander. I did not mean for this. No, this is not—"

"But—"

She put a finger over his lips. "You misunderstand."

Confused, Alexander strained. He stepped back. "You said you had something you must tell me?"

Julianna blinked. Her chin quivered. "My...my father." She looked away. "Last evening my father announced that he has betrothed me."

Alexander gasped. "Betrothed! To whom?"

"To a baron of the Von Gumppenberg family near Frankfurt-am-Main."

Alexander would rather have iron nails driven through his wrists than suffer this moment. He reached for her. "Let me abandon my vows! I will do anything."

Julianna raised a hand. "Say nothing more, dear Alexander. You shall be always near to my heart. I shall always love you and hope for you. But I am a nobleman's daughter and you a monk. Neither of us is free. We were never meant to be."

Alexander took a half-step toward her. Then another. What was happening? Where was the face of God now? "Julianna, I—"

Sounds of jangling metal turned his head. A troop of drunken guards was suddenly drawing near. Seeing the approaching soldiers, Julianna lunged at Alexander. She held him for one final moment, sobbing into his ear, "Surrender your masks and let God love you as I surely have."

Alexander embraced her until he could feel her pulling away. He then shared one more agonizing look before his princess turned and vanished into the shadows. Broken under moonlight, Alexander Horn fell slowly to his knees.

INGOLSTADT
FEBRUARY, 1783

Adam Weishaupt locked away his hieroglyphic decoding sheets and turned to face Johann Bode—initiated as the Illuminatus, *Aemilius*—recently arrived from Hamburg. After the Congress of Wilhelmsbad, the influential publisher had been rapidly advanced through the Order and now held the advanced degree of Regent. However, the only Illuminati that Bode knew were Philo von Knigge and Cato Zwack from the business in Wilhelmsbad, as well as six members of the Minerval church in which he studied.

Weishaupt shook his hand. "Welcome to my humble office. Please, sit." The professor struggled within himself, wondering if he'd been right to trust this man. Recent revelations about increasing opposition from the Rosicrucians, the Jesuits and an ever more conservative Duke Theodore had kept Weishaupt sleepless. After all, if the truth of his great plan were ever made public he would be dragged to the gallows. Lost in thought, he dropped some coals into his heater.

Weishaupt drew a long breath as Aemilius Bode settled into a chair. He remembered how unimpressive the man had looked in Wilhelmsbad, but seeing him again was worse. No wig. The man's dark hair was now combed back from his broad forehead and hanging along his collar. He was poorly shaven; his nose hung on his face pig-like, and his brown eyes were set far too wide for Weishaupt's taste. No, this man did not have the countenance of intellect.

"Thank you for coming," said Weishaupt in a measured tone. "You had a long journey."

"Baron von Knigge was insistent." Bode gaped about the office. He crossed his legs, disrespectfully. "It's cold in here. Do you have any wine?"

Weishaupt pursed his lips, offered a thin apology and poured the man a glass of Madeira. "Did Philo tell you why I summoned you?"

Aemilius grunted. "Philo? Summoned?" He leaned forward. "Who is Philo? And who are you to summon anyone?"

Weishaupt chafed. The man was being coy. Worse, Philo had not bothered to prepare this grunting Hamburger. "So, the baron did not disclose the purpose of this visit?"

Aemilius swallowed his amber wine and wiped his sleeve over his mouth.

The professor grumbled, "How old are you, sir?"

"Why do you ask such a rude question?"

"My task generally involves younger men."

"What task?"

"Your age, Herr Bode?"

Aemilius grunted again. "I am fifty-two."

Weishaupt poured a Madeira of his own, reminding himself how effective Aemilius Bode had been at Wilhemsbad. He sat. "I understand that you are a man of influence."

"Ja."

"You are the founder of J.J.C. Bode & Co. Publishers."

"Right."

Weishaupt's finger tapped along the rim of his glass. "You are a believer in Nature and the force of Reason."

"What is this about?"

"Your former partner accuses you of literary piracy."

Aemilius stood. "How dare——"

"You are an amateur cellist and play in a group instructed by Bach's son; you like poetry and you are a leader among the literati of Hamburg. You were once the tutor of Mendelsohn's wife; you are friends with our dear Goethe[1] and a confidant of the promising philosopher, Nicholas Bonneville."[2] Weishaupt sipped his wine. "Sit."

Bug-eyed, Aemilius obeyed.

"And you are quite the sinner." Weishaupt folded his hands. "I have read your confessional."

Aemilius paled. "But?"

Weishaupt was pleased to see the man sink into his chair. "Shall I recite your many blasphemies?"

Aemilius turned his face.

"More wine?" Weishaupt filled his own glass. "So, you see, my dear Aemilius, we know you well. And we are most grateful for your delivering the Strict Observance lodges to us. I can report that we are in utter control of at least six temples and are insinuated into many more. Beyond that, the Grand Orient in France is in complete alliance with our purposes. Are you pleased to hear this?"

Aemilius only stared.

"Hello? You have a question?"

The man cleared his throat. "Who are you?"

"Ah, finally!" Weishaupt leaned close. "For now, only eleven others know who I am. There had been twelve, but accidents do happen." He smirked.

Aemilius wiped a bead of perspiration suddenly rolling down his cheek.

"You have impressed Philo and have won the allegiance of Cato. And so, you are to be advanced into the rites of the Greater Mysteries and shall serve our noble Order as an Aeropagite." Weishaupt sat back. "Welcome to my Council. You should be pleased."

"*Your* Council? You are Basilius?"

Weishaupt laughed. "There is no Basilius. I am General Spartacus. And you shall never disclose my name to another without my permission."

Shaken, Aemilius rose. He offered his hand. "General Spartacus. I beg you to forgive me."

Seeing the man humbled before him filled Weishaupt with satisfaction. He stood. "And you thought I was simply a nuisance tagging along with Philo at Wilhelmsbad." He laughed again. "Indeed, I am your commander but together we shall save the world as equals. Now, sit."

Aemilius nearly collapsed into his chair. He poured a glass of wine and drank it down. "I am sorry for any disrespect in Wilhelmsbad—"

"Think nothing of it, Brother," said Weishaupt. "Now listen to me. With our present influence we are nearly positioned to strike. But our numbers must increase. Further, our higher degrees require more education. Therefore, today I seek your recommendations on more books, but also on plays and operas that communicate our primary vision: an enlightened government for the world, one properly ruled by the Order to make men happy."

"I have dreamt of this since I was a child." Aemilius took another drink. "Our enemies are many—and growing."

"And our friends plentiful, especially in France. You really must relax, Aemilius." Weishaupt felt suddenly better about the man. "And you have no reason to fear your confessional. It is locked away for none to see...so long as you remain loyal." Weishaupt picked a bit of lint off his knee. "And why would you not? As you say, the liberation of mankind is your dream."

"I was especially excited to read your five points," said Amelius. "We needed concise goals like these. They will change everything."

Weishaupt flinched, then quickly covered with a smile, his mind going to who could have shown him those. "Everything indeed." He studied the man. "But as you say, we do have enemies. Here in Bavaria, Duke Theodore is becoming a very real threat. And Cato is hearing more rumors about Jesuits spying under false names. But we also have strong allies. King Frederick still shares our vision in Prussia, the kings of Denmark, Sweden and Poland at least read what we want them to read. Our own dear Emperor Joseph is sympathetic to our ideas...what he knows of them. And most especially, France. May the Sun-god shine brightly over her."

"And the Americans?" asked Aemilius.

Weishaupt thought for a moment. "They were brave to challenge their king, and good work is being done for us there. At the moment, we are conspiring to take over masonic lodges in New York, Philadelphia and Virginia." He went on to ramble about other successes of his Order including his excitement over expansions into Britain, Poland, Italy and the good work of a Russian Illuminatus named Alexander Radischev.[3]

"I am confused on one thing, General Spartacus."

Weishaupt waited.

"Philo is a mystical man; Cato is a rationalist—a materialist if you will. Is the Order inclined to spirits and unseen forces, or to science?"

Weishaupt cleared his throat. It had taken him years to work through this same question. He looked squarely at Aemilius. "Must they exclude each other?"

Aemilius Bode wiped a large hand through his hair. "I think so, hence I incline toward the rational sciences—"

"As do I."

"But what of wisdom? Such a thing cannot be calculated or weighed."

Weishaupt raised a brow.

"Philo says that knowledge and wisdom are BOTH revealed by Nature. This accounts for the rational sciences as well as the immeasurable realities like happiness, beauty, love...and wisdom. He calls these the 'elemental *spirits*' of supreme Reason."

Annoyed, Weishaupt demurred. Philo always seemed to have a point.

Aemilius finished. "And so, he says that our disagreements are those of emphases *within* the service of Nature."

Weishaupt repressed his sudden vexation. Was Philo not surpassing him? He frowned. "We can linger in these discussions *after* we rule the happy confederation of mankind." But he was troubled for another reason. "Is there some risk that Philo could be confusing the brethren with this talk?"

Aemilius thought. "The average brother understands the divide. Among them are materialists who simply mock the Church and philosophers who argue to replace her. Cato is with the former; Philo with the latter. Yet, the average brother is aware that we all work toward the same end."

"So, in your opinion, we have no true divide?"

Aemilius hesitated.

"I feared as much. Philo's instruction must be to emphasize that we all have the same end." This was just the sort of excuse he needed to put a leash on Philo. Ever since Wilhelmsbad, the baron's shrewd influence over the Order had grown. Rumors of his ambitions had reached the professor's ears from more lips than he dared count. Weishaupt took a breath. "Tell me what other improvements we could make."

"Only what you have already said. Our churches need to be more precise on the matter of science and mysticism without disclosing too much for those still in the Nursery."

"Go on," said Weishaupt.

Aemilius relaxed. "But this takes so long."

Weishaupt remembered Kolmer. "Patience. We must be patient." He put a finger by the side of his face. "Also this: you must think of the Order as a dandelion. Our business is to plant ideas among enough men so that if ever scattered, the Great Plan cannot be destroyed. Our single plant will become a multiplying field."

The professor then stood and walked to a window. "Our is a most difficult task. The truths we protect are hidden within the great secrets of history but nearly extinguished by superstition. Yet the dream lives on, does it not? It is made safe by some sort of energy that cannot be quenched." He faced Aemilius. "Now, this: I insist that you insinuate Mr. Bergström of Regensburg. He has been carefully considered, and all distractions have been removed from his path."

"I have heard of him. But Philo is still suspicious. I am told he is a monk."

Weishaupt squeezed the arms of his chair. "I am in command, not Philo! Do you understand?"

CHAPTER FOURTEEN NOTES

1 **Johann Wolfgang von Goethe**, *Illuminatus Abaris* (1749-1832) was an extraordinarily influential German writer, philosopher, scientist and social critic. His many works include the well-known drama, *Faust*. Like other Illuminati and Freemasons, Goethe sought an enlightened future for mankind, free of nationalism and religious superstition. Called the 'Great Heathen' by some, he was beloved by the likes of Beethoven, Schiller and Weishaupt. Goethe found that symbolic expression (in his case, words) provided relief for the emotional losses he suffered in his youth. This led to his philosophical contributions toward an integration of science and art by way of imaginative processes. His membership in the Order provided Weishaupt with a great deal of credibility and philosophical direction, particularly in regard to ideas about dynamic, organic societies.

2 **Nicholas Bonneville** (1760 – 1828) was a French writer and philosopher deep in the stream of Illuminist assumptions. He would later support ideals such as communal ownership and a doctrine of love as the true religion of happiness. He was financially protected by the philosophical mathematician, d'Alembert and was a friend of Thomas Paine and the Illuminatus, Bode. As such, he learned to combine Illuminati purposes with the tools of publishing to inspire and support revolution by way of media. His future secret 'Society of the Friends of Truth' (aka *Cercle Social*—see Epilogue) would play a significant role in the French Revolution and elsewhere as one of the many offspring of the Illuminati.

3 **Alexander Radischev** (1749-1802) was a Russian nobleman credited with introducing Illuminism to the Freemasons of St. Petersburg. He would later write against the oppressive conditions of Russian society and lay the literary groundwork for future revolution.

"For by Christ all things were created, both in the heavens and on the earth, visible and invisible...and in Him all things hold together."

FROM THE BIBLE, *BOOK OF COLOSSIANS*

CHAPTER FIFTEEN

REGENSBURG
FEBRUARY, 1783

"THANK YOU FOR VISITING ME, HERR DOKTOR." ALEXANDER Horn rose from the tavern table and clasped hands with Dr. Karl von Eckartshausen. "It has been far too long. I missed you in Munich."

Karl shook the snow off his overcoat and sat on a hard chair across from the monk. "I had business in Vienna." He shouted for a pitcher of dark *Altbier* and black bread for both of them. "You do not look well, Brother Maurus."

Alexander was not well. He stared at Karl with dull brown eyes that revealed his exhaustion. His narrow face was especially drawn. He forced a smile but the charm was missing. "I am wonderfully happy, Karl."

"You are not."

Alexander's eye twitched. "Have you read the books I delivered?"

The charitable thirty-two-year-old academic folded his hands, fixing his discerning blue eyes on his younger friend. "I have." He waited.

Alexander wished the tray would arrive. Black bread and foamy ale would be the distraction he needed. He stared for a long moment into the man's face. Karl's normally ruddy cheeks were not the least bit pinked from the evening's cold air. What was wrong? "I think you are the one who is not well."

"My wife is in failing health."

"I am sorry." Alexander laid a hand on the man's forearm. "You still grieve the loss of your first wife, and now this."

Karl sighed.

He squeezed his friend's arm. The kindly scientist had become more than a buyer of books for the Munich library. Like Albert van Loon, he had become a reservoir of care, comfort and wisdom for Alexander that even rivalled Abbot Benedict.

"So, Brother Maurus, are you trustworthy?"

Surprised, Alexander sat back in his chair. "You do not know the answer?"

The ale-maid returned with the black bread and beer. Karl reached for a hard roll. "I have been approached by a deep circle within Lodge Theodore."

"The Minervals."

Karl raised a brow. "You know of them. Have you sold books to a Johann Bode?"

"Of Hamburg. No, but I hear that he travels with Dr. Weishaupt."

"Yes. Weishaupt. I perceive something is wrong with him."

"Why do you say that?"

"It is a feeling," said Karl.

Alexander blinked. "Well, he fascinates me. And he is good to me—"

"Because he buys books from you?"

Alexander grumbled. "Because he wants the world to be a better place. He and I share—"

"I suppose he only knows you as Mr. Bergström."

"He discovered me as Brother Maurus not long ago. But he believes that I am Mr. Bergström *pretending* to be Brother Maurus."

Karl tapped his finger on the warped table. "All rather confusing, even for me. Have a care. And the abbot?"

"He knows nothing of Mr. Bergström."

Karl took a long drink and dabbed his mouth with a napkin. "Does he know of Weishaupt and you?"

"No."

"Has he discovered your membership in the lodge?"

"No."

"I see. Now I understand why you look so lifeless. Secrets are exhausting."

Alexander set his jaw. "You do not look so lively yourself."

"Anyway, Johann Bode." Von Eckartshausen chewed, thinking. "He invited me to consider joining the Minervals and presented me with a long list of questions I've yet to complete. But he also asked about you and I gave him a positive report."

"You will join?"

Karl stared at his beer. "His invitation was persuasive, especially since they are using some of my philosophical books." He took a drink. "I think you should expect them to recruit you as well. I heard a mention of your American friend, Van Loon. I would expect these Minervals to spread their vision into the North American lodges."

Alexander smiled. "Van Loon is home in England." He went on to tell of Van Loon's British loyalties. Returning to the discussion at hand, he then said, "But tell me, what is the vision of these Minervals?"

Karl shrugged. "I am not really sure. As far as I can discern, they want to elevate Freemasonry to effect social policies. Make the temples more... meaningful."

Alexander's life returned. "Is Dr. Weishaupt a Minerval?"

"I do not know. The society only permits you to know the man who invites you in, and then the members of your immediate 'church.'"

"It is best the abbot knows nothing of this," said Alexander. "The idea of wheels within wheels would terrify him. He is already receiving letters about plots to murder the Pope from some secret society of revolutionaries somewhere."

Von Eckartshausen wrinkled his nose. "He would do better to keep an eye on the Jesuits. As far as I can see, the Minervals are men of letters, not poisons. I am told they want a world of virtue. It seems they are required to read a great deal. I overheard something of two authors: Adam Ferguson—who promotes a natural morality, and Gotthold Lessing. I am already familiar with Lessing's *Conversations for Freemasons*. Very controversial. He claims that the true desire of deep Freemasonry is to establish a world commonwealth." He took a drink. "That may be a purpose cloaked in our highest degrees. I would not know. But I doubt many actually would support this beyond a utopian theory. Nevertheless, it makes me wonder if the Minervals would sympathize."

Alexander was intrigued. "A single government for all mankind? But that would require a complete undoing of everything."

Karl waved the notion away. "Men's minds would have to be totally altered by an alien education. The idealists would have to indoctrinate the universities, the grammar schools and captivate every private tutor. They would have to control newspapers and publishing…even entertainment." He laughed. "Such a project would take hundreds of years, and it would have to be directed by spirits, not men!"

Alexander's mind raced. "But what if that really is the unreported purpose of the Craft?"

Karl shook his head. "The purpose of Freemasonry is to build better men who then build better societies—"

"And what if a better society is one of justice, of equality and brotherhood? A place without borders, without social layers, without religious differences—"

"Then you would have the Garden of Eden."

Thinking, Alexander's eyes narrowed. "But if that were the plan, then they would require a grand deception and finally force—"

"It shall never happen, and I doubt the Minervals—or the inside of the Craft—are about that business." Karl put a gentle hand on Alexander's shoulder. "Now, do you spend a great deal of time with Dr. Weishaupt?"

"Yes. He is wise, knowledgeable and eager to rescue mankind from its woes. He is a man who lives his convictions. I see no vice in him."

Karl listened, carefully. "And his excesses?"

Alexander shrugged. "We all have them."

"His arrogance?"

"Simply self-respect, maybe exaggerated a little."

"His heresies?"

"Misunderstandings."

Karl finished his beer. "I see. Well then, it seems he would make the perfect Minerval."

Alexander shrugged. "From what you say, he may share their vision of betterment, but he says nothing of them. I cannot imagine him following any man. He has trouble enough with the Grand Master at the lodge!"

Karl rose, chuckling. "I am delighted you have found a mentor. But study him, carefully, little brother, and watch for the fruit he bears."

MUNICH, BAVARIA
APRIL, 1783

"Come in," said Cato Zwack as he opened the door of his modest home. He stuck his broad head into the evening rain to be sure no one had followed. He pulled Adam Weishaupt into the room and locked the door. Wiping a large hand through his cropped hair, the lawyer snapped, "You're late. I have been stuck in here waiting with Philo."

Adam Weishaupt threw off his wet overcoat and laughed. He grunted to Philo, then searched the candle-lit room for wine. "Ah, there." He walked to a small serving table and helped himself to some French red. He thought Cato was nervous. "So, what is wrong with you?"

"We have problems."

Weishaupt was not interested in problems. He threw himself into a chair. "What sort of problems could we possibly have?" He cast a sideways glance at Philo now staring stoically into space.

Cato took a seat. "The Rosicrucians are mounting a real war against us—"

Weishaupt snickered. "Their silly superstitions cannot stand."

Philo cleared his throat and leaned forward. "General Spartacus, our secrets are leaking. Ever since that blasted sermon by Ignatius Franck the opposition has gained strength. We have revealed too much too quickly—"

"We?" Weishaupt abruptly stood. Insulted, he snarled. "We? No, not 'we.'" He aimed his forefinger at Philo. "YOU! I appointed YOU to design our insinuation. If it is failing it is on account of your stupidity!"

The baron stood, red-faced. "I follow YOUR commands—"

"How dare you blame me!" Weishaupt spun toward Cato. "Tell me what happened."

"A Minerval in Wetzlar has betrayed us. He revealed what he knows about us to the masonic lodge. The Grand Master spread the news and our church has been shuttered. An investigation for treason and heresy is underway by the magistrate."

Stunned, Weishaupt stormed about the room. "I thought we already fully controlled the Wetzlar Lodge! Philo, find this traitor. This is your mess." He paused. "And order that masonic temple to be burned. We must send a message and quickly."

Philo's eyes slid to Cato's and back. "Burned?"

"Yes!"

Cato then added, "Someone also betrayed us to Wöllner."

"Wöllner? The Margrave of Brandenburg?"[1]

Cato nodded. "He is also a preacher and a mad dog for his Christ. He has a large audience within the Rosicrucians. This is not good news."

Standing stiffly, Philo added, "I know him. He is an eloquent preacher able to stir the idiots."

Weishaupt scowled. "Two betrayals and now this." He began to pace again. "Wöllner. Why did you not tell me about him before?"

Philo cast another anxious glance toward Cato. "Our information is fresh, General."

Weishaupt was not so sure. He had been suspecting the baron of undermining his authority. He eyed Philo. "Is there anything else?"

The slender aristocrat flushed. "Ja. I was going to tell you this evening."

Was he?

"It seems Wöllner has just acquired control of the Lodge of Three Globes in Berlin.[2] He informed them that we are atheists and traitors who deserve the gallows, though we do not know what evidence he uses for this charge."

At the word, 'gallows,' Weishaupt chilled. He poured a fresh glass of wine and drank it, then another. The professor looked carefully at his two men. "You must not be discouraged. We are now more than one-thousand strong. Of these, more than two-hundred have risen into the highest degrees. These are our iron soldiers, committed to obey for the greater good. Our network is a growing web reaching into all of Europe."

His words stirred confidence in his own belly. "No, we've naught to fear. Among our benefactors are now the Dukes of Weimar, Gotha, and Brunswick. We have Von Dalberg, the governor of Erfurt. We have Counts Metternich and Brigida, Krisel and Banff! The chancellor of Hungary is ours, the Grand Master of Transylvania, Count Stadion—the ambassador to London, and our own minister of public education. All ours." The professor forced a smile. "This is to say nothing of Karl, Landgrave of Hesse[3] who is funneling Rothchild[4] money our way. And then there's our dear genius, Goethe." Weishaupt clapped. "You see? All will be well!"

It was then that Cato reached into his vest and retrieved an internal communique of the Rosicrucians. He handed it to Weishaupt with his face to the floor. "I am sorry, Spartacus, but there is one last thing."

Grinding his teeth, the professor snatched it away. *More?* He proceeded to read from a pamphlet, *The Illuminati Unmasked*. He began to stammer. "Look here...they say we are using Freemasonry to undermine Christianity...and are working to overthrow kings in favor of a new world commonwealth." Paled, Weishaupt turned to the others. "This is very specific. We have a third Judas, no doubt in our high degrees."

Weishaupt returned his eyes to the circular, now fearing he might find names, *his* name. He finally said, "At least they do not know *who* we are." His relief showed. He dropped the circular and walked to a wall where he stared at a bucolic water color of an inviting little farm cradled in the Franconia countryside. He thought of Friederika. He finally took a breath and turned. "Our cause is just, no matter the means. The spirits of history have destined us to rescue mankind. Our enemies must be destroyed. So, what do we do?"

Cato stepped close. "First, we find and execute both traitors."

Philo immediately objected. "We must have a care to not frighten away those yet training in the Nursery. Somehow, we must instill respect without terror."

Weishaupt raised his hand. "No. You are wrong, Philo. We need to instill a deep reluctance—even terror—in potential traitors. This will make our loyal brethren feel safer. If they do not feel safe, how shall they be expected to do more than talk of change. Why would they dare do what our vision requires?"

Philo sniffed. "Like forgeries, slanders, even assassinations——"

Cato interrupted. "I must access the chest."

Weishaupt's mind ran to the contents of Cato's chest. He wiped his brow. Vials of poisons, vanishing inks, the recipes for pestilences, powders for abortions—was it all really coming to this? He turned away. "Find our Judas' and do what you must do. They took oaths, after all."

"I have two men in mind for the hunt," said Cato.

Weishaupt thought for a long moment. "As far as Wöllner, remember that a ruined reputation may be as good as a corpse, after all. And it does not draw as much attention. Everyone believes that preachers are secret sinners. Make some inquiries. Ask about young women seen in his company. But if you must, invent some hideous sin and send a letter to one of our newspapers in Prussia."

Weishaupt turned to Philo. "You have proven yourself good at designing the sword, but it is Cato who will wield it."

CHAPTER FIFTEEN NOTES

1 **Johann Christoph von Wöllner** (1732-1800) was the Margrave of Brandenburg, a pastor, an economist and influential politician in Prussia. He was curious about the mystical arts such as alchemy, and sympathetic to the European Enlightenment. Concerned to make a difference in the world, he was an active Freemason and Rosicrucian, but became a champion for conservative Christianity against the Illuminati.

2 Founded in Berlin, the Lodge of Three Globes was the oldest of eight masonic 'Grand Lodges' in Germany, thus having jurisdiction over smaller lodges throughout Prussia.

3 **Prince Karl, Landgrave of Hesse-Kassel**, *Illuminatus Aaron* (1744-1836) was a key player for the Illuminati. Prince Karl governed a number of Danish and German principalities, was an occultist, and active Freemason immersed in teachings involving the conjuring of spirits. In 1773, Karl founded the important *Rite of Les Philalèthes* as an occult academy within a Parisian masonic lodge. He went on to develop an influential network of occultists and theosophists throughout Europe.

4 The Rothschild banking dynasty was founded by **Mayer Rothschild** (1744-1812). Some believe him to have been the principal financier of the Illuminati, but this is an unproven claim. Nevertheless, he is known to have been deeply involved with individual Illuminati like Prince Karl of Hesse noted above. Mayer's sons expanded the family's interests into France, Britain, Russia, the United States and other countries, making the dynasty a powerful player in global affairs for generations.

"Weishaupt seems to be an enthusiastic philanthropist. He is among those who believe in the indefinite perfectibility of man...The means he proposes are to enlighten men, to correct their morals and inspire them with benevolence."

THOMAS JEFFERSON

CHAPTER SIXTEEN

APRIL, 1783
INGOLSTADT

.

A RISING TIDE OF ANGRY ROSICRUCIANS WAS NOW a genuine threat, not only to the Order but also to Adam Weishaupt's own neck. He could not shake the terrors that now dogged him every night. He further imagined bitter Jesuits pulling strings behind the scenes.

Home was no solace. His deceased wife, Afra, had born him two sons and five daughters. One of his favored daughters had died mysteriously after he took her on an unwise stroll amongst the poor of Munich. Another daughter died from a fever that many said was on account of his neglect. The remaining girls seemed frail, and his sons failed to inspire his interest.

Was the universe punishing him? It seemed so. On most nights, dread began to rise as soon as the sun set. French brandy helped a little, English gin a bit more. But no sooner would he climb into bed than his mind's eye would be filled with the specter of Afra's face. Pale images of his dead daughters would follow. Before the bells of prime, he would then see an executioner. A rope would be fitted around his neck.

Deep into this particularly fitful night, Adam could bear the terror no longer. He left his bed and crossed his room. He retrieved a new timepiece—an expensive Breguet pocket-watch that Aemilius Bode had presented him just weeks before. He opened it in the light of a single candle. Three o'clock. He wiped the perspiration from his face and stared at the likeness inscribed on the closure. Aemilius told him it was the goddess of wisdom, Isis. He then held the watch close to his ear, hoping the steady tick-tock might center him. It did not.

Isis was useless.

He reached for his gin, then raised his candle. It cast an odd shadow over his shoulder. He chilled and threw on a woolen robe. Grasping the single candlestick in one hand and a bottle of gin in the other, he hurried downstairs to his library where he hastened to light a six-pronged candelabra atop a mahogany table. Holding the crown of light before him, the professor then made his way to stand at his wall of books: Plato, Plutarch, d'Holbach, Machiavelli and hundreds more. His eyes swept along the titles.

Where might he find peace among them?

Weishaupt heard a creak overhead. "What?" He looked up to see a dragon-like shadow hovering on the high ceiling. Unnerved, he drank quickly from his bottle. Wanting his fingers to feel something, he snatched *Candide* from its place. But Voltaire's great work suddenly seemed pathetically impotent. The professor's mind then returned him to child ghouls approaching from dark corners. His daughters? "Out! Out!"

The room cleared, he shuddered, took another drink and then reached for his books once more. He dragged his hand along their leathery spines until he fixed his sight on Adam Smith's, *The Theory of Moral Sentiments.*[1] "What useless optimism on a night like this…"

Anxious, Weishaupt glanced upward. The dragon had moved to the far side. He drank more gin and ran to light every candle in the room.

He returned to his books, but could Helvétius[2] shield him from his wife's ghost? Could Christoph Murr's[3] engravings chase the images of corpses? What use for David Hume's[4] fine logic from the gallows? Only Dr. Mesmer [5] gave him hope. Was *he* on to something?

The professor heard a step, then another. "Kolmer?" Frightened, he dared raise his candles. Nothing. No one. Trembling, Weishaupt sank slowly to his knees, wanting very much to pray.

Sunlight awakened Weishaupt from his awkward position on the hard floor. Confused, he stared into the struggling flames of those few candles that had not yet died in their own wax. He climbed to his feet and walked slowly to his desk. He faced the well-worn oak top, thinking. *What is this all about? These terrors, these visions?* A gnawing feeling crept through him. *An odd presence is at work. Something more powerful than reason.*

The professor stared into blank space for a time, and then began to pace the floor of his library with his hands clasped behind his back. He finally plucked *The Emerald Tablet* [6] off a shelf and began to read as he walked. Engrossed, he eventually sat and lost himself in Hermes for the next hour, finishing by reading aloud:

"'The father of perfection for the whole world is here.

Its force is above all force

The sun is its father, the moon its mother...'"

Finished, he closed his eyes. *Forces. Yes. These are the 'something else' that Lucius hinted at all those years ago in the Frankfurt coach.* He stood. *Should not my highest degrees incorporate this insight?* Unlike Philo, however, Weishaupt would not be considering modern mysticism for his Order. No. He had no need for charlatans and conjurers. Let the Rosicrucians and alchemists have those fools. Instead, he would return to his own early interest in the deepest secrets of the ancients. *Their* spiritual philosophies could be worth imbedding.

This idea pleased the professor. He now believed that his nights of terror may have been meant to reveal something that his purely materialist friends did not see—that reality was more than logic and far more than what could be deduced by the five senses.

This unexpected insight cleared the professor's mind. He adjusted his nightshirt. Everything was suddenly *right*. Clarity. Balance. Wisdom...Forces.

For all that Tuesday and through the night that followed, Adam Weishaupt dug through his books on the ancients. In so doing, he unearthed the esoteric blocks of stone that he now realized his Order had needed all along for the world they were destined to build.

Just before dawn on Wednesday, the exhausted professor then retrieved a stick of charcoal from his desk. Considering all of this, be began to sketch the Giza pyramid like he had done so often as a child. He stared at his drawing. About a hundred years earlier the English astronomer, John Greaves, had postulated that the Great Pyramid contained the dimensions of the earth, and its mysterious mathematics were hidden messages. "More than science," Weishaupt muttered.

The professor then began to draw stars. The mysteries and messages of Giza included alignment with stars of consequence. "There is something to all of this. Exactly what I do not know, but something..."

Weishaupt sat back. "But Giza is the key." He strained. "It is a monument to man's rescue of himself, like Babel." He leaned forward and traced the sides of his pyramid with his finger, following them upward. "Look and see. Rising to the sun; connecting the earth to the Source. Of course." He could feel his skin flush with excitement. "A symbol of natural man reclaiming his perfection. This is the message of the pyramid! The Americans knew it all along."

He poured himself some apple juice that a servant had tip-toed to him in the early hours. He walked to a window and stared at the lamplighters now dowsing Ingolstadt's street lanterns. "They extinguish false light because the true light is rising. And I bear its torch."

Enlivened, Weishaupt returned to his seat and tapped his fingers. Staring into a mirror he said, "Eden is ours for the taking." He then stared at the unfinished top of the pyramid. "It has been waiting millennia for its capstone."

A thought overwhelmed him. "And *I* am that capstone." He wiped his eyes. "Kolmer..." Barely able to contain himself, he grabbed his charcoal stick and hastily added the triangular capstone to his sketch. Inside the triangle, he drew the Order's circled dot. "By the gods, I understand." He pounded his desk. "Why is no one here to witness this moment!"

The professor ripped a blank paper from a drawer. He dipped his quill and began to scribble notes to himself like a man gone mad. A servant entered to deliver the professor hard cheese, bread and morning coffee. Ignoring her, Weishaupt pulled out more paper. Yes, this is what he must do.

For the whole of that day and into the night he wrote recitations, definitions, explanations and rituals for new degrees of his Order. These would be the highest degrees, the ones that opened the Order to the wisdom of the stars— the degrees reserved only for the most enlightened.

Covered in candlelight, Weishaupt finally opened his watch. Midnight. He wrote a final note to himself, an organizing summary of sorts.

I am finished and it is good, very good. To achieve a happy Oneness, we shall return mankind to its primitive state where neither private property or marriage divides. In the coming Eden, free men and women shall know what is best for themselves, and thus be gods. No boundaries shall exist between nations. No kingdoms, no families, no religion. All things are to be one. Mankind shall be happy and governed by the enlightened elite of a world commonwealth ACCORDING TO THE WISDOM OF THE ANCIENTS.

His purpose matured, Weishaupt staggered to his bed and slept soundly.

1 MAY, 1783

Just after a bright dawn, the professor was awakened by his servant's clinking of dishes in the downstairs dining room. He dressed, slowly. This was the seventh anniversary of his Order. He smiled to think of it. After all, the enlightenment of the past two days had finally delivered the Illuminati to its perfection.

Supremely content, Weishaupt made his way to the table and found his secretary, Socrates Lanz, seated and drunk from the night before. He was a square-headed, baggy-eyed, forty-eight-year-old originally from Freising which lay about two days south of Ingolstadt. Formerly a priest, he had a deep affection for spirits.

Weishaupt sighed. "What is it?"

Socrates handed the professor a coded letter from Cato Zwack, one signed with the Order's circled dot. He deciphered it, quickly. Weishaupt was pleased. "Good. Cato reports that the lies about Wöllner are taking effect."

Socrates handed him another letter.

Weishaupt deciphered that one as well. *One Judas has departed this world. Two more to go.*

"Your response to Cato, General?" Socrates helped himself to bread and butter, and a tankard of beer. The man was ferociously committed to the plans of the Order, and over the past two years he had proven himself to be loyal.

Weishaupt turned to look through lace curtains at the fresh Spring day. "Just tell him I am very happy."

Socrates snorted. "Happy? You? That is music to me."

"Ja." He turned. "I am happy. And you would be happier if you did not drink so much. Alcohol has a way of lubricating tongues." Weishaupt moved closer. "And wagging tongues—"

Socrates set his tankard down.

"Is there anything else?"

"Philo reports that your name is now widely known as the invisible hand."

"What?" Fear surged through Weishaupt. His throat tightened. He sat down, staring. "And?"

"That is all he said. I suspect the Rosicrucians are spreading this."

The professor could feel rough hemp around his neck. "My God." He tried to take a deep breath. "Summon Cato. Burn anything we have that could support a charge of treason. Not my books, though. They are just books. But I have letters." His name in the wind? But how could it *not* be? Seven years is a long time for men to keep a secret. He drew a deep breath.

Yet, what had he actually *done*? Teach men to think? Inspire men to change the world?

Would a judge warrant the gallows for these?

Weishaupt relaxed a little. His hidden purposes were veiled in symbols, sacred rituals and secret conversations. None of that would serve as evidence unless his upper degrees conspired against him.

But what of those necessary extremes for which he was being blamed? Forgery? Murder?

Unprovable.

"Wait, Socrates. Do not burn anything." He stared at his bread. "On the contrary, the time may have come for me to step into the light, after all." Weishaupt set his jaw. "Perhaps we should thank the Rosicrucians. Tell Cato to tighten our security, everywhere. We cannot have defectors creating trouble, especially if I step into the light. Do you understand?"

Socrates nodded.

"Now, I would like to eat in silence and take my walk. I expect you to be on your way when I return."

Before long, the professor was striding under sunshine past the familiar seven towers of the Kreutzor gate to enter the path of the green garden belting Ingolstadt. On this very day seven years ago, he had walked this same path with his original five initiates. "Seven years...the number of perfection," he said aloud.

The thirty-five-year-old professor tipped his tricorn to a passing couple. He thought the woman was beautiful and so he turned to study her as she passed. He would like to have a woman like that. The professor then bent his thoughts to his upcoming marriage. He would wed his deceased wife's younger sister, Anna Marie Sausenhofer von Eichstaat—a twenty-two-year-old, plain-looking blonde. He had calculated her to be sturdy enough to raise his surviving children, but he was somewhat concerned whether she could satisfy his natural desires. And did she have the brains to serve his destiny?

He then let his mind wander to his brother's widow. "Sofia could do both," he muttered. He had visited Sofia in her new Munich home twice since his brother's death. He liked the way her fair hair curled toward the throat of her long neck. Why not marry that sister-in-law instead of this one?

Weishaupt waved a squirrel off a bench, sat and closed his eyes. He let the sun warm his face and returned his thoughts to what should matter most. His eyes abruptly popped open. "Obelisks. We shall erect obelisks everywhere. They unite the heavens and earth; they point to the center of the circle." He shaded his face and squinted toward the sun. "Who knows what energies ride them?" Smiling, he imagined a great obelisk erected in Ingolstadt, one dedicated to him. "Ja. Maybe this really is the hour to unveil myself." He smiled. "By Christ, we need to get this revolution underway."

Lodge Theodore should have been a sanctuary for Adam Weishaupt. Many, perhaps most of its brothers were also Illuminati. Only Aeropagites like Philo von Knigge and Cato Zwack knew for certain that the professor was the puppeteer behind the curtain, but the Rosicrucians had spread their claims all over Europe. Tonight, the temple would certainly be filled with suspicion and clever questions. Who was the true commander, Basilius or Spartacus? Was Weishaupt either one?

He needed to decide whether he would answer or not. Was he ready to be unveiled?

Deep within, Weishaupt wanted nothing more than to march to the east wall of the masonic temple and shove the Worshipful Master to the floor. He could drop himself in the Oriental Chair and announce for all the world that he, Dr. Adam Weishaupt, was General Spartacus, founder of the Bavarian Order of the Illuminati!

But would that be wise?

So, on this otherwise pleasant evening, the professor stood at the door of the temple reluctant to summon the porter. If exposed, would the duke arrest him? He raised his hand to the knocker and paused. Considering how his forgeries had embarrassed the duke, would that not be likely? And how far might the despicable Jesuits go? He lowered his hand.

A moment later, Weishaupt shuffled away from the door to the thin cover of a barely budded walnut tree to think. A pigeon switched branches above, hitting Weishaupt's shoulder with a falling column of slick droppings. "Christ, almighty." He pulled a kerchief from his vest, then quickly realized that the pigeon's gift was enough excuse for him to abandon his arrival at the temple. Relieved, he called for a city cab and threw open the door to a single-yoke hackney with a broken spring. He shouted an address to the driver.

Within the hour Weishaupt arrived at his address and dismounted. The carriage pulled away leaving the professor with one boot placed squarely in a pile of green horse manure. He seethed, scolding the heavens with a string of profanities. He marched to a heavy door and slammed the brass knocker. Waiting, he dragged his sole along the boot wipe. Weishaupt then quickly adjusted his wig, his breeches and the sleeves of his coat. "Where the devil—"

A servant girl opened the door. "Herr Doktor, *wilkommen*," she said.

Saying nothing, Weishaupt swept by the girl and entered the home of Sofia Weishaupt. He kicked off his boots and tossed his hat.

CHAPTER SIXTEEN NOTES

1 **Adam Smith** (1723-1790) A Scottish philosopher whose works included an integration of economics with his observations of human behavior. His work was mandatory reading for initiates. Key to the Illuminati was his claim that humans are naturally interested in the happiness of others. This supported Weishaupt's optimistic insistence of the noble condition of primitive mankind. His optimism about a free society motivated many at the founding of the United States.

2 **Claude Adrien Helvétius** (1715-1771) A French philosopher who explained man's faculties as merely physical sensations. His work was used by the Order to challenge religious thought.

3 **Christoph Gottlei von Murr** (1733-1811) A German publisher who reproduced art discovered from the ancient world. The Illuminati idealized the wisdom and order of the ancients and so used their art to replace anything representing a traditional European worldview.

4 **David Hume** (1711-1776) A Scottish philosopher who made important contributions to the Enlightenment, one of which was the notion that science could meet metaphysics in an idea like a World Soul within which the universe effectively causes itself. He believed economics would ultimately control populations. He, too, was mandatory reading for Illuminati.

5 **Franz Mesmer** (1734-1815) was a German astronomer from whom we get the term 'mesmerize.' He claimed that nature operates through a flow of energy. Mesmer's work helped support a monistic view of the universe in which Reality was a self-contained unity. As mentioned elsewhere, such monism provided an alternative to Christianity.

6 *The Emerald Tablet* was an ancient esoteric work that was attributed to Hermes Trismegistus. It supposedly contains the essential secret wisdom of the ages.

"I will destroy the power of the wise…Has not God made foolish the wisdom of the world?"

FROM THE BIBLE, *BOOK OF I CORINTHIANS*

CHAPTER SEVENTEEN

A HALF-HOUR LATER, WEISHAUPT AND SOFIA WERE STANDING in a parlor behind a closed door with crystal glasses in hand. "I had no idea you were suffering so, my dear," said the professor. He poured Sofia a second glass of a fine Bordeaux and a third for himself. "First your husband, and now your sister lying near death? Tush. You must feel so very alone."

Sofia dabbed her gray-blue eyes. The young widow moved close to her brother-in-law and took his hand.

At the touch, Weishaupt could feel his hunger rise. "I am here with you. We suffer together."

Sofia was an intelligent woman of high culture. She squeezed Weishaupt's hand. "I so fear for my dear sister, Adam. I cannot sleep. This is more than I can bear."

"You need to receive comfort before you can offer it, my dear. Otherwise you will become a mere shell of a woman. That would be a supreme tragedy." Weishaupt lingered over Sofia's very German face. High cheekbones, fair skin, intelligent eyes. He thought of Friederika for a moment. That young woman was the archetype of the primitive humanity to which he thought Sofia should be returned. "I suppose you have priests praying over her?"

Sofia nodded.

Weishaupt thought as much. *Imprisoned by superstition.* He glanced about the room. His brother had provided well for her. He had grabbed far more than his fair share of the common wealth. Sofia's hand moved within his. He tightened his grip and smiled at her. "You are so beautiful."

Sofia blushed.

Weishaupt released her so that he might fill their glasses once again. "I always thought of you as the most beautiful woman in Munich."

She tilted her head, drinking. Face flushed, she smiled. "Is Anna Marie beautiful?"

"Who?"

"Anna Marie, your betrothed." Sofia tittered and emptied her glass.

"Ha!" Brows raised, Weishaupt refilled her glass. "The world goes away when I am with you." He walked toward a painting. "Your grandfather?"

She joined him, standing close. "Ja."

Weishaupt surveyed the image of a man stuffed into a decadent French suit. His hands sported four rings; his bonnet was pinned by a huge emerald held in a gaudy setting. A golden crucifix weighed heavy on one lapel. *Another world criminal*, thought the professor. He took Sofia's hand and kissed it. He then led her to a plush, eight-legged couch.

They said nothing for several minutes, each savoring their Bordeaux. Sofia spoke first, slightly slurring her words. "Nectar from the Gironde." She drained her glass.

Weishaupt smiled. He then followed Sofia's shapely young form as she curled herself into a soft ball against the arm of the couch. *Delicious*, he thought.

Sofia's eyes filled. "This has all been too much."

Weishaupt slid close. He leaned over her. "I understand." He handed her a kerchief.

Sofia wiped her eyes. "She is going to die."

"I cannot imagine what you are suffering, my dear."

Sofia lowered her face.

Weishaupt feared she might be withdrawing. No. He took her hand, firmly. He kissed her fingers and began to hum a soothing melody. His appetite increased.

He would have her.

And in the having he would strip her of her attachment to the illusions that enslaved her. He would be her blessing. The little professor began to rest the weight of his body atop hers. Sensing resistance, he recited a portion of a not-yet published poem from his famous new Illuminatus, Goethe:

> "'And the rough boy picked the rose,
> Little red rose on the heath
> And the red rose fought and pricked.
> Yet she cried in vain,
> And had to let it happen.'"

"I do not understand this," said Sofia.

"A friend of mine wrote it. He calls it, *Little Rose on the Field*. You see, the boy is in love. The object of his desire resists, but she surrenders in the end. His love proved worthwhile. It served them both." He kissed Sofia's neck.

She stiffened.

"Your very presence means so much to me."

"Adam, please——"

He put a finger under her chin and turned her face toward his. "You are so beautiful."

"I do not think so, Adam," said Sofia. "Please——"

Weishaupt kept his face close to hers. "I am lonely and very sad. And you are sad." He stared into her eyes, now wide. "You have awakened what is natural within us both. I desire you and you desire me. I see it in your soul."

"Stop. I will tell everyone." She pushed against him.

Weishaupt held her fast. "There is not a man in all of Bavaria that would believe you. Not even your father. Do you see a witness?"

Sofia struggled to breathe.

Weishaupt swept his eyes toward a statue of the Virgin Mary. "There? Ah, but she cannot speak. Pity." He pressed his body hard against hers and reached for the hem of her gown. "Now, little rose of the heath. I know what is best for us all."

Alexander Horn ran from the garden throwing his sleeveless scapular aside. Barefooted and dirty, he hurried toward his American friend now dismounting at the monastery's Schottenportal. "Albert! I have missed you."

"And I you." Albert van Horn stretched his hand forward. "I bring news from London." The man was perspiring within his high-collared *habit de ville*. He wiped his face with a kerchief, then removed an oatmeal-colored canvas bundle bound in twine along with a small leather satchel. "Nothing urgent. Perhaps over some food?"

Alexander escorted his friend to the guest foyer where he ordered beer, sausages and bread for them both. After hastily washing his hands, he rushed through the necessary courtesies to finally ask, "So, what news?" He pointed Van Loon to a table.

"Yes. Well first, I have been transferred to a new apartment near the Diet, but I must share it with two other agents from London." He lowered his voice. "I am afraid you cannot use my room any longer." He then tossed the bundle to Alexander. "I packed Mr. Bergström's clothing inside."

Alexander looked around. "I will have to hide this well. Can you not hold it another day or two?"

"I have already moved. It would be better for you to keep it." Albert leaned close, grinning. "Maybe Julianna can keep it for you?"

Alexander turned his eyes away. "I do not think so."

"No?"

The monk could barely summon the words. "She is married."

"Married? How did I not know this?"

Alexander struggled. "I never before said it aloud."

"Married to whom?"

"Baron von Gumppenberg from Frankfurt-am-Main." Alexander wanted to vomit.

Van Loon thought, carefully. "Ferdinand? He is a prince of Thurn and Taxis, and an admirer of Weishaupt—"

"Weishaupt?" Alexander tried to calculate the connection.

"I am sorry, my friend." Van Loon reached into the leather satchel and retrieved a pile of writings. "And anything about Weishaupt should trouble you. I have been in London for the last six months. Before that I was in Berlin, and then spent a month with old friends in Paris. Everywhere his name comes up." He glanced from side to side as if someone might be listening. "You must read all of these things."

Alexander focused on Van Loon. He knew the man was rarely this animated, nor this flushed for that matter. "What is this about?"

"Weishaupt is confirmed as the head of the serpent. He has been exposed. And I have information damning him and his Order of the Illuminati as heretical and treasonous. They are the wheel within the wheel of the Craft all over Germany and now beyond. They are also allies to French revolutionaries."

Alexander scratched his ear. "Weishaupt? Serpent? And this 'Order of the Illuminati—"

"Aye. Serpent."

Alexander shook his head. "No. This cannot be. But how does he know Gumppenberg—"

"No? What makes you so sure?"

"He would have told me if he were a member, let alone its leader!"

"You think so? I think you have been duped."

The monk blinked.

"We had it all wrong about the Minervals. They are only low degrees of this Order. All their secrets are coming out. You doubt me?"

"Ja. I do. Weishaupt is a good man. But—"

"Hear me. The Freemasons of Berlin do not doubt any of it. They are up in arms. The Pitts in England do not doubt. They are advising the Crown to raise the alarm against the Order generally and Weishaupt in particular. I have been instructed to use my position in Regensburg to gather information." He took a long drink of beer. "Members…especially from the Minerval degrees…are coming forward to confess."

"You mean men of low degrees who have betrayed their oaths? Their testimony is not credible."

Albert sat back, astonished. "I do not understand you."

"This is why the betterment of the world can only happen in secret. You and others are too quick to close down free thinking."

"Too quick? Not quick enough! And free-thinking? No, this is indoctrination. This is revolution for the sake of some mysterious upper strata."

"A revolution of ideas? So what? That is what makes history happen."

Van Loon took another drink and wiped froth from his lips. "This is not what I expected. Weishaupt has bewitched you. Think of the books he buys. Think of the teaching he offers you. Who are his friends? An aristocrat, a lawyer and publisher; they go by Philo, Cato, Aemilius. All Illuminati. And there are strangers from Berlin and Prague sneaking around the university every day, assigned to take on false identities in order to make introductions."

Alexander shook his head. "No one has bewitched me. What is wrong with wanting to be happy, safe and free?"

"Nothing."

"This is all I seek, Albert. Is it a crime for me?"

"No."

"Then why a crime for them?"

Albert said nothing.

"And how does Gumppenberg—"

"He is involved. I was a spy and I know how to sort these things. Trust me."

The monk bit his lip. "It just cannot be true. Dr. Weishaupt is a good man. He would not deceive me."

"You do not understand." Van Loon's tone had a sudden bite. "These men are *not* good men. They plot to overthrow the world as we know it. Their vision is not good, nor is it natural to the state of mankind. Theirs is a vision of ambitious despots. Some say they are doing the bidding of Lucifer."

To that, Alexander rolled his eyes.

"What they teach is the temptation that has seduced men in every age. The self-rule of men. It is that simple, except they enlarge it into a vision of some new order for the whole world."

Alexander stared at the papers piled in front of him, thinking. "Have you evidence that Weishaupt or this Order have actually *done* anything? Have good kings fallen? Have evil despots risen? Proof of forgeries, murders, blackmail?"

"Not yet."

"So, you simply fear ideas and slander good men?"

Albert fumbled with the buttons of his waistcoat. "The serpent deceived Eve with an *idea*. Look what happened—"

Alexander thumbed through a pamphlet of Van Loon's. "See here. This argument is from the Rosicrucians. They are rivals with their own motives." He picked up another pamphlet and read it, quickly. "And these charge Deism?" He laughed and returned to his seat. "Weishaupt is no Deist. He attends a Lutheran church. Franklin is a Deist. He and Washington and the American leaders are Deists. You would be right to worry about them. But the Illuminati? Ridiculous."

Van Loon thought for a long moment. "I fear both. Deep Freemasonry bends the knee to some unnamed Great Architect of the universe. The Illuminati worship the universe itself." He stabbed a sausage with his knife. "I should tell you that I have resigned my membership in the Craft on account of all this."

"You overreact, my friend. And that is always dangerous."

Albert answered, slowly. "I am not afraid of them. But hear me, to understand your journey, you must know who guides your steps. Think of the symbols in the lodge."

Alexander looked away.

Van Loon ate more sausage. "Remember when I furnished books to you? Books you had orders for?"

"And?" Alexander returned his gaze. "They are mostly by philosophers, educators and historians with notions of bettering the world—"

"But lovers of Voltaire who would have outlawed religion—"

Appearing suddenly, Abbot Benedict interrupted the pair. "Ha ha! Mr. Albert van Loon, spy extraordinaire." He winked. "What brings thee to our humble monastery?"

Annoyed, Albert adapted. He stood and bowed to the graying abbot. "I come to update Brother Maurus on the state of the world." He smiled.

"Ah, the state of the world," said Benedict.

"Would there a better place to ever be,

I would gladly go and see."

The abbot's eyes then rested on the papers. "And what are these?"

Van Loon proceeded to tell the abbot all that he had told Alexander. Troubled, Abbot Benedict began lecturing the walls. He then turned on Alexander. "Weishaupt! I always knew he was a devil! I told you to stop selling those books. Now I utterly forbid it."

"But—"

The abbot reddened. "But?"

Alexander scowled at Van Loon. What would 'Mr. Bergström' do now? These wild speculations were leaving him in a fine mess. He thought of the large order he was supposed to deliver to Weishaupt within a fortnight. "These rumors are just that. And my sales are funding our library."

"I no longer care. It is finished," barked Benedict. "We shall not be selling more of Lucifer's deceptions. Albert is simply confirming what I am hearing elsewhere."

"But what is proven?" challenged Alexander. "With respect, Father Abbot, the testimony of doubtful witnesses is all we have."

"Enough!" The abbot was red-faced. "Enough, Brother Maurus. Look again at the book lists. It all comes together." He laid a heavy hand on Alexander's shoulder. "There are no neutral ideas in this world. Only ideas that either nurture or destroy. Brother Maurus, thou shalt not sell another book to these evil men. They may be free to read them, but you must no longer be an accomplice. And one more protest shall merit thine confinement within our walls. Prayer and reflection might do you well. Do you understand?"

Alexander chafed.

"Well?"

How do I get out of this disaster? Alexander measured his words with a bowed head. "Father Abbot...em...Brother Maurus submits." Face to the floor, he licked his lips. "Brother Maurus shall sell no book, pamphlet or writing that is not approved by thee."

The abbot wrinkled his nose. "Why do you say it like that?"

He lifted his face. "Now you even object to the words I choose?"

Benedict sighed. "Very well, then, my dear little brother.

May Heaven shine brightly
And the air smell sweet
And the music of birds
Follow thy feet."

Softened, the abbot put his hand on Alexander's head kindly, and mumbled something. He then spotted the canvas bundle on the floor. "Yours, Brother Maurus?"

Alexander felt a start. "Eh?"

The abbot pointed to the bundle. "What is this?"

Albert intercepted. "Ah, pardon. It is mine." He bent over and lifted Alexander's clothing out of reach. "Items for the laundry."

*"We must acquire the direction of education, the professorial chair and
the pulpit. We must bring our opinions into fashion by every art."*

ILLUMINATI DEGREE OF PRESBYTER

CHAPTER EIGHTEEN

AUGUST, 1783
REGENSBURG

ALEXANDER HORN WAS LONELIER THAN HE COULD BEAR. His Julianna was forever
gone and his recounting that fact to Albert van Loon last month had torn open
the wound that had barely begun to heal.

Five months prior, Julianna had, indeed, married Baron Ferdinand
Augustus von Gumppenberg and was now removed to his estate just outside of
Frankfurt-am-Main. A Prussian diplomat thought that she was already pregnant. Alexander had also learned that the baron was close to key players of
the world stage, including Prince Karl, the Landgrave of Hesse-Kassel. What
he did not know was that both Ferdinand and the Landgrave were champions
of the Illuminati and in league with Weishaupt to destroy the Bavarian Duke
Theodore. Nor did Alexander know that Julianna was being recruited by Cato
Zwack for the women's lodge.

It was better the poor monk remained ignorant of these things. For months,
his nights had been filled with tortuous images of Julianna with her husband.
After his six o'clock morning prayers and his Chapter instructions, the monk
would walk to the monastery's fish pond and stare at his reflection. There he
would mumble to himself all manner of condemnation. What kind of man

chooses chastity? He *loved* her; would a real Christian not honor love above all things?

How foolish are rules that require obedience to Heaven in order to spite earth!

On the other hand, what kind of monk is not a monk at all...would a real monk not love the Holy Mother more than a princess?

How foolish is the monk who follows the flesh to scorn Heaven!

These struggles had smoldered deep within the young man ever since the night he had bidden Julianna farewell. But three words to Albert had poured fresh pitch on these smoldering coals: 'She is married.'

Exhausted, he awoke two days ago to curse his three fathers—Alexander Horn the Elder buried in Oyne, his Father Abbot who muzzled his joy, and his other Father no doubt despising him from Heaven. No. He would no longer suffer his fears of any of them. Their looming threats had suffocated his humanity for long enough; he had denied himself the natural love of a woman, the sundry joys of life and the freedom to just be Alexander Horn—an ordinary man.

And for what? For whom?

Them? He cursed them.

But as sure as the sun follows itself, yesterday he condemned himself for cursing them. Who was he to think such terrible things? What unbridled pride!

And so, while walking through Regensburg on this day, he stopped near a startled squirrel and recounted the many ways he had failed these three fathers. "I am a monk who craves a woman's body; I follow duty, but not with my heart. I obey, but I do so without joy."

Adultery, hypocrisy, insincerity. And that was just the beginning of long lists of failures he recited to the squirrel.

None of these charges were new to him. And whenever he doubted any of this, his brother Robby Horn had always been quick to call him to account. After all, Robby had already heard the confessions of Julianna.

For that, Alexander felt vulnerable and utterly naked.

Indeed, the man whom Alexander Horn wanted to be was being scourged by the man he was. His cross was now proving too much to bear. To whom could he give it?

Yet, shedding his suffering was a frightening thing in itself. A self-made cross was all that he had ever known. What would happen if he abandoned that?

As his brothers returned to the dormitory after their middle night prayers of Lauds, he walked weakly through the black corridors of quiet colonnades and into the private garth of his monastery where he lay down, deathlike atop the dewy grass. The air was moist, thickened by a summer night's fog gathering over the Danube. Above, the sky was square, enclosed by the walls of his cloister. A thin gauze of mist screened the stars. He closed his eyes.

The buzz of a few insects made his music.

The air did not move. Leaves did not rustle. The city beyond the thick stone walls was silent. His breath slowed to a steady rhythm, filling his chest like the easy draw of a deep bellows.

Before long Alexander Horn fell into a deep and dreamless sleep.

He awakened just before dawn for no good reason. His eyes opened to a starry sky from which some mystery seemed to summon his soul. On his back, he gazed beyond the square silhouette of the walled garden and into the eternal space beyond. Magnificence. Who said men should flee darkness?

Alexander suddenly wanted to absorb this night's bottomless skyscape. A tear formed. It slid along his temple. An ant tickled the hair of his arm. He moved to slap it dead, but paused, suddenly wondering about the ant. The little creature was experiencing him, and he was experiencing the ant. He smiled. "We are both part of something." He let it live.

A rising bird chirped.

Alexander liked this darkness. The Mystery had things to teach him. He sat up and let his hands drag through the wet grass. His finger caught a fallen leaf. He picked it up. "You have a story of your own." He smiled, laughing at himself. "Am I mad to think that?" A shooting star turned his head. *A spectacle just for me?* Distant thunder vibrated in his chest.

He smiled, glad that he had collapsed into this place where wonder had found him. Alexander climbed to his feet and stared at a tiny flower resting under starlight. Its colors were muted but yet enchanted him with hints of secrets to be revealed with the sun. He bent his nose to it and breathed, deeply.

Emboldened, the young Scot walked to the linden tree under which he often prayed. He climbed it. From high in its branches he stared beyond the stone wall to see the black sky turning to gray in the east. Filled with awe, he muttered, "The promises." He wedged himself safely in a notch for the next half-hour. The eastern sky brightened and stars began to fade. More birds chirped. He thought of hope.

The next promise appeared in an elegant flourish of pink and orange. He whispered, "Beauty." Alexander gripped the branch of his faithful tree and waited for more. He heard a voice. "Eh?" He looked down, fearing someone had discovered him.

No one.

Then, as clear as if it were a person speaking in his ear, he heard it again. "Alexander... my good and faithful servant."

The words filled him with some immeasurable wonder. But he quickly twisted on his branch, searching for some monk playing a trick on him. No one.

He heard it for a second time. A tear formed in his eye. "Love." The monk trembled.

His blurred eyes then caught the edge of the sun. He could not tear them away. The thin slice did not linger, however, as the sun quickly pushed upward to claim its magnificent place above the emerging green of the dewy landscape. "Might."

Shielding his eyes, Alexander let the morning sun cast its warmth upon his skin. A single bird swooped low from the river and arced alongside his linden. Friendship. The monk could only marvel.

The young man slowly climbed down from his tree. As his feet touched the ground, he found his body folding to his knees. He lifted the medal of St. Benedict suspended around his neck. He stared at its cross inscribed in the center of a circle. Comforted in the deepest places, Alexander kissed the cross, for in all of it Love had embraced him and Wisdom had filled him. He grabbed hold of the tree and prayed.

September, 1783
Ingolstadt

Adam Weishaupt was in trouble. Three weeks before, Professor Joseph von Utzschneider (*Illuminatus Seneca*) of Ingolstadt's very own Minerval church quit the Order, taking two other Illuminati with him. Uncertain of the depth of their betrayals, he and Cato now stared at their confessionals. Each contained embarrassing, if not utterly damning information.

Someone pounded on the door. Both men paled. Weishaupt rallied his courage and threw the door open to find his secretary soaking wet from the day's thunderstorms. Socrates Lanz thrust a message toward Weishaupt, then turned to run, shouting something about other urgent business.

The professor hurried to his desk. He cracked open the message and proceeded to read it. He began to tremble. He read it for a second and then a third time before finally letting it fall to the floor.

Cato picked it up and read it, quickly. One eye twitched. "I can take care of this, General," he said. "I have contacts beyond Achaia—far beyond the duke's reach."

Weishaupt held his hand up. "Silence." The professor unbuttoned his waistcoat and paced. He stopped to pour himself mint tea and then stared from his office window into the puddled streets of Ingolstadt. He closed his eyes, listening for some inner voice to guide him. All he heard was thunder. "Obstacles. Always obstacles, Brother Cato." He turned to face the lawyer. "Our duty is to the highest good."

"Ja, Herr General."

Weishaupt pursed his lips. "The highest good. And whom do you believe must determine this?"

"You, Spartacus."

The professor nodded. "Correct." He returned to his window. A streak of lightning flashed. "I bear a heavy cross."

"And what is the highest good in this circumstance?" asked Cato.

Weishaupt grunted. "The services of Marius Hertel.[1]"

Cato grimaced. "Marius? But this is about your sister-in-law—"

"Too much is at stake for sentiment. My honor is in danger and that is far more important than my personal attachments." He threw himself into his desk chair. "My name is already thrown about far and wide. No. I cannot risk everything for this. I must write to Marius. He and Celce have handled such matters before."

Weishaupt grabbed his cipher book. He proceeded to write a letter in hieroglyphics.

> *My faithful Brother Marius Hertel,*
> *I am almost desperate. My honor is in danger and I am on the eve of losing that reputation which gave me so great an authority over our people. My sister-in-law is with child. We have already made several attempts to destroy it...If you cannot restore me to honor I will hazard a desperate blow. She is only in her fourth month...*

He signed with his circled dot and handed the letter to Cato. "Make a copy for safekeeping. I will use it against him if he fails." Weishaupt paused. "Be sure he understands that he must do *whatever* is necessary to hide her disgrace."

The professor returned to his window again. *What does Sofia expect! She writes as if this is my fault.* He cursed. In two months, he would be marrying his other sister-in-law—the sister of his dead wife. *Does she dare think I would dishonor myself because she failed to prevent this! Did she think Rome would save us? Foolish girl.* He poured himself a gin.

Cato stood at the door. "The wedding is still planned?"

"Of course."

"What of the Sausenhofers? They must hear the rumors about you."

Weishaupt nodded. His father-in-law had demanded to know whether he was or was not the founder of the Order. He had obliged the man's direct question and, to his great surprise, he was embraced. "Of course. And they are very happy to know the truth."

Cato nodded. "Then you must know that Anna Marie's brother was insinuated in Regensburg. He is famous for singing the praises of 'Spartacus.'"

Weishaupt scratched the side of his nose. "It seems that I am surrounded by as many admirers as threats."

"No, no, no!" Adam Weishaupt slammed his fists atop his desk and threw ink across the room. "What kind of monsters are after me?" Philo stood in the professor's office, grim-faced and gray. Three more brothers had betrayed the Order. "*Seneca*, that pouty-faced shite. And *Archytas*? Even that idiot, *Xenophon!*[1] [2] Furious, Weishaupt threw open his desk and fumbled for a key hidden within his waistcoat. He inserted it to open a drawer leading to a secret panel. Another key opened the panel and from there he set aside a jar of *Aqua Toffana*—a poison Cato Zwack had distributed to key Illuminati. He cradled the poison in his palm. "What say you, Philo?"

The baron remained stoic. "This is Cato's provenance. As for me, I would say perhaps for the King of Sweden. We are told he is faltering and the vacancy could be profitable. But for three lowly Minervals? What do they really know? If you feel better, we can silence them with our damaging information from the scrutators.[3]"

"It is not about feeling better!" Weishaupt glared. "How can we know what they know?"

Cato burst through the front door and crossed the parlor. He was covered in mud from a long ride in bad weather. He retrieved a document from the lining of his tricorn. "See this!" He handed Weishaupt a copy of charges levelled against his name by the three defectors. "Traitors presented this to Duke Theodore's sister-in-law yesterday."

"Duchess Dowager Maria Anna!" cried Weishaupt. He flattened the paper on his desk. "How did you come by this?"

"An Illuminatus serves as her private secretary. He had no time to copy it in cipher, so he used our disappearing ink."

The professor's eyes strained to scan the slowly fading document. His heart raced with every word. "Christ." He pushed the paper at Philo. "How do they know these things?" He threw off his waistcoat and tossed it into a chair.

Philo and Cato stared at one another.

"They accuse us—me— of 'vicious moral sentiments...poisonings. As enemies of religion, approving suicide, declaring patriotism as childish.'" Weishaupt was suddenly faint. "They know plenty, Philo." He found a chair. "They have us, and they are clever. Notice how they accuse me of plotting with the Austrians to overthrow the Duke." He put a hand over his throat for a moment. "Everybody hates the Austrians." He closed his eyes. "They are blind to what is necessary for the common good. No. We must remain willing to do whatever we must, no matter the risk, no matter the sacrifice."

CHAPTER EIGHTEEN NOTES

1 *Illuminatus Marius* was **Joseph Anton Hertel** (1747-1828), a fellow professor, Areopagite and close confidant of Weishaupt able and willing to do things 'necessary.'

2 These three men were good examples of the kind of defector Duke Theodore enticed to bear witness against the Order.
Joseph von Utzschneider, *Illuminatus Seneca* (1763-1840) was a scientist and professor at the Marianum Academy in Munich. A Freemason in Lodge Theodore and active civil affairs, he was well-connected to numerous influential Bavarian elites.
Georg Grünberger, *Illuminatus Archtyas* (1749-1820) was a man of letters and influence, especially among the academics.
Johann Sulpitius, *Illuminatus Xenophon* (1762-1842) was a priest of sorts, and professor of French in Munich. His cosmopolitan airs and religious credentials made him an effective witness.

3 The Illuminati employed a position known as a 'scrutator' for covert spying on selected recruits and initiates. This went as far as studying sleeping habits, eavesdropping to transcribe private conversations and surveillance of social interactions upon which they then reported in detail.

"Mankind ought to think themselves happy in having superiors of tried merit. Supposing tyranny were to ensue, it could not be dangerous in the hands of men who taught us nothing but science, liberty and virtue."

FROM THE ILLUMINATI DEGREE OF REGENT

CHAPTER NINETEEN

DECEMBER, 1783
INGOLSTADT

FOR THE PAST MONTHS, ALEXANDER HORN HAD SKIPPED evening vespers to return to his linden tree. There he allowed himself the peace of the night lights that found him the branches. In that place he was able to see beyond. And by seeing beyond, he was beginning to see the close-at-hand just a bit more clearly.

He had told the whole of his experience to his friend, Dr. Karl von Eckartshausen. After all, the man was a wise mystic who understood such things. He did not yet bring it up with Albert, however. His American-turned-British friend was far too absorbed with his recent flight from Freemasonry and his obsession with the Illuminati. That and his constant looking over his shoulder; Van Loon was convinced that a former masonic brother had taken a wild shot at him from a passing carriage.

As for Abbot Benedict, Alexander was passively punishing him with silence. For all of his newfound reverence, Alexander maintained a bit of bitterness about the abbot's banning of his books. Of this he was not proud.

On that matter, Alexander had decided to walk a delicate balance. It was true that he had made a promise to the abbot that *Brother Maurus* would not

207

sell banned books. However, his wording to the abbot had been deliberate—most would say even deceptive—so as to not prevent *Mr. Bergström* from doing anything.

And so, on this cold December morning Mr. Bergström stood at the door of Adam Weishaupt's home bearing a very heavy bundle of books. He set the bundle on the frosty stoop and used the walking stick the professor had given him to rap on the door. A female servant of some eastern kingdom answered and ushered the young bookseller into the side parlor—the very same room where Kolmer had tossed his Spanish hat ten years prior.

"He will join you shortly, sir," said the servant. She took his coat, tricorn and walking stick. "Coffee? Christmas cookies?"

Barely able to take his eyes off her, Alexander nodded. "Please." He took a seat in the red chair and carefully adjusted his wig. He had never been in Weishaupt's home. Their meetings were either at the masonic temple in Munich, at the university office, or in the occasional tavern in Regensburg.

He looked about and calculated the professor to be a modest man of fine taste. His desk was neat, though piled high with correspondence. An enchanting painting of some Franconian farm hung over a green settee by the far wall. Heavy blue drapes were held open by braided ropes to let the gray light of the day struggle to brighten the room.

The letter the professor had sent 'Mr. Bergström' some weeks prior had been warm, like something an uncle would write to a favored nephew. And it invited him here—to his home—and just a week before Christmas. This led Alexander to imagine that his relationship was developing into an actual friendship. He was happy about that.

Alexander's sales calls had gradually become far more than transactions. Over time, Adam Weishaupt had begun using the occasions to share a great deal of his philosophical musings. These inspired Alexander to keep hope alive for the world and for himself. Such inspiration challenged the dark conclusions of Albert van Loon and the abbot.

Weishaupt entered the room with a flair and with a sturdy blonde woman on his arm. He was dressed in a fine suit, but she in a large gown that revealed her late-term pregnancy. "Ah, Mr. Bergström!" cried Weishaupt. "What a joy to see you. May I present my wife, Frau Anna Marie Weishaupt."

Alexander stood and offered a formal bow, foreleg set stiffly. "Of the Sausenhofers von Eichstaat." He did not think her as plain as some had said, but she was certainly huge. He took her hand.

Anna Marie smiled. "Ja. You know my family?"

"I have met your brother in Regensburg. He is a man of fine reputation." Alexander enjoyed the smile brightening her face. Something in her blue eyes conveyed strength. He liked her at once. "A very Happy Christmas to you."

Children's voices cried from upstairs.

"*Ach, mein Gott.* Already? I am sorry, Herr Bergström. Duty calls." Anna Marie lowered her face. "My husband speaks very highly of you. I am pleased to meet you."

Speaks highly of me? As she disappeared to tend the professor's children, Alexander was directed to a seat by the coal grate. He imagined an evil man would not have married a woman such as that. The thought assured him.

The young servant delivered a china tea pot and a fine silver platter of *Lebkuchen* and star-shaped butter cookies.

"My wife manages my children," said Weishaupt. "That way, she does not manage me!" He laughed and took a chair on the opposite side of the small hearth.

"I believe you have five children?" asked Alexander.

"Ja. I once had five daughters and two sons, but two of my daughters are buried and another lies ill upstairs."

Alexander was surprised by the matter-of-fact tone. "I am very sorry, Herr Doktor. I did not know—"

"Think nothing of it. I have my highest hopes set on the child soon to come. One should never abandon hope." Weishaupt switched his attention to the bundle by Alexander's feet. "Did you have any problems with my books?"

"It seems that others are gobbling up the same books you seek."

Weishaupt nodded. "I see." He sipped some tea and picked up a cookie. He bit the cookie in half. "If I may be direct, I was a bit put off by the monk masquerade you revealed in Regensburg. Tell me again how this works."

Shite. Not this. Alexander carefully returned his cup to its saucer. "Indeed. Well, the diplomats in Regensburg are suspicious of anyone in a fine suit. But their suspicions dissolve in the presence of a monk. Therefore, I can conduct business with greater ease as 'Brother Maurus' in that place." He did not like how carefully the professor was listening. "But here and in Munich it seems the clergy are held in contempt. Perhaps because of university learning? Perhaps political conflicts? I would not know. For whatever reason, I do better as Mr. Bergström."

Weishaupt tapped the side of his tea cup. "I see."

Why was the man still suspicious? Alexander calculated that it might be time to take a bold risk and end this. He lifted his cup to his lips, thinking. He worked to keep his hand as steady as a surgeon's. "Delicious. From England?"

"India." Weishaupt's tone was suddenly curt.

Ready, Alexander lowered his cup. "The problem I have with two personae is this—"

Weishaupt leaned far forward.

"The ladies."

The professor raised his brows.

"Yes. The ladies." Alexander set down his cup and saucer, then abruptly grabbed hold of his yak wig. Grinning, he jerked it off his head. "You see? I can never remove my wig!" He popped a butter cookie into his mouth.

Weishaupt sat back.

"Look at me. I wear a fine Italian suit-in-ditto, cordwainer English shoes with four pronged buckles, French silk hose…and then reveal this?" He pointed to his head. "It is not easy to bed a wench with a head shaved in the middle." To Alexander's relief, Weishaupt laughed.

"So, you see," said the bookseller. "My life is complicated. Quite truthfully, if trust is ever lost for the clerics in Regensburg I shall be delighted to abandon my 'Brother Maurus' and grow my hair back!"

Weishaupt eased back into his chair. "I understand." He reached for a Lebkuchen.

Color warmed Weishaupt's cheeks. Philo von Knigge had never budged in his suspicions about the bookseller. He had repeatedly badgered him to consider the possibility that Bergström was a spy for Duke Theodore or perhaps even the Jesuits. However, as complicated as it all seemed, the professor had always refused to believe that he could be a spy. Quite the contrary, he envisioned the young man as a supreme candidate for the highest degrees. He had been excited to draw Bergström closer, especially now that his efforts to remove Julianna from the young man's view had succeeded.

But Bergström had just lied.

Contrary to hiding his tonsure from women, Weishaupt's spies had reported the young man sneaking off with a princess while wearing his monk's costume...*with his shaved head.*

He surveyed the young man. It was not that lying, itself, was a problem. Far from it. But *Bergström's* lying surely was. Was he lying now? Fearing Philo may have been right after all made him suddenly sick. Weishaupt stared for a long moment before grumbling, "Men are not always consistent, are they?"

Alexander blinked. "I suppose not. Why do you ask?"

Weishaupt noticed the young man's shoulders tighten. "In my experience, men of religion fall the furthest."

Alexander hurried a cookie to his mouth.

"You believe that happens?"

Alexander swallowed. "I believe it *can* happen, sir."

Weishaupt narrowed his eyes, feeling the pulse of the hunt. "Do you believe it *should* happen?"

"I believe truth should reign."

Weishaupt sat back. *Then why do you lie about shaved heads and women? Who are you?* "Truth. Enlightenment. So, you really do read the books you sell."

Alexander nodded. He reached for another cookie.

"Do you find yourself in agreement with what you read?"

"A great deal of the time, yes."

Weishaupt paused, then said, "In my thirty-five years, I have found few men with the courage to apply the wisdom in these books. They would rather busy themselves with meaningless play and silly ceremonies. But apparently not you."

Alexander shifted in his seat. "In my twenty-one years, I have already discovered wisdom under moonlight, and knowledge under the sun. This is why I have always valued our discussions. You have helped to form me."

Weishaupt wiped his nose and reached for his tea, thinking. "Would you consider me to be sunlight or moonlight?"

Alexander hesitated. "In your joys I see the sun; in your sorrows I see the moon."

The professor felt a twinge. He liked that. Clearing his throat, he quickly said, "Tell me, Mr. Bergström, what is it that your heart most deeply longs for?"

The bookseller sat back in his chair. Weishaupt watched, carefully, as the young man seemed to strain. He could hear Knigge hissing, 'But will he give you an honest answer?' Would he? And how would he even know?

"I long to be a perfected man," said Alexander with convincing confidence.

Weishaupt was disappointed. Every initiate in the Craft blabbered something like that. Why could Bergström not have declared some noble ambition? Why not crave to be a leader of men, to be an invisible hand in the salvation of mankind!

Nevertheless, the professor remained curious. Maybe if he invited him to a Minerval church? Would others help discern what this young man was really about? The professor nodded. "I see. And is that all?"

Alexander avoided Weishaupt's searching eyes. Something was suddenly bothering the professor and it felt as if he were peering directly into his soul. Right now, the bookseller did not want anyone looking there.

Besides, hearing himself declare his longing to be a 'perfected man' sounded suddenly ridiculous. Over these recent years one failure after the other demanded his confession; his quest for self-perfection seemed more a fool's errand now than ever. And why did he cling to this temptation in the first place? He suddenly wished he could take back his words. But what would he say in their place? What *was* his heart's greatest desire?

He lifted his tea cup and stared into its dark contents. Avoiding Weishaupt's eyes, he then added a spoonful of sugar and stirred the tea slowly, losing himself in the slow swirl of the red-brown drink. *Julianna is gone. Perfection is unattainable. I am far from the man I thought myself to be. What is it that I want? What is it that I have always wanted? How do I answer him?*

His heart then swept him back into the linden tree and released him to the memory of the moonlit reverence that had filled him. Alexander considered the presence that lay beyond. He set his silver spoon aside. He then remembered the starry 'hem of the Almighty' and the warmth of his grunnie's lap. He had never felt so safe as in those places. Alexander exhaled and blurted. "I suppose in the end I want to belong to God."

"Eh?"

"I said, I want to belong to God."

"God?" The professor stood. "*God* is your aim?" His voice rose. "But you said you were reading my books!" He kicked the bundle. His fists clenched. "Are you a real monk?"

Alexander gaped.

Growling, Weishaupt stormed to his window. Outside, church bells began to peal. Whirling about, he shouted, "Belong to whose God?" He rushed toward the seated bookseller. "The Jehovah God of Eden who would keep mankind in darkness? That God?"

Alexander swallowed. Perspiration rose on his face. His mouth began to dry. What should he say? A passing cloud cast a shadow through the long windows. Alexander chilled as it swept the room. This angry man was not the Adam Weishaupt he had ever known.

Albert van Loon's desperate revelations ran through his mind. Could Albert and the abbot be right after all? Alexander shuddered to think so.

His breath became shallow. His chest tightened.

"Are you listening Mr. Bergström?" Weishaupt leaned close. "Or should I say, 'Brother Maurus?'"

Brother Maurus. He repeated that name to himself. He eyed Weishaupt blankly. The man said that name with such raw hatred. What to do? His mind abruptly jumped to the thousand pages he had read since a youth. He flew over them like a swooping owl.

He then realized that all he had said to Weishaupt was the word, 'God.' Alexander kept his eyes fixed on the professor's. Whose God was Weishaupt's? The professor claimed to be a Lutheran.

Alexander gawked. *Unless he is who Albert says he is.* He opened his mouth. But where were the words?

"You look like a dead trout," muttered the professor. "Say something."

Alexander blurted, "What do you think of Lucifer?" He was as surprised as Weishaupt with the question.

The professor stood upright. "Lucifer? Why do you ask that?"

Why did he? His fingers tapped on his knee. "It is written by some that Lucifer—"

Weishaupt touched his chin. "Lucifer the Light Bearer. Ancient wisdom says he is the wise serpent slandered in the Genesis myth—the dragon we should celebrate. He frees us to become the gods we already are." He leaned forward. "What say you?"

Alexander faltered.

The professor moved to his desk and withdrew the folio of Diderot's *Encyclopédie* that Kolmer had presented as a gift all those years before. He pointed to the title page, letting his finger linger on the image of Lucifer. "The Illuminator of mankind. One might say, the true Logos. He offers us the dignity to complete ourselves by the power nature has given us. But I ask again, what say you, Brother Maurus?"

Alexander chilled. "Why do you call me that?"

"Are you not him?"

"You know who I am."

Weishaupt returned to his seat, "Do I?"

Alexander braced himself. "Look at me. You know who I am, and I know who you are. You are 'Spartacus,' and you rule the Bavarian Order of the Illuminati. You are its Invisible Hand dedicated to the enlightenment of the world."

The professor remained quiet.

"You say you are my friend, yet you keep this secret?"

"Friend?"

"Yes. You invite me into your home as a friend," said Alexander.

"Well friend, you have not yet said which god you seek."

"From the bottom of his den in Ingolstadt, Weishaupt presides over his conspiring crew. Through them he commands Germany and might be called its Emperor of Darkness."

AUGUSTIN BARRUEL [1]

CHAPTER TWENTY

"Mr. Bergström? Did you hear me?"

Alexander gathered himself and stood. He realized that his whole relationship was in sudden jeopardy. "And you have not answered my claim that you command the Order."

Weishaupt measured his answer. "I shall disclose something to you, but you must vow to keep it a secret."

Alexander nodded, waiting.

"I am what is called a 'Minerval.' This means I have been invited into the secret Order of the Illuminati. As a Freemason, you must understand that I cannot say another word."

He lies! No mere initiate would be buying books, arranging meetings... Alexander took a breath. "I thank you, sir."

Weishaupt furrowed his brows and shook a fist. "Now, I ask again: what god do you seek? And what say you of Lucifer?"

"I wish to belong to the God of love."

"Bah! That is an easy escape. And what of L——"

Now wishing he *could* escape, Alexander blurted, "I am disappointed in your angry tone with me, sir. I no longer care to discuss this." He called for his coat. "You have treated me unfairly and now you parse my words."

"How dare you—"

The servant hurried in and Alexander grabbed his walking stick and coat. He moved toward the door. *Christ, get me out of here.* Turning, he said, "You are not the man I thought you to be."

"Wait!" Weishaupt's tone was commanding.

Alexander walked through the door and into the foyer.

Close behind, Weishaupt said, "When most men say 'God,' they refer to the God of the Church. For this reason, I reacted to your words." He laid a hand on Alexander's shoulder and turned him around. "I mean no disrespect. It is just that the Church steals men's happiness."

Alexander paused. "But what if a man could find happiness in the worship of Christ?"

Weishaupt scowled. "Do you?"

"That was not my question." Alexander then remembered something Van Loon had reported. "I ask because there are many rumors about this Minerval Order. One is that it wishes to annihilate Christianity."

"Did you ever hear me utter such a thing?"

"No," said Alexander slowly.

"I am only a Minerval. But I cannot imagine the invisibles who direct the Order would hold to such a purpose as that. No. However, I do believe that once properly enlightened, men are likely to stop believing the foolishness of that religion." The professor stood close. "Would that matter to you?"

Alexander bit the inside of his cheek. "I thought you were a Lutheran."

Weishaupt tapped a finger on his lips. "I assume you are viewing this as an objective man. That is good. I think you would enjoy meeting the Minervals in Regensburg, perhaps during an open discussion time at their church. There you are likely to find what you seek." He hurried to his desk and retrieved a sheet of paper. "I shall ask my superiors for permission to allow your attendance as a guest. No promises." He pointed to another envelope. "And take that with you. It is another book order."

Alexander just wanted to get away.

Weishaupt extended his hand. "I look forward to seeing you soon. I apologize for my overreaction. I am quite tired and it was foolish of me."

The bookseller took the professor's hand. It was warm and strangely inviting. "Accepted."

FEBRUARY, 1784
MUNICH, BAVARIA

"Did Bergström show up?" Adam Weishaupt snarled at Cato Zwack standing before him in a cold, rented room above a Munich tavern.

"He did. Thrice."

"And?"

"He impressed the whole of the Regensburg church. The Minervals have only good things to say." Cato retrieved a paper from his satchel and presented a report on the impressions of three spies assigned to the bookseller: the insinuator, the scrutator, and the Superior. "As you already know, he meets every standard of physiognomy: his eyes reveal a good spirit, his gait is firm, his countenance is open and noble. The scrutator could not find his apartment so we have no report on his sleeping habits or of women. He likes bakery treats. But Superior Pontius says he is an eager and liberal minded learner—"

Weishaupt's mind raced. He wanted to believe in this young man, but... "No information on his apartment?" He added a coal to the smoky hearth. "Something is off." He paced, chin buried in his palm. "Get a hold of Count Thaddäus. His family operates the postal network. I want him personally to include Bergström in the mail we read."

Cato nodded.

"This bookseller is certainly clever enough to be a spy for the duke. Or for the Rosicrucians for that matter," said Weishaupt. "Maybe the Jesuits. But I do hope it is not so."

"Philo thinks it is so."

"Enough about Philo! He wants Bergström abandoned. No. If Bergström were a spy, we would use him, not turn him away. So, treat him like a little bird. Do not frighten him. Do you understand?"

"Of course, Spartacus. He may simply be a complicated man as you have always believed," said Cato.

"Has the scrutator spied out the 'Brother Maurus' act?"

Cato shrugged.

The professor slammed his fist on his desk. "Must I think of everything!"

Someone knocked. Weishaupt stared at Cato.

"Hide," Cato whispered. He pointed to a closet. "In there."

Cato delayed, then opened his office door. "Finally," he said. "Come in." Dr. Karl von Eckartshausen entered with a polite smile. He handed Cato his overcoat and followed his hand to a wooden chair.

"Have you chosen your name yet?"

"*Attilius Regulus*—"

"The Roman general of the First Punic War. Yes. Good choice." Cato surveyed the new recruit. He and Weishaupt knew Eckartshausen to be a wonderful addition, most especially because the man had just been nominated to be the Keeper of the Archives of the Electoral House in Munich. This would keep him close to the hated Duke Theodore, to say nothing of his control of information. "And congratulations on your nomination. We have friends who can see that you secure that position."

"I am honored."

"How many books have you written, Attilius?"

"About fifty so far," said Karl.

Relieved, Weishaupt peeped through a tiny hole in the closet door, smiling. *This is a fantastic catch.*

"Including your plays?" asked Cato.

"Ja."

Cato began to circle him. "We have known each other for a long time at the lodge. You are a man of impeccable character."

Karl remained quiet.

"But our General reminds us that the Order has a higher purpose than the Craft. You shall continue to learn of it as we go along. I promise you shall be pleased." The attorney waited. "I am also happy to tell you that the highest degrees now move beyond Reason to make room for a priesthood of sorts. Something mystics like you should aspire toward."

"Philo has said as much." Karl said.

Weishaupt reddened behind his door. *Philo!*

"Really? What else has Philo told you?" asked Cato.

"Only that the Order is making great strides. We now have men positioned for powerful effect, especially in France."

Weishaupt hoped Cato would respond correctly.

"The French may leap too soon into extremes. Our Order recognizes patience as a virtue and education as the key. If we can control education, we can control the future. But we fear the French may terrify the general population with too quick a move. That would be catastrophic for us all."

Weishaupt smiled in the dark. *Excellent.*

"Of course," said Karl. "Influencing the young in their earliest instruction, and then through the universities would change everything. And in the meantime, if we can educate the elites everywhere through the literati—"

"Indeed. Newspapers, journals, magazines...plays, music, poetry, literature. You have keen insight."

Weishaupt was delighted. Attilius understood. He kept his ear to the door.

"I...I do have a question, Brother Cato," said Von Eckartshausen.

Weishaupt held his breath.

"You say the leader of our Order is the otherwise unnamed Basilius. But the whole world seems to insist that it is Professor Weishaupt—and that his actual Illuminatus name is General Spartacus."

From inside his closet, Weishaupt was oddly discomforted. The secret sounded suddenly silly. Why not just announce himself to the world?

"Brother, as you must understand," said Cato, "all deeper truths are revealed in degrees. In due time, you shall—"

"Say no more. I understand."

Cato continued. "You know many of our lodge members well. There is one man in particular that piques our curiosity—the bookseller, Mr. Bergström."

"Ja. Of course I know him. I have purchased books from him."

Weishaupt noticed the sudden unease in the man's voice.

"You introduced him to the lodge, if I recall?" said Cato.

"Yes. He was originally recommended by an Englishman."
Weishaupt had not known that. *Ask him, Cato...*
"Do you remember the Englishman's name?"
"I do not recall," muttered Von Eckartshausen.

MARCH, 1784
REGENSBURG

Since Christmas, Alexander Horn had wrestled with everything. His studies among the Minervals of Regensburg had surely piqued his curiosity. Imagining himself as an enlightened man ready to lead others toward deep happiness was an exciting thought. Further, knowing that his friend, Karl von Eckartshausen, had been insinuated into the Order assured him enough to keep Van Loon's persistent challenges at some distance.

Of course, unbeknownst to Alexander, the Order had barely revealed any of their true intentions to him. The Minervals were only Nursery degrees, and Alexander's attendance for their discussions a mere courtesy extended at the behest of the General. In fact, through Philo von Knigge, Weishaupt had directed the Regensburg elders to guide the topics carefully when the uninitiated 'Mr. Bergström' attended so as to not spook him away.

Blind to the whole truth, Alexander was sometimes uplifted by what he learned, but more often of late he was feeling uneasy. The teachers insistently claimed men to be as gods—evolving parts of a natural one-ness that may or may not include a supreme impersonal force within itself. He had quickly calculated that their notion of one-ness pushed love to one side. After all love needs an 'other.' Their resistance to his arguments gave him pause, suggesting that this may be why the Order so often emphasized the value of mankind rather than individual men.

Then there was the notion of *ruling* men's happiness. Alexander thought that felt a bit like a tyranny of joy. How would that work?

And in the background, he remained utterly discomforted by Weishaupt's apparent sympathy for Lucifer. Some of the Minervals toasted Lucifer in jest; others seemed quite taken with the notion. Were that not enough, a drunken Minerval had revealed his pledge. "'Inviolable obedience to my superiors and the statutes of the Order,'" he said. "If I betray the Order, I will have 'the rage of the Brethren prey upon my entrails.'" Inviolable obedience to Weishaupt? Upon penalty of death?

Alexander struggled to find either love or universal happiness in any of that. Quite the contrary, he was beginning to sense some kind of elite despotism and it made him afraid. Was Van Loon right? Was Von Eckartshausen blind?

So, on this bleak March morning, Alexander walked through the cloister garth deep in these thoughts. Hands folded behind his back, he spotted something from the corner of his eye. He stopped. There. One of his brothers was scurrying through the snow carrying an oatmeal-colored canvas bag that looked very similar to the one in which he had hidden Mr. Bergström's disguise. Alexander chilled. *No!* He began trotting a parallel course toward the far colonnades.

Grinding his teeth, he could not imagine how anyone could have found his clothing. He had put the bundle beneath wet kindling in an old wood box built against the outside wall of the latrine. That was not the sort of place where the brethren tarried, and no one had any business against the outside wall. It should have been safe.

Could it be something else? He ran a little faster until the brother made an abrupt right turn from the garden and disappeared into a corridor leading toward the library. "He's running to Benedict," groaned Alexander. He dashed across the frozen gardens, hoping to catch a glimpse of the monk's cargo before it was too late. A voice turned his head. "Eh?" Alexander spun around to find his brother, Robby. "What?"

"Why are you running?"

"Not now."

Robby hurried forward and grabbed him by the shoulder. He presented Mr. Bergström's yak wig. "Are you looking for this?"

Alexander stared. He was suddenly sick.

"Well?"

"Why would I be looking for that?"

Robby shoved his little brother. "I listen very carefully to confessions. I know so much more about you than you'd ever want to believe."

Alexander's heart pumped. "And?"

"I know the other who has been party to your deceptions."

Julianna. Alexander waited.

"So, do you wish to lie to me?"

Alexander looked over his shoulder. The monk and his bundle were out of sight.

"He discovered your disguise and is taking it to the abbot."

"My disguise?"

"Stop it!" roared Robby.

Was he ready to lie to his brother? To the abbot?

Robby shook his head. "You should have stayed home. Our mother could have saved the estate with you as manager. Here you are useless. I have no idea why you think yourself a monk. You do nothing but some garden work, and you barely pray. You read all the time, but who sees you with a Scripture in your hands? You sell books for the abbot, but why the disguise?"

Alexander shifted his eyes away.

"It must be for profit." Robby leaned close. Alexander turned from the garlic on his breath. "That makes you a thief. You will either be sent away on a penance to Rome or exiled to a hermitage or put out in shame. Prepare yourself."

"I am no thief. Nobody ever confessed that to you. I sell books for the profit of the brotherhood."

Robby shook his head. "I do not believe you. You pocket money for yourself—"

Alexander grit his teeth. "A little for extra expenses. But those expenses make for more sales."

"And why the disguise?" barked Robby.

Alexander chafed. *It was supposed to be about the masons, you dunce, not book sales.* Would he have to confess that, too?

"Enough of this," growled Robby. "There." He pointed across the garth to Abbot Benedict now walking slowly toward them, canvas bag in hand. A few weeks prior, the man had turned forty-seven. Still handsome and always glowing within a fresh complexion, his hair had grayed and his awkward gait belied arthritis in his hips.

Alexander braced himself.

What should he do? *I cannot lie to this man. He is too kindly, too gentle. He is slow to anger and full of mercy...*

"Brother Maurus." Abbot Benedict stomped some snow off his shoes and smiled. "I believe this may be yours." He handed Alexander the unopened bundle.

With a nervous glance at Robby, he accepted. But now what? To tell the truth would surely be the end of his service. He had deceived the brethren, skimmed a profit, lied, used his fancy clothing to inflate his pride. To say nothing of his other sins...of his doubts, of Julianna... "Father Abbot, I—"

"Shh." Benedict put a finger on his own lips. "You owe me nothing."

Robby grumbled and the abbot turned toward him. "Brother John, you wish to object?"

"Aye!" Robby pointed at Alexander with a wagging forefinger. "He owes you the truth."

Benedict said nothing. Instead, he turned and walked away.

Alexander was speechless. He held his bundle loosely, suddenly wanting to run to the abbot and confess everything. Robby's hard hand turned his attention.

"You see. You are incorrigible. He no longer believes he can save you."

Alexander released a deep breath. "On the contrary, he may have done just that."

CHAPTER TWENTY NOTES

1 **Abbé Augustin Barruel** (1741-1820) was a French Jesuit who wrote at length about the relationship of secret societies to social revolution. He famously penned, *Memoirs Illustrating the History of Jacobinism* which included an informed exposé on the Illuminati. See additional information in a later note.

"The means to work the redemption of mankind are secret schools of wisdom. We must therefore establish a legion which shall restore the rights of man, original liberty and independence."

DISCOURSE FROM THE
ILLUMINATI SCOTCH KNIGHTS DEGREE

CHAPTER TWENTY-ONE

20TH APRIL, 1784
INGOLSTADT

THE DAY HAD COME, AT LAST. PHILO VON Knigge had resigned. That man would hereafter be remembered only as Baron von Knigge. There would no longer be any doubt among the Council who was the absolute leader of the Bavarian Order of the Illuminati! Smiling, Weishaupt sipped some fine sherry in his university office and re-read the report from Cato Zwack.

> *'In the end, Philo accuses you of being a Jesuit in your despotism, utterly tyrannical and filled with the imagination of your own divinity. He writes, 'He is a pig-headed miscreant, an ungrateful and immoral man who deserves neither respect or the dignity of office. I shall never place my neck in such a yoke again.''*

The professor laughed out loud. He was overjoyed to be rid of him. Most of the Aeropagites had assumed that Weishaupt hated Knigge on account of vanity. After all, he had always avoided standing near the baron in public. In contrast to the diminutive professor, the baron was a tall, handsome aristocrat whose presence silenced most men and made women swoon.

However, vanity had only ever been part of it. Weishaupt's greatest frustration was the challenge to his sense of destiny. He and he alone had been chosen to breathe new life into the Great Plan of the ages. There could be no rival in that. But no matter, Weishaupt could finally rest easy on both counts. He would soon declare his identity, and then he would be flanked in public by Cato and Socrates; neither likely to distract others from their gaze upon the rightful leader.

The professor called for his secretary, Socrates Lanz, now fussing in the neighboring room. "Do you have it?"

The stout man quickly delivered a large, unopened envelope.

The professor opened Knigge's confessional with a zesty slash of a sharp knife. He scanned it. "Ha! If he violates his oath I will not need to have him gutted in his bed." He handed the baron's confessional to Socrates. "Read that. The Von Knigge family would be ruined forever."

Finished, Socrates blew air from his puffed cheeks. "I shall return it to the box. This is better for us than gold coin."

Weishaupt took more sherry. "Before you go, do you have Cato's report on Bergström?"

Socrates walked to a cabinet and retrieved an even larger envelope. "By all accounts he is clean and pure, of powerful mind and eager intentions. However, he does seem saddled with an attachment to orthodoxy."

Weishaupt grumbled. "And what of his other self... 'Brother Maurus.'"

"Ja. This is a problem. It seems Brother Maurus is, in fact, a very real monk in the Scots Monastery."

Stunned, Weishaupt cursed, loudly. "We know this for certain?"

"Ja, General. He is watched entering without leaving for days on end. Cato sent disguised pilgrims to the abbot's famous library. There they have seen the monk Maurus hard at work or walking to prayers."

Bursting, the professor paced. "What is he up to, and who are his friends on the outside?"

Socrates weighed the envelope in his thick palm. "It seems he spends a great deal of time alone, though he is beloved by Regensburg's high society and attends their balls and banquets."

"Brothels?"

"No. But he is seen in dark taverns with a Dutch American turned British diplomat by the name of Albert van Loon…and with our very own Attilius."

"Attilius?" Weishaupt ground his jaw. "Von Eckartshausen cavorting with our monk and a Froglander spy?" Could this be? The professor strained. "Of course! This means Attilius knows the bookseller as both Bergström *and* Brother Maurus." He paused, fists tight. "I want Attilius summoned here at once. He is lying to us, too."

"And what of the diplomat?"

"Van Loon. Van Loon. I know that name." Weishaupt sat. "Albert van Loon. Yes! He attended the lodge as a guest of…Eckartshausen! He's no Dutchman; he's American. And he resigned the lodge." Fearful, he immediately returned to his feet. "There may be more to this. Attilius said that Bergström was recommended by an *Englishman* whose name he did not recall." He snarled. "What if that was Van Loon? Of course. Bergström, Eckartshausen and Van Loon." Weishaupt whirled about. "They are all connected."

Socrates went pale. "Spartacus, you must remember that Attilius works closely with the duke. What if—"

A sickening, cold wave passed through the professor. "Say it."

"What if all three are in league with the duke as spies?"

Weishaupt adjusted his collar. "We have no information confirming this… yet. And of the American we know nothing. Though I heard rumors he was a British spy against America." He narrowed his eyes. "This is all terrible news." His mind raced. "I need more information on the three of them. Tell Cato to put his agents back in the field."

JUNE, 1784
REGENSBURG

Grace is a potent force, most likely because it makes no sense whatsoever. For weeks, Alexander had reeled from the unexpected kindness of Abbot Benedict on that snowy afternoon in the cloister. He now stared through the light of a single candle at the unopened bundle of Mr. Bergström's clothing, thinking.

He knew that the abbot remained ignorant of all his secrets, but Benedict now had proof that 'Brother Maurus' was up to *something*. Yet, Benedict seemed at perfect peace in his refusal to take hold of the matter. To Robby's chagrin, the abbot had not pressed in any way. On the contrary, it was Robby who was ordered to latrine duty for his public complaints.

In response, Alexander was slowly yielding to his heart's desire to seek out Benedict and finally bare his soul. Why not? The man had proven himself to be safe. In fact, he now realized that the abbot had always been safe. And if that were so, then perhaps his God was safe, after all.

However, on this pre-dawn day Alexander faced a more immediate problem. For the past few weeks he had an eerie sense that his every movement was being watched. While leaving his favorite bakery, he twice noticed the green, scuffed shoulder of a man's jacket protruding oddly around the edge of a corner wall. He spotted the same shoulder leaning beyond a tree near the entrance of the Imperial Diet.

Just yesterday, while running errands near the busy wine market, he was also certain that a one-eyed dandy in a blue French suit was pausing to one side each time that he, himself, paused. Imaginings? He had nearly convinced himself of that until he then rounded a corner to see the dandy and a huge man with a scuffed green jacket whispering together in the shadows of the Schottenportal. They were surely up to something.

It was then that he recalled Albert van Loon's stern warning. Albert insisted that Weishaupt's Order was developing a vast spy network to study recruits and investigate enemies; they had become expert in journaling men's habits as a way of investigating their characters.

Though without precedent among respectable men, Alexander did not think this necessarily warranted any great alarm. But Van Loon went on to say that they also collected sins to be used for extortion, blackmail or slander. Sometimes orgies and private debauchery were arranged so to gather evidence against even their own brethren if so needed. Further, they supposedly compiled lists of the targets' friends whom might also be exploited. Worse, he said this same network was not averse to assassination.

As persuasive as Albert had been, Alexander had remained unconvinced, particularly regarding the latter charge. As for the others, he admitted that the very nature of spying on potential recruits revealed certain inconsistences. For one, surveillance implied a need to know, and knowledge was a form of control. And control, by its very nature, stood opposed to the very atmosphere of freedom that Weishaupt crowed about.

Perhaps Weishaupt was simply being realistically cautious. The Church had, most certainly, persecuted free-thinkers. The Jesuits could be particularly ruthless and their history was beyond ugly. It would make perfect sense for the Order to be especially careful recruiting clergymen.

Nevertheless, the notion that he, himself, was being secretly watched troubled Alexander greatly. He had done nothing to suggest he could be a threat. Others might warrant caution, but Weishaupt had implied friendship with him, strained as it may have become since their last meeting. Unless he was simply being considered for admission?

Discomforted by the whole matter, Alexander decided he needed to find this out for himself if he could, and preferably before the late-morning coffee Van Loon had scheduled. He abruptly removed his habit to don his breeches and yak wig. Shirt on, jacket on, tricorn on and walking stick in hand, he carefully slipped from his cell and through the quiet corridors of the cloister. With his brethren praying in the chapel, 'Mr. Bergström' then stepped into the dim of the morning's first light. He took a position behind a wheeled baker's cart opposite the gray-stone Schottenportal on the guess that one of the spies might expect 'Brother Maurus' to exit that very spot within the next hours.

There he waited.

Regensburg awakened quickly, unencumbered by the river mist hanging heavy on this late spring morning. Alexander shifted side to side, peering through wisps of fog at passers-by from under his brown hat now pressed low toward the bridge of his nose. *Blue dandy or green jacket...or both?*

Unless the Order had sent an entirely new spy.

Unless there were no spies at all.

Hungry, Alexander glanced at the cookies now spread along the cart. His mouth watered. He raised his face upward and scanned the street once again. He noticed the baker eyeing him, suspiciously.

"I am waiting for someone," Alexander grumbled. He dug in his purse for a coin. "I'll take a sugar cookie."

The baker handed him a hard-baked cookie and tossed his head casually to one side. "He is waiting for someone, too."

Not ten yards away, the man in the green jacket had been standing behind a thick beech tree peering at the monastery gate. Chilled, Alexander shoved the cookie in his mouth and faded to one side. *What now? Should I confront this man?* He took a step from behind the cart. He hesitated. *Maybe it is better that they not know that I know.* He returned to his screen.

The man suddenly moved from one tree to the next. Alexander watched carefully. The spy then hurried a few more steps and toward the monastery. Alexander turned to see a monk under hood exit the Schottenportal and begin strolling along the street. He turned back to the spy who was now walking quickly alongside the screen of four-horse coach. Alexander followed.

Three hours later, Alexander ambled toward a vendor parked along the sunny side of the street. He was frustrated. The man in the green jacket had vanished somewhere in the fish market, still shadowing the unsuspecting monk. *Albert will enjoy this story,* he mused.

Buying a pretzel and a fistful of hard cheese, he moved to a stout cherry tree marking the entrance to a private house. He threw himself on the ground and placed his back against the trunk. He drew a deep breath, smelling river water and passing horses. "Does it really matter? I am making too much of it all," he muttered. "So what if the Order has spies? Eckartshausen must know they do and he's never complained." He ate his pretzel, then his cheese.

Alexander soon closed his eyes and dozed until the city's church bells rang ten o'clock. Awakened, he stood, adjusted his wig and hat, and began moving toward Albert's favorite coffee shop not far away. He paused to take a drink from a town fountain. Wiping his mouth on his sleeve, he noticed a blue blur move quickly to one side. He froze. Moving only his eyes, he searched the crowded street until he spotted the same blue dandy who had followed him before. His skin rose. "One eye patched…"

The dandy was tapping a cane on the cobblestones and staring far off. Alexander moved carefully behind a standing wagon and watched. "What is going on?"

He took a breath. The spy shuffled forward with eyes fastened to someone else. *Who is he watching?* Alexander followed the man's gaze to the form of a tall, broad-shouldered gentleman in the shadows. *Who is that?*

Crouched like a stalking cat, Alexander followed. He switched his eyes from the advancing spy to the gentleman and back again. It was then that an uncomfortable sense of being watched sent a feeling of dread through him. He moved to a safe hide behind a tied horse. *Green Jacket? Is Green Jacket here?* He scanned all directions.

Perspiration gathered along Alexander's upper lip. His mouth went dry. *Who is there?* He searched for the dandy with one eye and for the scuffed green jacket with the other. *The Order knows both Bergström and Maurus. They could be searching for either one of me.* He took a breath. *Green Jacket was following a monk…he must be looking for Maurus.* He exhaled. *Does the blue dandy think he found Bergström?*

Alexander licked his lips and stepped from behind the horse. *There!* Not far ahead he saw both spies now angling in on the gentleman who was sauntering along the shaded side of the street. *Both of them after him? They should know he is too tall to be Bergström. Who are they following?* He hurried forward.

The gentleman then emerged from the shade as he crossed a street. Alexander straightened. "Albert?" His head whipped back to the spies now moving closer. "Albert?" Should he cry out for him? Should he play the watcher? Why was Albert being followed?

Both spies then moved closer to Van Loon. Alexander hurried forward. He watched Van Loon turn into the heavily shadowed alley that he used as a shortcut to the coffee house. Alexander knew it well. "What do I do?" A vendor bumped into him from one side. *I need to warn him.*

He pushed ahead, quickly, and then cried out into the loud chatter of the street. "Albert!"

The blue dandy slipped into the narrow alley followed by Green Jacket. Both disappeared from view. Alexander raced ahead, shoving others out of his way and shouting Albert's name until he burst into the shadowed alley at a full run. He then spotted the murky shapes of two men ahead of him. The sight stalled him for just a moment. He heard an indiscernible shout. A tower of barrels collapsed some thirty yards away.

Then a cry.

Jolted, Alexander dashed forward, screaming Albert's name until he fell over a rolling barrel and crashed on to the bricks. He scrambled to his feet to see the two figures vanish around a distant corner. Just ahead lay a crumpled form. Alexander sprinted toward the heap.

He threw himself to the ground where Albert van Loon lay, groaning. Blood was leaking through his clothing and pouring from his scalp. "No!" Alexander cradled the man.

Albert lay still.

"Help!" Alexander jerked the man's jacket apart to reveal a surging slash wound. He tore off his own jacket and pressed it hard against the wound, crying for help. A shopkeeper came running. Within a quarter hour, two policemen arrived along with a dozen curious folk. Two burly peasants lifted Albert carefully into a wheelbarrow and another pushed him slowly to a physician's office near St. Peter's twin cathedral towers.

Not long after the bells of noon, Van Loon awakened and groaned. Alexander fell to his side. "Albert! It is me, Alexander."

Van Loon blinked.

"God be praised," Alexander said.

Albert ran his fingers gingerly along his belly bandages. Still stunned, he then lifted one hand slowly to touch the large lump on his head that was mounded under dried blood. He took a breath. He struggled to focus on Alexander's face, now leaning close. "I remember now."

A nurse arrived with a cup of tepid water. Van Loon leaned his head forward and drew a deep draught. Laying back on his pillow, he said. "Enforcers from Lodge Theodore? I think not; they mostly just threaten. But this Illuminati. They may have discovered that I am working with the duke. My corpse was to be a message about something."

Alexander struggled. "How do you know this?"

"I only know that Weishaupt is capable."

Was he? "I just...I just...it all seems so out of character for any of them——"

"Then you do not understand the nature of our enemies."

Alexander thought for a moment. "Regensburg is filled with spies and conspiracies from every government under the sun. You are a British diplomat, and..."

Van Loon closed his eyes.

"When the object is universal revolution, all the members of these societies must govern invisibly. Insinuate the same spirit everywhere, in silence, but with the greatest activity possible."

ADAM WEISHAUPT

CHAPTER TWENTY-TWO

28ᵀᴴ JUNE, 1784
INGOLSTADT

THE CITY WAS HEAVY WITH HUMID, EARLY SUMMER air. Adam Weishaupt paced in his university office, cursing. He paused only to re-read the terrible news. Six days prior, Duke Theodore had issued an edict against *'all communities, societies and brotherhoods in his lands that had been established without due authorization of law and sovereign.'* His Bavarian Minerval churches were to be shuttered at once, as were all masonic temples in the Duchy.

The duke had been heavily influenced for some time by various Rosicrucians and his sister-in-law, the duchess dowager. To support their fears of secret societies, they had recently provided yet more evidence from eager defectors of Illuminati-infected masonic lodges. These defectors claimed the Order to be heretical and spreading in dangerous ways.

Furthermore, the director of Bavaria's public schools— Minister Dantzer—had recently stepped forward to document how Weishaupt's Order had infiltrated education in order to promote revolutionary views on culture. Materials mocking religion and morality, as well as pamphlets proposing utopian solutions had found their way into curriculums everywhere. This, coupled

235

with the Order's boasting of influence in civil affairs—particularly in agitating Bavaria's relationship with its nemesis, Austria—had finally delivered the otherwise nonconfrontational duke to his limits. Weishaupt was now an official enemy of the state.

The professor dragged his finger beneath his collar and shouted for Socrates.

The secretary entered, grim and pale.

"This is an outrage," said Weishaupt. "A pathetic belch from an ignorant fool."

"Cato is on his way."

"Cato! That idiot has caused me enough trouble in Regensburg."

"At least that is out of the duke's jurisdiction," said Socrates. He poured them both some dark beer, then handed the professor his glass. He moved to the window where he stared over the green trees lining Ingolstadt's streets. "And nothing came of that business."

"Nothing? An attempted murder of a British diplomat—"

"Can never be proven that it was us." Socrates Lanz turned. "And Cato's thugs are in the wind. They will never be caught."

Weishaupt growled and swallowed his beer as he stared at his secretary's square face. He thought the man looked uneasy despite his heroic words. "They are in the wind along with enough rumors that we ordered it...that *I* ordered it. We may not hang for this, but it is a problem. Our enemies do not need proof, they only need suspicion to agitate their hatred." He dropped into his chair. "Bergström must know all about it by now. I am curious what he thinks." He leaned forward. "He and Attilius (Von Eckhartshausen). How they react to the rumors shall tell me whatever I need to know about both of them."

"Attilius may not have heard yet."

"Of course he has heard! He is in Munich. The whole city is buzzing," said Weishaupt. "I want Cato to keep spies on him. But I remain most interested in Bergström...or Brother Maurus, or whomever that damnable bookseller is." He swallowed a large gulp and wiped foam off his lip. *Whatever did I do to him? Why did he lie to me?*

"Might I offer an opinion, General Spartacus?"

Weishaupt grunted.

"We do not need to be taking chances in these times," said Socrates. "I think your bookseller is a risk. I think Attilius is a hopeless mystic. We've already learned that their common friend, Van Loon, is working for the Duke as a British spy."

Weishaupt turned. He studied his secretary's face, noting that the man's baggy eyes bulged red with exhaustion. "You look terrible." He wished all this would go away. "Go on."

"We turn away from them. We dismiss Attilius with threats, and we offer no more invitations to Bergström——"

Weishaupt stared. Each day seemed darker than the one before and now this. The truth was that he had little use for Eckartshausen other than his reputation, but now the man might be dangerous. "Attilius is one degree away from submitting his confessional. We can do little to control him until we have that in our box."

But what about his beloved Mr. Bergström? Weishaupt had dreamt of the youth's rising like a morning star to shine over his Order alongside himself. Oh, to see him receive his sword and crown alongside the skeleton in the black-draped room! Weishaupt expected the clever lad to easily ascend through the Greater Mysteries and attain the new degree of *Rex*—Man King. If the thoughtful young man preferred, he could have become a *Majus*—a Philosopher of the occult sciences guiding the esoteric dimensions of the Order. If only this bookseller would join the gods and carry the Great Plan forward with him. If only.

Of course, there was a time when Weishaupt had hoped the very same for Knigge.

The unexpected thought of the baron made his stomach turn. The baron's resignation was good news at first; he was relieved to be rid of a rival. But now, what if the baron was whispering to the duke or conspiring against him in Berlin? Maybe all this sudden trouble on Knigge's account?

Weishaupt shuddered. "Why no help from King Frederick in Prussia?"

"Eh?"

"Frederick of Prussia. He was a friend——"

"The Rosicrucians have gobbled him up," said Socrates. "You knew that."

Weishaupt stared into his glass. Did he? His mind turned toward the Rosicrucians and he clenched his teeth. "Jesuits could be disguising themselves as Rosicrucians. I hate them."

"Whoever they are, they are becoming more and more dangerous," said Socrates. "Cato insists they are aligning with the Church to oppose us. They have recruited unenlightened princes and have many friends in the lodges—"

"Who is *our* closest friend?"

Socrates paused. "Duke Ernst of Saxe-Gotha."[1]

The professor grunted with approval. "*Quintus Severus*. Yes, he is a good man. We still have many good men." He stared into his empty glass, thinking. "Tell Cato to keep our churches open. Duke Theodore will not press the matter beyond words."

"You are certain?"

"He is a timid man and timid men only push so far. Shrewd brothers of ours like Quintus will slowly counterbalance any others screeching at his table." He released a long breath. "Ja. I am certain of it." Weishaupt held out his glass and said nothing more until Socrates obediently filled it.

"The duke lives in a small world. He thinks he can stop us by denying us Bavaria," said Weishaupt. "He cannot limit us by interfering in this pitiful duchy. No, we are more than the *Bavarian* Order…we are cosmopolitan. Our brethren are in nearly every nook of Europe and Russia, even Poland." Assuring himself, he gulped some beer. "Now, where is Bode…er, Amelius?"

"In France again. He is working to infect the Parisian masonic lodge of the *Les Amis Réunis*, especially its circle of *Philalèthes*—"

"The occult masters of Europe. Yes, I know them. Their circle is powerful. We need them, but they are a bit too involved with magic. He must tempt them away from conjured spirits and the like." The professor set his beer aside. "He is to convince them that action, not spells, will change the world. But to do that, I told him to design a deeper rite that would appeal to both magic and power." Weishaupt smiled. He was delighted in Aemilius Bode's successes in France. "I confess a certain delight in my own genius." He sniffed. "Of course, I also instructed him to mask our identity by creating a new name."[2]

Curious, Socrates emptied the pitcher into his own glass.

Weishaupt scratched his arm. "Now, did you send my letter to *Lucianus*?[3] He is our most important tool."

"I gave it to our messenger two days ago."

"Good. Provide him with women or boys or money or whatever he craves. He is critical to providing books in great quantities to the reading societies. We are growing new ones in Mainz, Bonn, Coblenz, Cologne…all of this is as important as controlling education. Our literary societies are forming fathers, even as the schools form their sons. Can you see this?"

Socrates wiped a hand through his long hair.

"Lucianus has become our most important bookseller and publisher. I want him kept happy." But something else was still gnawing at Weishaupt, something he was reluctant to mention.

"General?"

Weishaupt blew a breath through his cheeks. "What about Knigge? Has he turned on us?" The fear of it had kept the professor awake through many a dark night. Weishaupt was well-aware that Knigge knew every secret, every lie and false claim hiding within the many degrees the baron had helped to write. More than that, the baron had never handed over the many documents still in his possession.

Socrates pulled on his sleeves. "I think he would not violate his sacred oath." He lowered his face. "If not for your sake, then for the sake of the brethren whom he still loves…and most certainly to save his own embarrassment."

Weishaupt listened.

"And I encourage you to show moderation. Your written attacks on him are doubtlessly being shared."

Who is this secretary to correct me! "Enough." The professor held up a finger. "Not another word."

Both men were abruptly startled by a sudden pounding on the door. Weishaupt motioned for Socrates to answer.

Socrates reached for the lock when a boot crashed the door in, knocking him to the floor. Three uniformed men burst inside.

"Dr. Adam Weishaupt?"

His legs nearly failed him. "Ja?"

One grabbed hold of Weishaupt by an arm. The others leveled bayoneted muskets. "Come with us."

Alexander stared across the cloister garden from the window of his monastery cell. News of the duke's edict against secret societies had reached Regensburg and the city was alive with rumors. Even the monks were buzzing about it, each with an opinion.

At his side lay his Bergström outfit, the jacket still stained by Albert's blood. In the week since the spies' attack, Van Loon had recovered dramatically. He remained in the care of an English doctor at the consulate offices near the Diet where he continued to send intelligence to Crown authorities.

Alexander had visited him each day, and each day the man filled his mind with more evidence of the Illuminati's 'real' plans for the world. But the stubborn Scot remained resistant. Though he had not seen Weishaupt since the attack, he was unwilling to believe the worst about the man. Van Loon argued that this was because he did not *want* to believe the worst. But now even Karl von Eckartshausen was alarmed. He insisted that someone was following him, fearful it could be either an agent for the duke or of the Order.

Uncertain what to believe, Alexander exhaled. Abbot Benedict had just summoned him to the library. He supposed the man's patience had expired. All of the intrigue surrounding Weishaupt and scandalous books and spies and attempted murders and the duke's decree surely must have forced him to finally bear down on the mysteries of Mr. Bergström.

"What shall I say about all of this?" Alexander asked himself. "How many sins do I confess?" He recited a long list to himself. "But none are without cause..."

But which cause? There seemed to be many: curiosity, fear, love, aspiration. He drew another deep breath through his nose, gathered up his bundle and began the agonizing walk to the monastery's library.

"Ha, my son," said Benedict with a smile.

"Father Abbot," answered Alexander. He bowed and entered the man's humble office.

The abbot rose from a wooden chair. "Brother Maurus. Always a joy to see you."

Alexander thought the forty-seven-year-old to look especially vigorous. His habit had been freshly washed, his ring of graying hair recently cut. "And a joy for me, as well, Father."

"Really?" Benedict winked.

> "The tongue forms a lie
> But the heart knows why."

Smiling, the abbot bade his monk to sit on a stool, avoiding any notice of the Bergström bundle tucked under Alexander's arm. "Be at ease, my son. I summoned thee for only one purpose. I want to offer Dr. von Eckartshausen sanctuary, and I want you to ready a room for him."

Alexander raised his brows.

"He is rightfully fearful," said Benedict. "He has conflicting positions as both an Illuminatus, a Freemason and an agent for the duke. The duke's recent edict makes him suspect on both sides. Given what happened to Van Loon, I think he should be sheltered here until this storm passes."

"He told you about—"

"The Order, yes. And his recent initiation and so forth." Benedict waited.

Anticipating the next question, Alexander blurted, "I am not an Illuminatus."

Benedict said nothing.

"Dr. Weishaupt belongs but says he is not the Spartacus everyone is talking about."

"Did I say anything about him?" said the abbot.

"No, but…" Alexander fumbled.

"My son, you are a mess." His eyes were soft. "You've spun a nasty web for thyself. You have been struggling since the day I met you. Over what, I am not exactly sure. But your striving…well, it exhausts even me." He laid an arm around Alexander's shoulders. "You still think far too much and you trust far too little. The good news is that you have no reason to struggle. All will be well."

"I…" The young monk was lost.

Benedict crossed his ankles. "I had a wonderful conversation with a Hindu mystic a few days ago. He came with some sort of delegation from India to the Diet. He said something that made me think of thee."

Alexander waited, wondering what on earth an Indian Hindu could say to catch the abbot's ear.

"He told me that baby monkeys must cling to their mothers, desperately. But tiger cubs simply enjoy the ride." Benedict put his feet up on a table.

Alexander scratched his ear.

"You look like a dimwit. Say something."

"I am happy for tigers?"

"What about the monkeys who fall?"

Alexander shrugged. "I am sorry for them?"

"You are not even trying." The abbot leaned forward. "Hear me. You live like a monkey. You cling desperately for your salvation." He pointed at the bundle. "You masquerade, you sneak about, you doubt, you lie, you cavort. You do not feel safe. I know more about your heart than you think."

A wave of unease came over Alexander.

"Are you not weary for all the striving?"

He surely was.

Benedict stood and walked to a window. "I think you are working with all thy might to feel safe and therefore happy. I suppose we all do to some point. But you—" He turned. "The serpent lies to us, you know; it tells us that we are monkeys." The abbot smiled. "But we are not monkeys. We are little tigers. We are children of grace and are secured tightly by love. Even that Hindu understands this." He drew a long breath. "Listen and hear me well. The good news is this: our rescue does not come from within but from beyond. Love and truth long to carry you as a gift of grace, little tiger. Learn to enjoy the ride." He smiled.

Alexander listened and he heard the abbot well. It all sounded very much like something Grunnie would have said. Warmth filled him as he remembered the power of mercy revealed in his linden tree. The young monk immediately began to open his bundle. "Father Abbot, I want to confess—"

The abbot stayed him with a raised hand. "I know all I need to know."

What do you know? Exactly? Or what did he think he knew? "I would rather I tell you, myself—"

"And I would rather believe that it all somehow serves a higher cause." Benedict dropped his eyes to a folded sleeve of Mr. Bergström's jacket sticking out from an opening in the bundle. "However, I do see Albert's blood stains all over that." Benedict extended his open hand. "Give it to me and I shall have the fuller wash it."

Alexander hesitated. "I use these clothes to enlarge my world, Father."

Benedict smiled. "Then at least go into that world clean."

He took a breath. What was happening here? Submitting, he handed the bundle to Benedict.

As the man received it, he said, "Brother Maurus, I would like to leave you with one final thing that I think shall serve thee well. Listen carefully:

Love and worry stand opposed,

Rarely friends, often foes."

Benedict paused for a moment, eyeing the young man. "As I have often tried to teach you, love casts out all anxieties. Thus, when such fear is present, love is not. I implore you to measure everything in this light." He shook his head. "I shout this at the Church but I find few to listen, even there. May God have mercy on us for it."

Another monk suddenly burst through the abbot's door and ran to Benedict's ear. Alexander strained to hear the whispers.

Benedict's face fell. "And he is here?"

CHAPTER TWENTY-TWO NOTES

1 **Duke Ernst II of Saxe-Gotha-Altenburg**, *Illuminatus Quintus Severus* (1745-1804) was considered an enlightened prince with lands located in central Germany. An active Freemason and patron of art, philosophy and natural sciences, he was initiated into the Illuminati under the name, *Quintus Severus.*

2 Bode eventually created the secret Lodge of the Philadelphes from members recruited out of the French masonic occult group known as the *Philalèthes.* The purpose was to promote the revolutionary intentions of Illuminism within French Freemasonry. This important move was the first example of the Order spreading beyond its original organizational structure, and established Illuminism squarely within the activities leading to the French Revolution.

3 **Christoph Friedrich Nicolai**, *Illuminatus Lucianus* (1733-1811), was an extraordinarily important bookseller and publisher from Berlin. His catalogue dominated the sale of media throughout Europe, thus giving him unique control over the information available to the elites of the continent. He was an active member of various secret societies and would eventually play a large role in projecting the principles of the Illuminati into the future. His taken name honors Lucian of Samosata (120-190AD) who famously mocked Jesus Christ and his followers.

"I will not confide the tragic secrets to you. I can only tell you that the conspiracy is so well designed that it will be impossible for either the monarchy or the Church to escape."

COMTE DE VIRIEU [1]

CHAPTER TWENTY-THREE

THE MONK NODDED. "YES, HE IS HERE."

"Then we come at once." Abbot Benedict turned to Alexander. "Karl von Eckartshausen was beaten just beyond our gates…"

The three men ran from the library office and found Karl bruised and bloodied in the refectory. His clothes were ripped and hanging off his body. Two monks were serving him soup, warm bread and honey. The cloister's physician was tending his cuts.

"Dr. von Eckartshausen!" cried the abbot.

The thirty-two-year-old melancholic stared into space. "My dear abbot. Today is my birthday. I hoped for better." He tried to smile. "Thank you for your hospitality."

As the abbot ordered a set of guest's clothing, Alexander fell to one knee alongside Karl. "Who did this?"

"Three men. It was all very fast. I was buying a cookie from a vendor just outside your gate. I was grabbed, dragged away and thrown into a dark cellar. As you can see, they handled me roughly. They ripped my clothing apart looking for something."

"Did you see their faces?"

Karl shook his head. "I only remember a one-eyed man in a blue suit. Like I said, it was all very fast and dark."

"One-eyed! Was another in green?"

"I do not recall," said Karl.

"What did they say?"

"Nothing that I remember. I think they were searching for correspondence or notes of some kind." Karl faced the abbot. "I am rather frightened by all this. I should have remained in this sanctuary."

Benedict laid a hand on his shoulder, assuring him he was safe and that his room would be available as long as he needed. "And when you are ready, we will see about an armed escort to return you to Munich."

Karl's hands began to tremble. He answered in a low voice, switching his eyes between the abbot and Alexander. "But what if these were the *duke's* men? I have not been very secretive about my membership in the Order, nor the lodge——"

Alexander stood. "It was not the duke's men."

The others turned.

"As I told the police, a one-eyed man in a blue French suit was one of two who attacked Albert," said Alexander. "The coincidence is too great."

Karl was drawn and pale. His cheek bone was swollen and red. "Why? Why would they do this?"

"They suspect you to be a spy for the duke," said Alexander.

Benedict leaned toward Karl. "Does the Order not use threats to keep your loyalty?"

Karl nodded. "They threaten to have us disemboweled." He shuddered. "I thought them to be colorful exaggerations as with the lodge. But I have betrayed nothing."

Benedict pressed. "I hear rumors that they keep members' secrets in some kind of storage. They use them as blackmail to keep mouths shut."

"Ja. Confessionals. But I have not progressed enough to provide one."

Alexander was no longer surprised. Confessionals? Blackmail? Van Loon had insisted the Order used these and more to mute men.

The abbot put his hand on Karl's shoulder. "There it is then. They calculated you might suddenly betray them, so without a confessional they fill you with another kind of fear——"

Alexander looked into the academic's gentle face. "Albert is stabbed and you are beaten." He began to grind his jaw. "Weishaupt." *Can it really be?* The young monk wiped his hand over his head. Anger rose. "It seems that for all his talk, he intends to enforce his so-called enlightened world with terror." He turned to Benedict. "Which means he is lying about everything——"

Karl von Eckartshausen stood, slowly. "I will be resigning at once."

Alexander began to pace. "No. I have another idea."

July, 1784
MUNICH

Adam Weishaupt had spent a humiliating fortnight locked in a dingy room at the magistrate's offices in Munich. The time had been spent in fear, and the man was tense as rough hands threw him into a hard chair in the office of the duke's interrogator.

Across from him at a cluttered desk sat a pie-face bureaucrat—an ex-Jesuit named Prosper Schwab who glared through heavy, red eyes. Behind the professor stood an armed guard. In another corner sat a large, disheveled man in a scuffed, green jacket whom Schwab introduced as a 'street agent' for the duke. Seeing him, Weishaupt nearly collapsed in relief. He knew exactly who the man was—a hired thug for the Order given the name of *Mars* by Cato Zwack. His presence was proof that Weishaupt had not been abandoned.

Thus assured, the professor reached for courage. He raised his nose. "What is the meaning of all this? You drag me here and serve me oat bread and bad beer."

Unmoved, Schwab reviewed a stack of papers. He then looked up. "You are a Jew."

"I am not. I am a Christian."

Schwab stared. "You were arrested in Frankfurt as a Jew."

Surprised that the Bavarians would have that record and from so long ago, Weishaupt squirmed. "They were mistaken, as are you. I was born a Jew but baptized as a Christian, sir, and loyal to Duke Theodore."

The inquisitor reached for his quill and ink to make a brief note. "Are you Spartacus, founder and commander of the Bavarian Order of the Illuminati?"

Weishaupt took a breath. "Of course not." *Knigge! Knigge has betrayed me!*

"I see." Schwab blew his nose into a rumpled handkerchief. "Do you admit to being a member of this treasonous association?"

The professor fell still. He quickly reasoned that his inquisitor must have no real evidence, otherwise he would be sitting in a courtroom. But, given that stack of documents, he also knew that an outright denial might provoke problems.

"*Herr Doktor?*"

"Ja." Weishaupt took a deep breath. "I am a brother in this Order, but it is not a treasonous association."

"I see." Schwab dug through his papers. "What degree have you achieved?"

Christ. Too low will make him suspicious. Too high will excite his questions... "I am only recently advanced to Illuminatus Minor."

"Is that so?" said Schwab. He scratched three fingers through along his jowl, then withdrew several papers from his pile. "Just above...um, Minerval."

How would the man know that? "Ja. Exactly."

"Tell me, professor. Is it true that the Minervals meet as secret philosophical academies in what you call, 'churches?'"

Weishaupt nodded. "Honorable men discussing their hopes for mankind. Our meetings are discreet, not secret."

"Monthly and always under a full moon...like pagans?"

"I object to 'pagans' sir, but otherwise, yes."

Schwab read something, then made a notation. "Apparently, your teachers suggest that suicide is morally lawful, and that in all cases the ends justify the means."[2]

"I do not know of which teacher you speak, sir." Perspiration gathered beneath his collar.

SIEGE OF EDEN: THE RISE OF THE ILLUMINATI

"Is not suicide a mortal sin for a Christian, Herr Professor? I ask, because you say you are a Christian."

"Indeed."

Schwab made another note. "Your churches go on to teach that theft and even murder can be considered worthy of commendation—when needed to further an otherwise good end."

Weishaupt remained silent.

Schwab said nothing for a few moments as he read another document. "A witness testifies that the objective of your present degree is 'to have all religious and political preferences stripped away,' and to teach one how to manipulate minds."

Perspiration now slid down Weishaupt's cheek.

"Further, you are to provide a list of all your deepest secrets to be kept safely hidden as a guard against your defection. Confessionals. Interesting. Have you provided such a list, Herr Doktor? Should we expect it to be a long list?"

The professor shifted in his seat. "I do not know where you are getting your information, sir, but—"

"Not your concern. Answer the questions." Schwab's eyes narrowed.

What to do? "I am only recently advanced into this degree. I have not yet provided such a list."

"Then you have no reason to fear, yet you are perspiring."

"The room is warm."

Schwab smiled. He glanced at Mars who remained stone-faced.

Weishaupt looked at the man, too. He wanted to command the ruffian to strike Schwab dead and then kill the guard behind. "Is that all?"

Schwab laughed. "You say you are not Spartacus." He folded his arms. "Then tell me, who exactly is this Spartacus?"

"I do not know. We only know the names of those in our church and our immediate superiors." Weishaupt had always wanted that to be true.

"I see. Is this you trying to manipulate my mind right now?"

The professor remained quiet.

"Then give me *their* names." He blew his nose again.

Out of the question. "I am unable to remember."

"You are lying." Schwab made a notation. "Tell me, what is your Illuminatus name?"

Weishaupt balked. He had not anticipated that question. "My Illuminatus name, sir?"

Schwab slapped his palm on his desk. "Do not play me for a fool. You all take a Latin name. This is common knowledge."

The professor's mind raced. For no good reason whatsoever, he then blurted. "Basilius." No sooner had the word left his lips then Weishaupt knew he had made a terrible mistake.

"Basilius? Fascinating. It seems 'Basilius' is the public alias given to the unknown string-puller; the invisible magician behind the whole Order otherwise known as Spartacus. It is a ruse—a code name behind which the mighty Spartacus hides." He suppressed a belch. "Therefore, you—Dr. Adam Weishaupt—really are Spartacus."

The walls were suddenly close. A cold clamminess covered the professor's skin and the world was fast fading white. "No, a misunderstanding. You misheard me, sir. I said, 'Basilas.'"

Schwab laughed out loud. "And who in hell's name was Basilas?"

"A teacher of Greeks on the island of Crete." Weishaupt tried to swallow.

Schwab roared.

"I swear it," said Weishaupt.

"I think we have you, professor." Schwab turned to Mars. "Tell me what you heard."

"The witness said, 'Basilas'" Mars' face was unmoved.

"What?" The bureaucrat cursed.

Weishaupt recognized this was the moment. He stood. "Am I free to leave? I have answered your questions."

Schwab ground his teeth. "Sit down!" He stared at another paper. "I have witnesses who claim your Order teaches that secret societies shall one day retrieve the fall of human nature, and that all kingdoms and political borders shall disappear. What say you?"

Weishaupt recognized that language from his degree of Priest. "It is not *my* Order. And as I have already testified, I have advanced through only a few degrees. I have no knowledge of such a notion, though I find it intriguing."

Schwab gawked at the professor like a baggy-eyed bloodhound eyeing a wary hare. "Your so-called churches are said to teach that religion is the slavery of free thought, and that reason is the only god to guide men into perfection. Is this so?"

Weishaupt swallowed. He was careful. "In my experience, Herr Schwab, these thoughts pervade the Freemasons and so—given that many of their members offer discussion at our Minerval gatherings—someone might have heard these ideas discussed. And again, these are not *my* churches."

"Do you believe these teachings to be true?"

"I would have to give the matter a great deal of thought. Reason as god and religion as slavery are very radical ideas to my ears."

Schwab sat back. "You are an incredulous liar."

Weishaupt remained still.

The bureaucrat held up another document, one with a seal. "A witness says *you* claim that the true purpose of Jesus was to 'reinstate mankind to its original state of liberty and equality,' and nothing more. No overthrow of evil, forgiveness of sins, restoration of God's peace...none of that. What say you?"

Weishaupt wished he could respond in no uncertain terms. *Religion is the great evil, you dunce. There are no sins; 'God's peace' is the peace of Nature!* "Your witnesses claim that *I* say these things? I have never said so."

"My witnesses are referring to the Illuminati Order."

"Oh. I cannot speak for the Order. Who am I to do that?" He forced a weak laugh, and glanced at Mars.

Schwab wiped his face. He shoved his pile to one side. "I can have you detained for trial."

A wave a nausea filled the professor's belly. "On what charge?"

"Treason and heresy."

Weishaupt remained outwardly calm. "You could." He took a breath. "But then you would look more stupid that you already do. What you have is an impressive pile of rumors and false testimony. You have nothing that could condemn this so-called 'Spartacus,' let alone a mere initiate such as myself."

Schwab reddened. He turned to Mars. "We are collecting more evidence?"

"No. You have everything in front of you."

Schwab groused. "I thought there was more."

"You see? Gossip and unsubstantiated claims." Weishaupt stood. *Dare I?* "Think what you want of me, but I am a man who is well-connected throughout the duke's lands. If I were you, I would tread lightly. Many of your superiors were my students. If you remember, I *teach* law, sir. And I will not let the law be abused another moment." Weishaupt turned to walk away, then paused. He faced Schwab. "But I do have a right to know my accusers' names. Tell me."

"I shall not."

"Then I shall file a complaint against you and this harassment. Two weeks in a stinking room—"

"Be glad you were not thrown into the city jail, Herr Doktor. *You* tread lightly here. This is not a trial."

Weishaupt quickly calculated his position. "I intend to go home."

Schwab stared at the professor for a very long moment. He wiped his nose, then one eye twitched. "I know you are lying. You are lying about everything." He stood. "I will soon prove that you are Spartacus, and I will see you hanged. Now get out."

CHAPTER TWENTY-THREE NOTES

1 **François Henri, Comte de Virieu** (1754-1793) was a French aristocrat and Freemason of the Martinist (see later note) Lodge at Lyon. He attended the Masonic Congress of Wilhelmsbad and left that event shaken. This quote is taken from his letter to a friend.

2 The primary questions posed in this scene are drawn from historical references found in the contemporary histories of Payson, Barruel, and Robison as per the bibliography that follows our story.

"The ancient symbols always had more than one interpretation. They always had a double meaning, and sometimes more than two, one serving as the envelope of the other."

ALBERT PIKE

CHAPTER TWENTY-FOUR

July, 1784
Regensburg

ALEXANDER HORN AND KARL VON ECKARTSHAUSEN STOOD IN front of a four-story townhouse two blocks from the Danube. Walking stick pinched under one arm, Alexander pulled on the sleeves of his new coat—a slim, cream-colored, Bavarian-made replacement for the one irredeemably stained by Van Loon's blood. He then felt for a small flintlock hidden in the small of his back just beneath the shorter hem of his new vest. He adjusted his wig and his hat. Alexander lifted his face toward the full moon of the July night and tried to calm his nerves. "May each of us learn the truth, *tonight*." He faced Karl. "Are you ready?"

Karl von Eckartshausen tried to breathe. The man was built for books, not espionage. "No, but I suppose that does not matter." He had experienced the dark side of the Order—or at least he suspected as much. And for the past days, he had listened carefully to Albert van Loon's well-informed exposé of Weishaupt's purposes. If anything that Van Loon had claimed was true, the aristocrat had every reason to be afraid.

The pair stared at the door. Inside, Regensburg's Minervals were gathered for their monthly meeting. Alexander had attended this very church on three prior occasions as a special guest and against the wishes of the dozen members. He had been given entrance only because of his letter of introduction. But to-night, he had come for a very different reason.

"Are we too early?" asked Alexander. He opened and closed a hand, unconsciously.

"No." Karl lifted his Minerval medallion away from his chest and stared at the image. The medallion was about three fingers wide and suspended on a green ribbon. Its gilded coin was etched with an owl sitting upon an open book. "By now they have already bowed to the pyramid, taken seats in the in-ner chamber, sworn to do business like owls in the night, and should just about be done reciting the *Ode to the Goddess of Wisdom*." The librarian wiped his high forehead with a silk kerchief. "I am guessing that at this moment they may be re-viewing some inevitable questions over symbolism. Last month an initiate asked exactly who the Grand Architect of the universe was. Most shouted, 'Reason.' A few others, 'Nature.' One cried out, 'Jupiter.' Others offered Hermes, Isis, Minerva, Athena, and one shouted 'the moon'."

Karl shook his head. "Hearing myself, I can suddenly see the dark void in all of this." He faced Alexander. "It is all connected, you know." He took a breath. "For example, the Romans knew Jupiter as the 'Light-Bearer'—*Lucifer* in Latin. [1] Their goddess of wisdom, Minerva, leapt from the head of Jupiter—wisdom emerging from Lucifer. Imagine."

Alexander took a breath and aimed the head of his walking stick at the door and rapped.

No one answered.

He rapped again. Someone approached from within the house. Alexander and Karl exchanged glances. He forced a brave smile. The door eased open, revealing a brother wearing a more advanced medallion around his neck. The porter said nothing, waiting for them each to offer the pass-phrase.

Karl took a breath. "*O procul este, profani* (Begone, unenlightened ones.)"

The porter turned to Alexander.

"I am Mr. Bergström." The bookseller handed the white-gloved porter his letter of invitation.

The porter looked back to Karl. "Your name, brother?"

"I am Attilius Regulus."

"You are late."

"I am."

The porter then read Alexander's letter. "Wait here, both of you." He slammed the door.

Alexander slid a worried glance at Karl. Something was amiss. What if he was denied entrance. Where would that leave Karl—

The door flung open. "Attilius Regulus, enter."

Both men took a step forward.

"Only Attilius is permitted."

No! Alexander noticed Karl twitch.

"But the bookseller has a letter—" said Von Eckhartshausen.

"The Superior denies him entrance."

Alexander fumbled for words. "I protest," he said, weakly. *This is not good...*

"Tell the duke your troubles," said the porter.

The duke? Alexander's breath quickened. *Why did he say that?*

Karl retreated a half-step. "This man is my guest. He has a letter and he has been here before. By now you could—"

The porter leaned forward. "Shall I tell the Superior that Attilius Regulus refuses attendance on account of a suspected spy in his company?"

Spy? A jolt of fear struck through Alexander's chest. "I am no spy, sir! I am a guest."

"We know who you are, Brother Maurus."

"What?" The young man's color drained. "Who is that?" His own words sounded pathetically weak to him.

The porter turned once more to poor Karl. "You are cavorting with a spy. The Superior was hoping to talk to you about it."

Alexander fumbled. He stared blankly at Karl.

Karl lifted his chin. "Who is this 'Brother Maurus?' You mistake my friend for someone else."

Would Karl's unexpected bravado carry the moment?

The porter wiped his nose. "I only know what I am told, sir. Perhaps you should come in and explain?"

Karl's body tightened.

How can I save him? Alexander's hand closed, tightly.

"Indeed," said Karl, surprising both the porter and Alexander. "I do not ap-preciate having my friends insulted. I will set this matter straight." He stepped through the door, bravely. "With apologies, Mr. Bergström. I will clear your name. Until then, may you abide like Zacchaeus."

The door slammed.

Zacchaeus? Alexander strained. He turned his shoulder to glimpse the moon-tipped Danube. *'Abide like Zacchaeus?' Whatever does he mean? Zacchaeus...* He walked slowly toward the river, wishing he had paid better attention to his Bible lessons. Something dropped from a tree just ahead. No doubt a bit of branch rustled loose by a squirrel. He stared up into an old sycamore. *Poor Karl. What do I do? What did he mean?* He took a few more steps toward the river, head down. The air was heavy. *Wait.* He spun about. *Sycamore tree...Zacchaeus. Yes!*

Alexander spun away from the river and hurried back. Zacchaeus, of course, had supposedly climbed a sycamore tree to see Jesus better; it was his way of staying close—of abiding. He remembered that such a tree grew high in the garden behind the Minervals' house. He had once left the inner chamber to seek some air at a rear window on the second floor—one located just above the tiled roof of an attached carriage house. The heavy branches of the old tree stretched over that same roof. "Yes, yes, that is it."

Arriving, Alexander quickly removed his new coat, his waistcoat, hat and wig. He secured his pistol in a deep pocket and tilted his head backward. He still loved climbing trees. Something about their silent authority appealed to him, and this one looked ready to help. He jumped for the lowest limb and grabbed hold with two hands. He then used his feet to scratch his way upward, grunting. He threw a leg over the limb. With a grunt, he rolled into a straddle position. He then placed his feet carefully, stood upright atop the branch and began to climb upward.

In moments, the monk stared across at the peak of the carriage house roof. A long limb hung over it, paralleled from above by another. He could slide his feet along the lower while hanging from the upper. "Here we go," he muttered. Alexander shuffled sideways, carefully. Closer. Closer.

The lower limb sagged a little and then a little more until it rested on the roof ahead.

Alexander inched closer. With a tentative stretch, he arrived at the clay-tiles. He eased himself lightly atop the roof. His weight cracked one tile, then another. Alexander grit his teeth. He lowered his body carefully, trying to get to his hands and knees.

Done.

Relieved, he caught his breath and removed his shoes. He then felt for his pistol, still stuffed safely in his pocket. Alexander crawled forward, slowly, until he came to the junction of the roof and the plastered wall of the house. Not far above was the window.

Pressing his hands against the wall, he unfolded his body upward. The window was at shoulder height and, as God was merciful, it was open. *Good!* With a quiet grunt, Alexander hoisted himself through the hole, and in another moment found himself standing in a dark corridor.

Heart pounding, he strained to listen. This second story was comprised of a windowless inner chamber built as a temple within the normal perimeter of the house, leaving a narrow hallway on all four sides. He leaned his ear against the chamber's outer wall and heard muffled voices within. He licked his lips, thinking.

Was Karl there, or had he been taken elsewhere for questioning? Alexander reasoned that he most likely would have been taken into another room. But which one? The first floor was far too subject to eavesdropping from the street. The fourth floor was a residence occupied by a jeweler's family. *He must be up on the third floor.* But if he was wrong?

Alexander made his way silently toward the front of the building where he remembered a stairway from a prior visit. He placed a foot on the first step. It creaked. "Christ have mercy." He took another step up and then another. His legs weakened with fear. The stairway was utterly black. Ahead he heard voices. He took another careful step upwards but then sensed a presence. He stopped, sure he had been heard. Someone was standing just ahead.

"Who goes?" said a man.

Should he pretend he was not there? Alexander crouched. He chewed his lower lip.

"I said, who goes?"

Alexander heard the man take a firm step down, a shoe landing heavy on the oak step.

"I can hear you breathing."

The monk wanted to run. "I am just a brother, reflecting in this darkness."

"You have a strange accent. What is your name?"

Alexander ground his teeth. *Weishaupt will hear about this!* His mind strained for a Latin name.

"No name?" The Minerval took another step down. "What is the passphrase?"

Alexander strained to remember what Karl had said. "*O procul este...*"

The man fell silent.

Alexander could hear his own heart pounding.

"I am coming down."

Tensed, Alexander moved against the bannister. Step, step, step. He heard the man's hands sliding carefully along the wall. *Mother Mary...*In another moment, Alexander could feel the heat of the man's body brushing by his own. He smelled of lavender and some kind of spice.

The man paused. "There you are."

Alexander held his breath. Now what?

He felt a hand on his shoulder.

"You feel young and strong."

Alexander's whole body tensed. What's this?

"And shy." The man's other hand found Alexander's chest. "No coat? No vest?" He exhaled. "Ah, now I understand. You are here for our pleasure. Pleasure on the dark staircase."

Pleasure on the staircase? A chill abruptly spread through Alexander. He cringed. The man's hand began sliding along the buttons of his shirt.

No. Alexander grabbed it.

The man laughed and leaned his face toward Alexander's.

"Enough!" The lad pushed away. He dug for his pistol which he jerked forward and jammed into the man's throat. "Stop!"

The man fell still.

Now what? Alexander remembered Van Loon telling him that one of Weishaupt's first recruits was a known sodomite named Sutor. He mustered an out. "Touch me again and Herr Sutor will destroy you."

"You're here for Sutor—for Agathon? The fat priest from Salzburg? He was put out years ago."

Van Loon had not told him that. Alexander countered. "Spartacus readmitted him."

The man hesitated. "Where are you from? Scotland? Ireland?"

Alexander shoved the barrel of his pistol hard against the man's throat. "I am Welsh. Now go away and not a word. Sutor will kill you."

Grumbling, the Minerval abandoned the anxious Alexander, slipping down the staircase and leaving the lad very little time to gather his wits.

"Christ, my Christ..." Safe for the moment, he returned his pistol with a trembling hand and made his way upstairs in the dark. *Karl. Help Karl.*

Alexander felt his way through the dark into the third story corridor, Alexander followed the sound of voices coming from a room at the back of the house. He slowly rounded a corner to find yellow light coming from the cracks of a closed door.

From inside he heard voices, but not his friend's. He stepped lightly along the hard floor boards in his stocking feet, then placed his ear against the door.

"Hear me, Cato. The duke is working tirelessly to destroy us. His accomplices in Berlin are ready to start a revolution against us. You must warn Spartacus."

"He already knows."

Alexander pressed his ear harder against the door.

"Are our confessionals safe?"

A Frenchman.

"Of course."

"Where are they?"

"If I told you, they would no longer be safe," answered whoever this Cato was.

Another voice—one with a Russian accent—then asked, "Can the work survive the duke's wrath and our enemies in Berlin?"

Cato answered, calmly. "The work cannot be stopped. Fate is with us. We have friends all over the world. The duke is a weak idiot, and this little Rosicrucian slander means nothing. Take heart, brothers, this pressure teaches us to be better. The Minervals must be advanced more slowly. Too many are sniffing out the deeper truths. Your superiors must be wiser, and defectors must be punished." Alexander clenched his jaw. Van Loon had worked very hard to convince him that 'deeper truths' did, in fact, exist.

"How do you want these defectors punished?"

"Poison, blackmail, forgeries, threats against wives and children. We do not care. The only thing that matters is the work. Do what you must."

The men murmured their approval. The Frenchman then commented on the activities of an 'Amelius Bode' in his country, assuring the others that the French monarchy would soon fall to enlightened elites. "We shall destroy the king and crush the Church."

Alexander clenched a fist. *Murder, blackmail, revolution, destruction of the church. It is all true. But what does Weishaupt know? Who is Cato? Who is Amelius?*

"What of Basilius?" the Russian said. "When will he be formally revealed? Are Basilius and Spartacus the same man? The rumors all ring the same, that he is Dr. Weishaupt."

What? Alexander strained. *Weishaupt? Can it be true?*

Cato finally answered. "The identity of our supreme commander is known only to the Aeropagites. When he is ready, he shall step into the light."

The Russian pressed. "We demand to know."

"You demand?" Cato's voice rose. "The General serves no one. No one demands anything from him, not princes, not rumors, not Rosicrucians. Your demands are irrelevant."

The room fell silent.

Cato then offered a gentle follow. "I can assure you that the time of revelation is nearly at hand. Until then, brother, be at peace. All that we do is according to the General's will, and all will be well."

The Frenchman then asked, "Then what of Attilius von Eckartshausen, his British friend...and that monk bookseller?"

Alexander caught his breath.

The room fell silent for a long moment. Cato finally answered, "We must kill the Englishman this time. He is a friend to the Pitt family and is likely to alert them to our movements in Britain. Further, he allies the British with the duke.

Christ!

"As for Attilius: He is being questioned by the Superior as we speak, but I do not believe he is a spy. He is a brilliant scientist, but too awkward and too timid to sneak about, pass messages and the like. However, he is too stubborn about his Christian beliefs to be advanced any further. For now, we just keep an eye on him."

Good. Karl is safe. Alexander released his breath. *But there it is: They plan to kill Albert.* He waited for more.

Cato then added, "As for the bookseller: He was at our door this very evening—"

"Mr. Bergström," grunted the Russian.

Alexander pressed his ear, harder.

"Indeed," said Cato. "We had such hopes for him." There was a pause. "We are almost convinced that he is a monk posing as a bookseller, and a likely ally of the British agent. However, in his eternal optimism, the General would rather we prove it beyond all doubt."

Alexander closed his eyes.

"Now, enough of this melancholy. If I am not mistaken," said Cato, "our benevolent and happy General has paid for some ladies—and others—to bring a bit of fun to our discouraged brethren."

Hearing the pleased men move, Alexander stood upright. *God help me. Get me out of here.*

He hurried to the top of the stairs, extended his stocking foot forward and felt desperately for the first step. There. His hand then found the baluster. Down, down.

He heard some commotion in the chamber just below. The inner temple was adjourning. *Hurry.*

Arriving on the second-floor, Alexander made his way hastily through the dark and toward his window. Doors were opening. *Go!* He sprinted. Men's voices filled the space. Some were laughing, some were shouting for wine. One was shouting for Agathon.

Alexander ran to his open window and nearly dove through. *Go, go!* He quickly lowered himself to the tile of the roof. No longer caring one whit about cracking tile, he scampered across the slope of the roof to the branch of his tree. He took a firm hold of the sycamore, retreated through its branches and finally dropped to the solid ground of the garden.

CHAPTER TWENTY-FOUR NOTES

1 Christian tradition has often associated Satan with the fall of a 'morning star,' or 'light bringer' from Isaiah 14:12. The term 'morning star' was translated in the King James Version as 'Lucifer'—a Latin word meaning 'light bearer.' Jewish scholars point out that this particular reference was to an evil king and not a cosmic entity.

However, the Bible does refer to a cosmic power known as the Satan who masquerades as an 'Angel of Light.' (2 Corinthians 11:14.) His false light shines in contrast to Jesus Christ who describes himself as the true light of the world in John 8:12. Jesus is further described as the authentic 'morning star' of Revelation 22.

The etymology of the word, notwithstanding, the historical use of 'Lucifer' and associated images are intended to represent spiritual sources of insight standing opposed to Christian experience.

"Were I to let them know that our General holds all religion to be a lie and uses even Deism to lead men by the nose...were I to tell the Freemasons of our designs to ruin their fraternity...were I to mention that our fundamental principles are so unquestionably dangerous to the world, who would remain?"

BARON ADOLPH (PHILO) VON KNIGGE

CHAPTER TWENTY-FIVE

OCTOBER, 1784
INGOLSTADT

IN THE PRECEDING JULY, BARON VON KNIGGE—FORMERLY THE Order's senior Aeropagite, Philo—had signed a formal agreement ending his awkward severance. The man had properly returned all papers deemed to be the property of the Order. He had sworn his silence in all matters. Nevertheless, Adam Weishaupt had spent weeks pacing. In Berlin, the masonic Lodge of the Three Globes was making war on him, revealing to the other lodges that the Order was exploiting Freemasonry for political revolution.

How did they know? Was it Knigge?

Or was it a spy, like the one now believed to have crept into the Minerval church in Regensburg just three months before? Weishaupt had ordered that mystery be solved, and quickly. Cato had been in the same building and had no answers. No one had an answer. All anyone knew was that a Welshman had been discovered in the dark of an unlit stairway, one who left his shoes on top of the shed at the rear of the house.

But Weishaupt was certain that he recognized those shoes.

On this damp October day, he sipped tea in his parlor. The heavy drapes were drawn, and an ashy fire glowed in the grate of the fireplace.

"Husband?" Anna Marie entered with little Wilhelm on her hip. "The girls are sleeping; the boys are playing upstairs. I thought you might want to see your favorite."

Something about Wilhelm had captured Weishaupt's imagination from the day he first saw him nearly seven months prior. At the sight of his son, he smiled. "Thank you. He lifted Wilhelm from his mother's arms and held him overheard. "You are the reason I do this," he said. "You and the memory of my own *Mutti*."

Weishaupt walked him to a corner where a small box sat atop a desk. He opened the box with one hand and retrieved a toy top. He then withdrew a sheet of paper from a drawer, one that he used to present the concept of Illuminism to others. On it was his circle and dot. Setting the point of the top on the dot, he gave it a spin. "See, Wilhelm. Watch it. The joy of perfection. I am spinning the whole world to bring you happiness." He turned to his wife. "Look at him. He loves it." Weishaupt smiled.

A knock on the door annoyed both husband and wife. Their servant girl answered. It was Socrates Lanz, Weishaupt's secretary.

"I am very sorry, sir," Socrates said. Removing his felt hat, he pinched it within tight fingers. "I have news."

Weishaupt handed his wife their son, then pointed them away. "Good news?"

Socrates moved to the fire and held his hands toward its warmth. "Philo sends his thanks for your letters."

"What letters?"

"You had me write letters to the Council assuring them that your fears for his loyalty were misplaced."

"I did no such thing! And call him 'Knigge.'"

Socrates shuffled. "You did, General. It was part of your agreement. He wanted his name cleared for any hint of disloyalty because he still values the friendship of the brethren."

Weishaupt turned away. Had he? Why could he not remember? "And?"

"In his thanks, he forswears his continued silence. I am convinced that he is too committed to his reputation among the others to betray us."

"This is why you interrupt me?"

"I thought it would be good news, General."

Weishaupt grunted. "What of Regensburg? Have we found the Welshman?"

Socrates shook his head. "Cato interviewed the only witness for a third time. The man is no longer sure it was a Welshman."

Weishaupt cursed. "I knew it." He strained, then opened his mouth. "The fool had the accent wrong. It was Scottish and I know exactly who it was."

November, 1784
Ingolstadt, Bavaria

Alexander Horn could barely stand still as he waited for Adam Weishaupt's door to open. An early snow had dusted the shoulders of his overcoat. He stomped his new shoes—a pair Abbot Benedict had provided after he ran home in stocking feet from the episode at the Regensburg Minerval church. Under his arm was a small bundle of books for the professor, the first the man had ordered in many months. Alexander suspected something was afoot but could not resist taking the bait. So here he stood, licking his lips and waiting to see the man.

The door opened and a lovely young woman bade him entrance. He followed her hand into the foyer and to the familiar environs of the professor's parlor. There she took his overcoat, hat, and walking stick. "My name is Inge Marie von Brunswick," she said.

Alexander marveled. He thought her to be one of the most beautiful women he had ever seen. "I am...Mr. Bergström of Regensburg." He bowed.

Adam Weishaupt entered with a flourish. He placed a light kiss on Inge's cheek, slapped her lightly on the buttocks, and asked her to hurry with some red wine. As she disappeared, Weishaupt offered Alexander a seat by the fire. He was dressed in a dashing fresh suit. "Did she tell you that she was a 'Von Brunswick?'"

Alexander nodded. He thought the professor might be a little drunk.

Weishaupt laughed. "She *wished* that were true. I rent her from a business-man in Frankfurt."

"Rent her?"

"Ja. I pay for her pleasures. My wife and children are with the Sausenhofers grieving the loss of one of my daughters. I thought sending them away would be a kindness. Besides, I prefer to grieve alone and in my own way." He took a seat. "Inge has a friend just a few doors away. Shall I send for her?"

The young woman entered with a tray bearing two glasses and a carafe of spiced wine. "Thank you, my dear." He pointed to Alexander. "Isn't he such a handsome young bookseller?"

Inge flashed her eyes. "Indeed."

"Your friend would like him."

"I cannot stay very long, sir," said Alexander.

"As you wish." Weishaupt waved Inge from the room. "The Order has been recruiting females, something you may or may not know.[1] This was an idea of one of the inner circle."

"I have heard the rumors." What Alexander did know was that Weishaupt was still being coy, though he was surprisingly candid.

Weishaupt took a long drink. "Not rumors. Whomever Spartacus is should be praised. The female lodges will support fine work. They are to consist of two classes: One is for the virtuous—they shall be taught how to provide proper in-struction to their sons. The other is for those—shall we say—free from prudish restraints. These shall instruct us all in what happiness looks like." He laughed. "Inge is a Minerval of the latter."

Alexander listened carefully. Van Loon had revealed similar suspicions. What Alexander needed, however, was *proof*— something he could lay on the magistrate's desk.

"Bergström?" Weishaupt summoned his attention. "Or should I say, Brother Maurus? Who are we tonight?"

The professor's tone was troubling. "Why do you ask me that?" said Alexander.

Weishaupt smirked. "I cannot remember whether it was the bookseller or the monk who lost his heart to Julianna, beloved wife of Baron Ferdinand Augustus von Gumppenberg."

The word 'Julianna' gave Alexander a start. How did Weishaupt know this? "Julianna Roth von Himmelsberg?" he said. "I remember her. I remember lots of pretty girls."

Weishaupt smirked. "Of course." He drank some wine. "I remember her affection for dear Brother Maurus." He took another drink. "She has been recruited into the Order along with her husband...or so the talk at church goes."

Alexander squirmed. Could this be true? Or was the professor goading him for some reason. "I assume for the first class? Does she have sons?" He knew she did not.

"Ha!" The professor slapped his knee, laughing. "I hear that many want her in the other group but I cannot say for sure. She is a lively one. Too bad her husband is sickly."

Sickly?

Weishaupt poured his guest another drink, wondering exactly how to proceed. Cato's spies had been following this monk and reported his regular rendezvous with the British agent. Furthermore, they noted the arrivals of local Minervals at the monastery. None of this could be a coincidence. His rational mind was convinced that his young friend could no longer be trusted. But his heart still demanded proof. "I see you are wearing fine shoes. They look like Italian leather?"

The bookseller stared at his feet. "I...I believe so. Milanese, perhaps. I recently bought them in Regensburg."

Weishaupt studied the young man, carefully. "I always consider the wardrobe of people I do business with. It is an old trick my godfather taught me. Wardrobe reveals character, standing, and priorities. It is something of a window into a man. If I am not mistaken, your former shoes had rare, four-pronged buckles. I remember thinking you are one who longed to be noticed."

Alexander stared, blank-faced.

Weishaupt's blood rose for the hunt. "And what about that coat? Looks Bavarian. That is nice. But I remember you in a stylish olive suit. Italian, I think. Am I right?"

"How would you possibly recall my wardrobe, sir?"

Weishaupt noticed the sudden strain in Alexander's voice. "As I said, my godfather taught me to notice. Besides, you always wore the same clothing." Was now the time to summon Mars?

Alexander tried desperately to control his breathing. *Shoes. They found my shoes. How stupid of me! Now what?* "I thought it time for a change. As you said, I wore the same olive suit for so long—"

"No matter to me, Mr. Bergström. I simply note my observation. Now, I need to use the latrine. When I return, let us discuss these books you have brought." Weishaupt stood and left the room, leaving the door open.

Alexander's mind whirled. *He knows something.*

Nervous, Alexander felt for the pistol secured in the small of his back. His eyes then fell on the professor's desk. *I cannot leave here empty-handed.* The young man licked his lips. Dare he? He took a breath and hurried across the room to stare at a drawer with a key inserted in place. He unlocked the drawer and pulled it open. Inside were envelopes written by various hands. He dug quickly for the bottom. A bead of perspiration fell. He lifted one, then another and finally another envelope into his hand. He hesitated, then stuffed all three within his coat pocket.

Alexander paused, straining to listen. *Take more?* He closed that drawer and opened another. On top he saw a sheet of paper with the familiar circle and dot. Beneath was a small, hand-stitched booklet. He opened it to find a cipher code. The sight of it caught his breath. Take it or not?

Footsteps.

The monk gaped. *It would be noticed.*

Did it matter?

Take it.

Footsteps came closer.

Leave it.

Alexander grabbed the book and stuffed it into his pocket. He pushed the drawer closed and rushed to his seat.

The doorway filled and all the strength fell from Alexander's limbs.

Adam Weishaupt paused at the threshold with the towering Mars by his side. The two men stared at the bookseller until the professor felt some urge to slide his eyes across the room and rest them on his desk. He then introduced Mars simply as a friend. *Something's wrong in here*, he thought. He waved Mars forward, then walked to his desk. He stood over it and lifted his face. *The monk is pale and stiff.*

He noticed the key in his drawer. *Stupid of me.* He opened the drawer and stared into its contents. Weishaupt remembered that his last correspondence was from Aemilius Bode. Something about successes in Paris. Before that he had received a letter from his friend, Duke Ernst of Gotha. He spotted Aemilius' letter on top where it should be. He lifted it to see Duke Ernst's just beneath. Weishaupt exhaled and closed the drawer.

But why did Bergström seem so nervous?

Walking toward Alexander, the professor said, "This man has a question for you." He tossed his head toward Mars.

The giant in his green jacket revealed a pair of shoes he had been hiding behind his back. "These belong to you?"

Weishaupt studied Alexander's reaction. He noticed one of the young man's eyes twitch, ever so slightly. "He asked if they belong to you?"

"They look quite similar to my former pair. Why do you ask?"

Weishaupt smirked. *Lying and good at it. What do I do with him now?* The professor paused. A sinking feeling filled him. The truth was that when the spunky monk was not here, it seemed easy enough to imagine Mars disposing of him. But now, seeing him in his home...A surge of pity came over him, that and sadness. "You say these are not yours, and yet, I have never seen another lodge brother, or bookseller, or even a gentleman on the street wear shoes with four-pronged brass buckles." He waited, watching Alexander's face fall. "I wonder if they fit? What are the chances of another of the same size with this exact design?"

"I assure you, these are not my shoes."

Trying so hard to be bold. Weishaupt paused, oddly impressed with his courage. *What must I do here?* He had taught his Order that above all else, the ends justify any means necessary. *If I do not abide my own teaching, will not Mars tell the others?* "Mr. Bergström. I insist you try them on. You would humor my curiosity."

Weishaupt watched the young man struggle. Would he do it?

Alexander's eyes fell to the shoes now dropped at his feet. He stood. "If you cannot take my word as your friend, I must beg my leave, sir."

Weishaupt expected as much. He moved close to the young man. A great part of him ached. He once loved this fellow as if he were a dear nephew. He set his jaw and said, "You, sir, shall not leave this room until you have put these shoes on those feet of yours." He motioned for Mars who revealed a knife within his coat.

Alexander retreated, backing into his chair and then falling into his seat.

Mars moved closer.

"What is this about?" the bookseller said.

"A reasonable question," answered Weishaupt. He leaned over Alexander. "A spy climbed into the Minerval church window in Regensburg just a few months ago. He left these shoes behind."

"A spy? Why would someone spy the church?"

"Do not be clever, sir. You were at the door that night and were refused entrance. Someone with your accent was come upon in a dark stairway. And you left *your* shoes behind."

Alexander kept his eyes on Weishaupt's, then blurted, "It is true. Forgive me for lying to you."

What's this? The professor raised his brows.

"Your porter forbade me entrance to the church, and that piqued my curiosity. After all, I had been permitted inside by your invitation on three prior visits. So, I climbed into the window and listened to the discussion."

Weishaupt leaned his face forward. "What did you learn about?"

"Jupiter. Jupiter and Athena...and how it is that the Morning Star gives birth to true wisdom."

The professor blinked. *What the devil! Is that all this is? A curious youth and not a spy!* "And these are your shoes?"

"Yes. And again, I beg you to forgive me for lying. I was embarrassed by the whole matter."

Weishaupt gawked. *There must be more.* "This is not the first time you have lied to me."

Alexander said nothing.

"So, you admit to being on the staircase. You admit to eavesdropping. You admit to climbing in and out of the window."

"I do. But only to learn." Alexander kept is face to the floor.

"You are lying, but I cannot prove it."

"I do not believe I would have willingly come to your home had I been up to some other mischief," said Alexander.

That seemed true enough. But what of his friendship with Van Loon? Weishaupt kicked the shoes toward Alexander and ground his teeth. "Take them. Take them and get out of my house."

CHAPTER TWENTY-FIVE NOTES

1 As mentioned earlier in the story, Franz (Cato) Zwack infamously organized the female lodges of the Illuminati to consist of the two classes described above. In his correspondence regarding this project, he writes 'The (two classes) must not know of each other, and must be under the direction of me, but without knowing it. Proper books must be put into their hands, and such as are flattering to their passions.'

"Then war broke out in Heaven: Michael and his angels fought against the dragon, and the dragon and his angels fought back…So that huge dragon—the ancient serpent, the one called Satan—was thrown down to the earth along with his angels…The dragon became enraged and made war on those who keep God's commandments and hold to the testimony of Jesus.

FROM THE BIBLE, *BOOK OF REVELATION*

CHAPTER TWENTY-SIX

January, 1785
Regensburg

ON A BITTERLY COLD NIGHT, A TROUBLED ALEXANDER studied Abbot Benedict's shadow-etched face. He sat in the library of the Scots Monastery at a table with an equally disturbed Karl von Eckartshausen and an angry Albert van Loon.

As snow piled up just beyond the stone walls, Eckartshausen hunched soberly within a wool blanket. Van Loon tightened the scarf around his own neck. To one side, a small fire struggled to chase the chill from its modest hearth. After five weeks of laborious deciphering, the foursome now stared at the three letters Alexander had stolen from Weishaupt's desk in November. The first was from an Illuminatus named '*Saturn.*' His letter was recent and concerned itself with the state of affairs in Britain and America.

To our Honorable and Enlightened General, Architect of Happiness,

We are sprouting in Italy, influential in France, in the Russian court, and throughout our own empire, but do we or do we not have agents working in the new United States of America? Their Freemasons dominate them, but do we dominate their Freemasons? It seems to me we shall have a mighty struggle liberating the minds of the stubborn heartlanders in that place.

And what of those snobs in Britain? The conservatives are committed to their superstitions and traditions, both of which shall keep us from reorienting their institutions. Their people remain ignorant, especially the bog-trotters of Ireland and the hard-heads of Scotland. Have we launched an offensive in London? Edinburgh? Cardiff? Dublin? If the whole world is to be governed as one, must that not include these soggy places as well?

This letter had Albert van Loon in a twist. He retained great affection for his one-time fellows in America, and he was ferociously loyal to the British Crown. To him, the missionary aspirations of 'Saturn' sounded very much like sinister plots.

The second letter occupied the abbot more than the first. "This one is a dark mystery," he said. "I have a sense about it that troubles me, greatly." He tapped his finger as he read:

"'My Supreme General,
This brief note is to inform you that the matter which you entrusted to me is settled.
Your Most Obedient and Willing Soldier,
Marius'"

Alexander suggested this was written either to conceal a terrible deed, or simply affirm the completion of an errand. "But we have no reason to assume something terrible," he said.

Van Loon countered. "You never cease defending them! If innocent, why did Weishaupt keep it in a locked drawer?"

The young monk shrugged, but a troubling truth had awakened deep within. No longer was any of this merely about fanciful notions. Something very real was emerging. Men had been injured and some might die. The Church was at risk. Was dear Julianna really caught up in it? He stood and set coals in the hearth. "I do not defend them, I am simply trying to be reasonable."

The third letter was the one which riveted Karl von Eckartshausen's attention. He held it to the candle and adjusted his spectacles as he read it to himself yet again. Finished, he said, "Brothers, listen to me. Saturn writes of plots, Marius remains a mystery, but this—this letter says everything I have been pondering since I forwarded my resignation." He eyed Alexander with uncharacteristic severity. "Sit down. I want you to listen very carefully."

Karl waited as the young monk obeyed. "This was written more than two years ago, a few months after the Order had stolen the power of European Freemasonry from Strict Observance at Wilhelmsbad." He cleared his throat. "If you recall, Strict Observance was committed to the occult and the 'Invisible Superiors' whom they believed directed the most ancient roots of Freemasonry. But Spartacus wanted to break them from any sense of something greater than himself."

Karl pulled his blanket closer to his throat, moving his eyes from one man to the next. "I contend that Spartacus Weishaupt *is* a tool of the very forces he tries to deny." He gathered his thoughts. "Weishaupt's Great Plan is not his at all, but has existed from the very beginning of history, itself." He sucked a deep breath through his long nose. "Permit me to read:

"*My Most Wise and Purposed General Basilius Spartacus,*

The brethren rejoice in our common successes under your inspired leadership. Whomever you are, you have been gifted by Nature to return mankind to its intended state of happiness.

However, our Order must remember that the Great Plan does not rely on the conspiracies of mere men. On the contrary, the reclamation of

Eden is a battle that has been waged by hidden forces from the very beginning.

We contend that the Order went too far at the Congress of Wilhelmsbad. Consider our symbols. The Order's circle-and-dot directs us to the un-named Source of all things; the triangle is ultimate order; the owl, eternal wisdom; the pyramid, perfect stability; the All-seeing Eye, the supervision of the Invisible; the torch, Enlightenment. Whether by symbol or by instruction, our beloved Order is rooted in the ancient Mysteries, themselves pointing beyond the limits of mere men, even yourself.

Your kind clarification of our respectful concerns is welcomed.
On behalf of the Brethren in Frankfurt, your most humble and admir-ing brother,

Mercury.'"

Karl set the letter down. He clutched both his trembling hands around the blanket at his throat. "Yesterday, I sat beneath the linden in your snowy garden. That is when I realized that all of this is about the tree in Eden. There the ser-pent of false light coaxed mankind away from the simple peace of God's pres-ence. 'You can be like gods,' the serpent said. Is not that same voice hissing from the very bowels of the Order?"

He turned to Alexander. "My courageous friend, we do not wage war against mere men. We are opposed by deceptions, temptations, and the tricks of our own pride. As long as men chase false light, they shall never enjoy the light of love. Do you understand?"

Did he?

Father Benedict stood. "My heart has seen the same in my prayers." He looked kindly at his friends. "But remember, we do not wage war alone. There are other forces afoot. Forces of the true light, and they are many."

6TH FEBRUARY, 1785
INGOLSTADT

Holding his letter of dismissal on this gray day, Adam Weishaupt stared into the mirror on his office wall at the University of Ingolstadt. "They say you are an evil man." He sneered. "Imagine, buying 'ungodly' books.' Can there even be such a thing?" He turned away and dropped coal into the stove to chase the chill. "Now what?"

Today was the now ex-professor's thirty-seventh birthday, but he suddenly felt so much older. Melancholy, he collapsed into a thick chair. Aemilius Bode had recently written to him that the seventy-nine-year-old American—Benjamin Franklin—still looked young. How could that be? That rascal had managed an armed rebellion, forged a new nation, infused wisdom, advanced science and drank deeply from the glorious excesses of Dashwood's Hellfire Club.

He, on the other hand, was like a man with one foot in the grave. He cursed. All he ever wanted was to form good men in order to save the world from the unholy trinity. His reward? Anonymity, betrayal, exaggerations, lies. Not long ago, Inge had even stolen his cipher book. None of this was just.

Discouraged, he closed his eyes. _A worthless failure. I have wasted my life._ He wanted to sleep. If only Kolmer would come and encourage him. Head resting on the back of his chair, his breathing slowed. An image of the man arriving in black robes and a Spanish hat came to him...

"It has been a long time. You have done well," Kolmer began.

"Where the devil have you been?"

"I have been busy preparing good soil for the seeds you have been spreading."

Weishaupt watched as Kolmer pulled a wooden chair close to say, "Faraway, little German school boys read from the books you have chosen for them. They will be men soon enough, men who will carry on. Your teachings have sharpened blades in France. Britain is stubborn, but your efforts will bear fruit. America is in your future—Russia, Poland, Austria, Italy...all in good time."

Weishaupt's spirits lifted. "But no one celebrates my name. How can I rule them without their respect?"

"Ah, my dear Spartacus. You do not sound happy."

Weishaupt snarled, "Do you not hear the irony? My Order was to bring happiness." He squeezed his fists. "But the Rosicrucians are inflicting pain... and Duke Theodore—"

"The Rosicrucians will be forgotten; the duke will die." Kolmer's voice was sympathetic.

"What of the Freemasons? They are such a tedious bother."

Kolmer paused. "The Freemasons serve the Plan in their own way. Be patient with them. In time they shall fade into silly clubs for old men."

"My wife and children are a burden to me...all but Wilhelm—"

"I have been removing burdens all along, you just never take the time to see."

The professor liked that. "Who are you, really?"

Kolmer laughed. "I have been guiding good men for a very long time."

A noise from behind gave Weishaupt a start. "What?" He quickly rubbed his eyes...

"Professor? Are you sleeping?" asked Socrates.

"Does it look like I am sleeping?"

The man shrugged.

Weishaupt straightened his sleeves. "What do you want?"

"I just received intelligence from Cato and his men in Munich. The duke is about to issue a second decree against us." He held up an envelope. "I have decoded Cato's letter for you."

Weishaupt rubbed his eyes. "Then read it to me."

Socrates began:

"*Duke Theodore is displeased that Lodges of Freemasons and Illuminati have disregarded his prior edict and are still meeting. He will soon issue a new edict, basing new restrictions on allegations that we are heretical, degenerate and revolutionary. He is planning to confiscate all our funds, giving half to the poor and half to any defector. I have advised*

*our financiers to get any money out of the duchy and into safety, prob-
ably in Gotha.*

*My spies inform me further that the duke will order your arrest as the
'head of the serpent' and has already sent guards to Ingolstadt. Flee
at once.'"*

Weishaupt held tightly to the back of a chair. "First I am dismissed from the university and now this?" He lowered his face. "I am so tired, Socrates. I am tired of foolish men, of evil priests and puppet princes. I am chosen to lead the world, and yet I must flee like a common criminal? Damn them all." He looked up. "Yes? What else?"

Socrates Lanz answered, timidly. "Mars reports that the duke's guards arrived in the city just hours ago. They are likely to arrest you tonight at your home."

Weishaupt drew a sharp breath. "Tonight? Is he certain?"

Socrates shrugged. "Mars is never wrong. He says they will also arrest others."

"My family is in Regensburg. I will flee there—"

"Mars says to not go to Regensburg yet. They already know your family is there so they are watching the gates and patrolling the highway."

Weishaupt sat. "Then what does our omniscient Mars recommend?"

"He already made arrangements for you to hide in the house of a brother. A commoner named Joseph Martin."

"My God, what have we come to?"

"The world is bigger than this duchy, Spartacus—"

Shaking his head, Weishaupt sighed. "I suppose that is true enough. And the duke will surely die in time."

CHAPTER TWENTY-SEVEN

MARCH, 1785
INGOLSTADT

"THERE, HERR MARTIN. DO I LOOK LIKE A workman now?" Professor Weishaupt was agitated.

He shoved a felt hat over his head and wrapped a leather apron around his waist. He scratched at his wool leggings, brushed lint off his coarse tunic and wiggled within his uncomfortable shoes.

The thin locksmith nodded. He had housed the important refugee for the last few weeks inside a small shed located next to the street's latrine. Mars reasoned that the duke's guards would never stoop to search for Weishaupt there. "You could be a cobbler, a mason or a smith," said Martin.

A cobbler? Weishaupt wanted to be a god. "Just get me to Regensburg."

Martin—an intelligent and well-spoken Illuminatus of middling years—answered quietly. "Mars says we are to flee to Nuremburg."

"What? No. A thousand times no. My family is in imperial Regensburg. Once inside, the duke cannot touch me—"

"The duke has men watching for you just outside its gates."

All hope drained away. Of course, that monster Mars was always right. But Nuremburg? "For how long?"

"Mars says for a very short time."

"Mars. Always Mars."

"He is well-informed by Cato and the others spying the court in Athens," said Martin.

Impatient with his entire predicament, Weishaupt blurted, "Just call it Munich. I have no time to fuss with codes." He tried to get comfortable. "Where is the mighty Mars, anyway?"

"Soon, General."

Weishaupt paced. "And what of our books? Has Socrates moved them?"

Martin nodded. "Most have been secreted out of Ingolstadt, many to the care of Duke Ernst in Gotha. But Dr. Schwartz has fled with the occult library. Cato reports that he is in Regensburg but fears the people there. He is likely to run to Moscow."

"Cato tells *you* and not me!" Weishaupt was more worried about the trove of his deepest secrets supposedly safe in Cato Zwack's care. He dared not mention them to this locksmith.

Martin lowered his face. "I was to give you the message, but I feared it would upset you."

Weishaupt slammed his fist against the wall. "Upset me! This is outrageous—" The sounds of someone arriving caught his attention. "Mars? Is that fool Mars finally here?"

The professor threw open Martin's door to find Mars dismounting a thick-chested warmblood. "Good. Finally," muttered Weishaupt as he hurried toward his bodyguard. "I want to be out of this miserable neighborhood." He gaped at the horse and then craned his neck to the ends of the alley. "Where is my coach?"

"Coach?" Mars gestured to the horse. "She is your ride. And you must go alone."

"Eh?"

"The duke's men are searching coaches."

"Alone?" The word gave Weishaupt a start. He would have to navigate the exit of the city, ride this beast for two-days, and then find refuge in Nuremburg— all without the instincts and ruthlessness of Mars.

"Ja. Alone. The guards are challenging all groups leaving. They assume you are too cowardly to try and escape on your own." Mars wiped his nose.

Cowardly? Weishaupt clenched his jaw. "Why can't you come with me?"

"There is a warrant for my arrest. I am too big to hide."

Weishaupt ground his teeth. The man had a point. "Why would they think I am a coward?"

Mars raised his brows. "Coward and traitor, heretic and goat molester. These are your new titles, General." He handed Weishaupt an address. "Find this house. We will send for you when Regensburg is ready."

Weishaupt snatched the address from his hand. He grunted something of a thank you to Joseph Martin, and demanded Mars help him into his saddle. Red eyes bulging, the small man faced forward on his large horse and tapped his heels.

April, 1785
Regensburg

A reluctant Alexander Horn entered the British embassy in Regensburg to discuss a plan. Finally convinced that Weishaupt's Order was truly a danger, he nevertheless had no stomach for the intrigue now swirling about his former friend. As far as the monk was concerned, the professor was an imperfect man who had been swept away by some sort of misplaced view of the world, a view perhaps insinuated by 'forces' not entirely understood by anyone.

"Brother Maurus," began Albert. "I would like you to meet Dr. John Robison,[1] the first general secretary of the Royal Society of Edinburgh."

Alexander extended his hand toward the forty-six-year-old Scots scientist. The man's grip began a slight movement into a Master Mason's which the monk promptly returned. Robison smiled.

"Dr. Robison has invented something he calls a 'siren.'"

The youthful looking Robison nodded. "It is a device that whines a loud warning."

Alexander could not miss the irony. "Sometimes the world needs a warning," he said.

Laughing with the others, Karl von Eckartshausen then escorted the Scot to the door and bade him farewell. Turning, Karl joined Van Loon and Alexander at a large walnut table where Abbot Benedict was quietly pouring tea from an English pot.

As the men took their seats, Van Loon said, "Duke Theodore has excited our Prime Minister Pitt[2] about the dangers of secret societies. With the minister's curiosity aroused, the embassy is instructed to 'pay more attention.' Robison is curious about what can be done, as are all of us."

Alexander sipped some tea. He knew he would not be able to walk away from this mess. "And what can be done, exactly?"

Albert retrieved a letter from within his vest. "I have here instructions to help gather documents and testimonies that support the duke's efforts. He wants to convict Weishaupt and his inner circle of treason, hang them and disband the Illuminati Order for good."

Alexander shifted in his seat. "I do not work for the Crown, nor does Karl or Father Abbot. And I am no subject of Duke Theodore." He set his jaw. "Furthermore, I do not think men should hang for ideas."

Van Loon pursed his lips. "Do you not want to see the snakes gathered up?"

"Of course—"

"You are still the King's subject—"

"I am a monk and I serve God."

Van Loon stood. "Sometimes I do not know who you really are! I wonder if you even do. If you want to serve God, help us defeat these devils!"

Alexander's cheeks went hot. His friend had poked a tender spot. "You do not tell me how to serve God!" he said as he stood. "I did not come here today as your agent, but as your friend." He took a breath. "Besides, you are off the mark. You can hang men, but you cannot hang evil. You cannot imprison it or exile it, and you surely do not defeat evil by doing evil! Evil is defeated by healing one soul at a time." He turned to Benedict. "As you so wisely teach, Father."

Albert paused. Sitting, he said, "And what of hanging men for deeds?"

Alexander liked nothing about hanging at all. "Perhaps for deeds, if it must be. But I would never celebrate such a thing."

"Then I ask you as my friend," said Albert. "I ask you as my Christian brother—"

"And as a man most well-informed," added Benedict. "Brother Maurus, we need you to help in your own way. You know Weishaupt, you have read his books, you have met the brethren. You may excuse their intentions as much as you need, but their methods reveal great danger. Have you no thought for the beatings of your friends?"

"Of course." Easing down into his chair, Alexander turned away. It was not only that. Weeks before, Van Loon had shared something even more troubling. He read a report to him confirming Julianna's initiation as a female Illuminatus in Frankfurt. The idea of it nauseated him. He pictured her in the dark shadows of some Minerval church with men who believed in 'holy sinning.' But to add this danger?

The young monk exhaled. Staring at the medal suspended from his neck, he considered his dilemma. "I will do what I believe is right to oppose this Great Plan of theirs, and I will do it with all the strength I have. But I do it according to the mercies of God."

"You are a stubborn Scot." Van Loon then filled Alexander's cup. "Join with us in whatever way your conscience allows. You have the protection of King George no matter what."

Alexander nodded. "Fine. Now what?"

"We are expecting Weishaupt to try for Regensburg. His family is here and another of his daughters is sick. Once arrived, we need to follow him. I have two agents assigned to help us. We want to compile a list of his contacts, and then spy them. The duke wants names."

Karl leaned forward. "Personally, I am not accustomed to following shadows in the night."

Albert laughed. "No, you are not. But you have become masterful with the cipher. Your task is to translate any documents we can steal." He turned to Alexander. "And that, my friend, seems to be your strength."

"A thief. It has come to that."

"A charmer and a thief, yes." Van Loon smiled. "And a very devout monk. Assuming Weishaupt is not captured before he enters Regensburg, do you think you could return to his good graces?"

"What?" The thought of that sent waves of dread through Alexander. "You want me to call on him?"

"Yes. At his apartment. We would have guards hidden in the street."

"Are you mad? For what purpose?"

"From what you say, he has always wanted to believe in you. No doubt he needs friends, now more than ever. He may tell you something…anything. And so I want you—"

"I believe he now thinks me to be a spy for the duke. I have no idea what he would do if I go to his apartment."

"He may know something about Julianna." Albert glanced at the others.

Alexander shifted in his seat, thinking. "You are appealing to a desire in me that the Church severely opposes. Is that not true, Father Abbot?"

Karl von Eckartshausen took control. He pointed to some papers sitting by Van Loon. "You said you had more information that would put some heart into our duty."

Nodding, Van Loon retrieved the papers. "On the third of this month, a defector—Marquis de Cosandey[3]—offered this in his deposition: '*When nature places too heavy a burden upon us, we are to apply to suicide for relief.*'"

Karl gasped and the abbot nearly dropped his tea.

Albert reached for another paper. "And just days ago, another confessor offered this: '*The Order is a college of the most able and honest men ruled by a class of Invisibles who believe that six hundred properly organized brothers could govern the whole world.*'"

"There it is," said Benedict. "Men who would encourage mortal sin, and yet believe themselves worthy to govern us all."

Van Loon then retrieved a circular from the stack. "This was sent to Illuminati in the jurisdiction of the German National Superior—some kind of office within the Order. It says that all members are released from their duties excepting that of secrecy."

Stunned, Karl said, "But? They have dissolved? I do not understand."

Alexander's shoulders lifted. "Then the duke has already won! Why are we even meeting?" He stood.

Van Loon raised his hand. "Sit, please. It is a ruse, a temporary diversion to have this very effect."

"How can you be so sure?" Alexander remained standing.

A knock on the door turned all heads. Van Loon hurried to answer and offered his ear for a whispered message. Nodding, he turned to the others. "Weishaupt has slipped through the net. He is here, in Regensburg."

CHAPTER TWENTY-SEVEN NOTES

1 **Dr. John Robison** (1739-1805) was a Scottish inventor, mathematician, physicist and philosopher. A ranking Freemason, he was interested in the betterment of mankind through the advancement of science and learning. He invented the siren and contributed to the invention of a steam engine. A few years after this scene, Robison became disillusioned with the whole progressive project of the Enlightenment, eventually authoring the influential book, *Proofs of a Conspiracy* presented to both George Washington and Thomas Jefferson.

2 **William Pitt the Younger,** (1759-1806) was the youngest British prime minister, beginning his tenure in 1783 at the age of 24. A highly educated reformer, Pitt navigated Britain through the effects of the French Revolution and the Napoleonic Wars. An early voice against slavery, he supported John Witherspoon's efforts to outlaw that moral outrage. Like his father, he was sympathetic to the American cause and grew suspicious of secret societies, eventually banning most in 1799.

3 **Johann Sulpitius, Marquis de Cosandey**, *Illuminatus Xenophon*, (1762-1842), was a professor and secular priest in Bavaria. One of many eventual defectors from the Order, he became a particularly important witness against Weishaupt with such revelations as noted in our scene.

"After the overthrow of civil society, its law and its leaders, the Illuminati shall develop a more liberal opinion of human nature. Our principles will become the foundation of all morality. Let Reason be the religion of mankind and the problem is solved."

ADAM WEISHAUPT

CHAPTER TWENTY-EIGHT

20ᵀᴴ JULY, 1785
REGENSBURG

"I AM CHOSEN TO CHANGE THE WORLD, AND yet I am chased from my home to live in this squalor!" Weishaupt looked around his modest apartment in Regensburg. It was located in a four-story townhouse on Engelsberger Street not far from the river. "Another daughter buried, my wife turned shrew…only one son worthy of my love—"

"Wilhelm will carry on for us all," said Socrates. The secretary dabbed his sweated brow. The summer day was stifling. "All will be well, Spartacus. We smuggled you into Regensburg safely, did we not?"

The professor chafed. "All is not well!" In truth, he feared that any day Kolmer might arrive with his carriage and sweeping cape to lecture him. *He will demand that I destroy the duke, punish the defectors, and put order to the Order*, he thought. He narrowed his eyes at Socrates. "I am a fugitive living on 'The Street of Angels,' of all places. Imagine that! Who arranged for this address?"

Socrates shrugged. "See it as an irony."

"You are an idiot." Weishaupt called for his son. His wife, Anna Marie, entered. She was drawn and pale from burying children and living with a husband supposedly chosen for higher things than her. The woman presented Wilhelm, now eighteen months old. The white-haired toddler giggled as Weishaupt lifted him into the air.

"My abiding joy," said the professor. He returned Wilhelm to Anna Marie with a stern warning. "If you let this one die, you will suffer wrath like you have never imagined." As his wife scurried away with Wilhelm, Weishaupt turned on Socrates. "Now you. You are to keep me informed of everything. Yet you fail me at every turn and we are on the run."

Weary, the former priest nodded. "I am trying, General."

"Trying? Do you think the Plan can succeed by men who *try*? No! I have been given a calling from the ages. A calling to focus a millennium of momentum to rescue mankind, and you say you are 'trying.'"

Socrates Lanz opened his mouth but nothing came out. To this, Weishaupt cursed again. "Enough, fool." The professor stormed to a table and leaned on two fists. "Tell me what is happening? Where the devil is Cato?"

"Cato is under suspicion, so he is fearing for himself in Athens."

"Call it Munich!"

"Munich, *mein Herr*. His men infect a great deal of the government and the military. They remain loyal, but they need guidance."

Weishaupt stood upright. "And that bacon-faced Aemilius Bode?"

"He is still in France and doing well. Our mission to insinuate the Freemasons there is on track. The French welcome our insights and, in Aemilius' opinion, are on the cusp of liberating the people from the monarchy and the Church."

Weishaupt was suddenly pleased. "Humph. This will encourage the Order everywhere. Finally, our teachings will bear fruit. Men will see what ideas can produce." The thought of it sent a wave of relief through his body. "This is good. Huzzah for Bode. Why have you not kept me properly informed?" He darkened, again. "Why must I have to beg for this news?"

Socrates wiped his brow with another kerchief. "You have been in crisis, sir. Flight from Ingolstadt to Nuremburg to here. The death of another daughter. Directing the safekeeping of the library and confidential information——"

Weishaupt raised his hand. "Where is my membership list?"

Socrates forced a smile. He held out the hem of his jacket. "Sewn within my own clothing."

The professor said nothing. *Is this a good idea?* Finally nodding, Weishaupt said, "Cato last assured me that our primary secrets are safely locked away in a secret chamber within his house in Landshut. Is that still true?" His mind ran to instructions, rites, seals for forgeries and recipes for poisons, explanations of symbols...

Socrates was not certain. "I was here when Cato told you that. I would expect it to be so. But Landshut is halfway between here and Munich——"

"And well within the duke's jurisdiction. I know." Weishaupt walked to a window. *Exploding chest or not, this is unwise. If the duke's police find it...No, this is not good.* Outside, the summer air was oppressive. The sky above was divided; a bank of thunderheads had seized the eastern horizon. "Meet me at the entrance to St. Peter's in an hour. I need to send you through the gates with a message."

Adam Weishaupt closed the door behind his secretary and threw himself into a chair. Cato had his deepest secrets tucked away right under the duke's nose. A simple decision by the police to search the man's house would get them all hanged. "I must get to Cato."

What had his life become? He closed his eyes and lost himself in memories of initiations and secret messages, of Baron von Knigge's early enthusiasm. He thought of Mr. Bergström and when he did, he shifted in his chair. *A loss to us. A confounding riddle. Bookseller as monk—or the other way around?* He wondered.

The professor turned his thoughts to Sofia—his deceased brother's wife. He had avoided her ever since that business with her abortion. *Too great a risk,* he thought. *But I do love her and I am sure she loves me despite all that inconvenience.* He released a long sigh, then sought comfort in his old fantasy. Friederika. He smiled. "Ah, *meine Liebschien...*"

A tap on his knee startled him. Weishaupt opened his eyes to see Anna Marie standing before him with a lemonade. He thought her to be ugly. Saying nothing, he took the drink, swallowed a long draught and stood. "I am leaving."

"Will you return tonight, husband?"

Who was she to ask this? "Why must you know?"

"Your children want to see you." Anna Marie lowered her eyes.

Weishaupt grumbled. "I suppose."

"Can you play with them?"

"I said, 'I suppose!'" Weishaupt headed for the door. "You all seem to forget who I am."

Anna Marie stiffened. "We know exactly who you are—"

The professor whirled about. "I do not like your tone. The whole world will know who I am soon enough." He threw open his door. "Someday you will honor me for the suffering I endure. Until then, my business is with forces you cannot possibly understand."

Slamming the door, Weishaupt trotted downstairs and emerged onto Engelsberger Street, grumbling. Glancing into the darkening sky, he made his way toward the twin spires of St. Peter's Cathedral. Arriving, he cursed at the church, loudly. He had recently been informed that Pope Pius had warned an Illuminatus bishop that the teachings of the Order were utterly opposed to the teaching of the Church. "Of course they are, you fool."

Weishaupt began to pace. "Where are you Socrates, you idiot?" The professor ignored a sausage peddler and a young girl selling cakes. "Fools and dolts. I am surrounded." A distant rumble lifted his head. "Good. Relief is coming—"

"What's that?"

The voice turned Weishaupt's head. "Finally. Where have you been?"

The perspired man shrugged.

"You are wearing the same jacket." Weishaupt leaned forward and whispered, "The one with the rosters sewn inside."

"Ja. I thought them best to be on my person. Would you rather keep them?"

Weishaupt chased a fly from his face. His apartment was more likely to be searched than Socrates. "No. Just don't lay your jacket about."

"So where am I headed?"

Weishaupt started walking toward an old Roman gate at the southern wall of Regensburg's city center. He looked carefully from side to side. "I want you to find Cato. I suspect he may have fled to his home in Landshut." He handed his secretary a small bag of silver coins. "This should be enough for your journey. You must find him quickly."

The professor noticed two men staring at him from yards away. "We are being followed. *Scheisse*." He paused. "See if you can spot Mars over my shoulder. He should be able to intercept them."

Socrates obeyed. "Ja. I see him peeking from behind a beer wagon—"

"Good. Then keep walking, but act like this is social."

The pair headed south on the city streets, stopping from time to time to buy a little something. First a cookie, then a beer. They pretended to laugh. Regensburg was busy and loud, and surly from the heat. Weishaupt lifted his face, begging for a cool rain.

He then glanced carefully about. There. At a far corner stood Mars. Across from him was another brother. Thus assured, the professor bade Socrates to continue toward the gate. A deep rumble echoed through the narrow streets. "Rain is finally coming." said Weishaupt.

Socrates grumbled. "You are happy for it, but I will need to travel in a downpour!"

"God's will be done," scoffed Weishaupt. He then leaned very close. "You must tell Cato to be absolutely certain that our secrets are properly secured. These times are too unstable. And I authorize him to destroy anything that might earn us the noose. Anything." Weishaupt slid his eyes from side to side. "Do you understand?"

Socrates nodded.

"You look uneasy," said Weishaupt.

"I do not like to think of the noose."

"None of us do." The two walked toward the gate. A few drops of rain began to fall. "We must separate here. The rain comes at a good time." Weishaupt thought for a moment. "Just act relaxed."

He glanced to see Mars following about fifty paces to one side. The rain began to pelt the cobblestones. People began moving for cover. Thunder clapped. Weishaupt looked about, thinking. What to do? He had second thoughts. He stared through the gate. Beyond was the dangerous jurisdiction of the duke. Would Socrates be stopped and searched? Would they take his jacket and find the rosters?

But who else could get this message to Cato? *Maybe a ciphered letter sent with some commoner that Mars could hire?*

"Spartacus?"

Weishaupt met Socrates' eyes. "Just wait a moment——"

Before either could add another word, a blinding flash knocked Weishaupt off his feet. Crashing to the ground, he gasped for air. Stunned, his ears filled with cries. To one side lay a horse, convulsing on the cobblestones. To another lay a child.

What? His world was a blur. He cried out for the pain in his head. He struggled to his feet as a mob of people stumbled about. There, directly in front of him, was Socrates Lanz. One of the man's shoes lay smoking two yards away. The cuffs of his jacket were smoldering. Dazed, the professor inched forward, gawking. Socrates had a gaping wound at the base of his neck and another wound by his knee. His breeches were scorched and blackened skin was smoking. Weishaupt fell to his knees. "My God."

Mars appeared from nowhere and grabbed hold of the professor, jerking him upright. "He's dead. Get out of here."

"No..." Weishaupt resisted. "But——"

"Now!" Mars dragged Weishaupt farther away.

Gaining clarity, Weishaupt abruptly resisted. "No!" He looked back at Socrates, now surrounded by a crowd of people. Police were running toward his corpse. "His jacket——"

"Not now," cried Mars. "You must get away from here."

"You do not understand," wailed Weishaupt. "The jacket——"

November, 1785
Regensburg

After some dispute, Socrates' body was released by Regensburg authorities and delivered to his home in Freising for burial. However, an observant official noticed an odd protrusion within the lining of the man's jacket. To the great shock of Duke Theodore, rosters of Illuminati from all over the German Empire were then discovered. Though not complete, the lists contained hundreds of names, many of whom were in extraordinarily high positions in various municipalities, military ranks, universities and even the Roman Catholic Church.

The news began to spread; men of stature and influence—all hidden behind the cloak of Freemasonry and seduced by noxious notions of heresy and revolution—had somehow managed to embed a conspiracy throughout Europe and beyond.

Armed with actual names and supported by an increasing number of defectors' depositions, the duke now furiously recruited defenders of the Church and guardians of social order. The war against Adam Weishaupt and his Order had escalated. It's primary weapon—exposure.

Gathered within Benedict's well-stocked library, Alexander now sat quietly alongside Albert van Loon and Karl von Eckartshausen once again.

"As we have feared, this is no mere competition for the minds of men," Benedict lamented. "Even Duke Theodore does not fully comprehend that this is something far greater."

"Ja," said Karl. "The same forces can be found behind the deceiving serpent of Genesis, the dragon of Hermes, the Light-Bringer of the Romans, and Lucifer. It is that which has filled Weishaupt's spirit with its Great Plan—"

"All of this because a lightning bolt killed Jakob Lanz?" blurted Alexander.

Karl lifted his hand. "This bolt from Heaven simply reminds us that things are in the wind that defy understanding. How unlikely for lightning to strike anyone, but yet it struck poor Lanz—"

"And missed Weishaupt," grumbled Alexander. "If he were the Devil's tool, why would he have not been killed instead of his secretary?"

"A warning, perhaps?" offered Benedict.

"Or a coincidence, Father Abbot?" said Alexander. "The whole city is in turmoil on this matter. The peasants agree with the priests that it is a judgment from Heaven. The duke and his allies are thrilled for that. But men who actually *think* see it otherwise."

The abbot and Karl looked at one another. "You believe we do not think?" said Benedict.

Alexander shook his head. "Dr. von Eckartshausen offers a sound argument, but the interpretation of this single coincidence is likely to make a mockery of all he says."

The abbot paused. "Brother Maurus may be right; our conclusions ought not rest on a bolt of lightning."

Van Loon clenched his fist. "The facts are plain. We have a list of names that should shock the world. Even the military is infected. What happens when Weishaupt calls for an armed revolt? How many officers would obey. Many!"

The three men fell silent. What would Duke Theodore do?

"The Order wishes to introduce a worldwide moral regime that will be under its control in every country. Its Council would decide on all matters...giving it the unrestricted right to pronounce final judgment over individuals."

JOSEPH VON UTZSCHNEIDER[1]

CHAPTER TWENTY-NINE

SEPTEMBER, 1785
REGENSBURG

AN ENRAGED DUKE THEODORE READ AND RE-READ THE rosters of Illuminati recovered from inside Socrates' jacket. The shocking lists of active members both within and beyond his duchy proved that the Order was of no mind to disband in Bavaria or anywhere else. Not only had his subjects disobeyed him, but Catholic Illuminati had also mocked the pope's pronouncement against the Order in the June just past.

But why was the duke surprised at their defiance? His counsellors had often reminded him that the Illuminati intended to *overthrow* governments and religion. Exasperated, Duke Theodore now issued his third edict against the Order, this time demanding repentance and registration of all members under 'severe threat.' If only he had jurisdiction within the walls of Regensburg!

But the Socrates Lanz incident also fueled rising discontent among the folk of Regensburg. Who was this Bavarian heretic named Adam Weishaupt to dare find sanctuary in their good city! Had not God clearly revealed his displeasure by striking down the man's personal attaché? Enough! The heretic and his followers should be exiled before God poured out judgment on the whole city.

Alexander Horn remained skeptical of all of that, but he had other reasons to approach the professor's house—five reasons, to be exact, although he was not yet certain which he would actually follow. The abbot, Karl, and Van Loon had proposed their own three-fold plan to bring truth to light. First, they wanted him to capture some sort of evidence—a stolen seal for forgeries, a letter, a code book—anything. Secondly, they wanted him to upset Weishaupt in such a way as might cause some kind of impulsive act—perhaps attempting an escape or sending a letter that could be intercepted. Finally, at the very least they wanted him to present Weishaupt with their own forgery—a false letter of safe passage out of Regensburg.

Then again, Alexander had two purposes of his own.

So, on this windy mid-morning, he pulled his monk's hood over his head to shield him from a swirl of dust blowing his way. He glanced at a group of drunken workmen milling about with staves in hand. They were shouting curses at Weishaupt's windows.

As Alexander drew closer, he then noticed the green-jacketed Mars and two other brutes standing guard in front of the arched doorway. *Him!* He drew a deep breath and walked directly to the door, glad that Van Loon and a soldier were hiding nearby.

As he approached, Mars moved quickly to block his advance. The giant stood wide-legged and with arms folded across his barreled chest. A blast of wind tossed his dark mane. "What do you want, monk?"

"I am here to see Dr. Weishaupt."

"Why?"

"Not your concern." Alexander stood firm. "But I've an important message for him." He tapped his forefinger at the side of his head as if to say, 'it is in here.'

Grunting, Mars turned, entered the house and slammed the door behind him, leaving Alexander on the street with the two other rogues. Both were filthy, one toothless. He suddenly wished Albert had a whole company of men in hiding.

The door opened. Scowling, Mars bade him inside and escorted him to the fourth floor. There, Alexander ducked through a small door at his left which led to a tiny office barely lit by a cloudy dormer window of poorly blown glass.

A wigless Adam Weishaupt sat in a worn, upholstered chair. Drunk, he was dressed in a yellow woolen banyan and thin slippers. Alexander was shocked; he thought the thirty-seven-year-old looked like he was eighty. He quickly scanned the musty room. On one wall, a mirror hung above a small, dusty table that was set with glasses and a smudged crystal decanter. Otherwise the room was sparse. He faced the professor. "I am happy to see you again, Dr. Weishaupt."

Adam Weishaupt stared at the young monk from eyes made red from sleepless nights and unabated anxiety. The world was turning against him and—despite Mars, the silence of the emperor, and the promised protection of Duke Ernst II of Saxe-Gotha—he was afraid. "Why are you here, Brother Maurus?"

Alexander glanced at Mars.

Weishaupt narrowed his eyes. "Speak, monk!"

"I am here for two reasons, Herr Doktor."

What is he up to? "Tell me the second reason first."

Alexander cleared his throat. "The second reason? Em, I want to ask what you know of Princess Julianna von Gumppenberg."

Weishaupt nearly laughed out loud. *Love sick fool. That's what this is about?* He waved Mars back to his station at the door. "Who told you this?"

"The whole world knows about you, and a great deal about your Order."

The professor liked the ring of that. Hearing that the whole world knew of him enlivened a bit of defiance. He stood. "Good. You have always loved her." He laughed. "But why do you ask about her now?"

Alexander wondered the same. Exactly what was it he wanted to know? And why? His Julianna was not his; she was another man's wife. He stared at the smirking little professor. "Is she well?"

Unsteady on his feet, Weishaupt took his hand and then directed him to a seat. He lifted an empty goblet. "The last I knew she was living an empty life with a sick husband. My informant reports that she spends hours staring at the Rhine, reading poetry, or walking in her garden."

Why is he spying on her? Alexander thought. *And how drunk is he?*

"But she is one of us and rising through the degrees rapidly." Weishaupt moved to the table and filled each of their glasses with an amber wine. He staggered to his seat and both men drank. "My informant also tells me that your Julianna expresses wishes to visit your beloved Scotland." Weishaupt winked, then held his wine to the light. "This madeira is somehow made by Scots: Cossart Gordon and Co. You should enjoy it." He raised his glass. "To Scotland."

She has not forgotten me! Alexander stared into his wine. "May I ask why you are spying on her?"

Weishaupt laughed. "Spying? No. My informant is what we call a 'scrutator.' He is assigned to observe this sister's progress so that we might serve her well. She is special."

Serve her? Alexander had his doubts. *Special?* In what way, exactly? The way he feared? "I understand the female lodges consist of two types of sisters. One is for the pleasure of the males. The other contributes to your cause by studying—"

"She is the latter," Weishaupt slurred. "Does that help?"

It did. Relieved, Alexander took a sip. "And she believes in your goals?"

Weishaupt hesitated. "Goals? What are my goals, Brother Maurus?"

Alexander answered directly. "Your Order wishes to destroy Christianity and replace it with philosophy. You hold common morality in contempt and encourage all manner of behavior that would end decency. You despise private property and wish to replace it with common ownership. You wish to replace kingdoms with a world commonwealth directed by your adepts. You oppose patriotism in all forms. Shall I go on?"

He thought Weishaupt to look suddenly anxious.

The professor tapped the side of his glass with a finger. He then stood and began to stagger around the room. From his hard chair, Alexander's eyes followed him until the man paused in front of his small window. "You have been told lies."

"I think not, sir. You have defectors in your higher degrees."

Saying nothing for a long moment, the professor drank more wine. "This is hearsay. I am quite sure you have no documents to prove any of it." *These goals were known only to my Regents. Who has betrayed me?* Weishaupt tried not to slur his words. "The Order exists to return man to a state of happiness. That is all. Do you find that offensive?"

Alexander shook his head. "Of course not——"

"Good. Then it seems we agree." He returned to his seat and collapsed into it. "Now, tell me the first reason for your coming."

Alexander fidgeted.

"Brother Maurus?" Adam Weishaupt waited, belly churning.

Alexander cleared his throat. "I have come to warn you."

Warn me? "I see."

"You may believe your goals are worthy, but your means are surely evil. Your brethren are committing serious crimes. Once proven, they will hang. And if heresy and treason are proven, you will hang with them. I do not wish to see men hang, especially someone who has been kind to me."

Weishaupt stiffened. "Ah, how nice of you. But there is that little matter of proof." He drained his glass. "You have none."

"You do not need to hate Christianity. You seek the very same happiness for mankind as does our Christ. You want men to be free from ignorance and superstition, to be educated and free—these are all things the Church——"

Weishaupt laughed. Standing, he tripped back to his wine carafe and refilled his glass. "Did you know that Jesus was the first true Illuminatus—a prophet of reason. But his followers abandoned his teachings. If you wish to follow that Jesus, welcome. But Christianity? Never."

Alexander paused. "We have sinned against you, sir. I hope you can forgive us."

Who is this man! Weishaupt took another drink. "Forgive you?" He snickered. "I will destroy you. You think my Order is finished. You think I should come running to the duke and beg his mercy."

Alexander waited.

Weishaupt laughed. "We have spread far beyond his reach. All his flapping has done is blow my seeds into the wind." Emboldened by his wine, the professor lifted his chin. "Already, I have Amelius Bode in full command of the French revolutionaries who will soon show the world what we are capable of doing. He has attracted hundreds of brethren, like Francois d'Aubermesnil[2] and his brilliant publisher, *Monsieur* Nicholas Bonneville of whom you will surely learn much." He walked close to Alexander and leaned over him. "We are spread across Europe, including a friendship with an Italian genius named Buonarroti.[3] Remember that name."

Alexander crossed his legs. "Three men? If this is all that is left—"

"By Christ, this is not all!" Weishaupt reddened. *I have hidden my hand long enough!* He drained his madeira. "My brothers are creating illuminated reading societies in Bonn and in Berlin, Mainz, Trier…all over the German states. [4] The great Beethoven himself attends! The Order has become more than itself—"

"Rich men with books, that is all."

Weishaupt's eyes swelled with rage. "Brother Maurus, you come here to mock me, to forgive me, to warn me? Who do you think yourself to be?" He threw his glass against the wall then rushed at Alexander shouting, "Everything you say about my Order is true! We do plot to annihilate your Church and your kings. We will violate your decencies and utterly ravage your vanities."

Wide-eyed, Alexander left his chair and backed slowly away as the professor leaned into his face.

"Do you hear me? I could have loved you, but you betrayed me."

The room quickly filled with an eerie silence. Weishaupt took a breath. *Now what?* He turned his back on Alexander. He had said far too much.

Alexander held his breath. *The man is turned inside out.* He watched Weishaupt for a long moment as the professor fiddled with a new wine glass. He could plainly see that the professor had become desperate about all of this, suddenly acting more like a wounded beast than a philosopher.

The monk then remembered his assignments. *I could now testify to his intentions. I have born witness with my own ears. And I have upset him.* He then carefully felt for the false letter in his pocket. *But do I do this? Trick him into an arrest?*

Sneering from his view in the mirror, Weishaupt finally said, "Look at you in your black robe, smug and self-satisfied. You think you are clever. You think you tricked me into a confession of my purposes."

"As I said, I came to warn you." Alexander dared a step toward the man. "I believe that if you surrender yourself and agree to abandon your methods, the world might actually listen to you. You do have something to say about injustice and—"

Weishaupt steadied himself with a long breath. *Something to say? Fool. They will hang me for what I have told you.* He said nothing for a long time. Another silence filled the room. A heaviness began to weigh his limbs. He considered what needed to be done, but it gave him no joy. On the contrary, a sudden wave of sorrow found him.

Weishaupt turned from the mirror and walked close to the monk. "So, you have come to warn me? I thank you for that." He felt an unexpected twinge of comfort in the monk's intentions. Sighing, he motioned for Alexander's empty wine goblet. He then returned to the little table and stared at himself in the mirror. *Is the dye cast?* A cold resolve crept through him. He shifted his gaze to Alexander's reflection. *Duty is upon me. I suppose he is a good man. A better man than me? But I am neither good nor evil, am I?* He pursed his lips. *Perhaps I am simply necessary.*

Still facing the mirror, the professor filled both glasses. "My dear Brother Maurus, I wish I knew you as the man you are instead of according to the masks you wear. Perhaps we could have found a way—." He noticed Alexander fidgeting with a small envelope. "What is that in your hand?"

Alexander returned the letter to his pocket. "Em, just an order for books."

The professor did not answer. *Oh, poor Brother Maurus. Good men cannot tell lies well. You are up to something.* Glasses filled with wine, he paused and stared into his own eyes. *If only...* He then slid his hand into a tiny pocket deep within his vest.

Returned to his chair, Alexander stared at the professor's back, waiting. But suddenly curious, he lifted himself upward from his chair high enough to see Weishaupt's hands in the mirror. The man was holding something.

The monk lifted himself higher still. When he did, he glimpsed the edge of a glass vial in Weishaupt's palm. A chill ran through him. He lowered himself, heart now pounding.

A moment later, Weishaupt turned and walked toward him with the two wine glasses in hand.

Alexander stood to accept his, mind racing.

"We each believe our path takes us to Eden, but there can be only one way to perfection. What say you?"

"Our paths are parallel, to be sure, Herr Professor. But the path of wholeness is the one that leads to love."

"Love? I am content to drink to that." Weishaupt raised his glass as a toast. "To love, then."

Alexander raised his glass. *He hands me a poisoned glass and talks of love. Is there no end to this man's deceptions?* "Love is the way of truth, sir. Love is kind. It is not arrogant, it is not self-serving, it does not rejoice in wrongdoing, and love is not afraid—"

"Ja. Of course." Weishaupt swallowed his drink.

Alexander stared at the professor, rage rising. "You toast love, yet you would poison me to serve some greater good?"

"What?"

He threw his glass to the floor and shoved the surprised professor across the room. "God forgive you!" The monk then made a dash for the door, scrambled down the stairs and burst into the street where Mars tried to block his escape.

Alexander dodged to one side. Mars and his two thugs lunged. He cried out, and Van Loon charged from his screen with his guard. In a moment, all six men were grappling and clawing at one another.

Too desperate to be afraid, Alexander snatched a stave from a drunken watcher. He smashed it against the head of the thug. The man fell away.

To another side, Van Loon's guard doubled in two, gasping. Mars jerked a knife from the man's belly.

Shouting, Van Loon swung his pistol forward and fired a wild shot, missing.

Mars ignored the shot and ran at Alexander. The monk swung his stave in empty air, then skidded to one side where the other thug grabbed hold of him. Mars cocked his knife arm—

"No!" Albert leapt forward, knocking Alexander out of the thug's grip. He then kicked a leg forward and swept Mars' legs out from under him. He spun to swing a punch at the thug's jaw, bouncing the brute against a wall.

Screening the fallen Alexander with his body, Van Loon then dug desperately for a second pistol buried in the small of his back. Getting hold of it, he alternated his aim between Mars and the stunned thug, both now climbing to their feet. "Stay behind me," he panted as Alexander stood. "Do you have your piece?"

"No. Christ——." Alexander had left his pistol behind.

"Just stay behind me," Van Loon ordered.

Crouched low like a lion, Mars slid an eye toward his accomplice. He smiled, wickedly, and with a deft motion he then caught his own man by the shirt and shoved him forward.

Startled, Van Loon fired, hitting the man squarely in the chest. But in that same moment, Mars jerked a short pistol of his own forward and fired.

A sickening thud filled Alexander's ears. Albert staggered backward, falling against him in a cloud of smoke.

Mars strode forward with his knife.

The stunned monk slid off Van Loon's collapsing body and dodged to one side. He ducked beneath a ferocious swipe of Mars' knife and backed up slowly until he was against a broken cart. Whistles filled the air and shouts. Regensburg police hurried forward. Cursing, Mars thrust his knife again, just missing Alexander's throat. He then turned, raced away and disappeared into the shadows.

Bewildered, the monk staggered forward and fell at Albert's side. "No, no!" He cradled his friend's head and gazed into his lifeless eyes. "I see you, Albert. I see you." Weeping, he then babbled a prayer for the eternal mercies surely extended to this good man's soul. Finished, Alexander gently gathered Albert van Loon close and rocked him to sleep.

CHAPTER TWENTY-NINE NOTES

1 **Joseph von Utzschneider** is noted earlier. This quote is excerpted from his testimony.

2 **Francois-Antoine Lemoyne d'Aubermesnil** (1748-1802) was an active French mason who was recruited into the Illuminati in 1787. He later became an important promoter of a new religion called 'Theophilanthropy' based on Deism and inspired by Weishaupt's desire to rediscover a perfect 'primitive' religion based on an occult apprehension of divine wisdom. His fellow Theophilanthropes included large numbers of French aristocrats, as well as Americans Benjamin Franklin and Thomas Paine. Decorated with the signs of the zodiac and scenes of nature, the churches of Theophilanthropy celebrated four sacred festivals said to bring into harmony wise men of all ages, one specifically honoring George Washington.

3 **Philippe Buonarroti** (1761-1837) was a second generation Illuminatus and Italian revolutionary carrying the Order's principles into Corsica, France and Switzerland. He eventually formed the first truly political secret society of the 19th century called the Sublime Perfect Masters. His organization modeled the various degrees of the Order and used nearly verbatim language in its communications. He later became a link to a third generation organization known as the Communist League of the Just which, in turn, hired Karl Marx to write his famous *Manifesto*.

4 The Illuminati had long before infiltrated existing literary clubs all over Europe. However, as pressure mounted directly on the Order, its members cleverly withdrew from the Order per se and re-formed into closed membership reading societies with the identical goals of the Illuminati in view. This was an important step in the ongoing life of Weishaupt's original Order.

"Conceal the very fact of our existence from the profane. If they discover us, conceal our real objective by professions of benevolence. If our real objective is perceived, pretend to disband and relinquish the whole thing, but assume another name and put forth new agents."

ADAM WEISHAUPT

CHAPTER THIRTY

November, 1785
City of Gotha, Duchy of Saxe-Gotha
Thuringia, German Empire

"You may have fled Regensburg, Spartacus, but your troubles follow." Cato Zwack slid his eyes toward a window.

"I killed no one," answered Weishaupt.

"No one cares. The emperor's agents are now poking about, and Bavarian spies are everywhere," said Cato. "No, this new house of yours is not going to work. You are nowhere safe except in the palace."

The professor stared at his lieutenant. "You tell me this house is not safe, yet you leave all our secrets behind in your cellar! Why did you not move them?"

Cato furrowed his brow. "It is all happening very quickly. But my cellar is secured with a secret chamber. To carry all its contents into a wagon and try to sneak away was a greater risk. Besides, anyone discovering it shall be blown to bits with our exploding chests."

Exhausted from his two-hundred-mile flight to safety from Regensburg, Weishaupt wanted only peace. "This must end," he said. "Look over there. Just beyond the wall is a green park, like in dear Ingolstadt. I want to walk my Wilhelm in that park without fear. Why can I not just be safe?" He studied the street. "Where is Mars?"

Zwack was in no mood for any of this. He, too, had become a refugee. After all, Duke Theodore of Bavaria was after every Illuminatus he could find in his duchy…and beyond. As might be imagined, the 'beyond' was creating a great deal of dissention. Nobles sympathetic to the Order—like Duke Ernst of Gotha—did not appreciate a foreign duke snooping beyond their borders. Nonetheless, as an attorney of significant influence in Munich, Cato was a prized target.

"Duke Ernst offers you the safety of the palace, and you insist on your own home!" Cato barked.

Weishaupt lifted his chin. "I am no mouse who needs to scurry into some little hole. In the palace I would be beholden to a prince. Have you learned nothing? I serve no man. Mankind will serve me—"

"Ja, ja. And 'in their serving you will bring them happiness.' So you teach us all. But until that day, you must stay safe. Theodore has men crawling all over Thuringia. Once he knows you are in this city they will snatch you away in the night. He will buy Duke Ernst a gift to say he's sorry for overstepping and you shall hang."

Weishaupt dismissed the warning with a wave of his hand. He then motioned for his family to disembark their waiting coaches, and as they did he paused to watch Anna Marie—now six months pregnant. "We do it for them, do we not?"

Cato drew a long breath, settling. "Ja, we do. Our children will have a happier life than ours." He faced the professor squarely. "The cause must prevail, which is why I beg you to take refuge in the palace."

"And what of you?"

Cato grunted. "Prince Frederick invites me to sanctuary in Augsburg, though Aemilius Bode wants me in France—"

"Amelius and the French," grumbled Weishaupt. He was torn about Aemilius Bode. The man's successes were impressive, but the glory he was enjoying… "This is all I hear about. Amelius is *my* man, yet I barely hear from him anymore. His successes there are on account of me!"

"Of course."

"He is moving too quickly and does not listen. King Louis will fall, but I fear for the chaos that might follow." Weishaupt shook his head. "Now, enough of this. Come, I am thirsty."

For the next weeks, the Weishaupt family lived peacefully in their new house— a two-story, half-timbered building in good repair and clean. The first floor offered a generous parlor and a comfortable kitchen complete with a large hearth. The professor's second floor room was an adequate space that included a small desk. His wife's room was adjoining, and the children shared the attic above. Outside, a half-dozen of Duke Ernst's men provided a covert guard spread about in nearby alleyways and sheds.

During this respite, the professor wrote to a university in Vienna in hopes of securing a position far from the threats swirling about him in the German Empire. After all, the Austrian despots also needed to be overthrown, to say nothing of the various princes suffocating the Slavic peoples. Vienna could be just the place to spread his Order eastward. Russia would be a prize, indeed.

He would need to wait patiently for a reply, however, and so on this dreary December evening, Adam Weishaupt was reading peacefully by a small fire in his upstairs room. The sudden banging on the downstairs door startled him. "No!" Jolted from his chair, he rushed into his wife's bedroom. "Answer the door!"

Anna Marie threw a robe around her pregnant body and shuffled down-stairs. The pounding continued. She drew a breath. "Who is there?"

"Me. Cato. Open the damn door."

She opened the door and Cato burst inside. He slammed the door behind him and slid the bolt through the latch. The man was soaked. His wig hung in dripping strands from under a soggy tricorn hat. "Bavarians are coming. They bribed Duke Ernst's men and will drag Spartacus away. Where is he? You have only minutes. Hide. He must hide."

Weishaupt inched his way down the stairway.

"Where? Where to hide you?" said Cato. Seeing no closet or even a large chest for the small professor, he pointed to the hearth that was quickly cooling from its earlier fire. "There."

"What?"

"There. I'll hoist you up there."

"But—"

All could hear a ruckus arriving at the door.

"Hurry, husband," said Anna Marie in a low voice. She rushed ahead to the hearth where she pushed ashy logs to one side. "Can you lift him, Cato?"

Weishaupt stared, blankly. "Up there?"

Cato quickly peered upward into the black chimney. "There are bricks at the base of the flue. I'll push you straight up the center, then spread your feet to stand on the bricks. They should hold you."

"If they don't?" Weishaupt moved into the hearth, growling.

"Then you'll be taken to Munich and hanged."

Fists now pounded on the door. Crouched, Cato wrapped the small professor within his arms and strained. Grunting, he lifted with all his might until Weishaupt clawed his way upward into the chimney. In a moment, the professor was in position. Cato backed out of the hearth and hastily threw off his sooty coat.

From inside the chimney, Weishaupt heard a window shatter and Cato mutter, "Here they come."

A Bavarian climbed through the window with a pistol in one hand. Cursing, he stormed to the front door and unlocked it. A half-dozen musketeers burst through.

Terrified, Weishaupt heard one of the men shout, "Where is he?"

"Who?" answered Cato, calmly.

All Weishaupt could hear next was a thump, a grunt, and a body fall to the ground. *Oh my God.* Unseen by the professor, a soldier had swung the butt of his musket against Cato's head, dropping him to the planked floor.

Weishaupt struggled to keep his feet. The sour soot burned his nose. He then heard a man assault his wife. "Where is your husband?"

Anna Marie's voice failed her. "With Duke Ernst, sir. They meet regularly."

"This late?"

Weishaupt bit his lip. *Do not betray me, woman.*

"I do not believe you. Who is that man?"

Weishaupt strained to hear. Anna Marie said nothing at first. Then he heard her say, "He is Johann Caspar. He sold us wood but never delivered it until——"

"Liar! He looks like a gentleman to me. He is your lover?"

Weishaupt heard a slap and his wife scream. *Do not betray me...*

"Search the house!"

For the next minutes, Weishaupt heard boots pounding all through the house. He then heard his children driven from the attic and herded down the steps. They tumbled into the parlor where they were interrogated. His eldest daughter, Nanette, insisted that *'Vati'* was regularly in the company of Duke Ernst and that the children had gone to bed hours before.

Good girl. Brave girl.

Weishaupt strained to listen, stifling a cough from an ashy downdraft. The men were clearly frustrated. He heard furniture tossed about. Someone broke some pottery. At last, one of them barked at Anna Marie again. "We are watching this house and this street. When your husband returns, we will seize him. After that, I suggest you take this devil's brood to France and put your curse on them."

The door slammed and Weishaupt dropped from his hide, coughing and covered in soot.

October, 1786
Regensburg

Just over a year had passed since Albert van Loon's death. The brave fellow had been buried in Regensburg's city cemetery with honors from the British Crown. An emissary from the Pitt family attended his services, as did Albert's brother and niece. An unexpected guest was Dr. John Robison of Edinburgh—the curious man of science briefly introduced to Alexander by Albert about a year-and-a-half earlier.

In these months, spies continued to warn the abbot that someone in the Order wanted Brother Maurus assassinated, along with Karl von Eckartshausen who was now under the protection of Duke Theodore in Munich. Therefore, Abbot Benedict continued to confine Alexander within the safety of the Scots Monastery where he was assigned duties within its impressive library.

The murder of Alexander would not have helped Weishaupt's cause, however. The monk had already divulged what he had heard in his tragic meeting to agents of Duke Theodore. Alarmed, the duke had then passed Alexander's testimony far and wide, eventually reaching Emperor Joseph II, as well as the Austrians, the King of Prussia, the British parliament, and most importantly, King Louis XVI of France. Some were alarmed, others ambivalent. The Americans apparently considered it all very far away.

As for the twenty-four-year-old, Alexander not only continued to grieve Albert's death, but he also remained disgusted with himself for failing to properly assess the character of Weishaupt in the first place. He had surely missed something, and had he not been so blind, perhaps Albert would still be alive. And why did he not bring his pistol that terrible day?

Concerned for the despondent young monk's well-being, the abbot responded in two ways. First, he had Alexander ordained as a priest. This would keep the young man busy offering mass to his brothers, hearing confessions and writing the occasional homily. Alexander did find some relief in the distraction of all of that, though he regularly complained that he was not worthy.

Secondly, the abbot permitted him to visit Albert's grave on the condition a guard followed. Grateful, Alexander did this faithfully. On this particular October morning, when the sun was warm and the air was cool, Alexander brushed fallen leaves to one side and laid a hand flat on the sodded earth of Albert's resting place. "'No one has greater love than this...'" He released a long sigh, sat back and thought of Grunnie Horn. He considered love.

Alexander then leaned far back until he lay flat on warm grass. He soon heard only his breath filling his chest, only to whisper its way out. In again, out again. His thoughts faded. He drifted away into an airy cavern of silence where he was filled with the peace of God's presence.

"Brother Maurus!" Abbot Benedict nudged the sleeping monk with an impatient foot, breaking the world in on Alexander like a crashing cymbal.

"Eh?" Annoyed, he scrambled to his feet.

"I have news."

Alexander wiped his face. "News, Father?"

Benedict leaned close to his ear and whispered, "The duke is sending men to raid Cato Zwack's house again. They have some kind of intelligence."

Alexander's mind went to work. "Is he arrested?"

"I do not know."

"Why do you tell me this?"

"Von Eckartshausen thinks you should join him there. If they find what they expect, they will need you both for deciphering and such——"

"Aye. How soon?"

Benedict was grave. "Very. You must say nothing."

11ᵀᴴ OCTOBER, 1786

LANDSHUT, BAVARIA

Landshut was a rich city within Duke Theodore's duchy. Lying not far from Munich, it sat on the banks of the River Isar with a view into the Bavarian foothills. Close to one of its arched gates stood the comfortable, red-tiled home of Cato Zwack.

Just days prior, Cato's wife had hired a stone mason to repoint loose bricks in a cellar wall. A nosey man, the mason had spotted odd drawings on a corner desk. More importantly, he calculated the cellar to be too narrow, given the dimensions of the first floor above. He quickly realized that the plank wall to one side was oddly placed. It was surely not original and no other houses in this neighborhood were so built. Aware of suspicions surrounding the Zwack family, he promptly notified the police.

Under bright sunshine, a dozen policemen—all armed with truncheons and a few with muskets—prepared to break down the heavy wooden front door.

Others guarded the back. To one side, Karl von Eckartshausen and Alexander Horn waited alongside a collection of empty trunks. Alexander stared at the trunks, hoping they would soon be filled with the evidence needed to put an end to the chaos, to arrest the villains and—perhaps most importantly—bring the light of truth.

A wagon arrived bearing four large men, a heavy timber and axes. The four quickly dismounted and lugged the timber forward. With a nod from the captain, they proceeded without ceremony and smashed the front door to bits.

"Search everywhere!" shouted the captain. "And bring axes to the cellar."

Alexander inched close. He could hear furniture tossed about and the distinct sound of broken glass. From the cellar he then heard the chopping of axes. His breath quickened. The house fell silent for a long moment. Alexander turned to Karl, now flushed with anticipation. "What do you think?"

"I think we have them," Karl answered. "Zwack is just arrogant enough to believe he was somehow invulnerable. That, or the net dropped more quickly than his options."

A shout came from below. Several policemen emerged. "Dr. Eckartshausen, come quickly."

Karl motioned for Alexander to join him and the pair hurried inside. They rushed down a steep flight of stairs into the musty basement now covered with splintered planks. Multiple lanterns cast a generous light through shafts of dust. Behind the shattered plank wall, they could see shelves filled with all manner of papers, locked boxes, vials, jars, and sundry books. Two men carefully carried a large chest away. An informant had warned of such an exploding chest in the possession of Zwack. Could they disarm it?

Wide-eyed, Alexander followed Karl forward.

"Let us break down the marks of private property; Let the Republic be the sole proprietor: like a mother it will afford to each of its members equal education, food and labor. This is the necessary law of progress."

FROM THE BUONARROTI-BABEUF *COMMUNIST CREED OF 1796* [1]

CHAPTER THIRTY-ONE

18TH AUGUST, 1787
GOTHA

IMMEDIATELY AFTER THE CHIMNEY SCARE, ADAM WEISHAUPT GLADLY abandoned his little house on Siebleber Strasse. Instead, he and his family now enjoyed a well-appointed apartment within *Schloss Friedenstein*—the palace of Duke Ernst that was built about a hundred years prior. The palace was a grand, three-winged baroque edifice with a central garden that brought joy to the professor.

Weishaupt refused to consider himself a fugitive. Instead, he told his wife that he now realized his arrival at the palace to be a fitting precursor to his ultimate destiny. In fact, the universe had wisely intervened to humble him within his chimney in order to refine him for his coming glory. "Ha! This place is precisely where I belong."

Anna Marie lowered her face.

"Whatever is the matter now?" Weishaupt scowled. "I grow weary of your doubts." But he knew exactly why she remained quiet. He, too, was secretly fearful. The raid on Cato's house had been a disaster. He had been assured by Duke Ernst and Illuminati from everywhere that all would be well, that whatever evidence was recovered might damn Cato Zwack but had no connection to Spartacus Weishaupt. They insisted that he was untouchable.

But was that so?

"I worry about the things rumored to be taken from Cato's house," said Anna Marie. "Does this not concern you?"

There should have been an explosion! The professor reddened. "Do not believe the gossip and the lies. Whatever mysteries Cato had buried in his cellar are his business and his problem. Which is why he is hiding in Augsburg."

But Weishaupt knew better. Whatever secrets were found would not be laid at Cato Zwack's feet alone.

In fact, the police now had in their eager hands an entire collection of ciphers and codes, symbology, over two-hundred letters, instructions for high degrees, tools for forgery and counterfeiting, recipes for poison gas, secret inks and notes on the value of a virtuous suicide. The police had been digesting it all for the past ten months…including one morsel the professor did not imagine was even there.

"I want to believe you, Adam, but—"

"Enough!"

"But what of the government's publications?" Anna Marie offered, timidly. "Everyone is reading them." Just three months previously, Duke Theodore and his ministers had published two volumes containing what they had learned so far from the Cato raid as well as a smaller raid on an Illuminati archivist in Sandersdorf.

Weishaupt wiped his brow and lifted a lemonade. "The public hates the Duke Theodore and will not believe his slanders."

Anna Marie reached for his hand. "But none of your brothers have challenged a single word that is written."

"Not yet, but surely soon." He withdrew his hand. "And I do not need your sympathy." His newborn child began to cry from another room. "Tend him."

The professor turned his face toward the large window filling his spacious apartment with good light. For the next quarter hour, he stared, listening to his wife coo their child back to sleep. Below, the duke's lush gardens were calming. Red roses and purple aster softened the trimmed edges of evergreen and boxwoods. A splash of native wildflowers lay like a carpet of colorful threads.

A trellis of white stood boldly against a Norwegian spruce. Still pools reflected the day's blue sky. It all pleased him so.

"I am chosen," the professor muttered to himself. "*Alea iacta est*, the die is cast. I have allies in high places. No matter what they do, we cannot be stopped." He smiled and sipped his lemonade. He then noticed a courier hurrying along a path bordering the gardens. Weishaupt leaned close to the glass and watched the man turn in his direction. Standing on his tip-toes, he then peered downward. The courier entered one of the arches of the promenade directly below.

Is he coming here? Weishaupt stepped away from the window. A mild dread came over him when a knock on the door turned his head. He licked his lips. *Good news?* He moved toward the door, warily. He opened it.

The courier bowed. "Herr Doktor Weishaupt?"

"Ja."

The man handed Weishaupt a small, sealed envelope. "From the private secretary of Duke Ernst, mein Herr." The messenger immediately scurried away.

Weishaupt stared at the envelope, shut the door and walked to a table. He put on his spectacles, slowly. He cracked the wax seal, unfolded the envelope and withdrew a short letter.

Finished reading, he put down the letter and removed his spectacles. "Wife."

Anna Marie entered with the baby.

"I must leave for the afternoon." Weishaupt stared into nothingness. Wilhelm came running from somewhere and ran toward his father on toddler's legs. The professor squatted to kiss the child's pink cheek, then walked to his room and dressed in his finest French suit—a handsome yellow coat with rich embroidery, a skirted waistcoat and snug breeches. He donned a new round hat which an Illuminatus from Poland had gifted him. Facing the door, he collected his silver-headed walking stick, checked his silk hose and low-heeled shoes, and then took a very deep breath.

Within the hour, an ornate, two-horse carriage arrived at the iron gates of the palace. The door opened, releasing the fragrance of sweet tobacco. A dark hand waved Weishaupt aboard. A large man under a heavy hood sat before the professor. Weishaupt balked. An icy chill climbed along his spine "Lucius?"

The coach lurched forward.

"Adam, old friend." The man threw back his hood, laughing.

"Kolmer. But—" An awkward silence filled the carriage. Perspiration gathered quickly under Weishaupt's shirt. Lucius was Kolmer?

"So, Lucius or Kolmer? Who do you say that I am?"

Weishaupt balked. Kolmer was Lucius?

Amused, Kolmer changed course. "Have you read *Agathon* lately?"

Agathon? Reeling, Weishaupt answered, "Not for years."

"Maybe you should."

What?

Kolmer reached under his seat and retrieved a bottle of scotch. "My tastes have changed, Adam. I once drank only Highland scotches, but now I prefer the Islay's. Smokey, peaty, wonderful. Have your tastes changed?" He poured both men a dram.

What is happening here? "My purpose is singular, sir. I have not the time to explore finer things."

Kolmer raised his brows. "A rebuke?"

"Rebuke? No, of course not." The anxious professor twitched.

"I see."

The clip-clop of eight hooves filled the silence that followed until Weishaupt could not bear another moment. "Why have you called on me, sir? And what of this Lucius masquerade?" He mustered a shred of courage. "Or is Kolmer the mask?"

Kolmer tapped the rim of his glass, watching the dark whisky vibrate. "It is not your concern." He stared through Weishaupt. "But I know something that should be." Indeed, he knew something that was about to turn the professor's world upside down. The Landshut police had discovered damning evidence in the Cato raid. A small envelope had been hidden away within the fold of a kerchief, itself tucked inside a box of random documents. The envelope contained the ciphered letter that Weishaupt had written to Marius Hertel some four years prior—a letter in which he admitted failed attempts to kill the unborn child he had sired with his sister-in-law, Sofia; a letter commanding Marius to try once again 'at all costs.'

"Did you order the killing of your unborn child?"

The color fell from Weishaupt's face. "Who told you that?"

"Do not pretend with me. The police have your letter to Hertel."

"Written in my hand, sir?" He struggled to sound indignant. "And with my signature?"

Kolmer sipped his scotch. "I do not know. Are you suggesting it is a forgery?"

A cold sweat now oozed all over the professor. He dabbed his bow. "Of course. Do you think I would be so foolish?"

"You do not look well."

"I am enduring a great deal. It is not easy being chosen."

Kolmer shrugged. "And it is not easy seeing you suffer. I always thought you to be a worthy man, neither good nor evil as some say, but surely efficient and quite necessary."

Something about that stuck in Weishaupt's belly.

"You have done well forming men's minds. They are a devoted lot—at least those in the higher degrees. You will find them to be defiant scoffers of Duke Theodore and his Jesuits."

Somewhat comforted, Weishaupt lifted. "Good. My faithful brothers know the truth and serve it well. I am proud of what I have built—"

"*You* built?" Kolmer raised a brow.

"Yes." The professor drank his scotch. *Who else?* Emboldened, he said, "The day comes when my name will be heralded."

"It is better to hide the hand. Your financiers are expert at that."

Scolded, Weishaupt turned his face to the window. "Of course."

Kolmer tossed his head at the passing scene. "Tell me, what do you think is happening out there, far beyond what a man can see from inside a chimney?"

The reference gave Weishaupt a start. *He knows about that humiliation?* Recovering quickly, the professor answered with a lengthy description of numerous successes from France, to the Netherlands, Italy, Austria, Russia, Scandinavia, Britain and a bit of news from his two lodges in the United States.[2] He praised his adepts, naming many and citing the scope of influence that the Order now enjoyed. He ended with a triumphant claim about devouring princes and priests, and upending common morality.

Kolmer listened, carefully, nodding from time to time and refilling both men's glasses. "And so, in sum you agree with me that you have served the cause, well, and that—"

"I have *led* the cause well, sir."

"Ah." Kolmer tapped the ceiling of the carriage and the driver reined his two horses. He pointed to the market street just beyond. "Yet, I still see men and women in rags."

What is his point? Weishaupt wiped his mouth. "Of course. This takes time. We must completely control education, entertainment—"

"I see. In France, Bode—or should I say, 'Amelius,' sharpens blades. Here, you print books. Which do you think these wretches would resort to first?"

Bode again! "France was prepared for us ahead of time," Weishaupt answered. "Her people already hated the Church and the king. But even there my Order gives necessary direction and discipline. In other places I move more slowly, as with Britain and America…the East as well."

Kolmer stared into the milling throng. "Do you wish to walk among them?"

Weishaupt cast his weary eyes across the milling throng. "Not today."

"I thought not." Kolmer stuck his head out of his window and ordered the driver to return to the palace. Settling back into his seat, he stared at Weishaupt for a long moment. "No matter what others might say, in my opinion, you have been a good investment. You succeeded in reviving something that will most certainly change the world."

Weishaupt wrestled with his comments. *Reviving? Investment?* "What are others saying?"

"Should a leader react to every barb, Spartacus?"

"Who is throwing barbs?" *What is happening here?*

Kolmer tapped a gold ring against his glass. "Well, I suppose a good example is Friederich Schiller.[3] He is not an Illuminatus, nor even a Freemason, though he is an important friend to our cause. Unfortunately, he now mocks you. And then there are the Mozarts—"[4]

Weishaupt raised his hand. "Mocks me! And the Mozarts—they know nothing of me! Fools. They are examples of the very ignorance I am stamping out."

Kolmer studied the professor. "I think you have lied to me about this abortion business. You ordered it believing you were protecting the greater good, did you not? It is the sort of thing a powerful leader might think to be an unfortunate necessity."

Weishaupt hesitated. *A trick?* "I have always believed in the greater good, sir. You know that. It is our single most important pragmatic principle."

"And since the end is good, any means that serve must also be good?"

"Of course."

Kolmer nodded. "I agree. But what is 'good'?"

Flustered, Weishaupt gaped. "Good is what serves our cause."

"I see." Kolmer took a sip. "Then what is wise, Adam?"

Now what! "Wisdom is seeing the good. Therefore, anything that serves the cause is wise *and* good."

"Whose cause did this child's murder serve?"

An uncomfortable dread washed through Weishaupt. "Murder? Did I admit a murder?"

"You do not need to admit it. In the eyes of your times you are guilty of exactly that. Now explain to me how such a stupid thing...such an unwise thing... served the cause."

Weishaupt could barely form a word. "I do not...I do not need to explain myself to you."

"Ah, but you do." The two traveled on in silence until Kolmer finally said, "Have you considered what is next for you?"

Next for me? All the professor wanted to do was survive long enough to reorient everything. "I have been working on some new ideas. From the palace I am able—"

Kolmer wiped his nose with a white kerchief. "New ideas are always welcome." He offered a paternal smile. "Yes. Write them down for us. Also, you should expose the ignorant hypocrites who have persecuted you. This will ease the pain of injustice you suffer. Do this here, in Gotha, and preferably from within the palace. Do you understand?"

Something was wrong. He was being somehow set aside. The professor's chest began to tighten. "I need to travel, to help my Aeropagites spread our teaching—"

"We have others."

Others? It is all falling apart! "No, you do not. I am Spartacus."

Kolmer's tone hardened. "You would do well to heed my words, Adam. Write your defense, feed your family and advise Duke Ernst as the doctor of law you are. If you need comfort, take heart in the seeds you have spread."

CHAPTER THIRTY-ONE NOTES

1 Buonarroti is mentioned in an earlier note. In league with fellow Illuminist François-Noël Babeuf (1760-1797) he created a second generation organization of the Order for revolutionary activities in France, Switzerland and Italy. This quote is from the credo of his high degrees.

2 The Illuminist Columbian Lodge of New York was chartered in 1782. The Illuminist Virginia Lodge of Wisdom was established in 1785. Each produced sister lodges and by 1799 there were approximately sixteen other Illuminist lodges in the United States.

3 **Friederich Schiller** (1759-1805) was a German poet and playwright who made deep philosophical reflections accessible to common persons. Devoted to the bettering of mankind, he did not join the Illuminati but kept close company with Illuminati brothers, including Goethe. He is a good example of the kind of man just beyond their membership that the Order hoped to direct in its goal of changing society.

4 **Johann Georg Mozart** (1719-1787) and his famous son, **Wolfgang Amadeus** (1756-1791) were not members of the Illuminati but were Freemasons and highly regarded throughout their homeland of Austria and beyond. Amadeus famously alluded to masonic imagery and purposes in his works, most especially in 'The Magic Flute.' Unfounded rumors persist that his revelation of masonic secrets finally cost him his life.

"Who among you is wise? Let him show by his good behavior and gentleness. But if you have bitterness and selfish ambition, such wisdom is devilish. For wisdom from above is pure, peaceable, and full of mercy."

FROM THE BIBLE, *BOOK OF JAMES*

CHAPTER THIRTY-TWO

AUGUST, 1787
REGENSBURG

"I NOW HAVE IT IN MY HAND," CRIED Abbot Benedict. He hurried into the monastery's library waving a paper. Arriving in front of Alexander and his brother, Robby (Brother John), he handed Alexander a copy of the fourth edict against the Illuminati that Duke Theodore had issued just days before. "The duke has banned all secret societies. He has issued nearly one-hundred warrants of arrest, and this time he orders death by the sword for anyone caught recruiting. "You, dear brother, helped bring us this day."

Robby—who had managed to remain aloof to this whole affair for most of these years—wrapped an arm around Alexander. "Now you can find peace, little brother," he said. "It is finally over and we can be friends again."

Alexander offered a half-smile. "We have always been friends. You have just been off doing God's work." He read the edict, quickly. Much of it was a rehashing of the prior three edicts. This one did, most certainly, give the monk clear cause to finally escape his membership in the Craft without fear of retaliation from the brethren. But it had gone a frightening step further. *Who should be put to death for ideas?* He wondered.

329

Then again, was Illuminism so corrupting—so vile a deception—that no other course remained? "I do not wish to disappoint you two, but the sword should be reserved for those who actually commit murder—"

"Like that vile Weishaupt!" cried Robby. He shook his head. "That devil ordered the murder of his own unborn child. He tried to poison you, his henchman killed your friend. Do these not move you?"

"I understand. Weishaupt is dangerous, and no one wants justice for Albert more than me. But now you seek vengeance against the whole of the Order for the crimes of a few. Most are good men who have shed no one's blood. They simply seek a better way for mankind—"

"You are hopeless," grumbled Robby. He moved close. "How far you have strayed. First, your curiosity draws you toward the temptation of secret knowledge—like Eve in the garden. Then you are seduced by that serpent, Weishaupt. You repent in part, only to now return to the defense of evil. How many poisonings has that wicked man inspired? How many suicides? Stabbings? Beatings?"

"You go too far, as usual. I do not defend evil, but only warn against our own evil in response. What evidence—"

"Chests full," answered Benedict.

"With respect, Father Abbot, they are chests full of ideas—"

"Evil intentions. Plots. Conspiracies. Plans," said Robby. "And very clear instructions on the mortal sin of suicide."

Benedict folded his hands. "Also poisons and recipes for murder."

Alexander gathered himself. "I do not say that the Order's secret intentions are not dangerous, even evil. You are not listening to me. I am saying we must have a care in the way we respond to evil. Are we not sons of Christ? Princes in his Kingdom? Are we not to love our enemies? You are a priest, Robby, and yet you lust for vengeance. Where is it written that we should love with the sword?"

Benedict interrupted, gently. "The sword is ordained to protect the weak. That is why Albert fought to save your life—"

The comment angered Alexander. He clenched his jaw. "Yes, yes, a thousand yes's, Father. But would you have me *hate*? Our hatred is why Weishaupt has an audience for his grand scheme."

"How dare you speak to Father Abbot like that!" cried Robby. "You attack the Holy Church." He crossed himself.

"Attack the Church? I call her to repentance, you dumb arse—"

Benedict raised his hands. "Silence, my sons." He turned to Robby. "Thy little brother is passionate for grace, whereas you chafe for justice—"

"My brother's so-called grace makes us weak," said Robby. "The Holy Church can never be weak."

Alexander bristled. "You are an idiot, and your justice is a cover for revenge."

"Enough!" cried Benedict. Patience gone, he pointed a sharp finger at the door. "Brother John, leave us."

Neither the abbot nor Alexander said a word as Robby Horn stormed out of the library. When the door slammed shut, Benedict turned to Alexander. He gathered himself, then lifted a hand over the young monk's head:

"God bless thee...for thy heart is golden.

God bless thee...for thy courage has been wrought from fear.

God bless thee...for thy suffering has borne wisdom from above.

But woe to thee for thy condemnation of God's Holy Church—"

Alexander wanted to burst. "Condemnation? You—"

"May you be as patient with those who love thee

As you are with those who hate thee.

Those who love thee will always be,

Those who hate thee shall never see."

Exasperated, Alexander answered,

"Their eyes might never see

Because of our hypocrisy!

"Hear me, Father Abbot. The logs in our own eyes are mighty timbers; the splinters in theirs but dust." He slammed his palms hard atop a table. "We have blinded them and now we would kill them?"

"You go too far," said Benedict, softly.

"These Illuminati want what we want. Justice, happiness—"

"My son, their utopian visions are counterfeits, and thus they inevitably lead the hopeful to very dark places."

Alexander swatted a fly on his arm. "Yes. Yes. But you would actually support the execution of men who simply hope for the best, even if they are blind to truth?"

The abbot looked away.

"No. In your heart you seek mercy."

"You are gracious to me, little brother." Benedict thought for a moment. "But I fear that they are severely corrupted and therefore dangerous." He shook his head. "You know as well as any the kinds of books that have insinuated into their very souls. The police found a good example in their raid: *Better than Horus.*[1] The book claims Jesus to be an Egyptian god. It puts Reason on the throne of creation. This is the sort of deception they believe."

"Your point?"

The abbot shook his head. "More is going on here than a contest of ideas."

"But we should never allow fear to extinguish the light of Christ."

The abbot wiped his brow. "You are right. And no man should be beyond grace." Struggling, he put an arm around the young monk. "But let us leave these matters to the state. I now require you to serve God in other ways."

16TH NOVEMBER, 1790
REGENSBURG

For the next three years, Alexander Horn submitted to his abbot's command and did his very best to attend his duties at the Scots Monastery in Regensburg. As France began to tear itself apart, the monk focused on his primary work as that of the monastery's librarian. His responsibilities included the acquisition of incunabula—precious books printed before 1501. His skill at discovering these was evident in shelves now heavy with the most amazing antiquities that drew hundreds of important visitors from around the world. The reputation of Brother Maurus now reached throughout the German Empire and far beyond.

In addition, he busied himself with private devotions, the hearing of monks' confessions, the offering of Mass, tending the gardens, entertaining visitors and so forth. His popularity as an engaging conversationalist, a charming guest and a clever wit had opened yet other doors. He was recently invited to conduct mass in private chapels and to hear the confessions of otherwise reluctant believers who were attracted to his heart of mercy. In turn, he was invited to a variety of balls and banquets, state visits and baptismal feasts.

In all of this, Alexander Horn grew in knowledge and in wisdom. Having seen love so powerfully available in the face of his grunnie and in the lifeless eyes of poor Albert, his own were opening wide to the goodness, the beauty and the truth all around him. Secured by such presence, he had become less restless, more centered.

Such confident grace then attracted yet other things. The British ambassador in Munich—a former friend of Albert van Loon—had recently begged the trusted monk to act as an official agent for the British Crown. After all, his popularity and welcome were unmatched in this city of intrigue. For the sake of his old friend, he agreed.

But then there was this: A confessor of Alexander's who was situated high in Emperor Joseph's court had recently learned through gossip that 'Brother Maurus' once had an eye for the former Julianna Roth von Himmelsberg. Thinking it would be a gift of gratitude, the man made some discreet inquiries. He had taken Alexander aside at a recent dinner to reveal that the woman's husband was 'a loathsome wretch fast approaching death.' Alexander found himself hanging on every word, only to walk away filled with both hope and guilt.

On this brisk day, Karl von Eckartshausen found Alexander in the cloister garden praying beneath his bare linden. "Brother Maurus?"

Alexander opened his eyes and smiled. "Ah, my friend!" Standing, the twenty-eight-year-old monk thought Karl looked oddly radiant.

The two shook hands. Just arrived from Munich, Karl glanced into the gray sky. "Rain is coming. I can smell it."

"I like the smell of rain. Remember, I'm a Scot! But I am curious, my good friend. What brings you to Regensburg?"

Karl adjusted his posture as if preparing for a long presentation. "I have spent the past three years believing the serpent's head had been crushed."

"Weishaupt? I am not interested. I have put my mind to other things—"

"Forget him. You should listen to me." Karl removed his hat and held it in two hands like a beggar holding a basket. "I implore you, Brother Maurus. The abbot closes his eyes. I have written to him over and over. But you. In this place you must hear many rumors. We need you to stay awake, perhaps now more than ever."

"Awake? Whatever are you talking about? And who is 'we?'"

"The Order is *not* dead. On the contrary it is alive and well, even in Bavaria. The duke frightened many away, but they are returning with a new boldness. He had to issue a fifth edict against them. His patience is utterly spent but I am told he lives in secret fear of what he cannot control."

Karl returned his hat to his head and reached into his coat with a gloved hand. "I have here a copy of the latest edict for Benedict to read." He waved it in the air. "You will see that it no longer refers vaguely to 'the sword' but rather says, 'any member attending a meeting, recruiting another, or corresponding shall be *mercilessly* punished by death.'"

"But why?"

"Why?" Karl was suddenly incredulous. "Do you not see why? France! That is why. The duke and other princes are accepting the truth that the Order's goals are not limited to reading societies and idle chatter over wine. They are not even about one man's murder of a child. No, the Order and its tentacles mean to bring blood to the streets *everywhere*—"

"We know nothing of Weishaupt's role in France. Besides, his vision of politics was generally temperate. Change over time—"

Karl darkened. "Weishaupt? He is no longer the issue. It is his Order that has multiplied. Weishaupt's protégé, Johann Bode—they call him Aemilius—is now in command worldwide. He has insinuated important French lodges, creating a wheel within a wheel known as the Lodge of the *Philadelphes*. The Philadelphes are busy cross-pollinating with that French Illuminatus, Bonneville, and his gigantic *Cercle Social*."

Alexander thought for a long moment. He quickly comprehended what all this meant and he groaned inwardly. "What you are saying is that a second generation is rising."

Karl nodded. "Exactly."

"I did not expect this."

"Of course not. None of us could have imagined what is happening. What one man has the skill to conspire like this? A single man can set a snare for a rival; he might join with a few others to plan the ruin of a reputation. But this? Never."

Confused, Alexander waited.

"Listen to me very carefully. I once said that it seemed to me that this so-called Great Plan could not be of men, alone."

Alexander waited.

"I made a journey to Switzerland last month and climbed into a high pass. There I met an unnamed man who walked with me for a time. He revealed more than I can say, though what I can tell you is very good news indeed. Last year St. Michael won a war in Heaven." [2]

The monk raised a brow.

"But the war on earth now rages. France is the present battlefield, many more are to come."

Alexander stared. *Has he gone mad?*

Karl smiled. "I am a rational man and so I understand your look of alarm. But when one perceives the whole beyond the parts—when one discerns with one's *heart*—one's mind can see differently.

"Do you remember how devoted the Illuminati are to the ancient mysteries? How they seek Hermes and adore Isis? How they worship Minerva in secret? Consider their attention to the zodiac and stars, to the symbols of the ancients." Karl took a few steps left, then right, thinking. "Their aim is set squarely on Omega—the final harmonious convergence of all things. They are utopians seeking to reclaim Eden in *their own strength*."

Alexander listened carefully. "Yes. I understand. It is Babel all over again." His vitality surged. "And so they follow a counterfeit light—"

"Directed by a dragon so clever, so cloaked in lies that they imagine an empire—"

"Like Babylon, preparing to overthrow the Kingdom of Christ!" *Do we go too far here?* Alexander stared into his barren linden. *But if we are right, then what terrible forces really do lurk behind these men?* He turned to Karl. "What do you propose we do?"

CHAPTER THIRTY-TWO NOTES

1 *Better than Horus* was a ciphered publication used within the Illuminati to promote the supremacy of Universal Reason over religious insight. Franz (Cato) Zwack's personal preference for materialism over the more mystical interests of many other members makes it unsurprising that this document was among his preferred treasures. I am unable to determine its author, though it appears to have been written in Amsterdam in 1785.

2 A true mystic, Karl von Eckartshausen reported meeting a man in Switzerland he described as 'full of wisdom and goodness, who was raised to a level of vividness.' This strange meeting was further supplemented by a series of instructive visions and dreams that ultimately prompted Eckartshausen's writing of *The Cloud Upon the Sanctuary*. This small book declares the presence of a spiritual force of goodness in the 'Celestial Church,' that stood in opposition to the secret societies and the counterfeit light of the occult.

The 1789 War for Heaven is catalogued in a great number of esoteric histories of the universe and is considered an important moment in the spiritual evolution of humankind.

Coincidentally, the French Revolution was sparked this same year, leading most historians to recognize 1789 as the end of the Age of Reason.

> *"One of the most ancient of man's constructive ideals is the dream of a universal democracy and a cooperation of all nations in a commonwealth of States. The mechanism for its accomplishment was set in motion in the ancient temples of Greece, Egypt and India. So brilliant was the plan that it has survived to our time and it will continue until the great work is accomplished."*
>
> MANLY HALL

CHAPTER THIRTY-THREE

20TH AUGUST, 1792
GOTHA

IN THE FIVE YEARS THAT PASSED SINCE ADAM Weishaupt's ride with Kolmer, the professor's world shrank. He would not admit it even to a mirror, but the raw truth was that his Order had not only survived, it had survived *him*. Spartacus Weishaupt had been sacrificed and his vision given to others.

"Anna Marie!" Surly on this hot summer day, Weishaupt rounded up his wife and children to walk through the Wednesday marketplace of Gotha. He had spent the night before trying to enjoy a drama at the duke's palace theater. It was supposed to be a delightful presentation of one of Schiller's works, yet knowing Schiller was the playwright made it another annoyance. That puffed up fool no longer respected him anymore than the many other Illuminati seated throughout the theater.

"Ja, ja, we come," said Anna Marie. Over these years, the poor woman had crumbled into a vague resemblance of her once sturdy self. The revelation of her husband's killing of his unborn child had filled her with secret terror, to say nothing of casting her to the edges of Gotha's society. But this paled against her abiding sorrow over the natural deaths of so many of the professor's children—whether Afra's or her own.

"Hurry!" Weishaupt tapped his walking stick impatiently on the ground. The forty-four-year-old wiped his face with a kerchief and climbed aboard the oversized coach provided by Duke Ernst's hospitality. His family filled the space and the coach lurched forward.

Ignoring the squabbling of his wife and children, Weishaupt considered recent times. In France, revolutionaries had imprisoned the royal family in the dungeon of the former Knights Templar. Without his guidance, who knew what hasty blunders might follow? Elsewhere, the Austrians now allied themselves with the Prussians to declare war on the new French government. And the French had recently declared war on the German emperor. In short, chaos was spreading across France and beyond.

Chaos excited him, of course. Weishaupt knew that out of chaos a new order could emerge. Such was a basic revolutionary principle. However, it was Aemilius Bode rather than he who was being credited for the Order's role in all of this—Aemilius and his blasted Philadelphes. And then there was that upstart, Nicholas Bonneville, of whom he had once boasted. Bonneville and his Cercle Social—the new heroes! Where was the glory for Spartacus Weishaupt as the hidden hand who had given life and wisdom to it all? Who was hailing *him*?

Enough of this. Now was the time for Weishaupt to reclaim his throne. He had already published his defenses as Kolmer had instructed. Nine of them, to be precise. But who was reading them? He had written to Massenhausen (Ajax) now in prison—one of his first four initiates—but the Berliner did not even have the courtesy to write back. Nor had most others. Money had moved elsewhere, and the duke was dining with him less and less. These things should have been obvious signs that the end had already come.

Saying nothing, the professor jostled atop the cobbled streets of Gotha stewing about the injustice of it all and how it was that he would reclaim what was his. By the time he finally arrived at the market square, he dismounted in a rage. He tossed the driver a coin, then directed his wife and children to the vendors. The professor watched his family disappear into the mixed throng of homespun and finery. His thoughts lingered for a brief moment on Anna Marie. He remembered that she had once respected him. Who had blinded her? His mind then turned to his first wife, Afra. Who had killed her? He shivered.

Weishaupt quickly searched for beer and a pretzel, and soon sat himself on a lonely bench at the edge of the market square. The broad branches of an old oak tree shaded him. He took a long breath. His mind drifted to the comforts of Friederika—his icon of feminine perfection. *She valued me.* He released a long sigh. *Ja. If only she were here.* Where was she now? And where was his sister-in-law, Sofia? What a beauty. *Was forcing her to kill the child such a terrible thing?* He let out a sob. *The world just does not understand.*

The professor wiped his eyes and stared into the tree above where a white pigeon hopped about. The bird dropped to the ground expecting a small charity of some sort. Weishaupt broke a bit of his pretzel and tossed it to the thing. More fluttered to the spot.

To one side, a violinist began a mournful tune. Weishaupt liked it. He removed his hat and scratched his scalp beneath the freshly powdered wig. He then looked at the red-brick face of the city's town hall. Inside, policies were being concocted. Outside, important men gathered along tables to drink beer and discuss the fortunes of them all. He belonged in both places.

The professor adjusted his wig, realizing that many of the gentlemen were now wearing their own hair. He considered his breeches. Were not the other men's more fashionable? And what of his shoes? Weishaupt smiled to himself. *Ah, if I modernize my appearance. With a fresh look and my defenses in place—with my Order and its children transforming the world from France, and the patient friendship of Duke Ernst—surely I shall reassert my rule as Spartacus Weishaupt.*

The thought was pleasing and filled him with hope. The professor relaxed and let the violin soothe him. *All will be well.* He drank a long draught of beer and then set his tankard on the ground. He finished his pretzel, noticing how gentle the light was that filtered through the heavy branches.

He closed his eyes. *Whatever melody is that man playing? It is beautiful...*

In another moment, the weary professor stretched himself along the wooden bench. His eyes grew heavy.

"Adam?"

"Eh?" The professor stirred. He blinked, smelling the faint aroma of sweet tobacco. He opened his eyes. "Kolmer?" Joy filled him. "You have not abandoned me?"

Towering over the little man under his Spanish hat, Kolmer smiled. "Abandoned you? No. I have been watching, Adam. Watching from a distance."

"Watching?" Weishaupt gazed upward, smiling. Hoping.

"May I sit with you?" Kolmer tossed his hat. He sat alongside Weishaupt and crossed his long legs. "I am very pleased to see you."

Heart fluttering, Weishaupt scanned the marketplace for signs of the man's entourage. Not far from City Hall stood the familiar six-horse, red coach with the white horse reined at the rear. A retinue of armed postilions stood near. He smiled at Kolmer. "And I am happy to see you."

Kolmer waited.

"I have needed you," said Weishaupt. Confidence rose, as did a sudden sense of indignity. "I have needed you very badly but you were nowhere to be found. My correspondence was rarely answered—"

"Needed me for what?" Kolmer wiped a hand through his long black hair.

"You must ask? Others are usurping my reputation—"

"Ah, that."

"You say it as if it were an easy thing…as if it were nothing at all!"

Kolmer shrugged. The pigeons flew away. "Let me ask you, Adam, what passion—whose voice—rules you now?"

"What passion? Whose voice?"

"I asked this of you once and you answered it was your hatred of the Jesuits."

"Oh. Ja. Well, surely not them any longer."

"Good. But there is a voice that you follow, a voice that rules you—"

"No man rules me! I serve no one; I am ruled by my own voice!"

Kolmer scratched his square jaw. "Hmm. I see." He fell silent for a long while, extending his arms wide along the back of the bench. "Do you remember my first instructions to you? I said we must deliver men *from* before we can deliver them *to*."

Wary, Weishaupt nodded.

"And I said that the strategy of the Order was to cast seeds into the wind like a dandelion. Do you remember that?"

"I have done that."

"Indeed." Kolmer watched the gentlemen mulling about the tables. "Look at them. Some may know what is coming, others soon will. We are slowly delivering the world *from* ignorance, superstition and fear, and *to* something very new. Ah, the joy of it."

Kolmer adjusted his posture and pulled a pipe from within his cloak. "Virginia tobacco," he said. "The Americans do not yet know what is coming for them, but they are being prepared. Their Freemasons are active; Illuminated lodges are working hard. Franklin is about to publish his autobiography—it dare not tell his whole story, of course." He laughed.

Kolmer withdrew his striker and spill holder. Lighting tow with his flint, he lifted a spill to the bowl of his pipe and drew on the tiny flame. He released a cloud of fragrant smoke. "Franklin, Mirabeau and you. What a wonderful trinity. Too bad Mirabeau is dead. All men die, you know." He drew on his pipe again. "Franklin's autobiography includes his creed, and his creed will serve that nation as a basis to turn the people *from*. Do you understand?"

Did he? Weishaupt nodded.

"But others will move them *to*." Kolmer touched the spill to the tobacco once more and sucked. "So it shall be everywhere. It takes time." Puffing smoke from his cheeks, he smiled. "What say you of our odd ally Cagliostro? I thought he was brilliant with his forgery on that matter of the Queen's necklace.[1] Ha. Right out of your bag of tricks. That simple deception set France ablaze. You see?

"But, I do fear France may be moving too quickly." Kolmer sighed. "Our Bonneville already knows that. I've sent messages to Aemilius Bode—but he has his hands full." He paused. "Nevertheless, I am pleased with how we just abolished the remaining orders of the Holy Wretch in that place. To see those foolish monks dashing hither—"

"That was done in haste and will raise more armies against us." Weishaupt crossed his leg. "I prefer transformation to revolution—"

"Indeed. But as you must know, your new German emperor thought he might attack our brethren. Poor Leopold.[2] Bravo on your assassination."

Weishaupt squirmed. No one had told him that his own had done this.

"And then King Gustav of Sweden.³ Ha, he should have known better than raise his hand against us. But to shoot him in the back at a masquerade ball? Brilliant. You have taught your men well."

The professor licked his lips. He knew nothing of this, either.

Kolmer drew on his pipe, thinking. "France will surely become a slaughter. But their disruption is changing the whole world. In America, your Illuminist lodges have spawned more than forty Jacobin Clubs in support. And the sons of the enlightened elites have formed a secret society within Harvard University.⁴ This is a good start; I am very pleased. You see how the Order is adapting everywhere? Even the Irish are waking up. The Order to them is known as the 'United Irishmen.'"⁵ He released some more smoke. "Can you see what is happening? Like a chameleon, the Great Plan appears one way in this place, and another way in that. Well done." Kolmer smiled.

Weishaupt knew very little of any of this and that fact was beyond insulting. He uncrossed his legs. "Yes? And where is my glory? I organized the purpose, I planted the seeds." The professor darkened. "If the atmosphere of the world has changed, it is on account of *me*. I need to be reasserted as the General, otherwise these 'adaptations' run the risk of becoming factions. No, no. Without my centering hand we shall move too far apart."

"*Your* hand?"

Missing the bite in the man's tone, Weishaupt nodded. "I think it is time to call for a convention."

"I see." Kolmer folded his arms. "And you actually believe that *you* are the organizing center?"

"Of course. And my convention could publish a unifying document from my new Council." Standing, Weishaupt went on to boast of how his persecutions had refined him, how his experience had uniquely qualified him, and how it was that the new world order would someday encircle him as its defining center. "I can see an obelisk in Ingolstadt."

Kolmer said nothing at first. At last, he stood and towered over the professor. "Do you forget our little coach ride in Gotha...what, five years ago? Did you never understand?"

"But—"

Kolmer laid two heavy hands on the little man's shoulders. "Adam Weishaupt, good and faithful servant."

Weishaupt hesitated. *Servant?* Pressed downward by the weight of Kolmer's hands, he lost himself in the man's hypnotic gaze. Struggling to absorb what the man was saying, he blurted, "Servant? I was no man's servant." He tried to pull away.

"Herr Professor, you have faithfully cast seeds into the wind...as instructed." Kolmer squeezed Weishaupt's shoulders.

Instructed? No, that is not it... A discomforting awareness began to crawl through him. Unable to move, he gaped upward into Kolmer's face. Images of the years appeared like a blurred mural in front of his eyes. Dread filled him.

Kolmer's face hardened. "I once told you that the Order would never end. It would live on under new names and in new places. Do you remember?"

Weishaupt felt smaller, still.

"My friend, you have never been the center." Kolmer removed his hands.

Nausea swept through the professor's belly. *What is happening here?*

"I also told you that, like your dear wife Afra, *you* would end. That time has come.".

The announcement landed on the professor with force. *No...*Adam Weishaupt shuddered. *Not now. After all I have done...* He could feel his chest tighten. He was faint. *It has come to this?*

Unable to speak, unable to accept any of this, Weishaupt closed his eyes. The world within then fell dark as deepest night. His limbs failed him, and the whole of him went numb. It was if he were spiraling downward into a bottomless pit. He spun in some eternal shadow until a deep-throated wail rose from his depths. His ears rang with his own cry and he awakened.

Weishaupt blinked. The whine of a lovely violin filled his ears. He sat up, bewildered. "Kolmer?" The man was gone; his entourage had disappeared. Wait. Had it been another dream? A white pigeon pecked around the professor's feet. "But—" His hand brushed against something on the bench. Adam Weishaupt turned his face and when he did, his eyes fell upon a sprig of acacia set neatly by his side.

CHAPTER THIRTY-THREE NOTES

1 'The Affair of the Necklace of 1786,' is believed by many historians to have precipitated the French Revolution. In brief: Queen Marie Antoinette's supposed signature was found on a purchase order for an outrageously expensive necklace. In an effort to defend the Crown from an outraged population, prosecutors charged a Freemason with Illuminati tendencies named Cagliostro (see prior notes) with conspiracy to defraud the royal jewelers through a forgery. To the chagrin of the French monarchy, the prosecution failed, leaving the monarchy disgraced. Of interest is that the prosecutor likely belonged to Cagliostro's own masonic Egyptian rite. Considering the fact that forgery was a weapon used by the Order to created disorder and mistrust, it is probable that the purchase order was, indeed, forged.

2 **Emperor Leopold II** (1747-1792) succeeded his brother, Emperor Joseph II in 1790 but was murdered two years later. Both emperors were brothers of Marie Antoinette, Queen of France. Despite Leopold's liberal views, revolutionaries saw his defense of his sister a betrayal.

3 **King Gustav III of Sweden** (1746-1792) was also considered an 'enlightened' monarch, though it seems not enlightened enough. His opposition to the French revolutionaries prompted Illuminists to assassinate him at a party.

4 One of the first secret clubs in American universities was Harvard's Porcelain Club. Originally named the 'Argonauts,' this exclusive inner sanctum of influence became a coveted membership for the sons of America's elite. Its eventual cousin, Yale's Skull and Bones (1832), similarly became an important, secret association that served (serves) to advance brothers within academia, industry and politics. The membership lists of these and other clubs suggests a persuasive claim that they are intended to perpetuate 'enlightened' leadership. An example is the Bush family—Bonesmen who overtly advanced the notion of a 'New World Order.' Interestingly, Skull and Bones'

membership requires initiates to present a sexual confessional—a clear example of the legacy of the Illuminati.

5 The 'United Irishmen' was created by foreign agents with Illuminati ties who exploited credible grievances among the Irish people. The organization mimicked masonic/Illuminati structures.

"The actual possession of Jesus Christ in us is the Centre toward which all the mysteries converge like rays to the circle eye."

DR. KARL VON ECKARTSHAUSEN

CHAPTER THIRTY-FOUR

September, 1792
Regensburg

ABBOT BENEDICT OFFERED A QUICK BLESSING AS ALEXANDER studied the food in front of him. "Do you see what I see, Father Abbot?"

Benedict reached for a spoon. "I see a beautiful meat pie, baked to perfection."

"Then you do not really see." The meat pie was a stew served within an oval bowl. Atop the bowl sat a baked puff pastry lid with a hole in the center. "The center of the universe is a portal. It is neither Reason or even God, but rather a portal TO God." He poked at his pie with a spoon. *Ha, my father was right!*

"You need more sleep," said the abbot. "And shave your head." He shoved his spoon into his pie. "Things are serious. I hope you are finally ready?"

For nearly two years Alexander had spent evenings organizing documents for a presentation to the British Prime Minister, Lord Pitt. "Just one more week—"

"Good. The world is falling apart. The new French Republic has pilfered the Holy Church. Their army defeated the Prussians at Valmy. They are said to be headed toward Frankfurt and Basel. I suppose they will march on the Netherlands." Benedict wiped his face. "None of this could have happened unless men's minds were infected by that Order—"

"And their hearts, Father Abbot. Do not forget hearts. Men's affections are more powerful than their thoughts. We need a way to return men—"

"Yes, yes. To the wise way of love. And only love offered in truth can do that."

A week later, Alexander Horn shed his black robes and donned a familiar set of clothes. The abbot was worried about plots against 'Brother Maurus,' so the young man was outfitted as Mr. Bergström once again. Ready, he clutched his well-worn, silver-knobbed walking stick—the one given to him by Weishaupt many years prior—and waited for a coach that would deliver him across the roiling continent to the presumed safety of Rotterdam. From there the thirty-year-old would sail to London where he expected to present his hard work to Lord Pitt. However, as always, he liked the notion of a reserve plan and he had one.

A four-horse coach arrived with three postilions and two personal body-guards. Alexander felt for the flintlock hidden within his coat. He then checked his purse of coins hidden deeper still. He hefted two leather bags that were secured by heavy canvas straps. Inside, were the documents that the wider world needed to see.

OCTOBER, 1792
LONDON, ENGLAND

The Crown's coachmen skillfully navigated Alexander's dangerous journey between Regensburg and Rotterdam, taking a circuitous route northward to Gotha, then through the cities of Kassel, Munster, and finally to Rotterdam. The five-hundred-mile jostle was mercifully uneventful, and Alexander soon found himself aboard a three-master which he sailed to London. The weary man then finally arrived at his lodging in Covent Garden.

One day later, Alexander and his guards rode through the City of London to his evening meeting with two secretaries of Lord Pitt scheduled in the Freemasons Hall on Great Queen Street. Arriving, Alexander was introduced, took his seat at a fine table and quickly proceeded to explain his purposes over a very fine claret.

As he revealed page after page of documents, Pitt's secretaries listened politely, sipping their wine from time to time, but mostly acknowledging friends drifting through the hall. Occasionally they slid glances at the clock tick-tocking atop the heavy mantel of a nearby hearth. One of the men yawned, then lit a pipe filled with sweet Virginia tobacco. Their rudeness was nearly too much for Alexander. *By the Saints! Do they not care what I've been telling them?* Apparently not. Frustrated, he labored on with his presentation for another half-hour.

Finally, one of the secretaries interrupted him. "I believe we have the gist of it, sir. We shall provide these papers to the Cabinet. I'm quite sure someone will be fascinated, but as you know, the world is in a bit of chaos."

The Englishman's condescending tone put the young Scot in a twist. "The world is in a 'bit of chaos' because of what I have disclosed! Can ye not see that? Lord Pitt should be made aware of these documents immediately!"

The men smiled, politely.

Alexander stood. "Listen to me carefully. There is a conspiracy to change the world as we know it. The end of Christianity, the end of kingdoms. They intend to replace your empire with their own."

"That is quite the claim." The men snickered.

"I do not intend to leave these documents with you. If Lord Pitt wants me to present them directly to him, I shall return." Fuming, Alexander collected his bundles and marched into the street.

Alexander's bodyguards abandoned him in London, leaving the disguised monk to implement his contingent plan by himself. With silver coins in hand, he made his way north by coach to Edinburgh where he arrived at the home of an interested party who lived along Castle Hill near Holyrood.

He glanced at some sea gulls screeching overhead, then tapped on the man's door with his walking stick. A maid answered.

"Dr. Robison's residence?"

She nodded and called for her employer. In a moment, the fifty-three-year-old professor came to the door wrapped in a wool blanket and looking very much annoyed.

Alexander bowed. "A good day to you, sir."

Not recognizing Alexander, Robison grumbled an answer in his strong brogue. "Do I know ye?"

"We were introduced some years ago at the Scots Monastery in Regensburg. You knew me as 'Brother Maurus.' We have corresponded a few times." Alexander gestured toward his own clothing. "I am traveling with some care."

The professor thought for a moment, then brightened. "Aye! Come in." Robison invited Alexander to his office and ordered his maid to bring tea. "Whatever brings ye to Edinburgh?"

"The times, sir. And the conspiracies of the Bavarian Illuminati."

The man's eyes arched. "God have mercy. I fear my beloved Craft is to blame. We were tricked. Please, sit."

Before taking his seat, Alexander opened his bundles and began stacking papers on the man's desk. "What I have is many months' worth of deciphered documents from the Order, as well as some samples of journals and pamphlets. In addition, I have written a detailed summary of my recollections of my times with Professor Adam Weishaupt."

Robison reached for his spectacles. "By the saints, this is exactly what I need! I have heard reports—"

"Mostly true. Murders, plots, schemes; heresy, conspiracies, treason. All of it. And their conspiracies continue."

The professor began turning pages, slowly. Murmuring, his hands finally fell to his lap. "This is God's gift. I have traveled the world with my suspicions, but now truth has found me."

Alexander was pleased. Finally, someone to listen. He sipped some tea. "It is my belief, sir, that what these men have begun is now spreading...adapting to time and place but grounded in a singular philosophy. Such a plot as this cannot be overthrown with arrests, hangings or even wars. Only the light of truth—"

"Aye!" Robison was clearly animated. "Can I have these bundles for a season? I will secure them until I can cast these secrets into bright light."

"How, sir?"

"I will publish a book exposing it all. I will discern and expose their hidden philosophy, purposes and players." He faced Alexander, squarely. "I shall first direct this book to the English-speaking world, as we are now in great danger."

This was exactly what Alexander had hoped. He had recently heard of a French cleric named Abbé Barruel who had plans of doing the same for France and the Continent. With two such books from two respected men, the weapon of truth could be loosed.

Professor Robison continued. "I have access to Lord Pitt, even the royals— I must also place this information into the hands of Washington and Jefferson, even Franklin—"

"Franklin?" Alexander shook his head. "He is likely one of them, and maybe Jefferson as well. At least in their sympathies."

Robison fell silent. "Then this is worse than I feared. Are we agreed, Brother Maurus? May I keep these documents?"

Alexander wanted to dance. *I am rid of this! I have passed the torch!* He extended his hand. "With joy, sir."

Robison was elated. "And one more thing. Might you remain here for the week? I should like to listen to every word that you are willing to confide."

November, 1792

Alexander remained with Robison for that week and the next. By the time he bade the elder Scot farewell, his heart was lighter than it had in a very long time. In his deposition he felt a great unburdening; he had put order to everything. All that he knew of the Great Plan of the Illuminati had now been turned over to another, and with it the very great weight of saving the world.

From Edinburgh he happily travelled to Aberdeen in hopes of visiting his mother, only to learn that she was enjoying Spain. Severely disappointed, he hired another coach and was soon dismounting before the familiar gray gables of Westhall.

A servant welcomed him home to the Horn family estate. The property was now owned by cousins scheduled to return within the week. Recognizing Alexander, an old gardener then directed other servants to prepare a room, some food, and to stoke a warm fire.

At the earliest light of a chilly dawn, Alexander hastily gobbled down a bowl of porridge and two biscuits, then borrowed boots and a set of clothing belonging to a groomsman. He soon set out on the morning's journey he had longed for over these many years.

Smiling under a fast-warming sky, the man strode quickly along the stony Huntly Road. He passed by the familiar rise of Bennachie Ridge to his left, then hurried past the curious villagers of Insch and arrived at the River Shevock. Standing at the river's edge, Alexander felt an urge to pause and listen, and so he did. In a mere moment, a lump filled his throat. He sat, marveling. "I hear it this time, Grunnie, your gurgling harmony—your 'Hymn of the River!'" For the next half-hour he laid back and let the river sing to him.

Inspired, he finally splashed through the cold ford and ran for the stone circle standing faithfully like it had for 2,000 years. Alexander put his hands on one stone and then the next. Something about the stones—maybe their gritty texture, maybe the solidness of them.

Alexander then strode up his beloved Dunnideer to arrive at the dolman of ruins. Laughing, he climbed into his seat like he had as a boy, resting in the power of the ley line running through the deep earth below. He studied the sky. "Christ above, I feel you here below. As it is in Heaven, may it be on earth."

He then dug his fingers into lichen, remembering. *Ah, dear Fiona, my angel, where are you now?* Sighing, he leaned back and thought of Julianna. He missed her so. Alexander murmured a prayer for her happiness. He then picked a dry wildflower from between two stones and lifted it into the wind. "I release you again, Julianna. It is how it must be." He opened his fingers and the brittle flower fluttered away.

Alexander turned his face toward the sprawling landscape running to the east. He rested in that sight for a very long time. Dollops of white clouds followed the blue sky into a distant horizon. Birds swooped, playfully. He was happy to be one with the beauty of this place—secured by the splendid might of all that was. The man's eyes filled. At long last, he understood that he belonged to the Presence—and always had.

An unwelcome gust returned his mind to matters-at-hand. He released a long breath, relieved that Robison had lifted his burden. He was glad to think of it gone. But was that entirely true? Was he no longer called to alert men to the deceptions of false light? How could the good news of Dunnideer be denied to others?

Alexander shifted his position in the notch. He knew that evil crouched at the door of every man, including his own. *And a troubled heart is not enough, is it?* He bit his lip. "But I am weary," he murmured. Besides, what was left for him to do?

From nowhere, an image of someone appeared in his mind's eye. He groaned. "Oh, no. I have had quite enough of you." A discomforting impulse moved him. A breeze then rustled through the brown grass around the ruins like a wandering hand. "I would rather not." An eagle screeched overhead.

Alexander closed his eyes. A cold blast of wind then flattened the brown grasses in a violent, wandering swirl. *But I was finally content, finished.* The inner voice then whispered, "A-L-E-X-A-N-D-E-R, good and faithful servant." He abandoned his seat. "Good and faithful?"

Then silence. Utter silence. The kind of silence that swallows one's heart into some great space. Alexander stood very still. A securing sense of deep wisdom settled him; Grunnie's? He closed his eyes and raised his face to the sun. Its warmth felt like love; its light, truth. The man's thoughts then returned to something that Abbot Benedict had taught him: *'Evil is defeated by healing one soul at a time.'* Knowing, he opened his eyes, inhaled a deep breath and took one last look across the rolling beauty of Aberdeenshire.

One week later, a 500-ton merchant ship rocked violently as it tacked away from Aberdeen against strong easterlies. The ship eventually delivered a now troubled Alexander back to Rotterdam where he vomited one more time before disembarking. Miserable, he took a room above a small tavern where he collapsed in a clean Dutch bed.

He awakened the next morning less ill but still utterly distracted from the mission that had found him at Dunnideer. This was all on account of a letter he had received at Westhall the night before leaving for the docks. Alexander stumbled downstairs and ordered some cheese, bread and coffee for breakfast. He flattened the letter on his table. It was from his brother and it informed him that Julianna was likely to become a widow any day.

But Robby's letter said more: *'I surrender. I am unable to rescue you. Your passions cannot be contained within the walls of a cloister. You were created to be a man of the earth, not Heaven. Relinquish your vows and spare us all.'*

Was that true?

Alexander turned his face to the window, thinking, until a frail old man approached his table from nowhere and surprised him with a heavy Scottish brogue. "Fix yer eyes on the path you've been put upon."

The fellow then rested an arthritic hand gently on Alexander's shoulder. "Whatever else weighs on yer heart shall take care of itself in due time." He grinned a wide, toothless grin and turned to leave. As he did, his leg caught Alexander's propped walking stick and knocked it to the floor.

Alexander promptly picked up his stick, and as he did his eyes fell on the tarnished handle with the deeply etched Minerval owl and faded 'B.' He sighed, then turned to the window where a small bird held the sill. "Well, little sparrow, how about that?" He scanned the tavern for the old man now nowhere to be found.

The next day Alexander began his hire of coaches shuttling across Prussia until he finally arrived at the Thuringian city of Gotha. Dirty, he took a small room above a timbered tavern near City Hall where he was able to arrange a bath and a washing of his clothes. It was also a good place to drink dark beer, listen to local gossip, and reassure himself that this was the right thing to do.

After three days, Alexander Horn was as ready as he might ever be. At midmorning he pulled on a blue overcoat, slowly snugged his tricorn hat atop his wigged head and made way for the door with his walking stick in hand. Once outside, he whistled at a plain-looking coach and gave the driver his destination. As the horses began their clip-clop atop the cobblestones, Alexander stared through the rain-spattered glass of his coach window. The city was gray, the people seemed lost. A smattering of Christmas greenery offered the only bit of cheer. "The seat of princes?" he muttered.

Bouncing hard over a hole, a twinge of doubt abruptly nagged him—the kind of doubt poised to put an end to purpose. An inner voice then whispered. *'Surely, justice must be served. Abandon him to the fate he deserves.'*

"He is only a tool, a marionette on a stage he does not understand," Alexander muttered.

'But his work has unleashed the seductions of evil. He deserves—'

"Why not mercy?"

'Dunnideer blinds you. This man caused harm—'

"But how else is evil defeated? Is not justice perfected in mercy?"

'And what of Julianna? Why not forget all of this and fly to her—'

To that, Alexander wiped his nose, thinking. "But would she not wish me here? Grunnie, too." He gathered himself. "Whose voice is this?"

Silence.

The coach shuddered to a stop. Inhaling damp air, Alexander dismounted slowly and paid the driver. He walked to a massive iron gate and peered through its black rungs to marvel at the sprawling stone palace of Saxe-Gotha. Platoons of disciplined soldiers patrolled the wide margins of its orderly central gardens. An assortment of fine carriages stood at the ready for unseen aristocrats. The whole world knew this place. Some thought it to be a haven of enlightenment; others feared it as the snake pit of the Illuminati. Whatever it was, the scene of empire made him feel suddenly small. Alexander looked at his mud-splattered shoes and summoned his courage. *Well, here I am.* He called for a guard.

The approaching soldier barked, "What do you want?"

Alexander squeezed the silver head of his walking stick. "I am here to see Dr. Adam Weishaupt."

"Who?"

Alexander raised a brow. "Dr. Adam Weishaupt. He is a guest of the duke."

"I do not know him." The guard walked away to check with two others.

Some said the professor had become a lonely wretch, tucked away and forgotten—disposed of deep within the palace. Rumors even had it that he had been reduced to a laughing-stock, a fool still captive to his own false grandeur. *So, no longer the center of the universe, after all?* thought Alexander. A quick succession of memories ran through his mind, ending at that terrible final meeting. He shifted on his feet.

After some delay, the guard sent a messenger boy to the gate. "Who is calling, sir?"

The question should not have caught Alexander by surprise. Stalled, he cleared his throat. Was he Brother Maurus? Mr. Bergström? Was he here as monk, bookseller, spy? He suddenly sensed Fiona—or was she Julianna—leaning close to his ear. He closed his eyes to listen. *'Be who YOU are. Step out as yourself, dear Alexander. Now is the time.'*

He opened his eyes. *Like a butterfly...* Ready, he removed his hat. He stuffed his wig into a pocket and presented his walking stick to the messenger. "Give this to the professor and tell him that Alexander Horn is here."

The boy turned the stick over in his hands and then asked, "And for what purpose shall I tell him you are calling?"

Alexander drew a slow, deliberate breath, and in the quiet of that brief moment Dunnideer filled him. He exhaled, smiling. "Tell Dr. Weishaupt that I bring him good news, and that it is very good news indeed."

THE END

"From the days of Spartacus Weishaupt to those of Karl Marx...this world-wide conspiracy for the overthrow of civilization and for the reconstitution of society on the basis of arrested development, of envious malevolence and impossible equality has been steadily growing."

WINSTON CHURCHILL

AFTERWORD

WHAT FOLLOWS IS THE NON-FICTION CONCLUSION TO THE lives of our two primary characters, as well as an overview of the Order's historical presence. The interested reader is encouraged to explore the exhaustive information available from the resources in the select bibliography.

Alexander Horn (28th June, 1762 – 16th April, 1820)
Biographical information on Alexander Horn is scant. However, in 1799 Alexander traveled to London as Brother Maurus where he was finally able to meet directly with members of William Pitt's cabinet to review the information already provided to John Robison. A few months later, the British Parliament outlawed all secret societies with its Unlawful Societies Act, though it was quickly amended to exempt Freemasonry.

Alexander then returned to the Scots monastery where he continued to live an extraordinary life. As Brother Maurus he expanded the library's reputation as a legendary repository of treasured books. He invested a great deal of his time in writing and research that resulted in published works exposing a wide range of conspiracies. However, his bookish devotion did not consume him. He remained a close friend to the powerful Thurn and Taxis family and was loved by the cosmopolitan dignitaries of Regensburg. An English visitor described him as 'such a wild young fellow...it is a shame that he should have a monk's habit.'[1]

The visitor did not know the half of it. In 1804, Brother Maurus was appointed as an official British diplomat to replace the English ambassador from Munich. This was a challenging duty given the dangerous climate surrounding Napoleon's maneuvers. But the Crown had more in mind for him than diplomacy. The position was a ruse for 'Mr. Bergström' to get to work, and as early as 1805 Alexander had his spy network in place.

In the course of his spying, Alexander soon learned that Pope Pius VII was conspiring with Napoleon. The news crushed him and he promptly abandoned his monastic vows; Brother Maurus was no more. Alexander Horn (as Mr. Bergström) now focused solely on clandestine work as the lone British *chargé d'affaires* roaming about central Europe. Within five years, he supplied nearly 900 secret dispatches to the British.

When Austria fell (in 1810), Alexander retreated to London where an indebted British government provided him with a generous pension. Three years later, he likely grieved the painful death of his presumed friend, Karl von Eckartshausen. Soon thereafter, he attempted to return to his beloved Regensburg, only to be expelled by the occupying French authorities.

Alexander's expulsion proved to be a blessing, however. The former monk moved to Frankfurt-am-Main where—no doubt surprised by sudden good fortune—he immediately courted and quickly married a Baroness von Gumppenberg of the Thurn and Taxis family. Our story names her Julianna and we assume she was a widow, though her exact identity is unknown. Regardless, one can only imagine his joy.

Alexander soon ached to return to Regensburg with his princess bride. He appealed to the French governors in Munich until his wish was finally granted. The happy couple planned their trip home for April, 1820. Sadly, on the 16th of that same month, our dear Alexander Horn died of unknown causes at age 57.

---

1 From the Oxford Dictionary of National Biography, 'Alexander Horn' by Mark Dilworth, on-line edition, 23 September, 2004.

Three days later, his spiritual father, mentor and friend, Abbot Benedict, also died.

Nothing more is known of our Julianna.

Despite Alexander's unusual life and his far-flung wandering from his monastic vows, the brothers of the Scots Monastery loved him and boldly included 'Brother Maurus' as one of their own in the monastery's roster of deaths. Surely, Alexander Horn was laid to rest as one who belonged to God.

Adam Weishaupt (6th February, 1748 – 18th November, 1830)
By 1787 Spartacus Weishaupt had already lost meaningful control of the Bavarian Order of the Illuminati to Johann (Aemilius) Bode. For one thing, Bode and his allies were proving to be better at adapting to rapidly changing times. But it was the scandal of Weishaupt's sister-in-law's abortion—an unspeakable crime in those times—that irredeemably exiled the founder from the entire movement he had set in motion.

In the tumultuous years that followed, Adam was increasingly marginalized from most intellectual and social circles, but was able to maintain an obscure position as a legal advisor to successive dukes in Gotha. This was apparently not satisfying, for he unsuccessfully attempted to obtain professorships in Vienna and Jena. In 1808 he was finally accepted into membership of the Bavarian Academy of Sciences—an honor shared by his father and godfather that must have helped soothe his sense of place.

In his later years, something quite astonishing then happened. We have no particulars, but it seems that some gift of grace healed Adam Weishaupt's wounds for he earnestly made his way back to the forgiving arms of the Roman Catholic Church. In fact, stunned priests happily deemed him "zealous" in his restored faith, and he was publicly honored for his tireless efforts in helping fund the construction of a church in Gotha.

Nearly forgotten as the tap root of the Illuminati dandelion, Adam Weishaupt died in Gotha at 4:30 in the afternoon of November 18, 1830 at the age of 82. The local parish chronicled his death by noting that he died "reconciled with the

Catholic Church, which, as a youthful professor, he had doomed to death and destruction."[2]

Adam was buried alongside his beloved son, Wilhelm, who had predeceased him in 1802 at age 18.

His second wife, Anna Marie (nee Sausenhofer) Weishaupt survived Adam by sixteen years and died in Gotha at age 85.

In all, Weishaupt fathered twelve children. His first wife, Afra (d. February 8, 1780), bore two sons and five daughters; all five daughters died young. His second wife, Anna Marie, gave birth to three sons and two daughters. In all, four sons and two daughters survived him and went on to lead successful lives.

The Life of the Order

Most historians agree that the Bavarian Order of the Illuminati formally dissolved sometime between 1787 and 1790, but the *movement* it founded did not. The scandal of abortion, revelations unearthed by Duke Theodore's investigations, and the severity of the Bavarian government's final edicts were enough to force a shift in identities. John Robison's book, *Proofs of a Conspiracy,* (thoroughly informed by Alexander Horn) was released in accord with a widely read exposé on the Order published by a French Jesuit named Abbé Barruel. These books prompted a wave of anxiety over ongoing Illuminati-inspired plots throughout Britain and the Continent. Robison's book also traveled to America where it found George Washington who abruptly labelled the Order as 'diabolical.'[3]

Robison's and Barruel's works motivated a Boston pastor named Jedediah Morse to raise enough of a fuss that on April 25, 1799 President John Adams proclaimed a national fast against conspiracies. However, Illuminism—defined here as the metaphysical/social/political movement inspired by the Order—was well-entrenched, especially in the media. On September 26, 1799 the *American Mercury* newspaper published a false document to discredit Morse.

---

2 *Catholic Encyclopedia*, 'Illuminati.' See www.catholic.org

3 Having been presented with Robison's book by a Rev. G. W. Snyder, George Washington—unlike Jefferson—expressed his concern about the 'nefarious and dangerous plan and doctrines of the Illuminati.' Calling the Illuminati 'diabolical,' he understood their expanding influence but he did not believe they had taken control of American Freemasonry.

Other Illuminist publishers quickly joined in and effectively suppressed the minister and his rising tide of alarmists for many years to come.[4]

The truth is that the Order had never been destroyed but had shrewdly morphed as conditions demanded. The *Catholic Encyclopedia* correctly observes that "The spread of the *spirit* (emphasis mine) of the Illuminati…was accelerated rather than retarded by the persecution in Bavaria."[5] For example, in France the Illuminati went to work under a new cover—the Lodge of Philadelphes— and embedded themselves within Nicholas Bonneville's powerful revolutionary *Cercle Social* where they helped drive the French Revolution. Illuminati in other parts of Europe hid within reading societies (their version of modern think-tanks) such as Berlin's influential Wednesday Society, and Karl Bahrdt's German Union of Twenty-Two. In North America, the brothers formed Jacobin Clubs and promoted secretive university clubs such as Yale's Skull and Bones which became means to insinuate Weishaupt's principles among the sons of the elite.

In short, Weishaupt's dandelion had multiplied according to plan. His commitment to a world where Christianity, moral convention, national boundaries and private property were no more, and where education safeguarded enlightened belief began to manifest through the centuries that followed. Illuminism's numerous tentacles, twists and turns are well-documented, but a few examples of what followed may serve to outline this fact:

In the **nineteenth century**, an Italian revolutionary and friend of the Illuminati named Philippe Buonarroti became the bridge between the Order and a new reading club known as the League of the Just. The League's London group included a German philosopher named Karl Marx, and it was the League that published the *Communist Manifesto* in 1847. The anti-Christian revolutionary effect of the *Manifesto* is commonly understood and needs no expansion here. But it is important to note that Marx's ten internationalist planks are expansions of Weishaupt's five, including such goals as the abolition of private property, redistribution of wealth, and the control of education.

---

4 See Stauffer, Vernon, *The Bavarian Illuminati in America* (New York: Dover Publications. Orig.1918, 2006) Pg. 313.

5 *Catholic Encyclopedia*, 'Illuminati.'

The Order's children also sponsored Europe's famous 1848 'Year of Revolutions' throughout the Italian and German states, Hungary, Austria, Denmark, Poland, Sweden and others. Later in the same century, the Fabian socialists of Britain would turn to Weishaupt's gradualism and insert incremental Illuminism successfully throughout the British Commonwealth. The Fabian Society exists today as one of many Illuminist think-tanks.

In the **twentieth century**, Illuminism's complex of organizations, publications, secret societies and financial interconnections formed the backdrop of the rise and revision of Communism, two world wars, a long list of regional wars, the spread of democratic socialism and the first efforts toward a world commonwealth.

As to the latter, Illuminist-inspired elites first organized the League of Nations and then the United Nations in order to advance the grand plan of global governance, otherwise known as the New World Order. In 1947 Sir Julian Huxley (British eugenicist and the first director of UNESCO) summarized the key tasks of the fledgling United Nations as "to help the emergence of a single world culture," and the "political unification in some sort of world government."[6]

Throughout that century, a long roster of other globalists advanced this cause through political, academic and financial machinations. An example is David Rockefeller who boldly declared the following: "Some even believe we are part of a secret cabal working against the best interests of the United States, characterizing my family and me as 'internationalists' and of conspiring with others around the world to build a more integrated global political and economic structure—one world, if you will. If that's the charge, I stand guilty, and I am proud of it."[7]

Of course, in our **twenty-first century**, Weishaupt's legacy lives on in communist and socialist regimes around the world. Illuminism is also

---

6   Newman, Alex, 'Education's Future Globalization of Indoctrination,' *New American Magazine* (Feb 4, 2019) p. 28.

7   From David Rockefeller's *Memoirs* (2002), cited by Thompson, Art, *To the Victor Go the Myths & Monuments* (Appleton: AOF Publishing. 2016) xxxiv.

active within a host of perennial secret societies such as the Bilderbergers,[8] the Bohemian Grove,[9] and the aforementioned Skull and Bones. However, the Order's goals are becoming ever more visible through the policies publicly promoted by numerous Illuminist-minded think-tanks like America's extraordinarily influential Council on Foreign Relations,[10] Britain's Royal Institute of International Affairs, The Trilateral Commission, The Club of Rome and The World Federalist Movement to name but a few. One only needs to read publications such as the CFR's *Foreign Affairs* to identify the players and document their intentions.

We should also remember Weishaupt's conviction to control the schools. In an ongoing effort to globalize education, UN Assistant Secretary-General Robert Muller recently published the World Core Curriculum, a "curriculum of our universal knowledge which should be taught in all schools of the earth." He boasts that the curriculum's underlying philosophy was heavily influenced by Alice Bailey. Bailey was an occult philosopher who created the Lucifer Publishing Company, channeled spirits, and predicted a new global religion that would crush both Christianity and national sovereignty.[11] It takes little imagination to hear the echo of Adam Weishaupt.

8 The Bilderberger Meeting was founded as a secret annual conference by Prince Bernhard of the Netherlands in 1954 to support the relationship between North America and Europe. Its far-reaching influence on business, finance, world federalism and the distribution of the world's resources is significant. The Bilderberger annual meeting is secret and the press is barred from attendance.

9 The Bohemian Grove was founded in 1872 and continues. It is a secretive social club of political, business and entertainment elites (including former American presidents) that meets near San Francisco to maintain key networks supposedly without doing business. The members participate in occult rituals under firelight at the foot of a giant Minerval owl.

10 The Council on Foreign Relations is an influential organization specializing in foreign policy. Its membership includes numerous secretaries of state and presidents, as well as key members of the military, financial services, industry, and academia. The Council is a prime advocate of economic convergence and global governance.

11 Newman, Alex, p. 29.

What Does This All Mean?

From 1776 to this very day, the ideological offspring of the Order continue alive and well. Adam Weishaupt's seeds have propagated a movement shepherding humanity toward a utopian vision of a *Novus Ordo Seclorum*—a New World Order. It is not surprising, therefore, that theories of a "master conspiracy" circulate.

Conspiracy theories can be ludicrous. Yet critics who believe men are unable to collude in such ways should recognize that the historical purposes of Illuminism are easily seen at work nearly everywhere. Whether generational conspirators have sustained a grand covert scheme remains a contended assertion.

Then again, who's to say David Rockefeller's "secret cabal" not only exists, but exists as the hands of something more...something *else*? Consider: Weishaupt's required reading was primarily metaphysical—even occultic—leading into deep theosophical speculation. He and many of his colleagues ultimately agreed that some sort of spiritual/energetic properties exist in the universe and they somehow govern the affairs of men.[12]

A century after Weishaupt, an influential theosophist named Madame Helena Blavatsky summed it up like this: "The whole Cosmos is guided, controlled and animated by an almost endless series of hierarchies of sentient beings..."[13] In later years, Alice Bailey, Allister Crowley, Napoleon Hill, Manly Hall, Corinne Heline, Mark Booth and others revealed a long-held and

---

12   The original Illuminati as well as current 'Illuminists' are non-monolithic in the particulars of their metaphysics. Everything from atheism to heterodox Christianity to neo-Pantheism has always been present; a tension within its membership between materialists and theosophists has continued from the beginning, though each group celebrated some form of ultimate Reason as center of all things. Communism/Marxist-Leninism adopted a materialist worldview, not unlike Bode and Zwack in our story. For these, the tenants of Illuminism take on a philosophical character. Western socialism is more open to theosophy such as Baron von Knigge's camp in his day. For these, Illuminism asserts various forms of spirituality. (Weishaupt, himself, seems to have alternated between the two camps, inclining in his later years toward theosophy). Either way, orthodox religious views—particularly Christianity—remain as the shared enemy.

13   Helena Blavatsky (1831-1859) was a Ukrainian occultist, writer and co-founder of the Theosophical Society. Though no longer widely known, her influence remains significant among those who embrace modern spiritualism and New Age mysticism. She is credited with

just-below-the-surface belief in a "Great Plan of the Ages" supervised by "forces." Readers are advised to seek out the 2016 ritual opening of the Gotthard Base Tunnel in the Swiss Alps, or do a bit of digging into the current fad of "spirit cooking," or read up on the Bohemian Grove to see how the elites of today's Order remain heavily invested in the occult.

Is it so unreasonable to wonder, then, whether it is *these* forces working through committed men and women over time that have led to an emerging, Illuminist New World Order? It may not be unreasonable at all. The apostle Paul wrote, "We do not wrestle against flesh and blood, but against principalities and powers in high places."

Such 'wrestling' from the counter-position of biblical Christianity has incited Illuminism's historic contempt. After all, in the name of Christ the world has suffered the Spanish Inquisition, book-burnings, Salem Witch trials, enslavement, genocide, rampant sexual abuse, institutional greed, religious arrogance...the list goes on. Yet something more fundamental than a proper revulsion against these abuses of Christ's name is at work in Illuminism's contempt, and it has to do with foundations.

The general metaphysical assumption of Illuminism is that the universe is the product of its own emanation—spirit/energy released from an unnamed Source occupying its center. This is Weishaupt's circled dot. The goal is for humanity to ascend to the Source for its ultimate completion/perfection. This can be accomplished through various paths of enlightenment, whether philosophical, economic, political, sociological, psychological, etc. In the end, hope is found within the potential of the human spirit.

Christian belief assumes the existence of a personal, loving Creator who is both within and beyond his creation. Unable to restore our own happiness, we are dependent on our union with Christ to experience the wholeness of love and truth.

The differences are irreconcilable: Illuminism presumes that human perfection is naturally attainable within the powers of humankind; Christianity relies on the perfection of Christ. For the former, perfection/completion is

---

introducing the West to eastern mystical philosophies. Cited by McLaughlin and Davidson, p.232.

achieved; for the latter it is *received* as a blessing. Therefore, Illuminism rejects the personal God of Christianity as THE rival for the center of their circle. And Christianity asserts the center of Illuminism to be a tragic deception. It is no wonder that history may be best understood as a record of spiritual warfare.

Whatever one thinks of these things, it should be apparent that some kind of movement is well underway. The siege of Eden is now upon *us*. Our world is being tempted toward something very different; one can feel it in the wind. The reader must decide for herself where the demons are gathered and where the angels stand.

SELECT BIBLIOGRAPHY

I have narrowed my bibliography to this 'Top Twenty' sampling of my research. Those titles that are **bold-faced** are my 'Top Three' picks for interested readers with limited time.

Barruel, Abbé *Code of the Illuminati* (Rooksley: Aziloth Books. 2012. Originally published 1798)

Blavatsky, Helena *Isis Unveiled* (Wheaton: Quest Books. 2013. Originally written in 1877).

Booth, Mark ***The Secret History of the World*** (New York: Overlook Press. 2011). Recommended for an in depth look at the spiritual secrets claimed to be behind the movement of history.

Brooke, Tal *When the World Will Be as One; the Coming New World Order in the New Age* (Oregon: Harvest House Publishers, Inc. 1989).

Corinne, Heline *America's Invisible Guidance* (Los Angeles: New Age Press, Inc. Reprint date unknown).

Dice, Mark *The Illuminati; Facts and Fiction* (San Diego: The Resistance. 2009).

Eckartshausen, Karl von *The Cloud Upon the Sanctuary* (London: William Rider & Son. 1909, Originally printed circa 1795).

Haggar, Nicholas *The Secret Founding of America* (London: Watkins Publishing. 2007).

Hall, Manly, *The Secret Destiny of America* (New York: Penguin. 2008. Originally published 1944).

Hall, Manly *The Secret Teachings of All Ages* (United States: Pacific Publishing Studio. 2011).

Hieronimus, Robert *Founding Fathers, Secret Societies; Freemasons, Illuminati, Rosicrucians, and the Decoding of the Great Seal* (Rochester: Destiny Books. 2006). Recommended for readers interested in the secrets of American's founding.

Hoar, William P. *Architects of Conspiracy; an Intriguing History* (Boston: Western Islands.1984).

McLaughlin, Corrine; and Davidson, Gordon *Spiritual Politics* (New York: Ballantine Books. 1994).

Melanson, Terry ***Perfectibilists; The 18th Century Bavarian Order of the Illuminati*** (Oregon: Trine Day LLC. 2009). Highly recommended as the quintessential research project on the Bavarian Order.

Ovason, David *The Secret Architecture of our Nation's Capital* (New York: Perennial. 2002).

Payson, Seth, *Proof of the Illuminati* (Woodbridge: Invisible College Press LLC. 2003, originally published in 1802).

Robison, John *Proofs of a Conspiracy* (Public Domain. 1798).

Stauffer, Vernon, *The Bavarian Illuminati in America* (New York: Dover Publications. 2006. Originally published 1918).

Thompson, Art, **To the Victor Go the Myths & Monuments** (Appleton: AOF Publishing. 2016) Recommended for a deep exploration of the ongoing legacy of the Illuminati.

Wasserman, James *The Secrets of Masonic Washington* (Rochester: Destiny Books. 2008).

OTHER BOOKS BY C.D. BAKER

Crusade of Tears
Quest of Hope
Pilgrims of Promise
Swords of Heaven; the Untold Story of Magna Carta
The List
The Seduction of Eva Volk; a Novel of Hitler's Christians
Becoming the Son; an Autobiography of Jesus
The Pursuit of Leviathan
101 Cups of Water
40 Loaves
Seedlings

For more information on C.D. Baker and his books, visit us at:
www.cdbaker.com

Made in the USA
Lexington, KY
27 November 2019

57717187R00231